TWO FOR ONE

Two For One

...a novel about having choices

Sean David Wright

iUniverse, Inc.
New York Lincoln Shanghai

Two For One
...a novel about having choices

Copyright © 2005 by Sean David Wright

All rights reserved. No part of this book may be used or reproduced by any means, graphic, electronic, or mechanical, including photocopying, recording, taping or by any information storage retrieval system without the written permission of the publisher except in the case of brief quotations embodied in critical articles and reviews.

iUniverse books may be ordered through booksellers or by contacting:

iUniverse
2021 Pine Lake Road, Suite 100
Lincoln, NE 68512
www.iuniverse.com
1-800-Authors (1-800-288-4677)

ISBN-13: 978-0-595-35448-1 (pbk)
ISBN-13: 978-0-595-79942-8 (ebk)
ISBN-10: 0-595-35448-3 (pbk)
ISBN-10: 0-595-79942-6 (ebk)

Printed in the United States of America

For the following:
My two daughters, primarily…
My two parents, next

Contents

BOOK I: Max and Danielle

Chapter 1 3
Chapter 2 8
Chapter 3 12
Chapter 4 23
Chapter 5 29
Chapter 6 37
Chapter 7 41
Chapter 8 49
Chapter 9 58
Chapter 10 63
Chapter 11 64
Chapter 12 70
Chapter 13 75
Chapter 14 87

BOOK II: Enter Katie

Chapter 15 91
Chapter 16 97
Chapter 17 102
Chapter 18 110
Chapter 19 115

Chapter 20 120
Chapter 21 131
Chapter 22 135
Chapter 23 141
Chapter 24 151
Chapter 25 158
Chapter 26 165
Chapter 27 169
Chapter 28 172
Chapter 29 176

BOOK III: Mixed Nuts

Chapter 30 187
Chapter 31 194
Chapter 32 209
Chapter 33 220
Chapter 34 228
Chapter 35 234
Chapter 36 239
Chapter 37 247
Chapter 38 259
Chapter 39 272
Chapter 40 276
Chapter 41 282
Chapter 42 288
Chapter 43 296
Chapter 44 304

BOOK I

MAX AND DANIELLE

CHAPTER 1

He would never have guessed that being rich would make him so horny, but it did. Unbelievably horny.

Max Bland was standing in his editor's office staring down at a check in his right hand made out for the princely sum of one-hundred and sixty-three thousand dollars. More specifically, a check made out to *him* for the princely sum of one-hundred and sixty-three thousand dollars. It hardly seemed real; he half expected the damn thing to dissolve in a puff of smoke like it was made out of the same paper the Mission: Impossible people use to send secret codes to their agents.

He gave Rachel a dubious look.

"And this is all mine?"

Rachel laughed and Max's heart stopped momentarily. But instead of "Gotcha!" Rachel said, "Well, I'm sure the IRS doesn't think it's all yours but, yeah, pretty much…it's all yours."

Max let out a relieved gasp and then sneered; he'd deal with the IRS later, those bastards, when he got back home to Arizona. Right now he started pacing. He had to. The surge of sexual energy coursing through his body needed an outlet. It was ridiculous, this horniness. Where did it come from? Was this normal? Do psychologists know that money has this effect on red-blooded males? It was so bad in fact that Max was even thinking of humping Rachel right here in her office which would have been fine had Rachel been an attractive thirty-something, maybe with long raven hair, green eyes and legs up to here. Instead, the editor was a woman who looked like an ex-NFL linebacker after sex-reassignment surgery.

"I just…I mean…wow!" Max stammered.

"The way things are going, hon, you'll be getting a lot more of those checks soon. Larger ones, even. You're the new star here at Sullivan. Actually, the only star. None of our books ever took off this fast."

"That so?"

"Absolutely. It's phenomenal. This thing is a monster. Bookstores are already running out and there's a waiting list two weeks long in some places. Our printers are having trouble keeping up with demand. Weren't you paying attention? Christ, I've been trying to get a hold of you for weeks."

The truth was, however, that Max hadn't been paying attention and he told Rachel so.

"I possess a low threshold for embarrassment, I'm afraid," he said. "Very low. Do you know what I've been doing the past six weeks, since my book was released?"

"Do tell," Rachel prodded and to Max her voice had the sultry seductiveness of a young Suzanne Pleshette.

"Hiding," he answered.

"Good heavens! What on earth for?"

"Self preservation, I suppose. The day my book was released back in March I was certain that I was about to be made a fool of. So I called my boss at work, told him I was horribly sick with some kinda SARS-slash-Ebola thing and that I wouldn't be back for weeks. Then I unplugged my phone, stuck it in the closet and basically lived the life of a hermit. I even unplugged the television and radio just so I wouldn't chance upon some critic calling me the anti-Christ because my book was so bad. I figured that at the end of six weeks or so I could safely re-emerge and resume my life as an anonymous systems engineer."

And the plan worked perfectly, he considered. The release date of his novel came and went with him not having the tiniest inkling as to how awful everybody thought it was. He remembered thinking that it was silly, really, this dream of making a living as a writer. There was a walloping amount of hubris involved, after all, in believing that people would plunk down hard earned money for something he'd written. So what that becoming a novelist was his one true ambition since high school? Big deal. When he was a kid his buddy Franklin Berman wanted to play in the big leagues but when Max last heard he was a CPA in Queens, and one of his high school sweethearts, Leslie Rosado, wanted to be an actress but was last spotted collecting tolls at the Bronx-Whitestone Bridge. For his part, it was probably best to just stick to systems engineering in Phoenix; it earned a steady paycheck and was a worthy occupation.

Then on Wednesday of his fourth week of isolation Max answered a pounding on his apartment door and upon opening it was immediately whacked upside the head by something hard.

"Whatsamatter with you?" bellowed the assailant. "Your mother thinks you're dead, for Christ's sake!"

"Dad?" Max said when his vision cleared. He felt a knot rising on his head where he'd been struck.

"Jesus, you don't answer the phone for weeks; we try calling all hours of the damn day; nobody's heard from you…what the hell's the matter with you? Your poor mother—you know how she is, always assuming the worst. And who's Sylvia Plath?"

"Sylvia Plath? She's a writer—was a writer. She committed suicide back in the sixties."

"Yeah, well, your mother's thinking you pulled a Sylvia Plath on us. Either that or you'd been murdered."

"Where is she?"

The elder Bland vaguely pointed west towards Oregon. "Back home, sedated. The doctor had to pump her so full of drugs there's no way she would've gotten past the dogs at the airport."

Max saw what was in his father's hand.

"You hit me with a copy of my book?"

"I didn't wanna wait for the paperback edition." Walter Bland had pushed past Max into the apartment. "Jesus, it's like I'm in a tomb," he commented. Max did, in fact, have all the blinds drawn and only one small lamp turned on. And because it was nearly six-thirty in the evening the effect was rather gloomy.

"So lemme get this straight…" Walter said, switching on the ceiling light, "I feed and clothe you when you were a kid; I put up with all your bullshit when you were a smart aleck teenager; kept my mouth shut when you dropped out of college to become a writer and now that you're a bestselling author I can't even reach you by phone?"

Max was caught off guard, still rubbing his head.

"What are you talking about?" he had asked.

His dad harrumphed. "What I'm talking about is that I didn't raise you to be a snob. Just because you're doing well for yourself now doesn't mean you get to brush off all us little people."

"No, I meant that part about my book being a bestseller."

"Jesus, leave it to you to write a book and not even know how it's selling. How could you not know that? What the hell did you write it for if you were going to ignore it? Yes, your book's a bestseller. Lucky for you, too, otherwise I would have knocked your head with a Louisville Slugger for all the aggravation your mother's been causing me. Also, I've been fielding calls from all our relatives back east, even one or two from someone claiming to be your editor. She's another one who thinks you're dead, only she used Ernest Hemingway instead of Sylvia What's-her-name."

Max, putting his hands on his father's shoulders, had stared the older man right in the eye.

"Listen, Dad, I want you to think very carefully. You're not just saying my book's a bestseller because Aunt Maggie bought forty copies of it like she said she would, are you?"

"Get a grip. You don't believe me, read the *Times*. Your book practically started out at number one on their list. And the review they gave it! Jesus! It's like they're ready to erect a statue of you in Central Park."

After all that time expecting failure Max was stunned.

"That's incredible," he whispered, more to himself than to his father. "You're sure it's my book?"

"*The Remarkable Reign of Pope Anne I*, that's your book, right? Then, yes, it's on the list. Now, would you please do a fellow male a favor and call your damn mother?"

🍁　　🍁　　🍁

After using his father's cell to call his mother and reassure her that no, he hadn't stuck his head in the oven or been the target of an Islamic *fatwa*, Max reattached his own phone to the jack in the wall and dialed into his voice mail discovering that it was full. In four weeks he had amassed a collection of messages that fell roughly into the following categories:

—His mother congratulating him on his book's release date.
—His mother worried because she hadn't heard from him yet.
—His mother hysterical because she still hadn't heard from him yet.
—His father swearing because "your damn mother is driving me crazy so pick up the fucking phone you ungrateful spawn of my loins and call her back to let her know you're not dead! *And who the fuck is Sylvia Plath?*"
And finally…

—His mother leaving a tearful message for the detectives stating that the body they found decomposing in the apartment belonged to Max Bland, thirty-eight years old, would never hurt a fly and was an organ donor. She also begged them to either find his killers soon or mail her his suicide note, and to apologize to his neighbors for the smell.

The rest of the messages were either from his good friend Danielle, or from Rachel Weiskaupf, begging him to fly to New York ASAP and in whose office he now stood with a raging hard-on listening to her ramble on about book signing tours and interviews.

"Interviews?" Max queried. News that his book was a bestseller was hard enough to swallow; news that people actually wanted to talk to him about it was nigh impossible. He was also noticing that for a fifty-nine year old woman Rachel seemed to have a perky set of boobs. The small fortune in his hand was making him crazy. A fantasy of tearing off Rachel's dress and burying his face in her cleavage flitted through his brain like a subliminal advertisement.

Rachel, apparently not at all aware of Max's lascivious ideas answered his question.

"Plenty of interviews, if you want to do them, which I would strongly suggest, hon. Publicity is publicity, right? Newspapers want to talk to you, *Time* magazine, *People*, *Newsweek*; you got Larry King, NPR, Charlie Rose…"

"Larry King? Really?"

Rachel arched her eyebrow in the way only Jewish women can. "Hon, when you write a book in which the main character is a lesbian who becomes pope and orders all Catholic priests to be castrated, people want to talk to you."

CHAPTER 2

❀

Returning home to Arizona from New York the day after his meeting with Rachel Max finally called his best friend Danielle at work to let her know he was still alive. She was genuinely relieved when she heard his voice.

"God, Max, what the hell?" she began. "How come you haven't been answering your phone? I mean, I guess I understand…it must have been something serious and you needed some time to recover but I've been scared to death and—"

"What're you talking about?"

"Your illness? The reason why you haven't been to work? Your boss, Todd, told me you were sick."

"Oh, that. That was a bunch of crap. I never felt better."

"Then what—"

"Listen, I have a perfectly good explanation for it but it's something I want to share with you in person."

"You mean you're healthy?"

"As a horse."

"You had me scared to death, you prick!"

"Yeah, you, my mother and a middle-aged editor who I came alarmingly close to making a pass at."

"What?"

"Forget about it. Are you free for dinner tonight?"

Danielle gave a little laugh.

"Sure, although Marc Dinglemann would prefer I wasn't."

"That guy from Engineering?"

"Yep and I shot him down. You know my rule about dating in the workplace. Besides, I don't want to one day become Danielle Dinglemann."

"I see your point. But he's a good-looking enough guy."

"He's *plain*-looking at best. Anyway, he's obnoxious but not in a cute way like you, and I have my eye on somebody else."

"Yeah, I know…Tom Cruise."

"Well, yeah, always. But this time I'm settling for someone just as good looking but not as rich."

"Whatever…Listen, I've already made the reservations. Compass Room at seven; I'll pick you up at six-fifteen."

"Compass Room? Funny, I don't remember ever giving you a blowjob. Did you win a radio contest or something?"

"Definitely 'or something.' Look, just be ready at six-fifteen, okay? And when I say 'ready' I mean I'll play the role of the person who knocks on the door and you'll play the role of the person who walks out the door, got it? Don't keep me waiting like you normally do while you try to match your eyeliner to your shoes. If you're good I won't make you pay half the check."

"I can't afford half the check at the Compass Room, sweetie."

"Then you'd better be good. Six-fifteen, bye."

After hanging up with Danielle Max eagerly opened a kitchen drawer and withdrew his checkbook. He had been looking forward to this since arriving at the airport this morning and the anticipation of what the next few minutes would bring was actually making him light-headed.

Up until his meeting with Rachel Max's finances were not in the best shape. In fact, he probably could have found ten-year old boys operating lemonade stands with better credit ratings than himself. He was several payments late on his student loan, had nearly four-thousand bucks worth of Visa card debt and owed the IRS eight-hundred dollars. His paycheck hadn't kept pace with the cost of living with the result that each payday his money vanished. Rent, car loan payments, auto insurance, utility bills—those were the essentials. What little was left purchased groceries, gas and the needed night out with Danielle in order to forget his woes. He worked for a company that didn't pay him what he was worth but because of the depressed job market his chances of landing a more lucrative position were about the same as him landing on the moon.

Ten years ago it was another story. I.T. gurus like him were in high demand and jobs paying 30 or 40 dollars an hour were seemingly everywhere. So Max spent four or five years during that period hiring himself out as an Oracle programming consultant, jumping from company to company whenever a headhunter would call to dangle more money in front of his nose.

Then the bubble burst. First, that whole Y2K scare proved to be nothing more than a bogeyman tale. The world's computers did not crash; the ATMs still worked; no nuclear missiles were accidentally launched. Second, the internet, still new back in '95 or '96, became commonplace and so user-friendly by the turn of the century that kindergartners could have been hired to design web pages if it weren't for the child labor laws. And finally, the dot-com industry imploded.

Suddenly Max was in trouble. The company he had been working for as an outside contractor laid him off in a cost-cutting maneuver. Initially he regarded it as but a minor setback and was as confident in finding another high salary position as he was in finding cocaine in a rap star's hotel room. But Max soon found that the market for guys who felt they deserved up to ten times the minimum wage just because they knew what things like EXEC SQL Declare $empcursor and FETCH Substr(%_) into db_ename meant had considerably dried up. For nearly three months he was jobless. Although he got plenty of job offers the salaries were deemed offensive by Max. The *least* he would accept was fifty-five grand a year and that was only if the company offered a benefits package which included certain services that could only be provided by bikini models. The most anybody was willing to offer, however, was forty grand, and many of them weren't even offering that.

Finally, economic reality set in. His optimism that things would turn around in the industry proved to be only so much false hope. His paltry savings were gone, he was falling behind on his bills and he was living off his credit card. Max was desperate when he interviewed with ProtoTech two years ago. That was part of the reason he took the job when it was offered for thirty-six thousand. The other part had to do with the delectably cute receptionist manning the lobby who flirted with him brazenly while he was filling out his job application and whom he dated for three months.

So now, Max was at his kitchen table signing a check made out to the U.S. Department of Education for just over twenty-eight thousand dollars. After applying his signature he kissed the thing and stuffed it in an envelope along with a note which simply said, "Kiss my ass." Next, he wrote a check for $3,791 made out to the good people at Capital One Visa, and for the good people at

Capital One Visa he included instructions to "Go Fuck Yourselves." Then another twelve-thousand and change was spent telling those cheery folks at Desert Schools Credit Union that once they got done sucking his balls would they be so kind as to mail him the title to his car.

But his masterpiece was saved for the I.R.S. Accompanying the check squaring his account with them was an epistle (to call it a mere letter, Max felt, would be to insult his talents as a writer) in which he wove such a poetic tapestry of foul language and anti-government sentiment not befitting a patriotic American that, unbeknownst to him, he was actually tailed by the FBI for three weeks and placed on a federal watchlist titled "Persons Suspected of Plotting Terror Acts Against the United States of America." His name appeared between those of Abdul ben Sistani, 25 years old, a Syrian native who was apparently once overheard telling a friend how to spell "jihad"; and Ethel Blickstein, 87, from Asbury Park, New Jersey, who wrote President Bush to tell him his new tax cuts for the wealthy were "stinky."

CHAPTER 3

The Compass Room was unique among Phoenix restaurants. Located downtown on 2nd Street atop the Hyatt the dining room revolved thus giving its well-heeled patrons a 360° tour of the Valley of the Sun. Dinner was pricey and back when Max was pulling in forty bucks an hour he didn't think twice about bringing women here just to impress them. Also, the food was very good. The best time to come, Max felt, was at night. During lunch the views weren't so great: Phoenix architecture, he felt, is about as imaginative and creative as an episode of *Friends*, not only is it boring but it's flat. With the exception of the skyscrapers downtown what you saw as the Compass Room slowly spun around at one in the afternoon was a metropolis of low-lying square buildings that all seemed to be painted the same shade of tan, and ribbons of traffic-choked highways. At night at least you had the glowing city lights underneath a canopy of twinkling stars.

The hostess who seated Max and Danielle was, apropos of these types of restaurants, rail thin, very pretty and seemed the type of woman whose one aspiration in life was to say the words, "As the new Miss America I vow to use my power to end world hunger and deliver Prada to poor people in Honduras." She provided them accommodations by a window.

"God, Max, this is beautiful!" Danielle gushed, taking in the view. It was a splendidly clear night and the earth and the sky both seemed filled with stars. "I've always wanted to come here but all of my boyfriends were too cheap."

"Ah, yes…you've always had bad luck in that area, haven't you?" Max said. "Who was the guy you went out with who took you to McDonald's on your first date and paid with coupons?"

"Evan, and don't remind me."

Danielle Edwards was Max's best friend in Arizona. She was a brunette of average height, slender and possessed an altogether enviable figure. She was twenty-six, very beautiful, always stylishly dressed and groomed but bore it all so easily she gave the impression that she woke up like that every morning. Tonight she was attired in black: a very classy mini dress with spaghetti straps and high-heeled sandals showing off pedicured toes.

"How many times have you been here?" she queried him.

"I dunno...six or seven."

"So I'm not special?" She feigned being hurt.

"Of course you're special, but you're more like Wendy's special, or maybe Jack in the Box."

"Fuck you."

They were interrupted when the floor captain arrived to inform them obsequiously of the night's specials. He was followed immediately by the sommelier who took the couple's wine orders before he in turn gave way to their waiter who of course told Max and Danielle that they had both made excellent choices and would have their dinners to them post haste.

"So," Danielle began when once again they were alone. "What's the big news? And you're sure you're in good health?"

"Positive. All systems operating within required parameters."

"What?"

"A little Star Trek humor."

"Geek. So, what's the news then?"

"I'm moving back to New York," Max said triumphantly.

Danielle raised her eyebrows. In what amounted to barely a whisper she said, "What?"

"Back to New York," Max said. His face was that of a man who was sublimely confident in his approaching future. "Took me twelve fucking years, Danielle...twelve years. Damn. I wasted a lot of time but now I'm set to do it. You've heard me talk about this before, right? Moving back to New York, I mean."

She nodded. In the two years she had known him Max had talked about returning to live in New York as often as politicians speak of lowering taxes.

"Anyway," Max continued, "I didn't really want to go back until I knew I'd be able to afford it, you know? New York's such an expensive city to live in. I dunno how my parents did it. I didn't wanna go back there and live hand-to-mouth; hell, I practically do that here."

"So what happened?" Danielle asked. She was already signaling the sommelier for more wine after gulping down her first glass upon hearing Max's news. Max thought she suddenly seemed a little out of sorts but before he could ask if anything was the matter she said, "I mean, I guess you found a pretty good job since you can afford to live there now, right?" She thanked the sommelier for her refill. "So what company are you going to be working for?"

Her companion smiled.

"Actually, no company and no job. At least not in the way you're thinking."

"You lost me."

"Well, here's the thing." And Max set about explaining to Danielle just what the thing was. First, of course, that he had written a book.

"It took me nearly three years," he said. "Well, if you count that I wanted to write one since high school then it took me over twenty years but for purposes of not becoming suicidal I choose not to look at it that way." He told her about how the book became an obsession with him, that the majority of his free time was spent writing it in parks, in libraries, in restaurants, even at work during lunch. "If I was home on the toilet taking a crap I'd be thinking about the book. When I was asleep I was dreaming about the book. Once, I was on an airplane flying to Portland to see my parents and I asked the stewardess for a pen and I wrote three paragraphs on those little napkins they give you with the complimentary drinks."

Secondly, how he used up another year trying to pitch it to agents.

"So you write a novel, right? You think the hard part is over and that it's good and something people would read. Ha! Trying to *sell* the stupid thing is the hard part. I spent a fortune mailing out sample chapters and a synopsis. If I saw a dime on the street I picked it up because it meant being ten cents closer to owning another stamp." And for all that trouble, he told her, he got rejection letter after rejection letter sent back to him. "Come over to my place and I'll show them to you; I kept them all. It's a stack this high."

Third, how after finally getting the manuscript accepted by an agent and then a publisher, he found himself in almost constant warfare with his editor.

"At first when I got news that a publisher bought the book I told myself I'd go along with anything they wanted just so long as they published it. Then my editor wanted to change this and change that and I got offended. I kept thinking, How dare she? Who does she think she is? It got to the point where every time my phone rang it was Rachel in New York wanting to 'make a suggestion' or needing rewrites, saying stuff like 'We have a problem in Chapter 17' and I'd be thinking, 'The only problem in Chapter 17 is that you need to get laid.' But I shouldn't complain. In the end it turned out good. I may have been resentful at times but Rach knew what she was doing. She actually made it a better story."

Their food arrived, Danielle being served the filet mignon, Max the salmon. Max immediately dug into his meal but Danielle seemed hardly to notice her own was there.

"I don't understand," she said, "what made you suddenly decide to switch careers and become a writer?"

Max swallowed his bite of fish before replying with, "I didn't suddenly decide. Like I said, I've wanted to be a writer since high school. I even dropped out of college my sophomore year because I thought it was a waste of time."

"How so?"

"Well, I'm one of these people who figure that when it comes to writing you're either born with the talent to do it or you're not. It's not something professors can teach you."

"Okay, so then how come it took you so long to write a book?" Danielle still hadn't touched her food.

"Laziness, procrastination, a combination of both," Max answered. "I remember thinking when I was in my early twenties that I had all the time in the world to write a book and so whenever I had free time I'd spend it having fun. Then when I was twenty-six my parents told me they were moving to Oregon to retire…"

Max told Danielle that he had had no choice but to face the prospect of leaving New York and moving with them. "I mean, when you earn five dollars an hour as a messenger, New York City is a bit out of your budget, unless you consider a park bench suitable housing," he said. This turn of events also opened his eyes to how much time he had wasted and he began feeling a little disgusted with himself. Not only had he not yet written a novel like he had planned to but he realized that if he had stayed in college he'd have graduated by now. Most likely he would have used the English degree to get a good job and been able to live on his own, like a true adult. His younger brother had a career and his own place over in Jersey; most of his childhood friends had careers and apartments; some were even married, owned houses…so he resolved to break from his parents, return to college, finish what he started. He'd somehow find a way to fit writing in with his schoolwork.

"That's what brought me here to Phoenix from the Bronx," Max went on, knowing that this was a part of his personal history that Danielle had never heard before. "I decided to attend Arizona State because the brochure they mailed me had all these pictures of cute co-eds in mini skirts and tank tops reading Proust. That was twelve years ago. Anyway, to make a long story short, while I was in college I learned a thing or two about computers, got a couple of part time jobs to make ends meet, and then dropped out when I started making a lot of money. But I still didn't write a book." Another bite of salmon disappeared into his mouth.

"So what finally made you do so?" Danielle asked. She was actually intrigued. Max was a very private man and in the two years that they'd been friends this was the most she'd heard him talk about himself. He usually deflected her inquiries with glib comments or vague details.

"I had a panic attack one night about four years ago," Max said. "There I was, sitting on my couch, watching *Coupling* on PBS and suddenly I got horribly cold, began shivering uncontrollably and had trouble breathing. I ended up on the floor on my knees hugging myself and realizing that just like that," he snapped his fingers, "I'm closer to middle age than I wanna be and I *still* hadn't written a book. I swear, Danielle, it was a wake up call. After the panic attack passed I went straight to Walgreen's, bought some notebooks and pencils, and started jotting down all the ideas I'd had for novels since, like, the tenth grade."

He went on to say that it had made him nauseous to consider the finished list and realize that not one word had been written for any of those stories. No outlines, no character treatments, no titles even. "I'm talking thirty, thirty-five, ideas, Danielle, and I had not taken the first step towards writing any of them." He then said he spent the rest of the night evaluating the list. Some of the concepts were immediately scratched, stuff he had come up with while a teenager and reflected a teenager's notion of a good story: the one about the monster from Hell who steals the souls of high school students; or the one about the science teacher who is also a secret agent. Others were discarded because they were too serious in nature: the tale about the last weeks of life of two AIDS patients; or the struggles of a poor family in the projects of the Bronx. Still others got the axe because they were just stupid: stories involving talking animals or superheroes.

"Anyway, I was left with this one idea I had come up with a few years earlier. The next day I called in sick and started writing it. I finished about a year ago. The rest, as they say, is history." He cut off another piece of salmon.

"How come I never knew you were writing this book?" Danielle pressed. "I thought we were good friends."

Max was quick to wave off her indignation.

"Truth is," he said after swallowing a mouthful of asparagus, "nobody knew I was writing a book. Not my parents, not my brother, not any women I dated during that time, nobody."

"Why?"

Max laughed dryly, "Have you ever told anyone you wanted to be a writer? Not a journalist, mind you, but a novelist. You see, in most people's minds a journalist can easily earn a living; you got the newspapers, the magazines, CNN, whatever. So therefore a journalist can bring home a paycheck, right? But when you tell people your idea is to be a novelist, fuhgeddaboutit. Right away they start trying to talk some sense into you. They tell you how hard it is to make a living as a writer, like they've ever tried. They say things like, 'How are you gonna support a family doing that?' They tell you they think writing would be fine as a hobby but that you'd better get a real job to pay the bills. My mother pretended to be supportive but I could tell it was fake, just something mothers are supposed to do, you know? And my dad…all he talked about was money. You could tell he didn't want a son who couldn't earn his keep."

"That's sad," Danielle said genuinely.

"It is sad but what are you gonna do? Besides, look at the evidence. There's a lot of people out there with unpublished novels gathering dust in desk drawers. And how many high school English teachers do you think really wanted to be high school English teachers when they grew up? My guess is not a lot. They're frustrated novelists or, even worse, poets, who discovered that it's hard to put gas in the car when nobody will buy your work for a dime. Let me have a bite of your steak."

Danielle looked down at her plate as if noticing the food for the first time. She cut off a morsel of her filet and held her fork across the table, letting him eat it right off the utensil.

"Yeah, they do filet mignon good here," he said, enjoying the bite. "They also have a good duck."

"Forget about that. So I guess somebody bought your book for a dime?"

Max laughed.

"A lot of people bought my book, are buying my book. And for a lot more than a dime; twenty-five ninety-five to be exact, tax not included."

"Fuck, Max! You mean to tell me your book is in the stores?"

"Since March, yeah."

Danielle rolled her eyes and looked away, an expression of consternation on her face, a huff of frustration escaping her lips. "That's such bullshit," she muttered.

Max stopped chewing. "Wait a minute, you're upset?"

"Yes, I am."

"We're here celebrating and you're upset?"

"Yes."

Max was puzzled. He replayed the previous few moments in his mind to see where exactly all this had gone wrong.

"And you have a good reason for this," he said upon failing to figure things out.

"Yes, you didn't tell me about your book," Danielle replied.

"What's that gotta do with anything?" he wailed.

"It's got everything to do with everything," she told him as if that answer made any sense at all.

"It does?"

"Yes. Why wasn't I important enough to share the news about your book with?"

"Well, it's like I said, I—"

"Am I not important to you?"

"Of course you're important to me. It's just that—"

"Just not important enough to share a life-changing event with?"

Now Max was getting upset. Pointing his fork at her he said, "Look, you twit, we're supposed to be celebrating, remember? You're supposed to be happy for me but instead you're giving me the 'pissed off girlfriend' routine, and we're not even having sex!"

"I can understand you not telling me you were writing the book," Danielle said. "That made sense and who knows? I might have ended up being one of those jerks who told you it was a pipe dream. But why wasn't I important enough to know the book was published *and* in the stores? What the hell?"

Max waved off her indignation again. "I didn't tell you anything because visions of disaster were running through my head. I was a wreck. The day the book came out I shoulda been the happiest guy on Earth but instead I just holed up in my apartment with the curtains drawn and my phone in a closet. I thought about telling you but then I also thought 'What if it flops?' And for some reason that really bothered me, you know? The idea of failing in front of you."

This caught Danielle's attention.

"Why would failing in front of me be such a big crisis?" she asked with more interest than she wanted to show. Before she knew what she was doing she had taken hold of his hand.

"Look, I dunno..." Max began. "I guess—"

"How is everything?" the floor captain asked, materializing out of thin air. Danielle shot him full of daggers with her eyes as Max released her hand.

"Well, other than my dinner partner going a bit psycho on me, superb," Max answered. "Except for one thing: we're supposed to be celebrating and I forgot to order champagne. *Cristal*...I've heard that's a good one, right? I've never had it."

"*Cristal* is an excellent champagne, sir. We have a 1997 available." The floor captain paused for a beat. "Of course, it's two-hundred dollars a bottle, sir."

"Is that all?" Max promptly replied, holding the captain's gaze. "Then bring me two bottles."

"Max!"

The floor captain bowed and shimmered away.

Danielle was looking at her companion as though he were a hybrid of lunatic and Greek god.

"Sorry," Max said. "I hope you don't think I was showing off but I hate it when people do that. Do you think if that old white guy sitting at the next table had ordered *Cristal* this jerk would have told him how much a bottle was?"

"Forget about him, just tell me how it is you're able to drop four-hundred bucks on champagne. I feel like I've stepped into some kind of parallel universe where suddenly you have money to spend."

"I mean, just because I've got a bit of skin color doesn't mean I can't afford the finer things in life."

"I know, but—"

"I mean, I'm well-dressed, very well-spoken...hell, my entrée costs forty-five bucks!"

"You're straying, honey," Danielle cut in. "What the hell is up with all the money you're spending?"

Max leaned forward across the table; Danielle did likewise. Their faces were no more than two inches apart. They looked like two schoolchildren about to impart secrets about the fat kid to each other.

"Look," Max began, whispering, "I know it's impolite to talk about such things but hell, I gotta tell somebody, just so I can try to make sense out of it all."

"What is it?"

"About ten days ago I had thirty-nine cents in my checking account and forty dollars in my wallet. And that had to last me till payday when I'd get to take home another pittance. But this morning when I got off the plane from New York I went to my bank and deposited a check for a hundred sixty-three thousand bucks."

"Holy motherfucking shit!" Danielle couldn't help the expletives coming out at more than normal volume, catching the attention of nearby diners who gave disapproving glares.

"I know," Max said. "You shoulda seen how the teller acted. A cute young thing who never so much as smiled at me before, but when I handed her that check she acted as if it was all she could do to keep from unbuttoning her blouse. Anyway, the money was royalties from my book; handed to me by my editor yesterday. The goddam thing is selling well. Really, really well. And get this: because the book is selling so well the president of the publishing company met with me when I was still in New York yesterday and told me he wants to sign me to a five book deal. Five books in four years for one million dollars."

"That's two-hundred grand a book! You said yes, right? Right?"

Max shook his head. "I told him I'd think about it. To tell you the truth I'm not sure how I'll feel writing with deadlines to meet."

"God, it must be nice to be in a position to consider turning down million dollar deals."

Max shrugged.

"So how does it feel to have all that money?" Danielle asked.

"It makes me horny."

Danielle laughed, so did Max.

"Seriously, it makes me horny." He related to her the scene in his editor's office. "My goddam genitals have felt electric ever since she gave me the check. Even now I can't help staring down at your cleavage."

Danielle arched her eyebrow. Leaning forward on her crossed arms as she was she knew there was a nice view straight down her dress; Max could probably even see the edges of the lace cups of her bra. She also knew her arms were pushing up her breasts making them look like they would overflow her garments. But she didn't move.

"Beyond horny...I dunno...I feel safe for some reason. I can pay all my bills and that's nice. Beyond that...I guess I just wanna shop! I feel like I'm going to get a headache with all the stuff whirling around in my brain that I can buy. On my way to your place tonight I passed a guy driving a brand new Mercedes and

I thought, 'Shoot, I can afford that; I can even afford to get the bigger one, fully loaded.'"

The champagne arrived. The sommelier handed Max one bottle that was wrapped in gold foil paper with a red velvet bow.

"I took the liberty, sir. For when you bring it home." Then the gentleman set about opening the other. Apparently the cost of a bottle of *Cristal* necessitated that the opening of one be treated like the unveiling of a religious relic. Forming a respectful circle around the sommelier was the floor captain, the hostess, all the waiters and the bread guy; all of them standing erect with hands folded. The bottle was gravely presented to Max who rolled his eyes at all this fuss and wished the chap would just get on with it. Danielle was served first, then Max. The staff waited until both had tasted the champagne and proclaimed it excellent, then they withdrew leaving the bottle behind in a silver-plated bucket of ice.

"Anyway," Max said, regaining the thread of their conversation, "That's why I'm moving back to New York; if the money keeps coming in like this I can finally afford it."

At this mention of New York again Danielle downed her glass of champagne at a gulp and had Max pour her some more.

"Are you alright?" Max finally got the chance to ask.

"I'm fine."

"It's just that I've known actual alcoholics who have seemed less interested in getting drunk."

"I promise you I won't get drunk."

Max seemed dubious.

"So when is this big move occurring?" Danielle inquired in order to change the subject.

Max shrugged. "That I don't know. As soon as possible, obviously. Let's see…it's early May now…I guess I'd like to be there by the end of July but I don't know if that's overly optimistic. From what I understand it's kind of hard to find a place to live in Manhattan, even if you have an excess of money to spend."

"Good, then you should stay here. Move to Fountain Hills if you want to live someplace fancy."

"God no. And it's not about living someplace fancy, it's about returning home. Look, Arizona's been good to me but I'm a fish outta water here. I've never gotten over leaving New York and now I can't wait to get back. I feel like hopping on a plane tonight, if you wanna know the truth." And he went back to enjoying his salmon.

CHAPTER 4

If Danielle sat down and really thought about it she'd realize that she probably said "fuck" nearly a hundred times that night starting when she said goodbye to Max after he dropped her off following dinner and she closed her apartment door on his retreating figure.

"Fuckfuckfuckfuckfuckfuckfuck!" she spat as she fastened the deadbolt and "Fuckfuckfuckfuckfuckfuck!" she repeated as she took off her sandals and trod barefoot into her bedroom. Unzipping her mini dress she let it slip down her frame and then she kicked it into a corner where a growing pile of laundry had been growing larger since last week.

"Fuckfuckfuckfuckfuckfuck!"

For several moments she had no idea what to do with herself. She merely stood there, in a strapless black bra and one of those new V-Strings from Victoria's Secret looking every bit like a very, very put out underwear model. A frown was creasing her pretty face and she seemed to be computing space shuttle trajectories in her head but all that came out of her mouth eventually was, "Fuckfuckfuckfuckfuckfuck!", angrily, with frustration, each successive "fuck" louder than the one before until by the seventh one the word was practically screeched. Finally, she looked at the Winnie the Pooh clock on her nightstand. Pooh told her it was almost nine forty-five. Still early. Normally, Max would have come in and they would have found a movie on HBO or watched *Cheers* reruns on TV Land. But tonight, after doing his usual gallant turn of walking her to her door, he had made some crack about going off to buy Bolivia and left.

"Fuckfuckfuckfuckfuckfuck!"

Okay, so Max didn't stay but it was still early, she considered. Syb and Liz would come over. She called; Syb answered.

"I need a powwow," Danielle said instead of hello.

"Ooh, sounds serious," her best friend said.

"Can you come?"

"Sure, Vic just fell asleep; he's working the early shift tomorrow."

"Bring Liz."

"Ooh, it *is* serious."

Danielle hung up. Once again she just stood there, staring into space, biting her lower lip. When she did do something it was simply to repeat her new favorite word:

"Fuckfuckfuckfuckfuckfuckfuck!"

Danielle and Max became friends because of something Max didn't do: make a pass at her.

Like Max, Danielle worked at ProtoTech Systems. Unlike Max, however, Danielle worked in the finance department making sure the company kept its head above water.

She'd started working there directly after college five years ago and because of her intelligence and initiative was considered indispensable and thus handled with kid gloves by her boss, a forty-ish woman named Cindy who let everyone know she was stuck in a loveless marriage and who secretly resented Danielle her beauty and youth but who nonetheless had enough crap in her life to deal with to not want to lose one of her top staff.

It was Cindy's own boss, the CFO, who was responsible for bringing Max and Danielle together. It was decided by him one day that what was needed was a complete revamp of all the database systems in Finance so he could better monitor ProtoTech's pecuniary performance. The CFO fancied himself a technophile and had grand schemes in his mind: slick systems, really cutting edge stuff, customized reports at the push of a button with full-color charts, the ability to dial in from home to check figures, single-click access to data from Singapore, London, Paris, South Africa, Mexico. Real top-of-the-line stuff. So the CFO talked to his golf buddy, the CIO, who in turn talked to Max, the new Oracle genius just hired. Max was told to talk to one Danielle Edwards, a "major babe in Finance" as the CIO put it, and whom Cindy assigned to liaise with the I.T. department on this project.

The night before her initial meeting with Max Danielle was over at Sybil's place for wine and conversation when suddenly she said: "God, I just remembered…I have a meeting with one of the computer nerds tomorrow about some new database project I got roped into."

"And I take it you're not looking forward to it?" Syb asked.

Danielle had rolled her eyes.

"First of all, tech guys are weirdos," she said. "This one probably has a partially built female robot in his garage because he can't get a real date. Secondly, you know how guys in general are. They can't control their hormones enough to work closely with a woman without trying to seduce her. This guy Max I'm suppose to see tomorrow will most likely spend the majority of the meeting making flirtatious comments and staring at my tits."

"Most likely," Syb agreed.

"And then, because this is a huge project that will take months to finish, he'll get around to trying to see me outside the office."

"Like for working lunches," Syb said knowingly, "so he can show you how good he is in a more social setting."

"Right, or happy hour at the end of the day, just to go over a few things while hoping I get buzzed enough to find him attractive. And then eventually he'll just happen to have an extra ticket to a Suns game or to a concert."

"And he'll invite you because his friend that was supposed to go suddenly can't make it."

"Right," Danielle said, and the two women laughed at the inanity of the opposite sex. Then Danielle said, "God, what is it with men? Why do they think that every attractive young woman they meet is amenable to being hit on? Even at work."

"That's easy," Syb had answered. "It's because a man's brain is in the wrong head on his body."

So Danielle had waited for Max in the fifth floor conference room two years ago with her guard up, ready to quickly rebut any ham-handed attempts he made at making at move on her. But Max did nothing of the kind. During that first meeting he treated her respectfully, put a surprising amount of value in her opinions and not once did she catch his eyes falling below chin level. There were no compliments from him on her perfume; no telling her that the color of her blouse looked good on her; no flattering tribute to how she was wearing her hair. He kept it strictly business. But he was also funny and his sense of humor appealed to her. He demonstrated a sarcastic disdain for all the bullshit that goes on in corporations of this size and for all the self-important people who swagger around the corridors thinking that making microchips was right up there with curing cancer. It was even funnier because he had this great New York accent. He sounded like Sonny Corleone from *The Godfather*.

"So…how bad was it?" Sybil had asked that night. "Did the computer geek bring his X-ray specs with him so he could see through your clothes?"

"No, not at all. Surprisingly, it went well."

There was something in the way Danielle said this which made Syb raise her eyebrows.

"Ooo! Do I detect a note of interest?"

"Well, he is attractive," Danielle had admitted. "Let's see…he's older, thirty-six I think he said but he doesn't look more than thirty, he's very stylish and well-dressed, very funny. And he's not a typical Arizona cowboy-wannabe white guy, you know? I think he's mixed or something…you know, interracial."

But as appealing as Max was to her Danielle wanted nothing to do with office romances, whether with men or women. A bisexual, she kept her relationships with both sexes limited to persons not in the employ of ProtoTech. It was too potentially messy otherwise and there were plenty of prospects elsewhere.

However, as time went on she began to feel curious as to why Max never made a move on her. Briefly she was sure he was gay. Had to be. Unmarried, in his thirties, very neat, well-dressed, knew who Anais Nin was. But that theory was crushed when she caught him eyeballing Megan Shuster from Marketing as Megan was sipping from a water fountain. Only straight guys eyeball women that way. The look in his eyes was purely carnivorous. Megan was cute, sure, Danielle conceded, but she was horribly flat-chested and had big feet; all in all Danielle thought of herself as the better package. The idea came to her that his interest in Megan meant Max had a thing for redheads. *Prick*, she had thought. *What is it with guys and redheads? Nearly all of them are extremely pale and covered in freckles.* She herself never fancied that breed in either sex. Then she noticed him giving Alison Frey from Engineering the once over. Alison was blonde. *Even bigger prick. What is it with guys and blondes?* Most of the blonde women she herself had dated had left her yawning in the bedroom. Then she caught him following Valerie Porter from Tech Support with his eyes when Valerie passed by Danielle's cubicle one day. That was the worst but not because Danielle herself wouldn't have minded spending a few hours in a bedroom with Valerie and was jealous but because Valerie looked remarkably like Danielle: same build, same hair color, same skin tone, same facial features. So if he was hot for Valerie why wasn't he giving any signs that he was also hot for her?

Telling all this to Syb and Liz one night about three months into the project it was Liz who said, "You are the type of woman I hate, Dani, you know that?"

"Why?" Danielle had asked, taken aback.

"Because you're one of these really cute women who complain all the time about guys making passes at you wherever you go like it's such a big bother and then, when you finally come across a guy who doesn't treat you like a piece of meat, you complain that he shows no interest in you. It is *so* self-indulgent and shows how needy your ego is."

Reluctantly, Danielle had to admit Liz was right. She was being self-indulgent. And so eventually she gave up trying to decipher Max's apparent lack of interest in her because it was indeed starting to make her feel alarmingly full of herself. Maybe, she rationalized, he already had a girlfriend he was happy with; maybe he'd recently gotten out of a bad relationship and was off women for a while; maybe she just wasn't his type. Eventually, as work on the project progressed and Max continued to simply treat her as a professional colleague she forgot the whole silly thing.

The way it turned out it was Danielle who ended up with the extra ticket to the Suns game. Sybil and Vic were supposed to go but Vic had the flu and Sybil hadn't wanted to go without him.

By then it was six months that Danielle and Max had been working together on the CFO's pet project, conferring daily by phone or e-mail, meeting in person twice or more a week so Max could ask questions or discuss screen designs or implementation strategies with her. Max didn't try to show off. He could add and he could subtract; he could multiply and he could divide. But when it came to the high level financial and statistical math that her department dealt with and which he needed to program into the new systems he threw up his hands in ignorance and relied solely on her expertise to help him. This impressed her because most guys she knew would rather eat used jock straps than depend on the assistance of a little ole woman. But then again, a lot about Max impressed Danielle. Not only was he smart but he was well read, extremely witty, urbane and very thoughtful. Somewhat exasperatingly, getting him to share information about himself was tricky but when compared to nearly all other men who couldn't shut up about themselves this also was a refreshing change. She was, in short, really enjoying Max's company and looked forward to their face-to-face meetings. And because he was a dozen years older she discovered that talking to him was happily unlike talking to guys her own age, his years giving him the ability to provide her perspective on issues she was dealing with, his opinions possessing a wisdom and maturity younger men just did not have. Before long, they had developed a nice "nine-to-five friendship": within the confines of ProtoTech good buddies but once they clocked out perfect strangers. Yet after work, at home in her apartment, there were many times she actually missed him and wished she knew his home number so she could call him up, invite him out for coffee and spend time laughing with him, telling him about a new book she was reading, getting his thoughts on world events or whatever…to develop, frankly, a real friendship extending beyond the workplace. She'd never had a close male friend before and she felt that such a relationship with a man of Max's caliber would be a positive addition in her life.

So when the Suns tickets became available Danielle thought about it for a bit and then figured why not? It would be a good first step towards creating that real friendship and she felt one hundred percent confident he wouldn't misconstrue the offer; in other words, that she'd say "Basketball game?" and he'd hear "Wanna fuck my brains out?"

CHAPTER 5

❦

When Syb and Liz arrived for the powwow Danielle answered the door dressed as she was: in only her black strapless bra and thong panties. An elderly man, one of her neighbors, happened to be passing by walking his pug when he looked over and saw this vision in lingerie. In addition to all the color draining from his face he dropped the dog's leash and the pug took off running for freedom. Sybil and Liz just stood in the door staring with raised eyebrows until Danielle finally came to her senses.

"Fuckfuckfuckfuckfuckfuckfuck!" she swore at her mostly nude body. She instructed her friends to come in and have a seat and then she popped into her bedroom, emerging moments later wearing pajamas that had little Eeyores all over them.

"Drinks?" she asked her guests.

"Absolutely, yes," Sybil said. She was a comely blonde with a somewhat pudgy frame attired in sweats. "I had a fucked up day at work. I wouldn't mind some of that wine you served me last time."

"The Moscato?"

"That's the one."

"Ugh, too sweet," Liz said. Like Sybil she was blonde but had streaks of chestnut dyed into her hair, and she was the tallest of the friends at six feet, very muscular and athletic. "You used to be a nice dry-red-wine-drinking girl and then you started in with all these sweet whites."

Sybil and Liz had known Danielle since high school and because they went to college together and even now lived only a few miles apart had remained close. It was Sybil whom Danielle actually felt closer to, though, owing to remarkably similar dispositions and tastes. Liz was a dear but it was Syb with whom Danielle spent countless late nights deep in counsel about life or love. However, when it came to red alert situations, a powwow like tonight, for instance, Danielle valued what Liz brought to the table with her more practical and logical nature, even if sometimes it hurt Danielle's feelings, which it often did.

Danielle handed Syb her Moscato, Liz a merlot. For herself she had a bottle of Bud, a sure sign to her friends that she wasn't happy. The three were in the living room; Danielle and Syb were sharing the couch with Danielle lying down, her feet on Syb's lap, and Liz in the armchair by the fireplace. At first silence reigned, then Sybil got the ball rolling with, "Soooo…what's on your—"

"Max is moving to New York," Danielle spat. "All the way to fucking New York."

Syb reacted as a best friend should, turning to better face her suffering friend and taking hold of her hand. An earnest look of concern was on her face. "He told you this?"

Danielle nodded as she took a swig from the brown bottle.

"Tonight. At the Compass Room."

A whistle from Syb. "Pretty fancy."

"Yeah, well, Max had no trouble paying the bill even though it was almost six-hundred dollars; he's loaded now." And she updated her friends on the change in Max's fortunes: best-selling novel, a huge wad of cash in the bank and counting, one million dollar book deal, the works.

"A-ha! So that was him!" Sybil said, then by way of explanation went on: "I was in Borders the other day and I saw this book…I forget the title, something 'Annie' or something about the pope…anyway it was by Max Bland. And I thought 'Hey, that's Max's name' so I picked up the book to see the author's picture, you know, to see if it was him, even though I didn't really think it was, and instead of a photo there was just a stick figure with curly hair. Then I read the author's bio stuff underneath the stick figure and it was all crazy bullshit: it said how the writer grew up on Easter Island and was raised by those giant stone heads; and how he was kidnapped by Mormon missionaries because they needed someone to marry their twelve-year old sister; and how he ran away and joined a radical Amish group that planned to assassinate the first President Bush but they could never find the time with all the barn-raising…stuff like that, it was hilarious."

Danielle laughed in spite of herself for it sounded just like Max; even the stick figure made sense: Max hated to be photographed.

"Yes, that's him," she said. "The man I love was raised by Easter Island heads."

🍁 🍁 🍁

Having drained the last of her beer Danielle got up for another.

"You know, I've seen the way he looks at you, Danielle," Sybil called out. "He's got the hots for you too. I think he's just as crazy about you as you are about him. In fact, I'm sure of it."

"Doesn't matter now, even if it is true," Danielle called back from the kitchen. She reappeared soon after, new Bud in hand, walking a little unsteadily now that she was adding beer to the wine and champagne from earlier, and took up her former position on the couch. Sybil began rubbing her feet. "You should've heard him tonight. He wasn't thinking about me; he wasn't thinking about any romance he could have with me; all he was thinking about was New York: when he was going to move back; where he'd look for apartments; going to Yankees games. It was obvious that as far as he's concerned Arizona and everyone in it is soon going to be a memory."

"But you two will stay in touch, remain friends."

"Yeah, but that's not really what I want is it?" Danielle sighed, took a long pull from her Bud, seemed at a loss. Then, "God, and he looked so good tonight, too. He'd went shopping with some of his new fortune and had on this great suit. And, I dunno, there was something very sexy about his attitude tonight. He was so…confident."

"Nothing sexier than a confident man," Sybil agreed.

"Fuckfuckfuckfuckfuckfuckfuck!"

Sybil once again took hold of Danielle's hand and squeezed it in commiseration. "Okay, I know this kind of advice is easier said than done, and I shouldn't talk because I always wait for the guy to make the first move, but this is an emergency: You need to tell him. You've waited long enough. Just tell him how you feel."

"And expect what to happen, exactly?"

"Look, I was serious before. I know for certain he feels the same way about you. It'll be alright."

"No, I mean, what do you expect him to do? Forget about going to New York simply because I tell him I love him? You don't understand, he's wanted this for *twelve years*. Twelve, okay? It's like his Holy Grail, his Mount Everest. He wants to get the fuck out of Arizona and he wants to do it ASAP. Hell, he's probably at the airport now with his extra bottle of *Cristal* and autographed copies of his book."

"So move with him," Syb suggested after a moment's consideration.

"What?" Danielle laughed. "Come on, I need real advice. You can't be serious."

"Why not?"

"But—"

"But what?" Syb pressed. "You found a man you're in love with who's running away to New York. Go along with him."

"But—"

"Think of how romantic it would be! Just like something out of a movie, right? And exactly the kind of thing you'd regret not doing when you're sixty."

"Okay, but—"

"But what? What argument could you possibly give for not doing this? Besides, you've been talking about leaving Arizona for years, Danielle."

This silenced Danielle and it made her sit up, for it was true. Both Syb and Liz had heard their friend mention this before because from a career perspective it made perfect sense. After earning her Master's degree three years ago by taking night courses at the University of Phoenix Danielle had had a firmer sense of what direction she wanted her career to go in and thus did she realize that she didn't want to spend forty years making sure two and two equaled four in a local company like ProtoTech before retiring on a pension in Sun City or Apache Junction. What really interested her were the international money markets, working for powerhouse banks like CitiCorp or CreditSuisse, outfits where two and two didn't always equal four because of the exchange rate. She loved finance, loved numbers and wanted to play in the big leagues, not the minors. The minors were fine for seasoning you, getting you experience before you moved onward and upward, she felt. The minors was Arizona, and staying here with her education and ambition seemed a waste. The bigs, on the other hand, was any one of a number of places Danielle had listed some time ago, where she could imagine having a nice corner office with a downtown view: London, Tokyo, Chicago, and the most important of them all: New York, the Mecca of world finance.

Suddenly a delicious idea was formulating in Danielle's mind. It was crazy, but delicious.

"If I told him how I felt," she said, "that I'm in love with him, and he reciprocates—"

"Which he will," Syb still insisted.

"Then I can just make plans to join him in New York."
"Right."
"Of course I'd have to find a job there first."
"Of course."
"Which shouldn't be too hard. I have a Master's and five years experience in a multi-national publicly traded corporation."
"Right."
"That's got to count for something."
"Right again."
"And I'm not talking about moving in with him," Danielle went on. "I mean, hopefully that would happen someday, but I'm not trying to rush things. I know how skittish men get when it comes to that."
"Don't want to scare him off."
"I mean, what have I got to lose, right? It'll be a bit of an adventure. If it doesn't work out romantically with Max then so what? New York is a big city. I can just focus on my career and hopefully he and I will stay friends."
"But it will work out with you and Max, honey."
Danielle looked at her friend.
"Are you sure?" she asked.
"Positive," Sybil gushed.
"So what I need to do is tell him," Danielle stated firmly after another long pull on her beer.
Sybil nodded her approval.
"Absolutely you need to tell him," she said. "If you let him move to New York and he spends time with those fucking trust fund Fifth Avenue-type women who say 'to-MAH-to' and wear all black like he does then he'll be gone for good."
"Right. So I'll definitely tell him," Danielle once more stated firmly.
"Right."
"Right."
"Bad idea."
This last came from Liz who up until now had said nothing, merely sitting in the armchair by the fireplace, sipping her merlot, and silently digesting all that she heard. In truth, when the three of them got together Liz was used to Danielle and Sybil going chattering off into their own world like Lucy and Ethel sharing juicy gossip. Indeed, when Liz spoke just now the other two were startled, jerking their heads towards her as though Liz had crashed a private party by sneaking in through the window.

"What was that you said?" Danielle asked.

"I said it was a bad idea," Liz replied patiently. "You telling Max. It's a bad idea."

Sybil made a face. Her reputation as an advice giver was on the line, after all.

Liz continued. "Am I the only one who sees the problem here?"

"Obviously," Syb said, perhaps a little too cattishly.

Liz leaned forward and held Danielle's eyes with her own.

"You've known Max, what, two years?"

Danielle nodded. "About that, yes."

"And in those two years, you and he have never been romantically or physically involved, right?"

"Right."

"Never talked about it?"

"No."

"No one-night stands after you both had too much to drink?" Liz asked.

Danielle stiffened.

"Max never has too much to drink and he's a perfect gentleman," she informed Liz. "He would never take advantage of me if I was drunk."

"So in the past two years you've never given Max reason to believe you wanted to be more than friends?"

Danielle hesitated a bit before replying. "Well, you know…he and I are always, like, flirting with one another, but it's just joking around."

"Joking around. So he's never misinterpreted any of it?"

"I don't think so. No. I can safely say he has no idea how I feel about him."

"So…"

"So what, Liz?"

"So how do you think it's going to look to Max when after two years of acting like he's just a buddy you suddenly tell him you're in love with him right after he tells you he's written a book that's making him rich?"

Another face from Sybil.

"Oh, come on…"

But Liz was quick to snap back in defense of her position.

"Oh, come on, nothing. It's a valid point. Think of how that makes you look, Danielle. Maybe Syb's right and Max has wanted to get in your pants since the beginning but even if that's the case it's going to seem pretty damn coincidental to him that you waited till now to start spreading your legs."

"God, Liz…" Sybil winced.

"I know Max, remember?" Liz pressed on. "Not as well as you, granted, but still. One of the reasons I love talking to him is because he's real. He has this attitude that most of what's in the world is crap and that most of what people tell you are lies. He doesn't take a lot at face value and he knows the meaning of the phrase 'too good to be true.' He's cynical. It's the New Yorker in him. Of course, if you told him first thing tomorrow that you got the hots for him then like most men he'd probably start wondering if you like it doggy style. But I'm telling you…Max is smart and Max is capable of thinking beyond sex. That's another reason I like him. I can have a conversation with him and not feel like he's undressing me with his eyes. Anyway, I think before you even got a chance to book a flight to New York he'd get suspicious, start thinking you're a gold-digger and tell you to stay here."

"Max knows I'm not a gold-digger," Danielle said sternly.

"Really? Because that's what most men think, you know. That underneath it all every woman is a gold-digger. And who can blame them? We're always saying that we want rich guys, that rich guys are the most desirable because they can buy us stuff and take care of us. Even in this age where women are independent we want the guy to pick up the check for dinner *and* pay for the movie tickets. And we'd rather date men with Jaguars than men with Mazdas even if the ones with the Mazdas treat us better. And what about that fucking show on television, *Joe Millionaire*? Twenty bimbos ready to marry a man they know nothing about just because they were told he's rich. We make fun of the show and call the women on it whores but what kind of message does it send to men?

"And you know what, Danielle?" A pause as Liz appeared to consider something. "Never mind," she ultimately said.

But at this point Danielle was in no state to never mind anything. Leaning forward on the couch she matched Liz' pose.

"No, what?" she prodded.

Liz waited a few beats before saying, "Well, you called a powwow and it's always been our policy that powwows are open and honest, right? So let me be open and honest."

"Go ahead."

"I will. If you want to hate me afterwards, fine." Liz took a breath. "I can remember when you first started telling us that you liked Max as more than a friend. You said you were considering dating him to see where it would lead because 'it might be something good'. Your words. But you made it seem like it was just something you may or may not do, the same way you may or may not buy a car after test driving it. That was just a few months ago; I remember it was around my birthday so it was what, five months ago? Now all of a sudden Syb and I come here tonight and you're in a tizzy, answering the door in your underwear and you're using the word 'love': 'I'm in love with him'; 'he's the man I love." Somehow you went from 'it might be something good' to being in love with him without any stops in between. And you don't even know what kind of boyfriend he'd be. Is he a possessive jerk? Is he overly jealous? Is he a good kisser? Is he any good in bed? Is he romantic? You know none of these things but suddenly you know you love him and you're ready to burst into tears because he's moving to New York. You're even ready to follow him there which, if you didn't know, isn't like moving to Mesa, it's all the way at the other end of the country! So what I want to know is, were you in love with him before he dropped six-hundred dollars on dinner, or immediately afterwards?"

CHAPTER 6

❀

So Liz had done it again. Brought practicality and logic to the table and stung Danielle with it.

But where did that word "love" come from? Danielle wondered, lying in bed after Sybil and Liz had left, staring up at her dark ceiling. It was after midnight now and she needed to get up for work in just under six hours but she was far from ready to fall asleep.

Certainly I love Max, she considered. But if I'm totally honest with myself, isn't that just as a friend?

There is a difference, after all, between loving someone as a friend and loving them as, well, a lover.

They occupy different parts of the heart. Loving a friend has more to do with comfort and familiarity whereas it's more of an emotional thing to love a husband or a boyfriend, and that's only if they earn it.

Max has definitely earned my love as a friend but as a mate? He's never been given the chance.

Liz is right: I have no idea how what kind of boyfriend he'd be or what kind of couple *we'd* be. So what the hell was I saying I love him for? That's so grade school. It makes me feel like I was acting like a little kid with a crush. I mean, I am attracted to Max. A lot. And it's probably safe to say I'm in lust with him but big deal…lust is easy. My nipples get hard every time I see the cute guy who works the deli counter at Safeway or that thirty-ish woman with the nice smile who lives two doors down. That's lust. But I've never considered myself in love with them.

Of course, Max is a different case, isn't he?

He's one of the best friends I have. But love? That kind of love? Violins and Valentine's Day? Why the hell was I talking like that? So grade school. I bet Liz thought I was acting like a twelve-year old.

And what was up with Liz making me sound like I just want Max for the money? I was ready to make Max my boyfriend when he was barely earning enough to pay his bills, before he sold this book he wrote, which I didn't know he was writing. I mean, yeah, the money he has now is nice and it certainly adds to his appeal but...

Adds to his appeal?

God, did I just think that? That his money adds to his appeal? Fuck.

But wait a minute. What's so wrong with that? What's so wrong with finding it appealing that a potential mate earns a good living?

Because it makes me feel shallow.

But why? Maybe the appeal of his money to me has nothing to do with material things: him buying me Gucci shoes or Tiffany jewelry. Maybe the appeal of his money to me has to do with a sense of security, of knowing that if we ever got married we'd be able to provide for ourselves and not end up living on the street.

I'm listening...

Who wants to just scrape by? Who wants to struggle? There's enough crap to deal with in this life already.

Fine. But is Liz right? Did his announcement of his new wealth make me start using the word 'love'?

No! I'm a little drunk so it probably came from all the booze I drank tonight. My IQ drops proportionately to the amount of alcohol I ingest and as a result my vocabulary shrinks. "Love" was probably the only word I could think of. I should start bringing a thesaurus with me every time I go to a bar.

Jesus, do you think Max knows how I feel? Liz is right, he is smart.

That's immaterial. What I have to figure out is whether or not to tell him.

And then move to New York? Am I ready for that now?

But if I don't...well, if I don't then he goes to New York not knowing how I feel and I risk losing him. But if I tell him how I feel and then turn my life upside down when I'm not quite ready, then...then I risk losing him because it won't work out.

Fuckfuckfuckfuckfuckfuckfuck!"

Danielle thought back to when she first realized she was falling for the New Yorker. It was in fact near Liz's birthday because Danielle remembered that Max had come with her to the mall to shop for a gift. Later, when they were lunching at Panda Express, he asked her if she wanted to go to the movies that night, something he'd done hundreds of times before, but this time she had to turn him down because it just so happened she had a date that night with some guy—who was it? Blonde. Green eyes. Southern accent—Tyrel! She had a date with Tyrel, someone she'd met at her gym. So she told Max that she'd go to the movies with him the next day.

As it turned out, Danielle now could not remember much about that date with Tyrel. She suspected they had dinner someplace but could not recall where or even what she ate; and she had a vague mirage-like vision of them at the Mesa Amphitheatre but could not recall why. Was it a concert, or a play? Nor could she recall anything much about Tyrel though she was certain they must have swapped personal histories at some point. The only clear thing she could remember about that date was how much time she had spent thinking about Max and wishing she were with him instead as well as wishing that he'd be the guy who would make an awkward attempt for a goodnight kiss on her doorstep when the date was over. And she remembered suddenly becoming flush with confusion and hiding in a stall in the ladies' room (the restaurant's or the amphitheatre's she had no idea) while she experienced the frightening/joyful/moving realization that perhaps the man she'd been looking for all this time had been right under her nose for the past couple of years.

🍁   🍁   🍁

The way it was supposed to happen, Danielle considered, biting her lip, still staring up at the ceiling, was that she would eventually tell Max that she wanted to take their relationship to the proverbial next level. In this version, Max wouldn't have written a bestselling novel and thus wouldn't have been ready to hop on the first plane to New York. So they would start dating and she would accept the promotion at ProtoTech she was up for; time would pass, her and Max would move into a condo in Fountain Hills or maybe Ahwatukee and decorate it with stuff from Ethan Allen and IKEA and have fabulous backyard barbecue parties even though Max can't stand parties, or people for that matter; then, after two or three years of managing the Overseas Investments and Properties division at work she'd be in a position to land any job she wanted in a city like New York or London. They'd live in a loft in Greenwich Village or a flat in Notting Hill and maybe they could both telecommute, staying home and working naked, taking breaks to have sex in the kitchen. *That* was how it was supposed to happen.

But now…

"God, this so…Aaargh!" she said aloud to her empty room.

But if she was hoping the walls had any advice to impart, she was sorely disappointed.

CHAPTER 7

❧

The way Max figured it, if you're going to burn a bridge, you may as well use a lot of fuel.

ProtoTech Systems sat on thirty acres of land in Chandler, a suburb of Phoenix. The company made microchips for computer motherboards and its Arizona workforce conducted their daily labors in three buildings, one of which was a frightening industrial-looking edifice with two huge water tanks alongside it and where the actual fabrication of the chips took place.

The day after his Compass Room dinner with Danielle Max crossed the lobby of Building B, flashed his ID badge to the ex-high school football star security guard and rode the elevator to the third floor, home of ProtoTech's I.T. department. It was a little after eight and so already there was the usual hubbub of business being conducted in this sea of cubicles: phones ringing, printers printing and programmers shouting out expletives as they debugged their code. Max gave half-hearted greetings to those who welcomed him back as he walked towards his cubicle but he did not stop to make small talk with anyone. It was pointless, really. If everything went according to plan he'd be out of here in fifteen minutes, twenty tops.

Max knew he was in an enviable position and indeed since last night he had been looking forward to this as much, if not more so, as he had looked forward to paying off those bills yesterday afternoon. Over the years a certain etiquette had developed for people who, for whatever reason, are leaving their place of employment: there's the two weeks notice; helping train the replacement; continuing to work on unfinished projects; sitting through an exit interview.

Max had no intention of doing any of that.

Arriving at his cubicle he cheerfully scooped up the pile of company correspondence waiting on his chair and dumped it all into the trash can. Then he turned on his PC, started the e-mail application and spent a moment staring at the screen composing his thoughts. When he was ready he addressed the message using a mailing list that would send it to everyone in the company and started typing.

🍁   🍁   🍁

A few minutes later he looked at his watch. It was 8:30. His boss, Todd, should be arriving just about now—in fact, yes, that was him saying good morning to Cecil a few cubes down. Finished with his e-mail Max instructed his PC to send the message in exactly ten minutes.

"Max! You're back!" Todd greeted his missing-in-action Oracle guru when he noticed him in his cube. "You're back! What a surprise!"

"Indeed." Max said.

Todd was a thin, sandy-haired fellow in his early thirties whom Max saw as nothing more than a prototypical corporate weenie.

"Been here long?" Todd asked Max.

"Nah."

"Good, good. So how are the Yankees doing?"

"Not too bad. In first place. Swept Boston this week."

"That's great! You know, I really expect them to win it all this year," Todd said.

Max smiled knowing that at some point today Todd would probably tell Bill, two cubes down, that he expected Bill's Padres to win it all this year.

"The season's still young," Max replied, "and their rotation is kind of suspect. We'll see where they are in July."

"Right, right. So, listen, now that you're back I guess you'd better come into my office and we'll go over a bunch of stuff."

Todd's "office" was not as structurally sound as the word implies. The whole thing could have been taken apart with a Philips screwdriver and five minutes of spare time. Todd's position didn't merit a real office with four solid walls and a door. Instead, he had what was derisively referred to as a "super-cubicle", which was basically the same thing Max and the others had but with higher walls. Max took a seat in front of Todd's desk, crossed his legs and waited with folded hands while his boss spent a few pretentious moments flipping pages in his Franklin planner and looking as if the future of the entire company rested on his shoulders. Finally Todd sighed.

"I'm glad you're back, Max. We've got a lot on our plate. The ball is in our court. The spotlight is on us."

Max felt sorry for Todd; the man didn't know how ridiculous he sounded.

"Well, of course, you've got the Sales Operations database that you were working on when you left," Todd continued. "But you shouldn't have too much more to do on that, right? They're screaming for it and I told them you'd have it ready a few days after you returned, so how about by next Thursday?" He made a mark in his planner. "Also, there's the SQL module for the customer survey pages on the website which the Java guys are waiting for." Another mark and then a pause as he turned a planner page. "Then we've got a request from Maintenance for you to create a Service Order Log for them; a request from Engineering for a system to keep track of blueprints." Another mark, another page turn. "Oh, and Facilities wants some changes made to that database you did for them a few months ago. They want the system to alert them whenever scheduled repairs on equipment are coming up. I don't know, talk to Danny about it." Todd looked up at Max to make sure his subordinate had digested all that. Then, "This is just the tip of iceberg, Max. You haven't heard about the new division they created in your absence; a complete restructuring of, like, five departments and it's putting the pressure on us. We got a lot of big stuff coming up. What the hell, job security, right? So I need you to knock out these small projects, get them out of the way so I can devote you to whatever needs to be done for the new division. Are we cool?"

Max didn't reply straight away. Instead, he picked a piece of lint off his black slacks, rubbed his fingers together and watched the lint slowly float down to the floor.

"You know, it's funny," Max finally began, when the lint landed on the gray carpeting. I told you I needed an extended vacation because of an illness I was suffering from. Now here it is, my first day back to work, I've already spent several minutes with you and yet you've not asked me once how I'm doing. You've asked me how the Yankees are doing but not me."

Max wasn't sure—because Todd normally was pasty white—but he could've sworn his boss's face lost even more color.

"I mean, I've worked here a little over two years now. I've never given you any trouble, never made waves. I've been a valuable part of this team since day one and yet the closest you've come to asking after my well-being is when you wanted an update on how the pinstriped baseball-playing millionaires I root for are doing. Why is that, Todd? Is Derek Jeter an Oracle programmer? Is Bernie Williams gonna show up here and rewrite the SQL queries for the Facilities database?"

"Jesus, Max, of course—"

"Correct me if I'm wrong, Todd, but didn't I make my condition sound pretty serious when I left? I seem to remember a lot of coughing and speaking in a weak voice. But I guess as far as you're concerned I'm just a handy-dandy programmer, a means to an end, a warm body to get the job done."

Todd was licking his lips and swallowing a lot. Sweat was moistening his forehead. Max realized that it had suddenly gotten quiet outside of the supercubicle. Just a few minutes ago he and Todd had been surrounded by an ambient noise consisting of fellow workers chatting together, speaking to people on the phone or tapping on their keyboards. Now, having overheard a taste of the conversation coming from Todd's "office" and finding it particularly juicy they were all hushed up.

Apparently Todd noticed this too. He leaned forward.

"Can we move into the conference room?" he whispered.

"Why?" Max countered in a normal volume. "As far as I can tell we're having a pleasant conversation. No, Todd. I'm actually quite comfortable here."

Todd held his hands up in front of him, palms toward Max, in a placating gesture.

"Max, I'm sorry," he said. "You're right, I fucked up. It's just that things have been kind of hectic around here, especially with you gone. I mean, you're my top Oracle guy so of course when you leave stuff starts to fall through the cracks, you know? And with the restructuring…Look, when I saw you in your cubicle I just got into business mode, you know? And I'm sorry. It's just been crazy around here. But you know ProtoTech cares about its people. We were all worried about you. Everyday people would come up to me and ask 'How's Max doing? Is he feeling any better?'"

"Is that so?"

"Absolutely. You know how much people like you in this company."

"Mm."

"It's just been crazy but you know you're one of my main men. You know that, right?"

Max let a few seconds of silence pass before he suddenly started laughing. An expression of relief took root on Todd's visage.

"Eh, don't worry, Todd," Max said, smiling his best. "You're off the hook. That whole illness thing was bullshit."

Todd blinked.

"Pardon?"

"Bullshit," Max repeated. "I haven't had anything worse than the sniffles the entire year."

Todd shook his head the way men do when they accidentally see their mothers naked and want to erase the image from their minds.

"What the fuck is going on here, Max?"

"The fuck is that I lied about being sick. I know, I know…" Max said, helping himself to some mints from a bowl on Todd's desk. "…it was wrong and I put myself at risk for some bad karma by doing so but what the hey. I needed a lot of time off and that was the only way I could think of to get it."

"By lying to me."

Max nodded. "Otherwise you would've tried to thwart my plans by talking about the Sales Operations database."

"And lying to me doesn't bother you?"

"Oh, fuck no. Quite frankly I don't see why it should since I'm quitting."

Todd's eyes were flashing with anger now and his cheeks flushed with indignation.

"You just walk in here after over a month and quit? Just like that? Six weeks off and you feel you can give two weeks notice with no warning?"

"Actually," said Max, "it's worse than you think. I'm giving you my two minutes notice. I am getting the hell out of here right now. I don't wanna spend another minute in this place and I certainly don't wanna spend another minute in the company of a guy the likes of you. Without a doubt you are one of the most two-faced, pretentious, brown-nosing, corporate zombie assholes I've had the displeasure to encounter and it is going to be a thrill to leave you wondering just how the hell you're going to get my open projects done. Better think hard, Todd. Better find a really, really, really good Oracle guy to replace me because that Sales Operations database that is almost but not quite done yet is one complicated piece of shit."

"You fucking—" But just then Todd's computer made a chiming noise that signaled a new e-mail message was arriving. All around them Max heard other PCs making the same noise. Out of habit Todd glanced at the screen and then turned his attention back to Max, but then he did a double take when his brain registered who the message was from. His face lost color again as his intuition screamed at him that this was not going to be pleasant.

🍁   🍁   🍁

From: Max Bland (MBland@prototech.com)
To: All Staff (GlobalStaffList)
Subject: Sayonara

My Dear ProtoTech Colleagues:

For those who do not know me my name is Max Bland and I am a systems engineer in the I.T. department at headquarters under the supervision of Todd Banks, which is kind of like working for one of those creeps who try to con old ladies out of their pensions over the phone. It is with the type of extreme elation normally reserved for lottery winners and those men fortunate enough to be married to centerfold models that I announce my resignation from this company. Indeed, if I ever have cause to darken these doors again I vow to kill myself by donning a Gay Pride t-shirt and walking into the Hell's Angels Annual Convention.

I now embark upon a new phase of my life:

——One that does not involve slaving for a faceless corporation with 31 vice-presidents (all of them men by the way, have any of you ladies noticed that? How long does it take for those bruises you get from bumping up against the glass ceiling to heal?) and who for some reason seem to want everyone to know the abysmally short lengths of their penises by showing up to work every day driving Porshes and Hummers.

——One that does not involve having to be courteous to people I don't like because I'm required to be a professional. For example, the colossally rude lunatics in Sales, who are all commission-driven conservative Republican assholes who would negotiate the sale of their children into slavery if they got a 20% cut; and the morons in Legal, who treat the rest of us like shit because they're bitter at not being able to earn $300 an hour in private practice due to the fact that law degrees from Everglades State College or the University of Lubbock aren't exactly like the ones Harvard or Yale award.

—One that does not involve wasting a third of every day in a cubicle, breathing recycled air and listening to Larry in the cube next to mine cough up a lung for eight hours and then watch him try to cure said cough by going outside for a cigarette break.

—One that does not involve sitting in pointless meetings…or having to buy fund raiser candy bars from people whose kids' schools need new lacrosse uniforms…or receiving chain e-mail letters promising me fantastic riches if I forward the message on to ten other suckers.

I'm especially pleased to never have to deal with the unjustifiably stuck-up attitudes of the women who work for the VPs. Hey, ladies…guess what?…you're *secretaries*—not *administrative* assistants, not *executive* assistants as you like to be known, but secretaries. You have no right to be snooty, and everyone here complains about how you all like to give us a hard time whenever we need to see your bosses for something. Keep in mind: your job descriptions include making coffee and reminding your boss his wife's birthday is coming up. Every one of you was hired because you have no ambition in life other than to not be waitresses and because you look good in skirts.

In conclusion let me just say that however good the quality of microchips produced by this company are ProtoTech nonetheless is lacking when it comes to fostering a good environment for its employees. I cannot say I have been ludicrously happy here. The pay sucks and the health benefits stink. Do you people realize that death would be a better option than going into the hospital for major surgery with our insurance plan? Look it up. So I bid thee all farewell. Forever. Bite me.

🍁   🍁   🍁

Todd didn't look too good. From the standpoint of a writer Max couldn't quite decide how to describe his ex-boss' face; it was both angry and nauseous; a cross between husband-coming-home-and-finding-his-wife-in-bed-with-another-man and husband-coming-home-and-finding-his-wife-in-bed-with-another-man-and-that-man-is-his-father. From the nearby cubicles titters of laughter were heard as the message was read. Soon there was a murmur of voices in the air that seemed to be encompassing the entire third floor. Max got up to go. Todd stared at him, tried to say something, anything, but failed to get the words past his larynx.

"Ciao, Todd," Max said in parting. Then he stopped by his cubicle but only long enough to reach down and yank the power cord to his computer from the socket in the wall. He watched the monitor blink off, winked at his reflection in the screen and then made a beeline for the elevators to the applause of his fellow programmers, except of course Larry, who was on a cigarette break.

CHAPTER 8

❀

Okay, this was getting ridiculous.

Danielle hung up the phone after once again hearing the start of Max's voice mail greeting: "You've reached 480-226..." She'd already left God knows how many messages over the past five days, she wasn't about to leave another. She was beginning to feel like a stalker, especially when she recalled how her last message went:

"Max, it's me, Danielle. Why haven't you called me back? Why haven't I seen you? I really, really, really want to see you so we can talk. I mean it. Call me back. I really, really, really need to see you. Call me at home or on my cell. Or you know what? Call Syb or Liz if you can't reach me. I really, really, really, want to talk to you. Wait. You have Syb and Liz' phone numbers, right? If you don't Syb's is 480-545..."

God. Danielle blushed at the recollection wishing she knew how to do that thing where you dial into someone's voice mail and erase the embarrassing messages you left because she truly wanted to erase that last one; and the others she left, come to think of it, which were equally desperate and only differed from the one detailed above in the number of reallys used.

It was evening and she had just gotten home from work. ProtoTech was still abuzz over Max's resignation a few days ago and his company-wide e-mail had assumed legendary status in part because it echoed the sentiments of a large percentage of the staff and in part because all the folks in the Sales and Legal departments had furiously descended on Information Technology en masse looking to tear Max limb from limb. It was even reported that more than one of the "executive assistants" working for the VPs had gone home in tears, leaving their bosses to make their own coffee. Over the past few days printed copies of the e-mail were surreptitiously taped to bathroom and elevator walls, the choice bits highlighted, and details of Max's last conversation with Todd, notably the part where Todd was labeled a brown-nosing corporate zombie were still fodder for water cooler chatter.

For Danielle, the most surreal part of the whole affair was when Valerie Porter, that almost-clone of herself whom Danielle had caught Max eyeballing back when they were working on that new financial system, ambushed her when she came out of the ladies room on the day Max quit.

"You're friends with that guy Max, right?" Valerie had asked.

Instantly suspicious (and noticing that Valerie wore the same perfume, *Manifesto*, as herself) Danielle said yes.

"Did you read his e-mail today? Wasn't that funny?"

"I thought so."

"Did you know he was going to do that?"

"No, it caught me by surprise also."

"You really have to admire someone who can speak his mind like that and not worry about the consequences. And his sense of humor...it's so wicked and clever. I love how he skewered those pricks in Legal."

"Well, they had it coming. Will you excuse—"

"Do you know if he's seeing anybody? And if not, do you think you can give me his num—"

"He's gay," Danielle had stated flatly and walked away.

Since then she had been trying vainly to reach him, even going so far as to call him one evening after midnight knowing he'd be pissed if she woke him up for anything less critical than "Max, Islamist insurgents are threatening to behead me unless NBC puts *Frasier* back on the air." But the phone had just rung and rung until, "You've reached 480-226..."

It took until the third day after his celebrated departure from ProtoTech for a rather unpleasant idea to coalesce in her mind, namely, could the fact that she received a copy of that e-mail be interpreted as Max telling her to fuck off as well? Surely he didn't group her in with the rest of the company, did he? she thought. With the assholes in Sales, the bitter snobs in Legal? That can't be it, can it? He and I are friends, she rationalized. Close friends. I only got the e-mail because he used the global list and he obviously used the global list to save time. There's no way he was bidding me farewell and telling me to bite him. Right?

Then, equally horribly: What if Valerie Porter did manage to get his number? She's chummy with Celeste in HR. And what if she called him, told him about the gay comment and now he's mad at me? And what if the only reason he hasn't answered his phone is because it's kind of hard to talk when you've got your face buried between Valerie's thighs? Which are exactly like my thighs!

Thus it was that after subsequent attempts to reach him—change that, make it *many, many* subsequent attempts to reach him over the following few days, Danielle was on the verge of panic, visions of Max and Valerie showering together running through her head. So naturally she called for another pow-wow, although, in truth, seeing how she did not invite Liz this time due to her heretical theories and only asked Sybil over, it was really more of a consultation.

"Okay," Syb said after the wine was poured and Danielle had brought her up to speed. "He doesn't have a cell phone?"

"He could never afford one," was the answer. "He always preferred spending forty bucks a month on his cable service."

Sybil took a sip of Moscato.

"Well, I bet he's able to afford one now, sweetie. You know, I went to Borders yesterday to try to buy that book of his and they were sold out. They told me there was a waiting list and it was going to take a week to get one. So then I went across the street to the Fiesta Mall…same thing. I called Barnes and Noble…same thing. The lady I talked to said that because this was Max's first novel the publisher must not have been sure of how well it would sell so they only distributed a minimum amount to bookstores. Now the publishers are scrambling to print more. Max is going to be one rich fucker."

"Fine, but why can't I reach him?"

Sybil glanced over at her friend. "So did you decide?" she asked pointedly.

"To tell him? Yeah."

"And the rest?"

"You mean moving to New York?" Danielle said. "Yeah, that too. I'm a bit nervous about it but you were right…if I woke up at age sixty knowing I could've done it but didn't then I'd hate myself."

"Good," Syb replied in a motherly manner. "At least one of our little group will hit the jackpot."

Danielle was taken aback.

"God, not you too," she moaned. "You think I'm doing this for the money?"

"I did not say that!"

"Because that's bullshit. If anything I resent the money now. *And* this best-selling book crap. Not only is it making him move to New York but apparently it's making him not call me anymore."

"Look, *I* know you don't want him for his money, sweetie but still…it's nice to see it happen to someone I love. I mean, Vic is never going to be rich, not working at Auto Zone, and he doesn't even read novels much less write them so you can count me out of the "Rich Boyfriend Sweepstakes" unless he invents a revolutionary new kind of muffler. I'll just have to live vicariously through you."

"Assuming it works out between us."

"Stop that! It will, trust me."

"And assuming I ever get to speak to him again. I just know he's off somewhere with that bitch Valerie. You know, she hasn't been to work the past two days. The two of them are probably in Vegas or Flagstaff ordering room service because they can't get out of bed."

Sybil shook her head. "You know, this is all your fault."

Danielle gaped. "Why do you say that?"

"Because it is, stupid. Max is hot, both Liz and I think so. In fact, remember about a year ago, when Vic and I broke up for, like, two days? I copied Max's number off your cell phone while you were in the bathroom and I was going to call him and pretend that I wanted to meet so he could explain why men are such assholes. But really I was going to lure him home and ride him like a stallion."

"And did you?" Danielle demanded.

"No. I got his voice mail and chickened out. Just my luck. Don't worry, I know he's off limits now but the point is I don't know why you didn't take him off the market a long time ago."

"We worked in the same company!"

"Fuck that," Sybil exclaimed, making a face. "Good men are hard to find, Danielle, and you had a good one in your clutches for two fucking years. I think you could've made an exception to your stupid rule. And while you were busy just being friends with him you kept going out with all these jerks who treated you like crap. Who cares if he worked for the same company? He's handsome, he's smart, he's considerate and I think we've established that he's got good earning potential. I mean, what were you going to do if he hadn't written a book? Wait until you both retired from ProtoTech and he needed Viagra?"

"He was sending out résumés because he wanted to find a higher paying job. I figured that once he got one it would be safe to…"

"Well he got one alright."

"…it would be safe to tell him that I wanted to be more than friends."

"You make it sound like a fucking business transaction."

"According to Liz it is." They both laughed, drained their wine glasses, poured some more.

Syb said, "No, the way to tell him is to invite him over, get some of this wine in him and just go down on him."

Danielle laughed. "I will admit that going down on him is on my to-do list but I'd like to work up to it."

"No, really, that's how I did it with Vic. Except instead of wine it was Coors Light and instead of being at my place we were at the drive-in movies. After he came he was like—" deepening her voice to a close approximation of Vic's tenor—"'So you wanna be my girlfriend?' and I was like, 'Duh…' True story."

Danielle was positively grateful for Syb and her irreverence. It felt good to laugh, it made her feel optimistic.

"So…" Syb started, "does Max know you swing both ways?"

"That I'm bi? God, no. Let's put it this way: after Daryl I'm extremely careful about telling men that I also like women."

"Ah."

Danielle dated Daryl for three months in college. For reasons which now escape her one night she had told Daryl about her bisexuality which had the effect of instantly morphing her boyfriend into a one-track-minded ass whose idea of conversation from then on was beseeching her to set up a threesome: "Oh, God, please! Pleasepleasepleasepleaseplease! Look, I'll do your laundry for a whole month! No! I'll do it for a whole year! Or how 'bout I make one of your car payments? Come on! Pleeeeeeaaasse!" The funny thing about it, Danielle considered now, was that even at his best Daryl lasted no more than a couple of minutes during sex; if she had actually invited another woman to join them he most likely would have ejaculated in his pants and been left at the starting gate.

🍁   🍁   🍁

The doorbell rang. Sybil, being nearest, offered to answer it but Danielle motioned her to stay seated and got up to do it herself. An "Oh, fuck!" escaped her lips when the door revealed Max.

"Do you need a kidney?" he asked wearily.

"What? What do you mean?" Danielle stammered, trying to get over the shock of seeing him.

"I mean," said Max, "I get home from the airport half an hour ago and I got forty messages from you begging me to call. Really desperate stuff, I'm talking about. So I'm thinking either A: you've lost your mind, B: you really need to get more friends or C: one of your kidneys failed and it turns out I'm a perfect match."

"I-I-"

"Are you gonna invite me in?"

Danielle stepped aside and Max entered.

"So I say to myself, 'Better not even unpack, better not even call her. Better just get over there and find out what's so urgent.'" He looked around the living room. "I must say I'm disappointed. I fully expected to find the place overrun with ghosts or something equally ridiculous. Hey, Syb."

"Hey, Max. Congratulations." Sybil got up and gave him a hug. At first Max seemed a bit confused but when he realized what the congratulations were for he said, "The book. You're talking about the book. Yes. Thank you, I appreciate it, that's nice of you. Danielle, I came alone so unless you think the moths outside are personal friends of mine it is now safe to shut the door."

This last was directed to the lovely Ms. Edwards who was indeed still holding the door open, looking at Max in stunned surprise. When she shut it she approached the novelist.

"Where have you been?" she asked.

Sighing, Max took a seat in the easy chair by the fireplace.

"Oregon. I left the day I quit my job."

"Why'd you go there?" Danielle pressed, certain the next sentence out of his mouth would contain the words *Valerie* and *multiple orgasms*. "And why didn't you tell me?"

"Why didn't I tell you? What are you, my mom's proxy in Arizona? I flew there to take care of a couple of things, alright? Lessee...first I saw my parents in Portland; let my maniac mother see that I was still alive and complain about how thin I am. Then we went to the bank and I paid off the mortgage on their house and bought them an RV. They've always wanted an RV although hopefully they won't ever want me to be seen in it with them. Then I drove down to Salem, saw my brother, paid off *his* mortgage and set up a trust fund for my two nieces."

"That's so sweet!" Sybil gushed.

Max shrugged. "Well, what I really wanted to do was buy myself a fully loaded BMW but I figured I'd appease the gods by doing nice things for my family first. Besides, I know if you had it you'd do the same for those you love. Anyway, after I did all that I went to California just to hang out."

"But you hate California," Danielle pointed out.

"True, but it's got more options for entertaining a guy than Oregon. I spent a night in L.A., a day in 'Frisco, drove down the Coast Highway to San Diego, ate nothing but clams and lobster the entire time."

"So you didn't see Valerie Porter?" Syb asked slyly, drawing a "cut it out" smack on the arm from Danielle.

"Valerie Porter?" Max asked Danielle in puzzlement. "You mean Tech Support Valerie Porter?" He whistled. "Yeah, I *wish* I just spent four days near the Pacific with Valerie Porter. Her in a bikini on a beach…that woulda been my kinda vacation."

Danielle pursed her lips and reddened slightly while Syb suppressed a chuckle.

"You know, Danielle," Max continued, "she looks a lot like you come to think of it."

"I never noticed." God, was she going to have to hear about goddamn Valerie all night? She wanted to smack Syb on the arm again except now Syb was standing behind the easy chair reaching over the back and massaging Max's shoulders, cooing about how fatigued he looked! And Max hated massages! Said that growing up in the Bronx meant he'd been tense since age five and he wasn't sure he'd be able to survive if his cortisol levels dipped below a certain point. But here he was, head back, eyes closed, letting Sybil's fingers knead his shoulders, looking for all the world like he'd gladly strip down and have her rub baby oil all over him.

"Yeah, I am pretty fatigued," Max told Sybil. "I haven't been sleeping well."

"Why's that, sweetie? Syb inquired, boring her knuckles between his shoulder blades.

"I dunno. It's kinda hard to explain but what it amounts to is this: I've wanted to be a writer for a long time and now I can truly say I am one. The excitement of finally being able to live the life I've imagined for myself makes me restless."

"I understand, sweetie."

"I can kiss database programming goodbye, thank God, and I can concentrate on writing all these stories I got whirling around my head."

"Right."

"And then there's this move to New York I'm making. Did Danielle tell you about that? Anyway, you can imagine how many millions of details that involves."

"Max," Sybil said, "I tried to buy your book but everywhere I went they were sold out."

Max nodded. "Yeah, I know. The publisher screwed up. It's a pain in the ass but I guess it's a good thing, right? Tell you what…" He dug into his pants pocket then reached up and gave Sybil his car keys. "You know what I drive, right? The silver Jetta? It's in the lot right next to those big palm trees. There's copies of my book on the back seat. Help yourself." He looked at Danielle. "Dare I ask if you've already bought a copy?"

"Well…I—"

Max laughed. "Do me a favor, Syb, bring one in for her, too. I'd do it myself but your fingers are magic. I don't think I ever wanna get up from this chair again."

"You'd be surprised at what else I can do with my fingers," Sybil said, making no attempt to hide the suggestiveness of the comment. She and he laughed heartily while Danielle fumed.

"I'll go out with you," she told Syb, pulling the woman by the arm and not letting her go until they were at Max's car in the parking lot.

"Go home," Danielle ordered Syb.

"What?"

"It's time for you to go home." She snatched Max's keys from her friend, used the remote to unlock the Jetta's doors. As promised, on the back seat were about ten copies of the novel. Danielle picked one up, finally holding in her hands the manifestation of Max's dream. In all the days that had passed since Max first told her about his new career as a writer this was the first time Danielle had even seen the book. The jacket was mostly black and the cover bore a shadowy, secretive image of a long-haired woman wearing a pope's miter. *The Remarkable Reign of Pope Anne I* was the title above the woman's head and below that, *by Max Bland*. On the inside rear flap of the jacket, just as Sybil had described, was a stick figure where Max's photograph should've been, and then the wacky bio featuring Easter Island and Mormons. Using her thumb, Danielle riffled through the pages back to front, amazed at all the words, all the paragraphs, all the chapters that had been written without her knowledge.

The book was finally real to her. It was this that was forcing her hand.

Danielle gave a copy of the book to Sybil and took one for herself. Then she once again started pulling her friend by the arm, this time to where Syb's blue Honda Accord was parked.

"Danielle! What the hell—"

"I told you, it's time to go."

"But I wanted him to autograph it for me."

So Danielle snatched back the book.

"I'll have him sign it and you can pick it up tomorrow. Goodbye!"

🍁   🍁   🍁

She paused before reentering her apartment, one hand on the doorknob, the other clutching the two copies of the novel.

So this was it.

It would be foolish to delay any longer. He had just jetted off to the west coast without so much as a word to her, who knows where he'll jet off to next time? And who knows if he'll come back? Her phone may ring tomorrow and it'll be Max saying something like, "I'm calling you from the box seats at Yankee Stadium; I flew here last night and I'm not leaving. It was nice knowing you; have a good life."

And why shouldn't she tell him now? Appearance-wise she looked fine because she was still dressed in the blue suit she had worn to work that day. She wouldn't mind touching up her makeup, maybe making sure her hair was all in place but how bad could it be? Max has seen her much worse.

So why wait?

What do I say? she asked herself.

You know what you're going to say. You've been rehearsing it for a week now.

But I've forgotten.

Figures.

No, really, I've forgotten. How was I going to start? Something about being happy, or being glad...

You were going to tell him you're happy he's finally accomplished his goal of becoming a writer.

Yes. Right.

And then build off of that. Is it all coming back to you now?

Yes.

So let's do this.

CHAPTER 9

❦

Yesterday, Danielle had done her research and according to the Rand-McNally Road Atlas her father insisted she keep in her car's glove compartment just in case she ever got lost in Saskatchewan or Death Valley there were 2459 miles between Phoenix and New York City. This was a relief because quite frankly this whole thing made her somewhat nervous.

Danielle rarely had cause to play the role of huntress, pursuing her male or female prey. She was sufficiently attractive enough that potential suitors of both sexes had no hesitation in asking her out. When, however, she did take matters into her own hands her form of aggression was very subtle. Upon spotting someone cute (male or female) at a party, in a nightclub, in the grocery store or at the gym she would set about reeling them in without so much as a single word being said: the right kind of look, a timely smile and game over. Now, however, she was about to embark on a voyage into completely alien terrain. For the first time ever as an available woman Danielle Edwards was going to have to sit before a man—*the* man, as far as she was concerned—bare her soul, tell him she wants to be his girlfriend, and hope he responds favorably. Not only that, but she was going to have to somehow work in the fact that she's willing to uproot herself from Arizona and move to New York, praying it won't send him running for the hills. Thus, for the past week she'd been rehearsing her lines, agonizing over the details of what she'd say, jotting down good points on Post-Its and then memorizing them, preparing herself as if she were about to appear before the Senate Select Committee on Human Relationships ("Yes, Senator, I do believe I'm qualified to be the girlfriend of Mr. Bland...Yes, of course I'll explain why...I'm attractive and witty with a triple-digit I.Q. I have a promising career, am independent and will be fiercely loyal to him. What's more, I'm an excellent kisser and am into light bondage.")

And if she totally bombed? Made a complete ass of herself? Well…that's why she was glad there were 2459 miles of the North American continent between here and New York City.

🍁 🍁 🍁

Entering her apartment she found Max now on the couch, TV remote in hand watching a Travel Channel feature about dining in London. She smiled at him when he looked over at her entrance.

"Syb had to leave, something came up. But she wants you to autograph your book for her." She handed him the two volumes. "While you're at it do mine, too. And what you write in mine better be sweeter than what you write in hers."

He nodded.

"Got it. Hand me that pen over there will you? See, I'll write 'Dear Syb, you really need to reconsider your opposition to waxing your upper lip' in hers."

"Max!"

"And I'll write 'Dear*est* Danielle, Here's…to…the…one-hundredth… wet…dream…I had…about…you' in yours. There." Max handed her the inscribed novels.

"Now what am I supposed to do with these?" Danielle asked through her laughter.

"Well, I would suggest not giving Syb hers, despite how true it may be, and being flattered with yours. A hundred wet dreams is a significant milestone, after all."

"Wait right here," Danielle instructed her prey and then disappeared into the kitchen. She may not have been sure about a lot of things when it came to what she was about to do but she was sure of one thing: she wasn't nearly buzzed enough. Thus did she set about bolstering her courage by the time honored method of quickly ingesting several swallows of wine drunk straight from the bottle. Then, finding it a little hard to balance on her high heels because she was so full of courage she teetered back into the living room.

Some blonde bimbo on the Travel Channel was cheerily telling Max about a fabulous new fusion cuisine restaurant in London's West End when Danielle sort of half sat/half fell on the couch next to him.

"Are you alright?" Max inquired, having reached up to help steady her before she dropped.

"I'm fine. Absolutely fine."

"You know, you're too young to be a washed-up drunken hag. Wait until you're at least thirty." He indicated the television. "I was just watching something about London. I can't wait to travel there. Maybe that'll be my first stop. I'm something of an Anglophile, you know, so I've always wanted to visit England. But I'd like to stay awhile. Not just two weeks like some fucking tourist but like a year; maybe even live there one day."

"No, Max, listen to me." Danielle took possession of the remote and clicked the TV off. It was silent now save for the humming of the refrigerator in the kitchen and the chirruping crickets outside. "Before you go running off somewhere else—New York, London, where-the-fuck-ever, we need to talk."

"Okay. Shoot."

"Fine. Let me start by saying how very happy I am for you that you have finally become what you wanted to become."

"A real boy?" Max quipped.

"Yes—no! No! A writer, you dummy. Stop that! Stop joking around."

Laughing, Max said, "I'm sorry. But I'm not used to you being this serious. I don't think we've ever had a serious conversation you and I. Even when we've discussed the plight of Third World countries we always managed to laugh at them at the same time. Is anything the matter?"

"No…I mean, I don't know…Not really."

"You know, I was joking when I asked if you needed a kidney but if you do then say no more. Call the doc and tell him to start sharpening his scalpel. Or what else do you need? You need some pints of blood? I'm full of the stuff. I'm not even sure I'm using it all."

"Max, cut it out with the jokes, okay? I don't need a kidney and I don't need blood."

"Then what is it? Whaddya need?"

"I need you."

"To do what?"

"Huh?"

"What do you need me to do?"

"Nothing. I mean…no, that's not what I meant. I meant that I need you—you! Not to do anything. Just you. I need…you, goddamn it!"

That shut him up but Danielle suspected it was only because he was confused.

Into the abyss, she thought and then decided to momentarily do away with the script as she rehearsed it. Emboldened by the wine and acting before her companion had a chance to distract her again with more wisecracks Danielle grabbed hold of his shirtfront, leaned in and kissed him, parting his lips with her tongue and leaving no doubt as to what was on her mind.

❦   ❦   ❦

The kiss over she held his startled gaze with her own and then, like a student reciting the Gettysburg Address, blurted out the speech she had prepared.

"Now do you understand? That's what I want. That's what I need. I've felt this way…I don't know, since around Christmas I guess. All of a sudden I realized that I was done searching. In all my life I have never, never felt this good with a man and I realized that every time I went out on a date with someone else I was comparing him to you and then I'd end up having a lousy time because compared to you they didn't measure up. Why do you think I haven't been dating much lately? It's because the only man I want to date is you. At first I tried to resist, you know? Because of our friendship. I didn't want to risk ruining it. But now I can't help it. I just know we would be good together, Max. As well as I know my name I know we would be good together. Think about it: we've been friends for a long time, we have respect for each other, we're comfortable with each other, we know our likes and dislikes—all that important stuff."

She hurriedly took a deep breath before continuing:

"And I'm sorry I never told you this before but it never seemed the right time. But now your book is selling well and you're making plans to move to New York and the last thing I want to happen is to see the man I've been waiting for all my life leave me just because he likes the hot dogs in Yankee Stadium. So I had two options, right? Option One: shrug my shoulders, let you go and just say it wasn't meant to be. Or Option Two: do whatever it takes to keep you. And that's what I've chosen because I wouldn't be able to live with myself if I didn't at least try to make something more serious than friendship work with you."

Another deep breath taken in a rush. She came alarmingly close to giving herself hiccups and wouldn't that have made a good impression?

"But listen, before you start thinking that I'm trying to force you to change your plans hear me out. I'm not asking you to give up moving to New York. But I don't want to miss out on having what I think will be the best and most meaningful relationship I ever had. So I've decided that what I'll do is move to New York also. Over the past few days I've been e-mailing contacts that I've made there through work and these people are telling me that because of my experience and education they can get me an interview with no trouble at all. I'm talking four or five interviews just like that, Max, at major banks, which is what I want. So I know I can get a job. Also, I'm still young so making a move like this is no big deal. It's not like I have kids or own a house or anything. Yeah, I'd miss my parents but that's what airplanes are for, right? And no, I don't already have china patterns picked out. I'm not talking marriage, I'm not even talking about living together. I would get my own place and we would date just like any other couple and we'll see how it goes. I know that there are no guarantees that this will work out but personally, though, I can't see how it can go wrong. We're perfect together! *We* feel right and I'm willing to do whatever it takes to give this a shot.

"Anyway, that's that. If the idea of being my boyfriend doesn't totally repulse you then let's do it, let's try to make this work."

🍁   🍁   🍁

There. She had done it! Honestly, it was easier than she imagined and she was quite proud of herself. And why shouldn't she be? Using a firm tone of voice which belied her nervousness she had made her feelings towards him known while at the same time making it clear to him that this was a matter he himself should offer no objection to. She had left out nothing: how great she felt with him; how optimistic she was about their future as lovers; her willingness to move across country…nothing was omitted. A lawyer couldn't have argued a better case. What's more, she had added some special little touches along the way—for *oomph!* Like taking hold of his hand as she told him why she hasn't been dating much lately, and stroking the back of his neck when she mentioned them being perfect together. And of course, that improvised kiss at the beginning she now considered nothing less than a stroke of brilliance on par with all other strokes of brilliance in mankind's history, like the wheel or waterproof mascara. In short, Danielle was a woman in whose shapely form there existed not one speck of doubt that she could now look forward to a bright future with Max as her soul mate.

Finally, after several moments, he seemed to overcome his initial shellshock and was opening his mouth, getting ready to speak. So Danielle smiled her encouragement, letting him know she was all ears.

CHAPTER 10

❦

"What are you, crazy?" Max said incredulously.

CHAPTER 11

❀

Of course, he knew right away he could've handled that better. Questioning a woman's sanity when that very same woman has just opened her heart to a man and expressed her true feelings was not the stuff of Shakespearean sonnets. It wasn't even the stuff of limericks. Max knew this, of course, and it was at times like this when he wished he had better control over that impulsive shoot-from-the-hip New Yorker mouth of his. But what he didn't know was how else exactly he was supposed to respond.

"Where the hell did all this come from?" he asked.

"What do you mean?" Danielle replied, wounded.

"What do I mean? What I mean is that this came on kinda sudden didn't it?"

The suspicious tone of voice he was using made Danielle think of something.

"God, you're not imagining that all the money you now have is making me do this, are you? Because that's exactly what Liz was saying the other day."

"Oh, really? Well, Liz is pretty smart, no? I mean, didn't you tell me she was valedictorian of your high school? Maybe I should listen to Liz. Maybe Liz has a point."

"Max! God...this is me you're talking to; you know me. Have I ever struck you as the type who was a gold digger?"

Max's mouth dropped open.

"Is this a joke? Are you joking? Yes, yes you do strike me as that type!"

"What!?"

"You're kidding me, right? You spend ninety-percent of your income on shoes and clothes. You shop at Saks Fifth Avenue and Macy's, even though you can barely afford it. You own more pieces of jewelry than Liberace did. You talk about having a really big house on Camelback Mountain and one day owning a Mercedes. You'll spend three-hundred bucks on a fucking purse just because it's made by some Italian designer and you bitch about how cheap your boyfriends are. You want the fine life, Danielle and there's nothing wrong with that but something tells me that given a choice you'd prefer to hook up with a guy who can either help you get it or, better yet, hand it to you as a wedding present. Not that I blame you…I mean, I'd marry for money."

"Really?"

"Why not? It'd be nice to be pampered for a change."

"Sure, but—"

"Live off someone else's bank account; let her pick up the check when we go out."

"Okay, fine, but—"

"Have an allowance; spend her money shopping for big screen TVs or Maseratis. Take trips to—"

"You're straying, honey…listen to me now. Max, you know I'm not after you for your sudden wealth. I would not do that to you."

Max shrugged and it was obvious he was not convinced. This was proven when he said: "Then why is it that we've known each other two years without you once giving me a sign you were attracted to me?"

"That's bullshit!" she exclaimed. "I have given you signs. Plenty of them over the past few months!"

"You have not!"

"I have to! What about that night a few weeks back when I asked you to sleep in bed with me?"

"You were drunk, you twit! We had just come back from a bar and you were blotto. The only reason you wanted me to sleep with you was so that I could be there to make sure you didn't choke on your own vomit!"

"Fine. Then what about that night two weeks ago, huh? We went to the movies, you drove me home, walked me to my door and I kissed you goodbye."

"You call that a sign? No, better yet, you call that a kiss? My grandmother—God rest her soul—used to kiss me like that. That was a peck. That was Marcia Brady kissing Greg. If you wanted it to be a sign then you would have shoved your tongue down my throat like you did a few minutes ago."

"Fuck! Why are you being so irritating!?"

"It's a gift. If you plan on moving to New York with me you'd better get used to it because there are about eight million more people there just as irritating."

This caught her attention.

"So, you're accepting my moving to New York with you?" she asked.

Max hesitated. Something about this whole enterprise made him pessimistic about its success. Like being told that all he had to do to pick up a billion dollars in cash was walk into downtown Baghdad wearing an American flag t-shirt and a George Bush rubber mask while carrying a sign saying "Iraqis Like It In The Back Door."

"Boy, that's just my luck, isn't it?" he finally said. "The woman of my dreams tells me she's got the hots for me but the only catch is that she has some crazy notion of moving to New York in order to be with me. That's just great."

Danielle pointed.

"Ha! You said 'woman of your dreams.'" she exclaimed. "You just called me the woman of your dreams. Ha!"

"Of course, I did, you idiot," Max replied. "Why shouldn't I? Hell, on looks alone you qualify as every man's fantasy. Even those guys who only like fat women or amputees probably wanna sleep with you. But for me it goes way beyond your looks, trust me. I mean, you're right, you know…you and I?…we're perfect for each other. I've thought so for a long time, in fact. And I guess if you twisted my arm I'd admit you're the woman I've been searching for all my life."

"This is exactly what I wanted to hear! Oh, my God! Why didn't you tell me this before?"

Max knew that was coming and he was ready with an answer.

"I figured you only liked white guys."

"What? Why?"

"Because I've only seen you date white guys." He pointed to a shelf where she kept a stack of photo albums. "The evidence is right there. All those pictures you have of you and your exes…they're all blond, blue-eyed, captain-of-the-football-team types."

"Yeah, but…this is Arizona, Max. It's like a white guy outlet store. I've got nothing against dating outside my race, it's just that there aren't many options here. Besides, wait a minute…I know you've heard me say how hot Denzel Washington is."

"No, no, no," Max said, shaking his head, "Denzel Washington doesn't count. He's not a real person, he's a fantasy. Every white woman I know wants to fuck Denzel but when it comes to giving their phone number to an equally good-looking black guy who sends over a drink in the bar they're all of a sudden immune to jungle fever. But look, that's not the problem, alright? If you say you're attracted to me then fine, you're attracted to me. I'm not gonna bust your balls about it."

"Then what *is* the problem?" Danielle asked earnestly, having a hard time deciding whether she should be happy or heartbroken. She tried to take hold of his hand but he kept it away.

"What's the problem?" he threw back. "What's the problem?" He stood now and began pacing in front of the couch like an irate father reading his child the riot act after the school principal called. "You're planning to move to New York just like that, huh?" He snapped his fingers.

"Yes, because I know it's what I need to do to be with you."

"Uh-huh. So the only way I get to be with you, a woman who's perfect for me, is if you uproot yourself from the place you've called home all your life, right?"

"Well…sure, I guess…yes. I know you don't want to stay in Arizona. What are you getting at?"

🍁   🍁   🍁

This is what Max was getting at:

"I like the idea of you and I being together, I really do like it. But this idea you have of joining me in New York, it's mad. You people from Phoenix like to think you live in this great big, fast-paced, thriving metropolis. And that's a laugh. This place is a one-horse-town compared to where I come from, okay? Have you ever been to New York?"

"Once, when I was twelve. There was a family reunion at some great-aunt's place in Buffalo."

Max harrumphed.

"First of all, Buffalo is nowhere near the city and, secondly, Buffalo is a piece of shit, okay? Their biggest contribution to the world has been barbecued chicken wings. Buffalo, Albany, Syracuse, Rochester…they all may as well be in Canada for all I care."

"What's your point?"

My point is, what if you move there, end up being miserable and wanna move back? And then you give me an ultimatum: stay with you and return to Arizona, or give you up and stay in New York. That's exactly the type of unfair bullshit you women like to pull."

Danielle said, "Max, what do you want me to say? Besides, I'm not only moving there for you. Ask Sybil and Liz, they'll tell you New York has been on my list for a few years now because it would be a big boost for my career. New York, London and Tokyo, those were my top three. I know what I'm getting into—"

"Yeah, sure you do."

"God, is this your idea of sweet talking me?" Danielle shot back with some irritation. "I had every hope that by this time we'd be making out on the couch."

"Making out on the couch? I ain't making out with you until I've had my say and get this cleared up. You must think this is some kind of joke."

"I do not! How dare you! I'm the one sitting here ready to completely change my life—in large part because of you—and I don't see anything funny about it. I'll be leaving my family, all my friends, everything I know, everything I've grown up with. Jerk."

Max returned to couch. "Alright, alright. Calm down." This time, he tried to take hold of her hand and this time she kept it away. "Look, I just wanna know how solid you are about this, Danielle. I mean, I showed up here tonight expecting that all we'd do is hang out and watch TV. Next thing I know I might have a terrific girlfriend who wants to move across country with me, and she's being handed over on a silver platter. It just sounds too good to be true, is all."

Max paused a moment, gathering his thoughts, wanting to elucidate just what it was he was nervous about.

"It's just that…you're used to a certain type of lifestyle here: sunshine, palm trees, a swimming pool in every backyard, friendly people. You've never been crammed on a subway car with thousands of strangers during rush hour; you've never been told to fuck off by someone on the street because you asked her what time it was; you've never had a waiter tell you to hurry up and order, lady, when you can't decide between the lasagna or the veal. It's never rained for more than two days your entire life here in Arizona and you've never once had to get up in the morning during a blizzard and trudge to work like an Eskimo. You southwest people think you can move to New York and life will be like an episode of *Seinfeld* or *Will and Grace*, complete with laugh track. But you just don't know what a ball-busting place it is."

Sighing, Danielle replied, "I know all that, Max, I'm really not that naive. Rude people, bad weather, noisy crowds, root for the Yankees or else you'll be killed. This isn't a decision I made a few minutes ago. I've been turning it over in my head since the night you told me about your book and how many days ago was that? If you'd just trust me and take a chance I think you'll find that this will be the best thing to ever happen to you."

Max, however, wasn't ready yet to let this go. He opened his mouth to continue his argument but Danielle suddenly decided this matter needed to be dropped. She shushed him by putting her finger on his lips.

🍁 🍁 🍁

Right there on the couch while kissing him Danielle unbuttoned his black shirt, running her fingers over the soft curls covering his chest. Then she unlocked her mouth from his, brought her head down and bit his nipple. Instantly he was hard. Abandoning himself to desire, forgetting everything else, he let her take the lead, allowing her to show him how far she wanted this to go but he did grab hold of her head, pushing her mouth tighter onto his nipple and sighing in response to the pain/pleasure she was eliciting with her nibbling. A few moments later Danielle made her intentions perfectly clear when she pulled away, shucked off her suit jacket and lifted her burgundy blouse over her head. When her breasts fell free from the bra that she practically yanked off Max gasped at how perfect they were. Suddenly he grabbed her by the waist and in a flash had her laying on the couch, himself poised over her, returning the favor of stimulation by sucking her breasts until her own diamond-hard nipples were sore from the attention.

"Hold me down," she ordered in a whisper and so he grabbed her arms by the wrists, pinning them over her head while she humped her pelvis up to grind against the bulge in his pants.

Somehow moments later they ended up in the bedroom with Danielle kneeling before him on the floor, unfastening his pants. She uttered a delighted and hungry growl at the size of the erection which sprung out from his briefs. She tried to take the entire length of it into her mouth but found it impossible, so she made do with engulfing only the first few inches with her lips, hoping he'd be content. After several minutes she pulled him over to her bed, scrambled to finish removing his clothes, slid off her own skirt and ordered, "Now!"

He offered no argument and laying beneath him she reached down, guiding his erection to her opening. As soon as he began pushing in and she felt the lips and walls of her vagina stretching as they never needed to before to accommodate a man Danielle orgasmed hard around his still-invading member.

"Oh, fuck," she cried. "Oh, fuck!"

CHAPTER 12

❀

Out of habit Danielle had stolen a quick glance at the clock on her nightstand the moment she had taken hold of his penis to guide him into her. In her opinion the male half of the population was comprised mostly of big talkers incapable of living up to their promises of showing a lady a good time in the sack. Their assurances of "I'll rock your world all night long" and "We'll make love until the sun rises" were as reliable as a declaration from McDonald's that their food is good for you. So, over the years, Danielle had started to play a kind of game: whenever possible, she would note what time it was when a guy started making love to her and then note what time it was when he started making goofy faces and collapsed on a heap atop her. Later, she'd share the results with the girls over wine: "Only four minutes last night. Hardly worth getting undressed for." or "He must have been taking his vitamins; he lasted a whole seven minutes." Until now the record had been held by Brad Zygalski, a boyfriend of three years back. On a night during which Jupiter must have been rising in his sign of Aquarius Brad had given Danielle a whopping eleven minutes of show time. But now...

"I was beginning to get offended," a flushed and exhausted Danielle confessed to Max after they were done and they both lay panting on the bed staring up at the ceiling.

"Why's that?" he queried.

"Because it's almost one o'clock in the morning and when we started it wasn't even ten-thirty. I was beginning to think I didn't turn you on enough to make you come."

He laughed hard at this, turned and gave her a playful bite on the shoulder. "Don't be ridiculous. Of course you turn me on, it's just that I really, really like sex and so I prefer to make it last. If that's gonna be a problem you can bring a magazine into bed with us next time."

She assured him no, that wouldn't be a problem. No problem at all. And she was ready to sign affidavits to that effect. In fact, she thought while laying there trying to get her heartbeat to slow, there was nothing he did to her tonight she had any problems with. In addition to his staying power Max had shown himself to be a very selfless lover, one with an understanding of a woman's body. For example, after she had prematurely come right at the start he had thrust himself entirely into her and then simply held it there, telling her to wrap her arms and legs around him, letting the contractions of her orgasm convulse around his penis, knowing that her vagina would be too sensitive for enjoyable intercourse now that she had come. All the while he kissed her or sucked on her neck, biding his time, patiently letting her genitals recover. Then after several minutes, when he sensed she was ready, he started moving his penis in and out again, slowly at first, then faster and harder till she came a second time.

Max had also shown a remarkable appreciation for her body. Patiently he explored her form and she put herself completely in his hands, allowing herself to be admired like a work of art. He sucked on her toes, licked up and down the entire lengths of both legs, turned her over, covered her back with kisses and spent several thrill-inducing moments rimming her anus with the tip of his tongue—an entirely new experience for her. And unlike previous male lovers who only gave her clitoris cursory and clumsy attention with their tongues out of some sense of obligation, Max showed just how much he loved oral sex by expertly going down on her and coaxing another orgasm from her body that caused her vagina to tighten around the three fingers he had inserted inside.

When it was all over she had wanted nothing more than to doze off into deep slumber, happy now that she'd finally found a man worth shaving her legs for.

🍁 🍁 🍁

Max pulled Danielle closer to him, enjoying the warmth of her flesh against his nude body. Their exertions done they were both immodestly laying atop the bed's covers and Danielle was periodically drifting off to sleep. Every now and then she'd jerk awake and during one of those conscious moments she tightened her grip on him and purred, "Mm…why haven't we done this before?"

"Because I wasn't rich before, remember?"

"Shut up."

She dozed off again. The next time she awoke she went to the bathroom and when she came back and resumed her snuggling position Max, who had yet to even shut his eyes, asked, "Danielle...what if you can't handle it?"

She took hold of his soft penis and said, "I think I handled it pretty well, don't you?"

He smiled. "No, I meant moving to New York."

"God, are we on this again?"

"Yes, yes we are. And you should be thrilled, quite frankly. It shows a depth of concern on my part for our future together that you women always say men are lacking."

"Okay, fine," she sighed. "Continue to bore me."

"I mean, I'll give you that for the first few months or even the first whole year you'll do just fine in New York because everything will be new and novel. What I want to know is what happens after the novelty wears off?"

"Sweetheart, I know you're just trying to be sensible or whatever but really, stop worrying about it. Right now, at this point in my existence, I want to move to New York because it feels like the best thing to do and it's pointless to talk about something as abstract as a year from now. Before we did this," and here she grabbed his flaccid penis again, "I was pretty scared about leaving Arizona..."

"Aha!" Max interjected.

"But now I'm not," Danielle went on. "It's the right thing for my life now just as I know it's the right thing for yours."

She sat up.

"Besides," she said, "you need me."

"How do you figure?"

"Because even here in mild-mannered Arizona you're a bit of a grouch. When you move to fast-paced New York you'll be a perfect candidate for a heart attack. Won't it be nice to have a woman you can turn to when you need mellowing out?"

Max cocked an eyebrow.

"Mellowing out? Here's a tip," he said, "when a man needs to mellow out he doesn't turn to a woman. Women are usually the reason he needs to mellow out. So what else you got?"

"Look, you prick," said Danielle, "why don't we stop this silliness? You're making me less inclined to give you a blowjob."

"A blowjob, huh?"

"Mmmm-hmmm."

"Yes, well…I suppose I could just trust you know what you're doing."

"Mmmm-hmmm."

"Put aside my God-given talent for pessimism and—"

"That would be best," she interrupted, kissing her way south on his body. "Now shut up and enjoy."

🍁   🍁   🍁

The next day Danielle called in sick to work and she and Max spent much of the time in bed, two people each with a new sex toy to play with. So focused were they on each other, in fact, that both breakfast and lunch were forgotten and they were only able to stop themselves when the noise from their growling stomachs got too loud to ignore. By then it was nearly three in the afternoon and they were famished. So, finally getting dressed, they drove to a nearby diner where they not only ate their fill but went over what would happen during the upcoming weeks and months. The discussion went well because Max had reached a decision. Outwardly, he expressed the same kind of enthusiasm as she did, and really, it wasn't that hard. Danielle was a knockout, after all, not to mention very sexy and, as he pointed out to her last night, the woman of his dreams. Inwardly, however, he was choosing to remain partially skeptical of this scheme, at least until time proved him wrong.

Later in the day Sybil came to Danielle's apartment and was surveying the brand new couple on the couch.

"You two look so cute together!" she gushed.

"Don't we, though?" Danielle gushed back, giving Max a peck.

"Wait a minute, Syb, you've seen us together a million times before," Max pointed out.

"Yeah, but not as a couple," the blonde replied.

"There's a difference?"

"How could you not think there's a difference?" Danielle asked.

"I dunno…I—"

"There's totally a difference," Syb insisted.

"But I look exactly the same as when you saw me last night."

"But you weren't her boyfriend last night."

"Duh," Danielle said.

Max was about to continue seeking clarification on this point but a sudden prophetic vision appeared wherein he was in a straitjacket being led away by men in white coats. He took it as a warning and kept his mouth shut.

"Sooooo…" Syb began, "you two are really moving to New York? That's so romantic! And exciting!"

"I know, I can't wait," Danielle said and she gave her new acquisition another peck.

"So when are you leaving?" Sybil inquired, still enthusiastic and eager to learn all the details.

Max spoke first. "I'm leaving straight away. I'm booked on a flight in two days and when I get to New York I'll start looking for a home."

"But he also has loads of interviews to do," Danielle bragged. "He's going to be on David Letterman!"

"NO!"

"Yes!"

"Can you get me his autograph, Max?"

But the author held up his hands.

"Wait a minute…I haven't agreed to do Letterman yet. On the one hand you're talking about being in a studio with an audience full of frat boys who think Steinbeck is a German beer; but on the other hand I'm told that Salma Hayek will also be a guest that night and, let's face it, I wouldn't mind being stuck backstage with—ow!"

"Sorry," Danielle said. "I hope I didn't leave a bruise that Salma will find unattractive." Then she told Syb her plans.

"First I'll get some job interviews set up, fly to New York for those, hope one of them turns into an offer, fly back here to pack up and then stay with Max at his new place while I apartment hunt. So, basically, for me it's a waiting game."

"And while she's waiting," Max added, "Salma and I will be going over the details of my new book in our underwe—ow!"

CHAPTER 13

❀

The Remarkable Reign of Pope Anne I was a runaway bestseller and the book everyone was talking about. One pundit made the comment that it was the literary world's version of Michael Jackson's *Thriller*. The important critics adored it, book clubs put it on their summer reading lists and at colleges throughout the country professors teaching Contemporary Fiction classes added it to their syllabi for the coming semesters. Websites devoted to the book appeared overnight and the character of Anne became a cult heroine for people with whom the story had a particular resonance: gay women; disenchanted Catholics; religious reformers; new age philosophers. A graphic novel adaptation of the book was done and Patrick Stewart was hired to read the audio version on CD. Added to all this, Miramax Pictures, smelling a potential hit and with a verbal commitment from Cate Blanchett to play Anne, further fattened Max's coffers by outbidding Paramount for the film rights and paying him a record-breaking sum for them. Max's agent then offered to bear his children.

Of course, not everyone liked it. *Pope Anne*, in addition to being an entertaining and comical yarn was also a thinly veiled attack on the Catholic Church and on Christianity in general. Max had used his novel to highlight the hypocrisies of Catholic doctrine as well as poke fun at what he saw as the outlandish beliefs of the countless people filing into churches every Sunday in this modern age to worship a man so light on his feet he could walk on water. As a result, while most of the country was embracing *Pope Anne* for the fun read it was, others were busy vilifying the name of Max Bland. But if they were hoping he'd repent they were sorely mistaken.

The day before he was to be a guest on David Letterman's show Max appeared on *Larry King Live* and was asked for his reaction to the *Pope Anne* book burnings taking place across the nation.

"I love 'em," Max said with no hesitation. "And I'll tell you why: first of all, I love to see religious fanatics publicly make fools of themselves. Just the fact that they would organize something as repressive as book burnings proves that these are the type of people who still believe there should be 'Whites Only' signs on all the best public restrooms and the vote taken away from women. The other reason I love 'em is because in order to make a worthwhile bonfire these zealots have to go from store to store buying every copy of the book they can get their hands on. At twenty-five ninety-five a pop. So the only problem they're really causing is forcing me to choose which Italian sports car I'll buy to drive my heretic self around in."

The next day he was asked by David Letterman how it was he came up with the idea for a lesbian pope.

"To tell you the truth, the idea came to me when I was in the bathroom after eating a burrito," Max replied to uproarious laughter from the audience. "I do all of my best thinking about religion when I'm on the toilet. There's something about expelling waste from your body and ruminating on religion that go hand in hand. Listen, do you think Salma Hayek is free for dinner?"

Needless to say, Sullivan Publishing was delighted. They were a firm founded by a former Random House editor and like Max they too shrugged off any controversy the book brought with it. What's a few death threats when the profits from this one book were stratospheric? What's several dozen members of the religious right protesting in front of the Sullivan offices when Sullivan was able to thumb its nose at Viking, Signet, Knopf, Bantam and all the other giant publishing firms who had rejected Max's novel and were now green with envy? In fact, in addition to pushing forward their plans to distribute the book in the European market, Phil Sullivan, the company's founder, showed his eagerness to keep Max writing for him by sweetening the offer made earlier. Instead of five books in four years for one million dollars it became three books in five years for four million, payable in advance, no deadlines to be set.

Thus when Max arrived in New York to apartment hunt he was a man of means and had the satisfying pleasure of knowing he could live pretty much where he wanted. Unlike those many years ago when he was a college dropout working as a messenger and earning five bucks an hour, now he was able to feel as if nothing was beyond his grasp. For his future home he considered all options: lofts in the Village, brownstones on the East Side, duplexes and studios in all-of-a-sudden trendy neighborhoods like the Bowery or the Meat Packing District. Max even had the romantic notion of returning to the Bronx albeit not to the blue-collar neighborhood he was raised in but rather the posh high-brow realm of the Riverdale section. But he decided against that. Manhattan was New York and he knew that if he didn't make his home there he may as well stay in Arizona. So, after twenty days of living at the Plaza and being led from one end of the island to the other by a chain-smoking realtor named Penelope it turned out that where Max wanted to live was in a brand new luxury high-rise recently opened on Fifth Avenue just two blocks south of the Metropolitan Museum of Art.

"The tenant board will love you, hon," Penelope assured him between puffs. "A nice quiet writer, very distinguished. And you're a perfect gentleman. They don't want rock stars living here with their wild parties and sex and drugs and stuff like that. You'll be the perfect neighbor."

Seems she was right and after the board approved his tenancy and the building's management company approved his penmanship on a check for 2.5 million dollars Max Bland was once again a resident of the City of Greater New York.

❦ ❦ ❦

Danielle became a resident herself two months later, after she finally found employment. Those contacts she had told Max about did indeed manage to get her a handful of interviews with a number of the big players in corporate finance: CitiBank, CreditSuisse, UBS-Warburg and some others—each of them outfits that do business with ProtoTech. But it was one of those only-in-New-York type chance meetings that actually netted her a job.

An elegant fifty-ish woman was awaiting the elevator along with Danielle as the latter was leaving Citibank's offices following a grueling interview. A conversation started when the woman complimented Danielle on how well Danielle's handbag matched her suit.

"Do you work at Citi?" the stranger asked.

"No, ma'am. Well, at least not yet, fingers crossed. I just interviewed for a position."

"I see. I suppose then I shouldn't tell you what a collection of dumb-asses I think they are?"

Danielle laughed. "Why not? I'm not officially one of the dumb-asses yet."

The lift arrived and both women boarded. As it began its descent to the lobby the woman asked, "And what is it that you do?"

So Danielle gave her a quick rundown of her career thus far, being sure to mention her professional motivations for wanting to relocate to New York. Quite frankly, she had been glad for the distraction of conversation. The CitiBank offices were on the ninety-second floor of this particular skyscraper and, truth be known, she was terrified riding that quickly plunging elevator.

"Hmmm," Danielle's companion began thoughtfully, maintaining a seemingly disinterested gaze on the floor indicator. "This may very well be your lucky day."

"How's that exactly?"

"Well, let's just say that Dave Carlson's coronary thrombosis, while most unfortunate for that wheedling little prick, could possibly be a godsend for you." She looked over at Danielle. I wonder, do you have time to join me downstairs for a cup of coffee?"

And there it was. On an elevator ride between the ninety-second floor and the lobby Danielle had secured another job interview. And between the first sip of her latte and the last she had secured a job.

Turns out the elegant lady was Margot Vermeers and she ran the North American Division of the Dutch banking giant, ARCL. She had been to CitiBank to scream at one of its regional managers for screwing up a wire transfer. It further turned out that Dave Carlson was dead, and Danielle, she of the well coordinated handbag/suit ensemble was the perfect fit to replace him.

"He died two days ago," Margot informed Danielle after perusing her résumé and grilling her on her education and experience. "I can't say I'm happy with the circumstances, though. I would much rather he had a stroke and suffered for many years as an invalid. In any case, we haven't even had a chance to advertise for the position yet and there is no one in-house who I feel is right for the job so why shouldn't I offer it to you? Saves me the headache of placing an ad. I'll check your references, of course, but barring any revelations that you're connected with Al Qaeda I don't anticipate problems. In the meantime, take a couple of days to think it over and I'll call you in forty-eight hours."

Afterwards, when she and Max were riding back uptown to his place in a cab Danielle shared her story of good fortune.

"...and I'll have my own office *and* a staff of three! Margot told me she's wanted to have someone my age in that position for a long time because she thinks a younger person will be more creative when it comes to problem solving. I guess this Dave Carlson dude—who she hated!—was a backstabbing two-faced son of a bitch—her words—who was just interested in keeping the waters calm until his retirement. And guess how much she wants to pay me, Max! Go on…guess!"

"Lessee…minimum wage plus tips?"

"No."

"Thirty pieces of silver?"

"Very funny. Now, keep in mind I was making thirty-two thousand at ProtoTech. But Margot told me the position starts at eighty-five thousand! Eighty-five fucking thousand, Max! Can you believe it!"

"Wow, that's great, honey," Max said exuberantly, giving her a kiss. He didn't have the heart to tell her that when one considers the costs of living and working in Manhattan and then combines that with her taste for expensive clothes along with her predilection for buying shoes at an Imelda Marcos pace eighty-five thousand a year was pretty much the same as thirty-two thousand a year, maybe less. Instead, he took her out for a celebratory dinner at Sardi's and when she offered to pick up the triple-digit tab at meal's end he shrugged and let her feel like a big spender.

❦ ❦ ❦

Though she tried not to show it by putting on a brave face the complexity and enormity of New York was actually a bit daunting to someone raised in the Phoenix suburb of Fountain Hills where, as Max put it derisively, "people blow kisses to each other as they skip merrily down gumdrop-paved lanes."

"Okay, crash course," Max said one Saturday afternoon in the Delacort Theatre while he and Danielle were waiting for a *Shakespeare in the Park* production to begin. Only a week earlier she had "officially" arrived in New York, Max meeting her at JFK when she disembarked off her flight from Phoenix.

"Write this down," he instructed.

"Write it down? Are you serious?"

"Listen, your pain-in-the-ass mother called me and wasted twenty minutes of my life begging me to make sure you wouldn't end up killed here in the Big Apple so, yes, write this down. That way, if you do end up dead I can say it wasn't my fault." He waited until she had fished her day planner out from her purse and had pen in hand. "Okay, first off, when you're waiting for the subway don't stand right at the edge of the platform otherwise you might get pushed in front of the train as it's pulling in."

Danielle was horrified.

"People do that?" she asked.

"More than you think. Why aren't you writing it down?"

"Sorry."

"Next, if you have to ride the subway late at night always ride in the middle car, where the conductor is, it's much safer. Ideally, though, you won't be stupid enough to be on the subway late at night but if you do find yourself out late and I'm not with you then take a cab. If you don't have enough money for a cab call me and I'll pick you up in my car, unless, of course, I recently walked in on you in bed with another guy in which case you can go to hell."

"Got it."

"Later tonight I'll give you a list of neighborhoods to avoid after dark, even a few to avoid in broad daylight. Remind me."

"Okey-doke."

"But here's a good rule of thumb: avoid all city parks after sunset, no matter what."

"Fine."

"I'm serious, Danielle. Even if there is a sale going on at a fabulous boutique directly across a park from you and you only got ten minutes before the store closes don't cut across the park if it's dark."

"Fine, I got it…"

"Next, always carry your purse with the strap crossing over your chest, like a bandoleer of ammo; it deters purse snatchers."

"Got it," she said, scribbling in the planner.

"And never count large sums of money in the middle of the street. In fact, don't count any sums of money in the street. If you come home to me crying because some punk snatched a wad of cash outta your hand while you were counting it in the middle of the street I'm not gonna have any sympathy for you."

"Wonderful."

"And when you eventually get your own apartment never answer the door without first asking who it is and checking the peephole."

"Makes sense."

"Of course it makes sense, but let's count how many times I catch you not doing it. Also, never trust anybody from Brooklyn."

Danielle looked up and asked why.

"Because Brooklyn used to have a major league baseball team and anybody who comes from a borough stupid enough to let a major league baseball team leave for California can't be trusted."

"You're kidding, right?"

"Fine, don't write it down but the first time you trust somebody from Brooklyn and you end up getting mugged don't come crying to me. Now, repeat after me: 'Take a hike.'"

"Take a hike," Danielle said.

Max shook his head.

"No, no, no. Put some malice in it, like I did. Sound tough. Get the Fountain Hills outta your voice."

"Take a hike," Danielle tried again.

"Better but you need to work on it."

"And why am I doing this?"

"Well, after decades of trial and error real New Yorkers figured out that the most efficient and sure-fire way of getting rid of someone who's bugging you is to say 'Take a hike' with an appropriate amount of menace. Never fails. Not only will it work great on all the guys who'll hit on you but it sends the Jehovah's Witnesses scurrying."

"I see."

"Now, this last bit of advice is the most crucial. Be sure you write down every word I'm about to say."

"Okay, okay, wait a minute. '…sends the…Jehovah's Witnesses…scurrying.'" Danielle turned to a new page. "Okay, shoot."

"Don't ever, ever embarrass me by walking into a New York pizzeria with me and ordering pizza with pineapples on it like a moronic Arizonan. If you do that I'll kill you myself."

Initially, Danielle had to rely much on her boyfriend for showing her around and teaching her how to get from point A to point B. Max proved to be a willing enough guide but after the first two or three months of her residency Danielle would often eschew his services and instead opt to spend a few hours on weekend afternoons exploring the streets on her own, and even if she took a couple of wrong turns and got lost there was an education in finding her way home again. It was thanks to such outings that she learned that Madison Square Park was nowhere near Madison Square Garden, and to mind the cyclists when walking across the Brooklyn Bridge otherwise you'll get creamed. Thus did she discover that the Korean grocery three blocks east from her apartment had better fruit than the Korean grocery three blocks west, and that the absolute best place to read a book on a lazy autumn day was at a particular bench that was shaded by a towering oak on the edge of the Rambles in Central Park.

It took some time for her to get over Manhattan's sticker shock, however. While originally delighted at how "higher tax bracket" her salary at ARCL sounded she quickly realized what Max already knew: that eighty-five thousand a year doesn't go all that far on this particular island. The same income in Arizona, she ruefully considered one night while balancing her checkbook, would have gotten her a 2000 square foot house with brand new appliances in a gated subdivision and a Lexus in her driveway. Here in New York she had to settle for a smallish one-bedroom apartment on the second floor of a converted town house in Chelsea—the rent for which was more than three times the $650 a month she had paid in Tempe. This left her enough money to cover the expenses of commuting roundtrip on the subway five days a week; the occasional power lunches with her associates at ARCL; shopping for groceries at stores where everything was twice as expensive than in Arizona; cab rides here and there; utility bills; et cetera, et cetera, et cetera. Yet once she got used to it and adapted her budgeting skills she had no regrets. Besides, the vibrancy, diversity and cultural bounty of Manhattan far surpassed anything Arizona had to offer and this, coupled with the huge step forward her career had taken, made it all worth it and whenever she made the acquaintance of somebody new and that somebody new said he or she lived in Flushing, Queens or Richmond, Staten Island or (even worse!) somewhere in New Jersey, Danielle felt a smug satisfaction in stating that she herself lived "in Chelsea, right here in Manhattan."

🍁   🍁   🍁

While Danielle was spending that first year in New York becoming acquainted with her new surroundings and losing her Arizona ingenuousness bit by bit, Max was adjusting to life as a literary celebrity. And not liking it.

When he took the time to think about it he realized that all he had really wanted out of life was to be a published author (done); earn enough from his books to write full-time (done and then some); and spend the remainder of his days on Earth in relative obscurity enjoying his hobbies and coming home each evening to make love to a beautiful woman (the making love part: done; the relative obscurity: not even close.) *Pope Anne* was enjoying success beyond all expectations; it was the biggest selling book since *The Da Vinci Code* and although Max loved the money she was generating for him Anne was also proving herself a major nuisance. Her creator was a sought after figure, an overnight literary giant. His agent's and publisher's offices were flooded with fan mail and requests for personal appearances, die-hard fans would lurk outside his apartment building hoping to catch a glimpse of him and he was even being heralded as a hero in the lesbian community, which saw in Anne a symbol of progress and in Max a progressive-minded writer capable of sparking real change in society.

Almost as soon as he got phone service in his apartment the instrument began ringing off the hook. For starters the majority of the calls were from the publicity rep at Sullivan requesting he put in an appearance at some benefit luncheon or some publishing organization's annual black tie ball. Sullivan themselves threw him a welcome home party, swore to him beforehand that it would be a small intimate affair when in fact it ended up being two-hundred strangers specially selected from New York's literary elite, gathered in the ballroom of a swanky hotel all slapping him on the back and acting as if Max was the second coming of Salman Rushdie. Then there were the numerous booksignings, talk show invites and magazine interviews. Personally, Max felt *Pope Anne* didn't need any more publicity; when he heard Jay Leno make a reference to the book in his opening monologue one night Max was of the opinion that any further efforts on his part to promote the novel would be overkill. But he felt obligated to Sullivan. After all, they had taken on an unknown writer and then showed their faith in his work by aggressively marketing *Pope Anne* when it first came out. So off he'd go to this soiree or that with Danielle as his date. While she invariably had a blast he would spend the evening grumbling under his breath and pretending to be interested in what people were saying to him.

Whom he didn't feel obligated to, however, were the various Witherspoons, Davenports, Vanderhavens, Montgomerys, Sloanes and Fitzgeralds, fellow Upper East Siders who came out of the woodwork and were apparently rich enough to obtain his unlisted number with very little trouble. This, apparently, was the cream of New York high society: really, really, really old money, from back in the days when being a railroad baron was considered cool. When they first called Max they stated their names as if they fully expected him to automatically know who they were (which he didn't) and as if they imagined he was genuflecting on the other end (which he wasn't.) Max soon realized that these people collected notable artists such as writers to add a certain bohemian flavor to their coteries the same way they collected summer homes. They called inviting him to dinner parties or brunches or weekends at their cottages at the

Cape. Max would have liked nothing more than to politely decline their offers and save himself the trouble of rubbing elbows with people who think the poverty line hovers around the 100 million mark. Besides, he didn't like the idea of being an accessory. But his efforts at avoiding them were stymied by Danielle who had actually heard of these people and salivated at the opportunity to move in their circles. She begged him to accept their invitations even resorting on occasion to waiting until she had sucked him to a hard-as-steel erection and then saying, "You know, sweetie, I'd really like to go to Mayzie Witherspoon's brunch on Saturday. I promise we won't stay long." So off to rub elbows he'd go. Eventually he conceived the idea of no longer telling her they called but this was thwarted thanks to Danielle's natural charm: the Witherspoons, Davenports, Vanderhavens, Montgomerys, Sloanes and Fitzgeralds simply began calling her in Chelsea with the invitations, relying on her to tote Max along.

He had counted on finding some measure of solitude and anonymity on the crowded New York streets whenever he stepped out for his favorite exercise of walking. After all, it's not like a writer is a movie star, he reasoned. But in this modern age of the internet, multimedia promotional campaigns, specialty magazines and 200-channel cable TV service *Pope Anne* had assured that the face of Max Bland was easily recognizable. He may not have been accosted for autographs on Manhattan's sidewalks as often as, say, Robert De Niro or Al Pacino, but it occurred enough to make him wish it wouldn't. Especially when he came to realize that a lot these people were either:

A) wackos…

"Hey, Mr. Bland, can I have your autograph? You know, your book really inspired me and because of it I've started my own church where women are the ones in power and every Sunday we show our thanks to Jesus Christ by drinking the breast milk from a lactating parishioner. I'd like to make you a bishop."

B) wanting something…

"Hey, Mr. Bland, can I have your autograph? You know, I'm a writer too and I just happen to have a copy of my manuscript here with me. Would you mind reading it and maybe even pass it on to your publisher?"

Or C) Republicans…

"Hey, Mr. Bland, can I have your autograph? You know, I think your book is horrible and an insult to God our Father who with Ronald Reagan has watched over this country so faithfully. Books like yours are evidence of the moral decay plaguing this nation ever since the Clinton administration. You can keep your autograph."

Soon enough he began thinking that J.D. Salinger had the right idea of being a recluse in New Hampshire.

🍁 🍁 🍁

Often he was asked by friends, family, fans, Davenports or Witherspoons when his next book would be finished and indeed by the time his first year in New York had passed he was well on his way to completing it. This time it was a science-fiction epic doubling as a satire on American politics and contained not one lesbian. Max wrote Mondays through Fridays in a little studio apartment he bought within walking distance from his huge home on the sixtieth floor of the new luxury high-rise. The studio was sparsely furnished with only a desk, chair, lamp and couch for napping. He kept some foodstuffs in the kitchen but did not have a TV to distract him or a stereo to listen to. No computer even. He wrote entirely in longhand in spiral notebooks and then once he had a couple of chapters done he'd go home and transcribe the work into a word processor, editing it as he typed. How much time he spent writing each day was dependent on several factors: how he was feeling, his mood and whether Inspiration was staying for dinner or had only dropped in for a cup of coffee. Sometimes he wrote for hours; sometimes for minutes.

Thanks to Anne, however, this new book had gotten off to a rough start. Having a successful first novel was all well and good. So too were the accolades he was receiving for his skills as a writer. But Max knew that in everybody's mind was the intriguing question: Can he do it again? The phenomenal triumph of *Pope Anne* assured that his sophomore novel would carry the heavy burden of Expected Greatness and thus would be diligently scrutinized to see if it measured up to its predecessor. At stake was the risk to Max of being labeled a one-hit wonder. Max knew this and quite frankly it messed with his head when he started writing the new book. He must have rewrote the first two chapters a dozen times; spent who knows how many nights lying awake worrying about concept, plot structure, characterization; second-guessed word choices and chapter order; added passages only to delete them; deleted passages only to add them back again. In short, it was hell.

Finally, in November, having managed to compose only three usable pages in two months and desperate for some way to break free of the stranglehold, Max packed his things, kissed Danielle goodbye and flew all the way to the Solomon Islands. Checking into his hotel he asked the front desk manager, "Have you ever heard of a book called *The Remarkable Reign of Pope Anne I*?"

"No, sir, I haven't."
"The name Max Bland mean anything to you?"
"Only that it is on your credit card, sir."
"What about Mayzie Witherspoon? Is she known to stop by here from time to time? Particularly for brunch?"
"I'm afraid not, sir."
"She doesn't own this island, does she?"
"Not to my knowledge, sir."

Max nodded. "Excellent. I'll want a room for about a month. Please make sure I'm not disturbed and I'll need a supply of sharpened pencils. Also, have the kitchen send up a huge pitcher of iced tea…has anyone ever told you it's hot here?"

CHAPTER 14

❈

One Sunday morning in August, over a year after he and Danielle had moved to New York, Max was over at Danielle's apartment in Chelsea reading the Arts section of Times in the easy chair by the bay window where the light was good despite the fact that a misty rain was falling outside. Danielle was reclining on the couch, mug of vanilla coffee in one hand, the World Business section of the paper in the other. Both he and she were content, at rest and sated from the breakfast of bagel sandwiches picked up from the deli on the corner and the sex they'd had when they woke up.

Suddenly, Max interrupted his perusal of an article about a new Basquiat exhibit opening at the Modern that week to ask Danielle, "Doesn't your lease for this place expire this month?"

Danielle nodded but kept her eyes glued to the newspaper.

"Mmmm-hmmm," she responded. "And I've already gotten the letter from the landlord reminding me to renew."

"Ah," Max replied and then fell silent. For several minutes nothing more was said between them. When he was done with Arts Max picked up Sports and winced at how many errors the Yanks made in their loss to the Blue Jays the night before. Meanwhile, Danielle, her woman's intuition tingling, was waiting patiently, resisting the urge to prod.

Finally…

"You know, I've been thinking lately," Max began nonchalantly. "Things have been going good between us…"

"Yes, they have. Very good," she agreed, still reading the paper.

"Right. I love you, you love me."

"I love you very much, sweetie." Eyes still glued on the paper.

"Absolutely. Turns out you were right when you said back in Arizona that our friendship would give us a good foundation to build a romance on."

"I am a genius." Eyes on the paper.

"Originally I thought you were crazy, remember?"

"Vividly."

"But you've been here over a year now and you put all my stupid fears to rest."

"Told you so."

"Right. And we've been practically living together ever since you got settled here in New York. I mean, think about it...except for the rare occasion now and then I'm either waking up at your place or you're waking up at mine."

"Mmmm-hmmm."

"And I know I snore horribly but then again so do you, for a woman."

"Thanks." Shooting him a withering look but then returning her eyes to the paper.

"Especially after you've had a few drinks. I mean, it's like, whoa!"

"I get the point..."

"Anyway, look...I'm no good at saying mushy things so I'll just put it this way: I would consider myself the luckiest man in New York to be able to see you walk through my front door each night after work and know that you're home. I wanna see mail addressed to the both of us; I wanna decorate a Christmas tree with you; I want your *Cosmopolitans* and *Crain's* to be on my coffee table with my *National Geographics* and *Smithsonians*. I want Mrs. Krutoy's annoying little poodle to sniff *your* crotch on the elevator. So, why don't you tell your landlord to kiss your ass and come live with me?"

She was on him in an instant, on his lap, arms around his neck, kissing him full on the mouth, her eyes glittering.

"Do you mean it?" she asked.

"Absolutely," he assured her. "We had sex this morning therefore I'm not horny and so I know it's not my dick talking. I really mean it. Let's make a life together."

BOOK II

ENTER KATIE

CHAPTER 15

The envelope was addressed to both of them, so naturally he opened it. Inside was an invitation, the details of which he had to read over twice just to make sure he wasn't seeing things, and a note written in a woman's flowery script:

D,

I got your address from Syb, I hope you don't mind but I really wanted you to come. It's been too long since we've talked and my special day would be less special if you were absent. Time has healed my wounds, how about you? Tucson seems like forever ago. Please come and see me off on my new life. Please.

L

P.S. I can't believe you live with Max Bland!!!! How cool are you?

Max frowned, suddenly feeling guilty for having read it but, hell, his name was on the envelope, too. How was he to know there would be private messages inside? He'd just explain that to her when she got home tonight. No problem. In the meantime he was going to fix himself a sandwich and, since it was a warmer than usual April day, sit out on the balcony reading Wodehouse for a bit.

🍁　　　🍁　　　🍁

Max was dozing in front of the television as the Yankees played their season opener against Anaheim. He had tickets to go to the game at the ball yard in the Bronx but the warmer than usual April day had turned into a typically lousy April evening complete with a spring shower and he hated sitting in a stadium in the rain. He awoke with a start when he heard Danielle shut the apartment door.

"Hi, babe," he greeted her through a yawn.

Danielle blew him a kiss from the foyer where she was busy removing her coat and stepping out of her boots. "How was your day?" she asked, selecting a hangar from the closet.

"So-so. Had a better day writing yesterday but I won't complain."

Max was now on his third book, at the very beginning of it. His second novel had been completed by Christmas and was due to be released the week before Memorial Day. He tried not to think about it because it tied his stomach in knots with worry.

"By the way," he said as he watched the Yankee left fielder stroke a double, "we've been invited to a gay wedding."

Danielle said, "Really? How do you know it's gay?"

"Because both the bride and groom are named Lisa."

Max heard something drop. Looking over to Danielle he saw that she had let fall her coat and hangar and was staring at him as though he'd just told her he'd gotten her mother pregnant. She stayed like that for a while, in a kind of stupor, and then she snapped out of it, calmly picked up the coat from the floor, hung it up and, trying to appear normal but failing because her voice was just a little higher than usual, asked, "How did you hear about the wedding?"

Max pointed. "The invitation came by mail today. It's over there on the telephone stand."

He watched her step over, pick up the opened envelope and remove the invitation. The handwritten note almost fell to the floor but she caught it in time. As she read it he could practically see the color drain from her face. Max's guilt from earlier came back. Danielle looked over at him, this time she seemed frightened.

"You read this?" she squeaked.

"Yeah, but…look…" he began, getting up from the couch and joining her, "…it was addressed to both of us, see? Look on the envelope. It says, 'Danielle

Edwards and—*and!*—Max Bland!' How was I suppose to know there was a private note inside? At first I thought it was driving directions to the church or maybe something telling us what gay-friendly store they're registered at."

Quietly, she asked, "So, what do you think it is now?"

Max shrugged.

"Beats me. I guess I figure you and one of the Lisas (bride or groom, I don't know) were good friends once and you had a falling out in Tucson—which makes perfect sense because Tucson is a dumb-ass town and I can imagine that anyone who stays there more than an hour would get cranky—but now she wants to patch things up and see you at her wedding."

"There's a little more to it than that," Danielle said softly. She had the invitation open and was gazing at the text inside announcing the upcoming happy event. Then she reread the note. "She really wants me to come," she said mostly to herself.

"Well, you'd better make sure things are truly copasetic between you two," Max said. "I'm not traveling all the way to Flagstaff just to break up a catfight."

🍁 🍁 🍁

It was later that night, when they'd gotten back from dinner at a Japanese place two blocks over and Danielle had once again bolstered her courage, this time with sake, that she said, "Do you really want to go to that wedding?"

Max shrugged. "Do I ever wanna go someplace where there's gonna be more than ten people? Although…I guess I wouldn't mind seeing a gay wedding. I've never been to one. Why shouldn't they be allowed to marry? If two people love each other, let 'em do it. It's not like us straight people are so good at it, right? I mean, what's the divorce rate at now? Fuckin' sanctimonious conservatives should mind their own business. Anyway, if you wanna go see your old friend's wedding then sure, I'll come with you. As long as I don't have to talk to anybody."

"You know that'll be impossible," Danielle told him. "It's a lesbian wedding and you're Max Bland."

"Goddammit," the writer swore. "I guess you're right. Maybe I'll just stay home after all." He looked at his watch then picked up the cordless phone. "I promised my mother I'd call tonight."

"Wait," Danielle ordered, pulling him to the couch and sitting down. "Not yet. We need to talk."

"Uh-oh."

"It's not like that. There's something I need to tell you."

"What? Is it about my mother? What have you heard?"

She took his hand. "I'm sure your mother is fine, Max. Still in good health and still thinking I'm not good enough for you."

"A theory I have not yet dismissed."

"Fuck you. Now listen…you know I love you, right?"

"Uh-oh."

"Knock it off with the uh-ohs, there's nothing wrong. Listen…I have to tell you something about myself, something that I've kept secret."

Max was about to make some crack about her being the shooter on the grassy knoll in Dallas but then stopped himself. She seemed very anxious and a little frightened. He pulled her closer to him to make her feel safe.

It did the trick. In a torrent of words, the equivalent of ripping off a bandage, Danielle finally confessed to Max that she was bisexual, had been for many years, felt no shame whatsoever about it but that it was nothing she broadcast. Then she told him about Lisa who, it turned out, Danielle had been seriously involved with several years ago until they had a bad breakup during a weekend in Tucson during which all sorts of accusations were made and name-calling done. When she was finished Danielle felt compelled to apologize to her boyfriend for not revealing this aspect of herself earlier, either during their "just friends" phase or after they became romantically involved. But Max shushed her.

"Please. What do you have to apologize for?" he chided. "It's not like you voted for Bush in the last election." He kissed her forehead. "Still though…I gotta admit, this is quite an unexpected bit of news."

"I know."

"So. You're…"

"Attracted to women? Very much so."

"And you've…"

"Had sex with women? Yes. Plenty."

"Ah."

Danielle took a deep breath. "I was seventeen the first time. That was the year I also lost my virginity to a guy, Richard Bogath—hardly an experience worth talking about. Anyway, a couple of months later I really wanted to see what sex was like with a girl and as luck would have it I had a friend who was gay. She wasn't a close friend like Syb or Liz, she was just someone in the neighborhood who I hung out with from time to time. Very pretty, very feminine, that's how I like them. I went over to her place one night when her parents were out and I, like, really started flirting with her. One thing led to another and we started kissing and then next thing I knew I was going down on her."

"Just like that?"

"There was a brief stop off at her breasts but, yeah, pretty much, just like that."

Max was intrigued. "Did you know what you were doing?" he asked. "Because to tell you the truth it took me a while to figure it out."

Danielle thought for a moment. "Me too. I started doing it too hard, you know? Too much pressure and too fast. She told me to slow down and soften up. I was also just, you know, licking her clit; she had to tell me to suck on it as well. And, of course, she taught me the importance of inserting fingers."

"Yeah, the fingers," Max said. "It took me a few years to catch on to that. In fact, it's such an important step they really oughta cover that in sex ed. So, did she go down on you?"

"Oh yeah, and I came in like a minute." She laughed.

They sat silently for several moments, Max stroking her hair, Danielle drumming her fingers on his thigh, allowing him time to absorb all this information. Finally, Max asked, "So which did you like better? Sex with the guy or sex with the girl?"

With no hesitation Danielle said, "Definitely the girl. It was no contest." It took a long time before she started to like having sex with a guy, she told him, adding that at one point just a few years ago she considered becoming a card-carrying lesbian—women being the only ones able to make her come. But despite that she wasn't able to completely turn off her attraction to men. "Yet virtually all the men I picked were horrible in bed," she said. "It was a catch-22. You don't know how good a lover you are, Max. You're well endowed and you last a long time. Those two facts alone put you above most men. But you also appreciate a woman's body; you know how to tease and build up anticipation; and you're very creative: that position you had me in last night and all the nasty things you were saying to me while we were at it…I'm getting wet now just thinking about it. You've made me obsessed with you. Just the thought of you with another woman is enough to ruin my day."

Max laughed. "Well, fear not, babe…having one woman is aggravating enough; I can't imagine what having two is like." Then he said, almost as if dreading the answer he'd receive: "What about now? I mean, which do you like better now? Sex with a man or sex with a woman?"

"It's not that easy, Max. I like them both. It's like you liking the Yankees and the Knicks. The Yankees are baseball, the Knicks basketball, different sports, different rules, but you still enjoy both teams." She got up, saying she needed a glass of water. "I will tell you, though," she continued as she made for the kitchen, "now that I think about it, this is the longest I've been without a woman."

CHAPTER 16

✤

In the kitchen Danielle poured herself a shot of Scotch and drank it before pouring a glass of water with ice. She then stood by the window staring out at Central Park across the street.

That had gone much easier than she could've hoped, she considered. No surprise, really. Max is such a liberal-minded guy that a slight deviation from the norm such as a person being attracted to members of both sexes was hardly enough to faze him; just look at how accepting he was of gays marrying. And he was right, it's not like she voted for Bush in the last election. Yes, she was glad she finally told him. It took away the possibility of him finding out through other sources (such as Syb's big mouth) and it also relieved the guilt she'd been feeling lately. When she and Max were just friends Danielle did not even consider broaching the subject of her bisexuality, but as soon as they became lovers that part of her female nature which yearns for the kind of intimacy with a mate that can only come from full disclosure began to open her mouth and spill the beans about a bunch of stuff. Over time she told him about all the tests she ever cheated on; her brief affair with one of her college professors; the approximate amount of money she'd ever stolen from her mother's purse; her experimentation with marijuana during high school; and her secret crushes on Lyle Lovett and Paul Giamatti. Junk like that. But never the big one, not until now and it felt good to get it off her chest.

She frowned suddenly, swallowing another sip of water.

On her way to the kitchen she had told Max that this has been the longest she's gone without a woman.

Why did I say that? she asked herself.

Because it's been on my mind, that's why.

But why? she insisted. The sex I have with Max is phenomenal. Last night he made me come so hard I lost all feeling in my left leg.

True...true...but as good as the sex is with Max it does nothing to satisfy that part of me which desires women. Yankees and Knicks, remember?

Okay, fine. But how do I get over this? I'm committed to Max, after all, therefore I certainly don't want to do anything behind his back, like cheat on him with a woman.

In that case, I'm stuck. I may not know now how to get over it but I'd better get over it, start up a lesbian DVD collection or something. I've known all along that people like me inevitably have to make a choice: either we have to stay single and enjoy men or women according to mood, or, if we find ourselves in a committed relationship with one sex, give up the other. And I'm the type of person who likes committed relationships.

Of course, there's a third option.

I know. If I get to craving a woman so much I can't stand it then I can always invite one over for a threesome with Max and I. Then I can enjoy her guilt-free.

That's probably what Max is sitting in the living room hoping for right now. Just like Daryl.

But I didn't want to have a threesome with Daryl.

Do I want to have one with Max?

I'm not sure. I know it's every guy's fantasy and I love him enough to want to give him a mind-blowing sexual experience he's never had before but...

Could I handle seeing him have sex with another woman? Could I handle seeing him pleasure another woman?

What if he liked doing it with her more than with me?

What if she was tighter than me?

What if her tits are bigger than mine?

What if she's better at giving blowjobs?

What if she called him up one day, suggested they get together for some fun without me? What if he said yes?

Okay, this is crazy. A threesome is out. I'm having heart palpitations just thinking about it. I'm too jealous. If I heard another woman moan like I do because of what he's doing to her I'll probably scratch her eyes out. Much safer to buy lesbian porn. Maybe there's a subscription service I can sign up for. A new DVD every month. Buy eleven, get the twelfth one free.

But the cat's out of the bag. I've told him I'm bisexual...there's no way he's going to let this opportunity pass him by. It's, like, part of the Guy Code. If his friends found out that he didn't try for a threesome they'd probably report him to the proper authorities and he'd get his penis taken away. I bet when I go back in the living room he'll start campaigning. How much do I want to bet that he insist I set something up for this weekend?

Great. Just great. I've probably taken that sweet, charming and sexy man and turned him into Daryl. Just great.

❦   ❦   ❦

In the living room Max was watching a *Cosby Show* rerun on Nick at Nite. It was nearing eleven o'clock and Danielle had an early meeting tomorrow but she just knew the threesome discussion was coming and she wanted to nip it in the bud. Sitting on the couch she snuggled up against him and waited it out.

But for a long time he said nothing. Just went about watching the episode and every now and then stroking her hair, the way he does when he's preoccupied. It wasn't until near the end of the show, when Danielle was dozing off, that he said, "Hey, sweetie…"

Suddenly alert Danielle thought, *A-ha…*

"I've been thinking…"

Of course you have, Danielle thought. *You're wondering if for your birthday you can have me and a double-D blonde gift-wrapped in bed.*

"About that analogy you made earlier…"

Danielle furrowed her brow. "What analogy?"

"You know, the one about the Yankees and the Knicks and how you used it to compare liking sex with men and women."

Totally confused, because this wasn't going the way she imagined it, Danielle sat up and asked, "What about it?"

"It's just not a very good one, that's all," he said, picking up the remote and channel surfing. "You see, the professional baseball and basketball seasons don't really overlap. So, even though I do like both teams I typically only have one of them available to me at a time; in other words, under normal circumstances I can't catch a Yankees game in the afternoon and then go downtown to the Garden and catch the Knicks that same day. You follow? Unless, of course, the Knicks make the playoffs but, come on, who are we kidding? They suck. Whereas you, being bisexual, can presumably choose to have sex with a man in the morning and then have sex with a woman later on, after dinner perhaps. So it's not a good analogy. A better analogy would have been to compare you liking sex with men and women to me liking pistachios and cashews. You see, different nuts, different flavors, but if I choose, I can enjoy both of them whenever I want. Don't you have an early meeting tomorrow?"

Instead of answering Danielle just stared at him, open-mouthed.

"You are such a nerd," she finally said.

🍁   🍁   🍁

Over the next several weeks Danielle kept anticipating that her confession to Max would somehow change their relationship. It was either a sign of how much she loved him or a sign of how much being in New York affected her personality but she really did become paranoid for a while. Unbeknownst to Max, he was suspected of always harboring fantasies of a threesome and anything that came out of his mouth, no matter how innocuous, no matter how far removed from the general topic of sex, went through a process in Danielle's brain of first being heard as a blatant bid by him for some three-way action before being understood as what he actually meant. As a result, Max began noticing disturbing symptoms of what he thought was mental retardation in his girlfriend because there was always a time lag now between when he'd say something and when she'd respond. He considered calling her parents. But the time lag was only because a question like "Hi, honey, how was your day?" would enter her ears, travel to her brain, and be detoured straight to Fear and Paranoia Control where it was translated as "Hi, honey, did you find us a new playmate yet?" which would then send orders to her heart to beat faster and commands to her palms to start sweating. While the folks at FPC were laughing their heads off at their little joke spies from the Normal Reason and Logic Division would steal the question, perform an accurate translation and rush it to the Speech Center with orders to hurry up and make her say, "Fine, dear, I got a lot done" before she looks like an idiot. Very often they were too late and for several weeks the couple's simplest discussions were affected.

Max: "Instead of going to Montauk this weekend how 'bout we take the drive to Mystic Seaport?"

Initial translation: "I've heard Connecticut women are really hot. How 'bout we go to Mystic and find one to have sex with?" Body responds with increased heart rate, sweaty palms and panicked look in eyes. Finally, accurate translation performed.

Danielle: "Um…that's fine, I guess. We've already been to Montauk twice this spring, right?"

Max: "You sure you haven't bumped your head recently?"

Or...

Max: "I ran into Phil Sullivan on Madison Avenue today and somehow got us roped into having dinner with him and his wife on Thursday."

Initial translation: "I ran into Phil Sullivan today and remembered that his wife is absolutely gorgeous. I'm gonna call her and invite her over Thursday to have some fun with us." Beginnings of a panic attack and then, accurate translation.

Danielle: "Um...great. Great. We haven't seen him and Gloria since, what, March?"

Max: "You're losing it, you know? A shame, too. So young."

For two months it went on.

One night Danielle called Syb in Arizona and confessed all this.

"Obviously it's a good thing that you told him, right?" Syb suggested.

"Yeah, obviously, but it's still driving me crazy," Danielle said. "I can't help thinking that I *broke* him in some way. I had the perfect man and then I go and do something stupid like bring up the word 'bisexual.'"

"Just give it time, you'll get over it."

"I hope so. Remember that episode of *Sex and the City* where Samantha's boyfriend tells her he wants a threesome for his birthday?"

"Yeah, the jerk. And he tells Samantha he wants the hostess at that restaurant."

"Right. Well, last night, Max and I were at one of our favorite restaurants and there's this absolutely gorgeous hostess who works there and who just really hits it off with Max for some reason, and all through dinner I kept expecting him to ask me if we could bring her home in a doggy bag."

Finally two separate factors forced her to stop seeing threesomes around every corner. First, Max never brought it up. Not once. Not even in jest. Unlike that creep Daryl who made a complete ass of himself begging for one, Max never even uttered the word *threesome*. So, little by little, her mind returned to normal and Max stopped thinking she was retarded.

The second factor was that she met Katie.

CHAPTER 17

❦

It was in June. At work one day Danielle was interrupted tallying some figures by Margot entering her office.

"Bad time?" the elder woman asked.

"No, just a sec, though." And Danielle input the last three amounts into the computer before instructing the machine to tot them up. "Okay, what's on your mind, Margot?"

Danielle was glad to see her boss, whom she really admired and who had been overseas for the past couple of weeks at the head office in Rotterdam. Ever since that impromptu hiring over coffee nearly two years ago Danielle's star had risen rapidly in ARCL, earning her a promotion to division head and justifying Margot's decision in offering a job to someone she met while waiting for an elevator. The two of them had also become close personally as well, due to the shared experiences of being smart, driven women in a male-dominated industry. Many times Danielle had tortured Max by dragging him to some do at Margot's house in New Jersey with lots of people and during which Danielle was often held up by Margot as the heir apparent. In part because of this friendship and in part because of her new high-ranked position Danielle was one of only three people among ARCL's two-hundred strong New York work force permitted to call Margot by her first name. To everyone else it was Ms. Vermeers, usually uttered with a smattering of fear.

"How was your trip?" Danielle asked when Margot had taken a seat.

Margot sighed. "Crap, darling, crap. Next time I will send you and you can deal with those idiots."

"I think I would be thrilled just to be in the Netherlands. I hear it's beautiful."

The other woman shrugged.

"So what's on your mind?" Danielle asked again, sensing that her boss was not really in the mood for small talk.

"Well, it's like this…" Margot began. "That damn scandal ARCL has gotten itself involved in over in Europe has headquarters worried about image."

"It's not as bad as all that, is it? It was, like, on page 46 of the *Journal* today."

"It's bad enough," Margot said. "For three-hundred years we manage to keep our noses clean and then a couple of assholes in Germany decide to fake some numbers. Our stock prices are down in all major markets and many of our biggest clients want independent audits done."

"Stuff like this blows over quickly," Danielle said. ARCL was so big, she knew, that it would take more than a few pages of manipulated numbers to put the company in any real harm. Besides, the culprits were in jail. "Who will be talking about this in a month?"

"I agree, darling, I agree. But headquarters wants damage control from all angles nonetheless. That's what I'm here to see you for. In addition to allowing the audits the geniuses in Rotterdam think more of an effort needs to be made to improve our public image all over the world. Community service, charitable donations, et cetera. At first I figured on letting someone else handle all this but then I had an idea of where we could start. Not too long ago I was at a benefit dinner for the homeless and heard of an organization here in Manhattan that helps homeless people find jobs. Now, maybe we could help that organization out by hiring some of their charges. Put them in the mailroom, use them as in-house couriers, give them clerical jobs, you get the idea. It could be an on-going thing. I'd like you to get it started because you've got the brains to do so but once we've got a system in place you can pass ownership of it to that namby-pamby Gail Pender, she's got nothing better to do anyway."

"Sounds easy enough," Danielle offered.

"It should be. I'm giving you full reign with my blessings which means that if any of the jerk-off department heads give you a hard time about putting a homeless person on their staff tell them to come to my office to beg me to keep their jobs."

"Got it," Danielle said.

"The magic number is twenty."

"I beg your pardon?"

"Twenty homeless people, darling. You see, we have about two-hundred employees working here now and twenty is ten percent of two-hundred. I want to be able to say to anyone who will listen—like the local news, for example—that ten percent of our workers are homeless people. It sounds impressive. So at all times I want twenty homeless here."

"Got it."

"And tell those shrews in HR that we don't want to look cheap. We'll hire these people at more than minimum wage."

"Got it." Danielle was writing all this down.

"But not a lot more. A buck or two."

"Right."

"And make sure the dunderheads in Marketing get a press release out once the first person starts working. I want to read about what a saintly company we are while I'm having my morning coffee."

"Got it."

"And inform the Nazis in Security of our plans. Tell them to be extra vigilant but not to *look* like they're being extra vigilant."

"Got it."

Margot took a Post-It note out of her suit pocket. "I called around and found the name of that organization; it's on East 47th Street. The lady you contact is Katie Shaw; here's her number."

🍁   🍁   🍁

East 47th Street being on the way home Danielle decided to knock off work early. It was a lovely summer's day, not very humid, and she figured that after meeting with Katie Shaw she'd walk the rest of the way home, maybe stop off at Gristede's for some groceries and then cook Max dinner.

Danielle had called Katie as soon as Margot departed and after briefly explaining herself arranged to meet with her at The Homeward Bound Center to learn a little bit about the operation and to start the process of getting some of their clients into ARCL.

The address Danielle was given directed her to a dingy storefront on a seamy stretch of 47th between Fifth and Madison, and when she pushed through the door she found herself in a noisy waiting room whose two dozen or so seats were all occupied by members of that segment of the population who did not have jobs paying a hundred grand a year or whose boyfriends weren't bestselling novelists.

Like most people who relocate to New York Danielle had quickly developed an indifference to the plight of the homeless and the ability to brusquely ignore them each day as she was out and about. She thought it was sad, of course, seeing a man in rags sleeping on a park bench or a woman picking through a city garbage can for scraps, but she also knew that in this city the problem of homelessness was greater than any possible remedies she could provide and so upon seeing the man in rags on the bench or the woman pawing the trash Danielle would (like most of her fellow Gothamites) mentally shrug and think *Not much I could do about it.*

Now, however, Danielle found herself in this small waiting room surrounded by the very people she had always treated as invisible and she was feeling extremely self-conscious. For the first time ever she became aware of how prosperous she must look. And for the first time ever it felt shameful. None of the shabbily-dressed folks here presumably had a dwelling to call their own and yet here she was decked out in Versace and Jimmy Choos. And although it might have been her imagination she could swear that many sets of eyes were boring into her with resentment. So she was very grateful when the receptionist sitting behind bulletproof glass finally got off the phone.

"What can I do for *you*?" the receptionist asked Danielle in a cutting tone, scanning the expensive clothing and looking as if she'd like nothing more than to kick this rich bitch to the curb.

"Um...Katie Shaw, please. She's expecting me."

The receptionist looked like she doubted it but after giving Danielle's outfit another derisive once-over she got up from her chair. Danielle watched her walk past a row of desks where Homeward Bound workers were interviewing homeless people, helping them fill out job applications, to a large filing cabinet on the back wall. A curly-haired blonde was filing some papers with her back to Danielle when the receptionist approached with news of her visitor. Katie Shaw looked over her shoulder towards the waiting room and the instant the two women's eyes connected over the forty or so feet separating them Danielle knew that one day they would end up in bed together.

🍁   🍁   🍁

About as tall as Danielle Katie Shaw had an earnest, girl-next-door face; very cute with flawless skin bearing just the hint of freckles on her cheeks. Like Danielle she was slender but with more apparent grace to her movements, and she was far less bosomy and had her hair cut short in a stylish bob whose wavy curls caught glints of the fluorescent lights. Her most notable features physically were her eyes, the irises of which were a pleasant sea-green with flecks of gold. Evidently because working with the homeless doesn't pay very well Katie was not attired in anything that came close to matching Danielle's high end couture, yet she did justice to, and looked very professional in, the gray pantsuit she wore that may have been bought from K-Mart.

The attraction between the two women was palpable and when they shook hands the contact was maintained perceptibly longer than what Miss Manners suggests. And while their mouths were saying such things as "Pleased to meet you" and "How are you?" their eyes were already enjoying after-sex cigarettes.

Katie's "office" at Homeward Bound was much like Todd's "office" at Proto-Tech: basically just a high-walled cubicle meant to give the perception of importance. But in this case the perception actually worked. It was the only such enclosure in the entire place, everyone else working at desks that were out in the open. When Danielle entered and sat down she was amused to see a copy of *The Remarkable Reign of Pope Anne I* with a bookmark a third of the way through it on Katie's desk.

"So...Ms Edwards, you—"

"Call me Danielle, please."

Katie smiled. "Fine, Danielle...you're with ARCL; that's like a bank or something, right?"

"Exactly. A very old bank in the Financial District. We're not far from where the Trade Center once stood."

"Well that's cool. I wish more of you Wall Street types would participate in our program."

"You mean they aren't? It seems like such a good cause."

"It *is* a good cause but are you kidding? As much as we want to help the people who come in here we're having a hard time doing it. You call up a company and say, 'Hey, how would you like to hire a homeless person to fill the file clerk position you've got advertised in the paper?' and they treat you like you asked them to wear your dirty underwear, you know? And it's a shame because it's not like we round these people up off the streets just so we could look busy. *They* come to us; these are people who *want* to work but it's hard placing them unless it's for really menial jobs like scrubbing toilets or scooping up dog poo from the sidewalks." She paused. "You're not looking for toilet scrubbers or dog poo scoopers are you? Because if you are, we'll take it, sanctimonious speech notwithstanding."

Danielle laughed. "No, we're not looking for anything like that." She liked Katie's enthusiasm for her work and empathy for the people she served. Of course, she decided not to mention that the only reason ARCL was getting into this game was to polish up its recently tarnished image, and that if you held guns to the heads of senior management, Margot included, they would tell you they didn't give a flying fuck about the homeless. "We're looking for office workers," she went on, "nothing fancy, mind you, but definitely not toilet scrubbers."

Katie smiled again and Danielle was sure there was more to it than professional satisfaction. The two women held each other's eyes for a long moment until finally Danielle broke the spell by expressing an interest in the various photos Katie had framed on the wall.

"Are these your success stories?" she asked. All of the twenty or so 3x5 photos were of men or women smiling happily into the camera and holding up a key.

"Mmmm-hmmm. Every one of those people you see got permanent full-time jobs through this office and now live in their own apartments. I like to take pictures of them holding up the keys to their apartment doors. The word 'success' has been bastardized by much of society, you know? It now only applies to people with millions in the bank who have maids for their butlers. But here our definition of success is what you see in those pictures: off the streets and in a home." Katie's pride was evident.

"And the lighthouse?" Danielle asked, referring to the one oddball picture, an 8x10 of a lighthouse on a craggy coastline.

Again the smile. "That is my favorite place in the whole wide world. It's Inverness Lighthouse on the coast of Maine, outside of a really cool town called Windemere. You'd love it. It's small, very artsy with lots of cool boutiques and little galleries. Very laid-back people, very liberal-minded, you know? Unless you're a skinhead or a member of the Klan they don't care what you do or who you do it with."

"Sounds nice."

"It is. But the best part is a bed-and-breakfast on the shore which is superb for romantic getaways. You know, two people who don't want to do anything more than open the windows, let the chilly air in and then spend the day snuggling under the comforter."

"I see."

"Sounds lovely, doesn't it?"

"Very."

"Well, maybe you'll find yourself there one day."

"I'm expecting to. If you can promise me I won't be disappointed."

God, this is crazy, Danielle thought. She was amazed at how easily she was flirting. The funny thing was, ever since she got involved with Max she'd been as welcoming to other men as the sight of Lorena Bobbitt sharpening her scissors, quickly snuffing out any hopes they had of having their flirtatious attentions reciprocated because when it came to men she was perfectly satisfied with the one she owned. But now in the presence of this blonde, obviously gay, bi or curious *woman* it was as if Max didn't exist. Danielle had to remind herself that he was probably awaiting her at home and that just this morning he had gotten her off hard by going down on her as soon as she woke up. Even so, she found herself once more locking eyes with Katie and communicating desire silently.

This time it was Katie who broke the spell.

"So…um…you want to use our services. That's cool. Um…the way it works is you tell us what kind of jobs you have available, we go through our files to find matches and then you interview them to see if they'll work out. Our clients are all fingerprinted and they've had background checks run on them, and we provide you with complete dossiers on each individual. On occasion we ask that you give someone the benefit of the doubt even though he or she may have a police record but whether or not you do so is entirely up to you. And like I said before, these people want to work. There have been a few bad apples but trust me, we operate on a three-strike rule; once those strikes are used up we stop trying to place a person."

"Sounds good so far," Danielle observed.

"So…what kind of jobs do you have?"

Danielle told her she didn't know that yet, that this was the very beginning of what was sure to be a complicated endeavor involving multiple departments at ARCL and—more aggravatingly—multiple department heads.

"Well, how many of our clients do you anticipate hiring?" Katie asked.

"I'll need twenty," Danielle answered.

Katie's eyes lit up and she could not help an expression of exuberance from taking residence on her features.

"Twenty! Really? That is so cool! Are you serious?"

Danielle didn't understand what the big deal was. "Those are my orders. ARCL is to have twenty homeless people working for it at all times. That's almost a direct quote from my boss."

"Jesus! I mean, that's great. Do you realize, Danielle, that if this works out, I mean long-term, your bank may ultimately be responsible for getting twenty homeless people off the streets? I know it doesn't sound like a lot but it is! It's a lot to those of us who work here and spend our days hoping to make a difference but usually end up going home frustrated."

The passion for her work that Katie was exhibiting made her that much more attractive to her listener. "I'm glad you're excited about it," Danielle said, smiling.

Katie leaned forward in her chair, and piercing Danielle's brown eyes with her sea-green ones said, "Excited? God, I could kiss you."

Danielle blushed and instantly felt herself getting wet.

🍁 🍁 🍁

Outside on 47th Street once the meeting was over Danielle walked a couple of paces in the direction of Fifth Avenue but then had to stop to catch her breath. Her heart was pounding, her nipples were granite and she was so lubricated she wanted nothing more than to throw Max on the floor, straddle him and impale herself. All thoughts of walking the rest of the way home were forgotten, as were the plans to stop at Gristede's. On Fifth she hailed a cab and fidgeted in the back seat the entire journey. She found the apartment empty when she arrived and mentally cursed Max for not being there for her to use carnally. However, after a glass of wine failed to steady her nerves she went into the bedroom, put on a lesbian DVD recently purchased and masturbated herself to such an intense orgasm she couldn't help but scream out.

🍁 🍁 🍁

Meanwhile, at Homeward Bound Katie had to cope with calming her own nerves as well. She felt as if she didn't know herself. It had been so instantaneous, that yearning for Danielle, that attraction between the two of them. It was frightening, almost. And because it had been so long since she'd felt anything remotely close it was also shocking. There wasn't a single detail about their encounter that Katie forgot. Given a pencil and paper she was sure she could accurately draw the arrangement of every single hair on Danielle's head.

Sitting behind her desk Katie sighed deeply and then repeated it when she noticed how calming it was. She looked at Danielle's business card and without being fully conscious of it ran the tip of one finger over the letters spelling out the woman's name.

CHAPTER 18

❀

A week later, on a dreary Tuesday, the phone on Danielle's desk rang.

"Danielle, hi. It's Katie Shaw from Homeward Bound."

Suddenly this particular Tuesday didn't seem so dreary. Danielle signaled to her secretary to come and shut the office door.

"How are you, Katie?" she greeted the caller.

"Fabulous. I just received a fax from your HR lady with a listing of job positions that you'll consider for our clients. I still can't believe that you're set to hire twenty of them! Everybody here is totally jazzed and we've spent the morning trying to select the people that we think will make the most of the opportunity."

"I completely trust your judgment," Danielle assured her.

There was just the slightest of pauses before Katie replied with, "Does that include my judgment in restaurants? I mean, look…um…there's obviously a lot of details in a project of this size, right? And, I want to be sure you guys are happy because of what's at stake, you know? So, why don't we meet sometime this week after work, have a meal and while we're eating I can go over with you the dossiers of the people we're considering sending your way."

Danielle decided to play along with the cover story though she made a bet with herself that if at this proposed rendezvous she and Katie invested ten words on business she'd wait another week before buying the new Manolo Blahnik Mary Janes.

"How 'bout it?" Katie prodded.

"I don't see why not. What time are you getting off tonight?"

"Depends on how competent you are," Katie purred, and then: "Shit! I'm sorry! I totally did not mean to say that out loud! Shit! Please forgive me. Have you ever done that? Just blurted something out before your brain has a chance to censor it? Shit!"

Danielle laughed.

"It's my fault for giving you such a wide opening," she said through her chuckles. "Actually I'm glad to see you have a quick sense of humor."

"Just as long as my quick sense of humor—not to mention my assumption—doesn't turn you off of helping the homeless," Katie said sheepishly.

"Don't worry. Keep my order open for twenty poor people."

"They prefer the term 'Victims of Right-Wing Spending Policies.'"

"Ah, so it's the government's fault?"

"According to most of them."

"So are we on?" Danielle asked. "I could swing by your office."

"I have a better idea," Katie came back with. "Do you like Szechuan? Because I'm thinking of a place on Spring Street in the Village, Yen Ching. We can meet there. Is six too early?"

🍁 🍁 🍁

Katie did in fact bring a briefcase full of client files to Yen Ching's but it was never opened. In fact, unbeknownst to her, when Danielle met her in the restaurant's vestibule before they were seated in a booth by the window Danielle purposely made sure the conversation stayed clear of business matters. She really wanted those Manolo Blahniks.

The two women made it through dinner on getting-to-know-you talk: Danielle told Katie about growing up in Arizona, Katie told Danielle about growing up in Marcano, Nebraska ("The most boring town in the most boring state in the union. For fun we used to go cow tipping. The sad part is, we found it entertaining.") They discussed favorite foods, favorite movies, favorite bands while avoiding anything to do with politics, religion or abortion rights. Though it was only their second meeting, to any of the other patrons in the restaurant who happened to glance over at the attractive twosome occupying booth 4 it appeared as if it were a reunion of old friends. In fact, they were having such an easy-going good time that they broke rule number one of figure-conscious women by ordering dessert after their entrees were finished.

It was while they were waiting for it to arrive that Katie leaned forward on the table, deciding the time was right for venturing into more interesting subject matter. "My luck can't be this good," she said. "I'm guessing the bad news is you're taken?"

Danielle nodded.

"Well, she's a lucky girl," Katie said.

"It's not a girl," confessed the Arizonan.

"A man?"

"Yep. His name is Max and we live together. In fact, you were reading his book the last time I saw you."

Katie's eyes widened.

"Your boyfriend is Max Bland? The writer? I'm impressed."

"So are most people."

"No, really. He's actually one of my favorite authors, if not *the* favorite. Do you know that when his second book came out a couple weeks ago I called in sick, bought it as soon as the store opened and spent the rest of the day on my fire escape reading it?"

"Max spent that day in Nepal, hiding from all the attention."

"No!"

"Swear to God. He sent me a picture of the Sherpa who carried his luggage."

"Wow. Well anyway, I've read *Pope Anne* twice now. I even wrote him a fan letter about it. And you're dating him?"

"We've been together over two years and we were friends before that, when he lived in Arizona. I knew him when he was just 'max bland' not 'MAX BLAND'. He's the reason I came to New York when I did."

"I'll have to thank him for that," Katie said. Talk was suspended when the waiter arrived with their dessert. As soon as he was out of hearing range Katie said softly: "But I wasn't getting the wrong signals from you, was I? You're definitely into women, right?"

"Absolutely. Specifically, I'm definitely into you."

Katie arched her eyebrow.

"I'm glad one of us finally admitted it," she said. "I'm definitely into you, too, which brings me to my next question: is it a case of you being bi or is the great Max Bland living with a closet lesbian?"

"Bi."

"Positively?"

"Let's put it this way: if Max were to lose his cock in a freak piranha attack in the Amazon you'd have a hard time convincing me that life is worth living. It's why I don't let him travel to South America."

"Fair enough, fair enough."

"And you?" Danielle asked.

"Let's put it this way: if all the women in the world except me were kidnapped by aliens from another planet you'd have a hard time convincing *me* life is worth living. It's why I hope E.T. stays the fuck home." She took a sip of sake and then a bite of cake. "I don't have anything against men as a group, though. They just don't do it for me sexually."

"Have you ever been with a man?"

"No, but I've gotten to know a few dildos quite well. They're a nice bunch, actually, always ready to go and waiting for me in a box by my bed. I was hoping to introduce you to them sometime soon."

"Mm."

"I'll tell you my story," Katie said. "The first time I saw a penis I was thirteen. My best friend Maggie Simmons found her father's secret stash of porn videos in the barn and brought one over for the two of us to watch, you know, just for giggles? Anyway, I barely noticed the men in it but I couldn't take my eyes off the women. I was, like, hypnotized. That's when I knew what I long suspected: that I wasn't destined to have a man carry me across a threshold one day."

Danielle used a few moments to gather her thoughts before continuing the conversation.

"This situation," she began, "has never presented itself before. I mean, in the past, whenever I was in a relationship with a guy the opportunity to also be in a relationship with a woman never came up. And vice versa. It was always one or the other. Maybe it's because my romances with either sex never lasted extremely long. Now that I've finally landed the man of my dreams I suppose it was inevitable that God's sense of humor would kick in."

"I bet God used to pull the wings off flies when he was a kid, you know? Cruel bastard."

Danielle laughed.

"Anyway…look, Katie…I'm not here with you because I'm expecting you to want to be my fling or because I think you'll want to share me with Max. I'm sensitive enough to know how colossally unfair that would be. And when I left you last week after our meeting I was thinking that I didn't necessarily have to see you again, but when you made the dinner invitation this morning I couldn't resist." She grinned sheepishly.

Katie took hold of Danielle's hand and stroked the back of it with her thumb. "I'm glad you didn't resist," she told her.

Danielle's sheepish grin morphed into a sardonic one and she said, "Yeah, but what good did it do us?"

"Well, we found out we got the hots for each other. It's always nice to know you're on the same page with somebody about that."

"Even nicer if you can do something about it."

The other woman nodded assent and then said: "I guess we're stuck being friends."

"'Stuck' is right," Danielle murmured. "I have to admit that there have been times lately when I feel trapped. I mean, I love Max and I certainly don't want to be freed of him but…this bisexuality of mine now feels like a curse, and it never did before. But despite how I feel about Max it's impossible to ignore my desire for women." She fell silent for a moment or two. "I don't know…maybe it was a bad idea to join you here tonight. It was like throwing gasoline on a fire."

"But I am glad you joined me," Katie said.

"Fine, but before you called this morning I had actually succeeded in spending an hour not thinking about you. I mean…is it just me or when we met did it, I don't know…feel perfect?"

"It wasn't just you," Katie assured her and then the both of them went back to drinking their watermelon sake, eating their cakes and watching the passersby on the sidewalk outside.

CHAPTER 19

❀

For a long time after that dinner at Yen Ching Danielle remembered the sensation of Katie's hand in her own. It was all she had, really. Both women had parted that night wanting to act upon the intense attraction between them but both also had no idea of exactly how they would go about doing it. The hang up, of course, was Max. Danielle had felt guilty just having dinner with Katie knowing that if Max had done something similar with some woman he was attracted to she would have been devastated and spent hours in front of the mirror, nude, wondering just what part of her now twenty-nine year old body was betraying her by showing its age and turning him off. Katie, sensing Danielle's guilt with that uncanny ability women have of detecting emotions, herself felt guilty about thus wanting to figuratively give the great Max Bland the finger and ravish his girlfriend.

So when they said goodbye after dinner their words of farewell contained with them an unspoken understanding that, given the circumstances, it would be best if they kept things within the parameters of the strictly professional goal of getting twenty homeless people off the streets.

That said, between June and November Danielle and Katie did not see each other once, a testament to their will power since many times during that period each of them was sorely tempted to call the other and invite her out for lunch, cocktails, or stolen kisses in the ladies room at Macy's. Instead, they kept their contact limited to e-mail, although, quite frankly, they did little to hide their feelings for one another in their electronic correspondence, to hell with the parameters of the professional goal of getting twenty homeless people off the streets:

∾

From: Katherine Shaw (shaw.kate@homewardbound.org)
To: EdwardsD@ARCL.com
Subject: Re: Lonnie Sullivan
Sent: June 22 1:00 p.m.

My Dream,

So sorry about Mr. Sullivan not working out for you guys. I suppose that in the future Homeward Bound needs to not only perform fingerprint and background checks but also checks on whether they tend to "see" Redd Foxx chasing after them with scissors and yelling "Lamont, you big dummy!". (Is there a test for that?) In any case, I have a replacement in mind. She will report on Thursday.

Still hoping,

K.

∾

From: Danielle Edwards (EdwardsD@ARCL.com)
To: shaw.kate@homewardbound.org
Subject: Re: Lonnie Sullivan
Sent: June 22 2:35 p.m.

Hey you,

Darn! I was under the impression that per our contract when one of your people didn't work out the Director of Homeward Bound would fill in temporarily. That's you, isn't it? I rather like the idea of having you as my wage slave, although I seriously doubt the Dept. of Labor would approve of the type of work I'd have you doing. ☺

Me

∾

From: Danielle Edwards (EdwardsD@ARCL.com)
To: shaw.kate@homewardbound.org

Subject: Being territorial
Sent: August 29 9:35 a.m.

Hey you,

Remember when I wrote you to say that I had passed control of our little project here to Gail Pender? Well, that twit came to me just now and asked me where your office was located because she wanted to meet you in person and check out your operation there. I told her that was no concern of hers and any face-to-face matters would be handled by me.

The truth is Gail is very, very cute and I am very, very jealous. I want to be the only one at ARCL whom you lust after. ☺

Me.

From: Katherine Shaw (shaw.kate@homewardbound.org)
To: EdwardsD@ARCL.com
Subject: re: Being territorial
Sent: August 29 9:51 a.m.

My Sweet,

Have no fear. I once had a girlfriend named Gail and it was a disaster, so that name has bad associations for me. Just like I could never date a woman named Sharon (my mother's name. Can you imagine having an orgasm and screaming out your mother's name?!? Can you imagine the therapy bills? Uggh!).

However, now I'm very, very jealous that there is someone in your office who (or is it "whom?" I always forget. You'll have to ask the great Max Bland for me) you deem "very, very cute!" Just remember, if it turns out Gail is gay she can have you ONLY after I'm done with you!

K.

From: Katherine Shaw (shaw.kate@homewardbound.org)
To: EdwardsD@ARCL.com

Subject: Dreaming...
Sent: October 31 8:40 a.m.

My Star,

Last night I dreamt about you but I cannot go into particulars as it would cross the bounds of professional etiquette.

K.

From: Danielle Edwards (EdwardsD@ARCL.com)
To: shaw.kate@homewardbound.org
Subject: re: Dreaming...
Sent: October 31 10:31 a.m.

Hey you,

Don't tease! Tell you what, I'll go first because I dreamt about you recently, too. It involved a certain bed-and-breakfast in Maine, that box you say you keep by your bed, a lot of nibbling and some mild spanking.

By the way, Happy Halloween!

Me.

❦   ❦   ❦

And so it went. Hundreds of e-mails over several months; two women play-acting the roles of lovers. For actual carnal release Danielle had, of course, Max; their sex life never suffered, but when that other side of her sexual nature began jumping up and down begging for attention she'd wait until Max was gone somewhere, taking one of his long walks, perhaps, or up in the Bronx bowling with his buddies from the old neighborhood, and then she'd make a selection from her growing Sapphic-themed DVD collection and find relief at her fingertips.

Katie didn't have a steady lover herself, a female equivalent of Max. Her needs were met by a series of brief flings with women she met socially. But her attraction for Danielle never waned. In fact, very often, when a woman's head was between Katie's thighs and Katie's eyes were closed as the surges of pleasure swept upward over her body it was, in her mind, Danielle responsible for bringing her to orgasm.

Then, over the Thanksgiving weekend that year, something interesting happened.

CHAPTER 20

❀

That year, Max and Danielle spent Thanksgiving in Arizona. Since leaving her home state for the Big Apple Danielle had, of course, made several return trips back for quick visits but Max had never bothered to accompany her. Arizona had no interest for him anymore. None of his family lived within its borders; he'd made no lasting friendships and during his residence there he'd seen pretty much all the state had to offer: the Grand Canyon, the Petrified Forest, various Indian ruins, that great big crater made when a meteor slammed into Earth way back when...Now Arizona was just a hot, dry place filled with too many golf courses and too many retirees who still remembered when you could get a hamburger, Coke, fries, shave, haircut and new Ford all for a nickel. So, over the various long weekends throughout the year Danielle would make the trip to the southwest on her own, Max staying behind.

Her family never took umbrage to this. Max was an artist and therefore allowed his eccentricities. More importantly, he was a very rich and well-known artist and because this mattered to people like them they would have forgiven a lot worse just for the distinction of counting him as part of their clique. In fact, Max's agreeing to come for Thanksgiving dinner set off a flurry of activity in the Edwards household in preparation for his arrival. Danielle's mom spent the weeks leading up to the holiday calling her daughter seemingly every hour to acquaint herself with the finer points of hosting the celebrity author.

"Hi, dear, it's Mom. What does Max like to drink?"

"Mom, I'm sure he'll be fine with whatever you have."

"No, I want him to be happy; he's my guest. Now, come on, what does he like, soda-wise?"

"Ginger ale."
"How elegant!"
"Since when is ginger ale elegant, Mom?"
"It's just not as pedestrian as Coke or 7-Up."
"Whatever. Oh, he also likes a lot of water."
"You mean Perrier?"
"No, I mean cold."
"Okay, thanks. Bye, love."
An hour later…
"Hi, dear, it's Mom again. What about foods?"
"What about them?"
"Well, is there anything Max doesn't like? He's my guest."
"Peas and mayonnaise."
"Peas, huh? I was going to make my pea salad as a side."
"He won't touch it."
"It's really very good."
"I know but what are its two main ingredients?"
"Peas and mayonnaise."
"Aha."
"I see your point. So I shouldn't make it?"
"I didn't say that! I just said he won't touch it so don't expect him to eat any. But I'm sure everybody else will."
"So no on the pea salad. Okay, thanks. Bye, love."
An hour later…
"Hi, dear, it's Mom again."
"Mom, I'm at work."
"I'll keep it quick. Dessert."
"For Max?"
"Of course, he's my guest."
"Along with a bunch of other people, Mom."
"Yes, yes, yes…but he's special."
"Whatever. He likes ice cream. Nothing with nuts in it, though, and nothing with fruit."
"Got it. I'll only buy chocolate chip and the stuff with cookie dough."
"You know, *I* happen to like Butter Pecan and Cherry Jubilee."
"Maybe next time, dear. Bye, love."

🍁   🍁   🍁

While Danielle's mother was driving her crazy her father spent that same time period expanding the guest list a bit despite his daughter's warnings that Max hated crowds and if Thanksgiving dinner was anything more than an intimate family affair he would be miserable. But as her father worked in the cut-throat world of academics where prestige is gained in a variety of ways he could not help but let it be known among his colleagues at Arizona State University that someone of Max's stature would be gracing his dinner table.

"Max Bland is coming to *your* house for Thanksgiving?" one of his fellow professors asked.

"That's right. Say, aren't you planning on including his first book on your sophomore lit syllabus next semester?"

"I am."

"What a coincidence, huh? So who do you have coming for Thanksgiving?"

"Just some relatives from out of town."

"Well, if you'd like you're welcome to join us. I'm sure Max will be talking about his new book."

And on another occasion:

"Max Bland is coming to *your* house for Thanksgiving?"

"That's right. Say, didn't you tell me a while ago that you lectured on his use of something or other in your Gay Studies class?"

"It was medieval iconography. And yes, I did."

"What a coincidence, huh? So who do you have coming for Thanksgiving?"

"My in-laws."

"Well, you're free to join us, of course. I'm sure he'd love to hear about your lecture."

And on yet another occasion:

"Max Bland is coming to *your* house for Thanksgiving?"

"That's right. Say, didn't you have your Examining Popular Culture students do some kind of project about one of Max's characters?"

"They had to write a 2000 word essay on the similarities between Pope Anne and Princess Leia."

"What a coincidence, huh? So who do you have coming for Thanksgiving?"

"Some friends I went to college with."

"Well, don't be shy about dropping by if you'd like. I'm sure Max would love to hear what your students wrote in their papers."

🍁   🍁   🍁

The resulting affair from all this was a Thanksgiving dinner which Max found as enjoyable as one of Mayzie Witherspoon's brunches. Although there was plenty of ginger ale to drink (in fact, there was only ginger ale to drink) he had to contend with being the main attraction for a group of fawning relatives and acquaintances who filled the Edwards's Fountain Hills home to bursting and seemed bent on treating him as if he were Armstrong just back from the Moon. It was far from the intimate family gathering promised and Max even began envying one of Danielle's cousins: he may have been a garbage man but at least no one was bothering him.

But every cloud has a silver lining and for Max that lining was revealed later in the guest bedroom. For most women, Danielle included, few things are more of a turn-on than bringing their man home to meet the family and seeing him revered and treated like royalty while all the other women's husbands or boyfriends are generally ignored. There are hardly any creatures on this planet more competitive than the human female and so her landslide victory in the age-old game of "Whose Man Is Best?" made Danielle fidgety with desire for her trophy mate. Thus, at bedtime Max never knew what hit him. Danielle was so horny they needed to sleep till noon the following day to recover from their carnal exertions.

🍁   🍁   🍁

Upon awaking at noon and then sharing a shower together the day after Thanksgiving Max and Danielle got back into bed with the contentment of two people who have a whole day ahead of them free from responsibility. Danielle was snuggled against her boyfriend and using her cell phone to read her e-mail; Max was trying to concentrate on a Zola novel, but something was forcing his focus on another matter.

"Sweetie?" he began.

"Uh-huh?"

"When was the last time you were with a woman?"

Danielle pretended to continue reading her mail. "A woman? Why do you ask?"

"Just curious."

She snapped the cover of her phone shut. "Okay…um…let's see…Oh, I know. Do you remember that night back when we were just friends, when we saw Bill Cosby's show at the Orpheum? After you dropped me off at home I called this one girl I had been kind of seeing and invited her over."

"Bill Cosby? That was, like, three and half years ago."

"Yep."

"Hmmm." Max said as if he were about to spend considerable time pondering a particularly knotty question about quantum physics put to him by Stephen Hawking. But almost immediately he said, "Alright, I'll tell you the real reason this is on my mind. It has to do with something I saw yesterday during that publicity stunt your parents called a Thanksgiving dinner."

"I'm sorry about that, by the way."

"All I did was write a couple of books. It's not like I cured cancer or solved the oil crisis."

"I know."

"Was it too much for me to expect a nice civilized dinner?"

"No, it wasn't."

"And what the hell was up with all the fucking ginger ale? A Vanilla Coke would've hit the spot. Or maybe some coffee. And why did your mother keep telling me there wasn't a single pea in the house?"

"Long story. You're straying, honey…what did you see yesterday?"

"Well, it was while I was listening to some moron telling me something about Pope Anne and Princess Leia. Since I wasn't really paying attention to what he was saying I happened to catch sight of you over on the settee talking to some woman. Anyway…maybe it was my imagination but it seemed to me that there was this look in your eyes, like you were very attracted to her, I mean physically attracted to her, and that you were trying to let her know it."

Danielle remembered the woman in question. Her name was Ashley. She was a relative of some sort of one of her father's guests and yes, Danielle had been very drawn to her. In particular, she recalled having this overwhelming desire to suck on her toes.

Deciding not to deny anything Danielle said, "You're right, Max. I was attracted to her and I probably was being a little obvious about it." She snuggled closer to him. "I'm sorry," she said contritely.

"No, no, no…don't apologize. You did nothing wrong."

"You're not upset?"

"Why should I be? She was a cutie, after all; really nice legs. Quite frankly I'm relieved. When you told me you were bisexual I was afraid I'd find out you only liked fat chicks."

Danielle playfully punched him in the ribs.

"Anyway," Max continued, "that's not the first time I noticed you checking out women."

"No?"

"Nah. Ever since you told me about that part of you I've been kinda watching."

"Oh, God," she moaned, burying her face in his chest. "How bad has it been?"

Max thought a moment. "Well, you've never made an ass of yourself, if that's what you're thinking. But it's pretty clear to me that you haven't been able to turn off your desire for women even though you're involved with a man. Am I right?"

She had to admit that, yes, he was.

"Must be a bitch of a problem for you bisexuals," Max went on. "How did you handle it in the past?"

"Never had to," Danielle said and then she told him pretty much the same thing she told Katie several months earlier, that her romances with men and women had never overlapped previously.

"So, do you resent the longevity of our relationship?" Max asked. "Because it hasn't allowed you the chance to explore romances with women?"

"No!" Danielle was quick to respond. "Honey, no. I love what we have and I love you. God, please believe me. If I lost you I'd be crushed." She had propped herself up on one elbow and was looking him in the face, letting him see the devotion in her eyes.

Max smiled and stroked her hair soothingly.

"Alright, alright, no need to get all panicky. I knew that. Although it is nice to hear you say it."

Danielle searched his face, hoping not to find doubt. "Max, listen…this whole me-liking-women thing is not going to affect us, alright? I knew a long time ago that one day I'd have to make a choice: if I fell in love with a woman I'd have to give up men. If I fell in love with a man—and I have!—I'd have to give up women."

"Ah, well, you see, that brings me to my point," Max said. "I don't think you should have to."

❁   ❁   ❁

Sitting up fully in the bed Danielle eyed Max with confusion.

"What do you mean?" she asked.

"Well, I mean this: you're bisexual; that's something you can't turn off and something you can't have surgically removed. No matter how much you love me and no matter how great our sex life is you are always and forever going to also desire having sex with women."

"That's just my bad luck," Danielle said.

"I don't think it has to be," Max countered.

"Meaning?"

"Meaning that I don't see any reason why you shouldn't continue having sex with women."

Danielle stiffened, and with a very affected tone huffed, "Oh, really?" Despite her rising ire at what she thought Max was leading up to a part of her admired his patience and underhanded sneakiness. It had been, what, seven months since her confession to him of her bisexuality? And he had craftily led her to believe that he had no interest in using that information by parlaying into a sex-capade featuring himself and two women. A brief thought flitted through Danielle's mind that Max was in the wrong line of work. She was certain the State Department could use someone like him.

"And I suppose," she started in, "the only condition to me having sex with all the women I want is that you get to play along with us, right?"

"Not at all," Max replied calmly.

"Oh, come off it, Max! I'm not stupid! You want a threesome, plain and simple. Every guy does, so don't expect me to believe you're not trying to get one. And gee, aren't you lucky? You have a girlfriend who likes eating pussy as much as she likes sucking dick. How convenient."

"Danielle, sweetie—"

"I'll admit I am surprised it took you this long to bring it up, though, but I suppose it makes sense. Last night my family pissed you off so you figure I need to make up for ruining your holiday, *and* you caught me flirting with another woman, so you figure you can cash in on my guilt. Well, listen…and this is the final say on the matter: I decided when I told you about being bi that I didn't want any threesomes in my future, end of story."

Max made an attempt at holding her hand but she snatched it away and folded her arms across her nude torso. Max chuckled.

"Danielle, you're right. A threesome is every straight guy's fantasy and I do like the idea of being in bed with you and another girl. But I also know it's never gonna happen."

"Good, you were listening."

"No, that's not what I meant. I know it's not gonna happen because neither one of us is emotionally strong enough to have a threesome."

His girlfriend frowned. What had started out as confusion and then clarified itself was now confusion again. She gave him leave to explain himself by the perplexed look she offered.

"Look," Max said, "let's start with you, alright? Do you have any idea how jealous you are? You're borderline psychotic. Remember a couple months ago when you dragged me to Phil Sullivan's housewarming party in Connecticut? That really good-looking blonde lawyer was talking to me and she was one of these touchy-feely types, always stroking my arm or squeezing my elbow, remember? You were all the way on the other side of the room when you saw us together and you shot like an arrow right for us and then grabbed hold of me making sure the blonde knew I was your property. Then you spent the rest of the night following me around, scowling at every woman who was even marginally attractive. And that's just one example; believe me, I could spend *days* talking about how possessive you are. So I have no realistic hope that you'd be able to watch me fucking another woman even if you were right next to us waiting your turn."

Danielle said nothing.

"As for me," her boyfriend went on, "there's two problems: Number One, how would you expect me to enjoy having sex with another woman knowing how jealous you are and that you might kill me in my sleep later on? Number Two, I'm far too cynical to think I'm that lucky. How can I enjoy having sex with another woman if I'm busy trying to figure out why you agreed on having a threesome in the first place? Was it because you're bored with our sex life? Is it because I no longer satisfying you in bed? Are you trying to get something out of me? A puppy, perhaps? One of those Chinese babies you can adopt over the internet? Are you guilty of something? Maybe of cheating on me with another man? In short, I would analyze the thing to death—while it was happening, no less!—until my erection disappeared and I gave up. I'm not stupid either, Danielle. The guilt-free, no strings attached threesome is a myth perpetuated by the porn industry. The real thing, I imagine, is fraught with a lot of fine print and hidden costs. Like tax relief."

🍁 🍁 🍁

What he said made sense, so much so that Danielle softened her defensive attitude by a few degrees. She remained skeptical, though.

"So if you don't expect to gain anything by it," she said, plucking lint off the bed sheets and stealing quick glances of him from under her eyebrows, "namely a threesome, why are you saying I can have relationships with women?" Quite unbidden, an image of Katie entered her mind.

"Because you're bisexual!" he said patiently.

"But I already told you: I had to make a choice and—"

"And I'm telling you that you don't," Max interrupted, "that the way I see things it's not fair for you to have to choose."

"But I do have to choose, Max! That's the way this works, remember?"

Max shook his head. "Look, to hell with the current societal paradigm of one person/one mate, alright? That may be fine for most people; it may be fine for completely straight or completely gay folks but for someone like you it's too confining. Your bisexuality won't allow it. It's a variable that alters the equation."

"So?"

"So? So if the equation is altered let's embrace the new result. Just because you, a bisexual, are in a relationship with a man, me, doesn't mean you should have to give up women."

"Yes, it does!" Danielle insisted.

"No, Danielle. The notion that someone like you has to ignore a full fifty percent of her sexual cravings in order to 'fit in' with society's outdated and narrow-minded definition of what makes a couple is absurd. You have a right and an obligation to yourself to satisfy your sexual needs completely. And for you 'completely' means finding a female partner to go along with the male one you already have."

"This is insane," Danielle muttered, but again Katie appeared in her head and suddenly she couldn't find the words to continue arguing against Max's points.

"No, it's really not," he said. "I've been thinking about this for a while now, Danielle, and I dunno what the current medical research on this topic says but maybe people like you can't make the kind of choice you keep talking about because it's unnatural; like me trying to choose between breathing and suffocating. Besides, every time I see you undressing a woman with your eyes I'm more and more convinced of this one immutable fact: for your own benefit and for your own sexual well-being you need to have sex with women as well as with me and I'm telling you that I have no problem with it. Simply put, if you wanna get a girlfriend, do so."

🍁   🍁   🍁

Danielle felt she had wasted her "This is insane" comment from a few moments ago because now she really wanted to say "This is insane" but hated being repetitive. Yet she was having trouble choosing an appropriate substitution. The oddity of this conversation—and the fact that she had never seen it coming—was such that Danielle, normally quick-witted and articulate enough to engage anyone in worthwhile debate, was flummoxed. It was as if her brain were a soup pot full of questions and remarks in a boiling broth and all she could do was dip in a ladle hoping to scoop something out.

"Why are you doing this, Max?" Danielle asked after the first dip.

"Pistachios and cashews," Max said as if that explained everything. But when it was clear it did not he went on.

"Remember when I said that you being bisexual was similar to me liking pistachios and cashews?"

"Yes."

"Well, suppose one day I couldn't eat one of them anymore, let's say pistachios, because society has decided that 'normal people' can only enjoy cashews. So…there I'd be with cans of cashews in my kitchen but do you think I'd never crave eating pistachios from time to time? That's what's at the root of this whole thing. You fell in love with a man, me, thank God, and according to society you need to stop there, feel happy and content and forget about anything else you may desire. And you tried. But you can't can you?"

She didn't answer.

"Of course you can't," he answered for her. "And I know this because every time I turn around you're sending 'fuck me' signals to every woman prettier than Martha Stewart, and that's a hell of a lot of women. So what I'm saying is, stop the flirting already and just go get yourself laid by one of them."

"You can't be serious," Danielle uttered but she realized that she so wanted him to be serious. Added to the soup pot now were all sorts of delicious possibilities. "You're giving me permission to have sex with a woman?"

"Absolutely."

"To cheat on you?"

Max made a face. "I don't know that I'd call it cheating, honey."

Danielle was a little stunned.

"Sweetie, having sex with a person other than the one you claim to love is cheating," she said.

"No," Max replied. "Having sex *deceptively* with a person other than the one you claim to love is cheating. You, however, would be doing this with my full knowledge and blessing."

"Semantics," Danielle said dismissively.

"Maybe, but let's not argue about that now."

"Fine, but this whole idea of me finding sexual gratification with other individuals should bother you a lot more than it seems to be."

"And I'll tell you why this is not bothering me: the other individuals in question aren't men. I dunno…it's hard to explain but I'll try. You having sex with another man would make me question why you did it. Is he better-looking than me? Is he taller than me? Does he have a bigger dick? Is he more romantic? You see, it would really fuck with my self-esteem. But the way I look at it, you having sex with a woman is simply a case of you getting relief for an itch I can't possibly scratch, no matter what I do in bed with you."

"Ah," Danielle began, "but what if I like sex with the woman more and decide I no longer need you? You may be taking a big chance."

Max gave her a wry little grin and when he answered he tried not to sound too overly confident.

"No. You like cock too much, sweetie. Specifically, you like my cock too much. I have no fear that some woman will snatch you away from me by convincing you that you're really a lesbian. If that did happen within six months you'd be back at my door telling me to put my spurs on and saddle you up."

"Arrogant prick!" Danielle said giving him another playful punch in the ribs to which he responded by grabbing her. In a flash he had her pinned face down on the bed and giggling beneath him. She gasped as but a second later she felt the tip of his erection brush against her anus and then stab into her dry vagina. He let it stay there, not moving it while he sucked on the back on her neck, causing her to moan, feeling her canal respond by coating his penis with lubrication. When she began using her Kegel muscles to clutch possessively at the penis stuffing her he whispered in her ear, "There is no way you'll be able to give me up."

"I know," she gladly admitted through clenched teeth and then let him have his way with her.

CHAPTER 21

Finally going stir crazy in the bedroom Max and Danielle dressed after sex and, opting to leave their rented Mustang behind, took a stroll into the center of town, enjoying the mild November weather which is such a far cry from the blistering heat common in the Arizona desert from May to September. While window shopping on Fountain Hills Boulevard Danielle thought it best to regain the thread of their earlier discussion. She still wasn't sure whether or not to believe or even hope that Max would freely allow her to have sex with women, an act she was ready to equate with being paroled from prison.

"So what are the rules?" she asked, peering at a pair of red leather pumps in a shoe boutique's window.

"I gather then you're interested in taking advantage of my offer?"

She smiled. "Maybe. First I want to hear how much of my soul this will cost me."

"Fair enough. By the way, I don't really like those pumps. Remember, I have a foot fetish so my approval is necessary; I much prefer the blue sandals. As to what the rules are, well…I believe the first rule should be honesty." He led her inside the store. "Since I'm giving you permission to indulge in your taste for women I see no reason for you to be deceitful—Yes, hello," he said now to a pretty clerk who approached to service them upon their entrance. "…those blue sandals in the window, we need to see them in a size six, please." He guided Danielle to a set of chairs where they sat awaiting the shoes. "I mean," he continued, whispering now that they were indoors, "if you're gonna be late coming home one night because you have a rendezvous with a young lady then say so; don't tell me you have a meeting at work or a pottery class to attend. If I get the feeling you're sneaking around then I'll imagine you're doing all sorts of horrible things."

"Okay. What else?"

"Well, I think that our relationship should take priority—Thank you, miss," he said to the clerk. "We'll let you know how we like them." Max took the proffered box, opened it and extracted one sandal. He then gently placed Danielle's foot in his lap and after fitting the shoe on admired how it looked. He bent and gave her ankle a kiss. "How does it feel?" he asked.

"The kiss felt wonderful and the shoes are very comfortable. I like them."

"See anything else you want?"

She pointed after taking a look around. "Those brown pumps are cute."

So Max signaled for the clerk, gave the order and when the shoes arrived the ritual was repeated. After the brown pumps earned his approval Max handed the clerk his debit card and told her to ring up the purchases. Back on the street, shopping bag in hand, Max asked, "What was I saying?"

"Priority."

"Yes. Absolutely. Our relationship should take priority. I mean, if you wanna have flings with women, fine. Just don't forget that we've managed to build something nice, you and I, despite the fact that I'm anti-social and you're incredibly high maintenance. I don't wanna feel as if you're neglecting our relationship and by extension neglecting me."

"Don't worry," she said, stopping to give him a reassuring kiss. "I like what we've built also. Are those all the rules?"

"Just one more: no picking up skanks at the Greyhound station. I don't want you bringing home some disease that'll make my dick fall off. That and the fact that the reading public has questionable taste about what it considers great writing are the only things I got going for me."

"Darn. I heard the bus station is a hot spot for girl-on-girl action," Danielle joked and then, more seriously: "Will I be expected home by a certain time or am I allowed the occasional sleep over?"

"Sure, why not? Spend the night with a young lady anytime you'd like, particularly if there's a good baseball game on or you're PMS-ing."

They started walking again and after several steps Danielle shook her head. "God, I can't believe we're talking about this," she said. "You're serious?"

"Uh-huh."

"Something doesn't feel right about it, Max," she confessed.

"That's because you've been brainwashed into believing this type of thing is wrong. I experienced the same feeling. When you first told me you were bisexual I thought to myself, 'Oh well, she's outta luck 'cuz I'm not sharing her.' But the more I thought about it the more I saw how shockingly selfish it would be for me to deny you completeness."

"No, I mean that I feel like I'm being set up. You're not agreeing to all this because you've found somebody yourself that you want to have an affair with, are you? One of those undersexed housewives who I notice practically throwing themselves at you during your book signings?"

Max laughed. He did, in fact, have a significant female fan base in part because of his exotic good looks and in part because of his proven ability to create believable female characters in his novels. The autograph queues at his signings were thus mostly made up of women and many of those who weren't gay had no qualms about flirting with the author or slipping him notes asking him to call when they handed him their copies of his book.

"Jesus, no," he said. "Look, as much as I love women do I really strike you as being patient enough to handle more than one of you at a time? No thank you. I got enough problems. Quite frankly, I'm just hoping you'll find somebody you really like and start taking her to Mayzie Witherspoon's brunches instead of me."

"Mayzie is sweet, Max."

"Mayzie is a spoiled heiress who's too old to collect dolls so she figures she can collect people. But that's neither here nor there."

They walked in silence for a while then, continuing to window shop and occasionally stepping inside a store to browse. Max could tell his girlfriend was particularly pensive; she had reached into her purse and extracted her Tic Tacs, keeping the little box in her hand and popping a fresh one in her mouth every minute or so as if the tiny mints were full of wisdom and answers instead of sugar and artificial flavoring. And when they entered an antiques shop Danielle immediately wandered off from him to contemplatively thumb through a set of vintage postcards.

Max understood. What he was proposing, after all, was quite unorthodox—especially because, as Danielle had put it, he wasn't trying to gain anything. It was natural, then, that she should look this gift horse in the mouth by being wary and suspicious. But Max saw no choice. Lately, he had been wary and suspicious, too, but for completely different reasons: he was getting tired of noticing Danielle devour an attractive woman with her eyes and then wondering if the orgasm she had that night or the next day was in fact caused by his skills as a lover or by some fantasy involving said woman that Danielle was playing in her head. Sure, he meant all that stuff today, about wanting to give her the freedom necessary to enjoy both sides of her sexual nature. It was the only thing that made sense if one looks at it in terms of ensuring Danielle's happiness and well-being. And he was open-minded enough to not see anything weird about it. But he also wanted peace of mind. He wanted, simply put, to always be sure that when they lay together it was indeed him she desired.

Or to put it another way, he didn't want Danielle craving pistachios when she was supposed to be enjoying cashews.

🍁   🍁   🍁

They returned home the Monday following Thanksgiving. The flight from Phoenix landed at La Guardia that afternoon at 3:15, the hired car dropped them off on Fifth Avenue at 4:47 and they entered their home at 4:52. Exactly ten minutes later while Max took a nap Danielle was ignoring the unpacking to be done and was sitting in front of her computer.

    From: PopeAnne@bigappleweb.com
    To: shaw.kate@homewardbound.org
    Subject: !!!!!!
    Sent: November 29 5:03 p.m.

!

Call me!!!!

CHAPTER 22

❀

Katie Shaw was passionate about helping others. Growing up in Marcano, Nebraska Katie was the type of kid who brought home birds with broken wings while leaving out saucers of milk for stray cats (in one instance leading to disastrous results when the stray cat ate the bird with the broken wing.) Her adolescence found her in Girl Scouts, energetically picking up trash in parks or reading to the blind, and in high school she was the one organizing canned food drives and protests at City Hall against proposed cuts to the handicapped services budget. Her parents, obviously, were very proud, but secretly wondered why their daughter didn't put as much energy into chasing boys.

What brought Katie to New York after she graduated from high school was an aspiration to put her charitable instincts to work on a larger scale. Marcano just didn't have enough problems; Katie sometimes found herself making up causes to avoid boredom: Students Against Newt Gingrich, for example, or Satellite Television For the Elderly. New York City, though, had always been her promised land because New York had slumlords and overcrowded prisons and huge welfare rolls, not to mention an understaffed social services infrastructure, corrupt politicians and overwhelming homelessness. Often, after yet another day spent going door to door collecting cans of mixed vegetables on behalf of the local United Way, Katie would watch the evening news, hear of some horrible injustice being perpetrated against yet another subset of helpless New Yorkers and sigh longingly.

"What was that for?" her mother inquired after one such sigh.

The seventeen-year old Katie had pointed at the television.

"I just wish stuff like that would happen here in Marcano," she answered rather sulkily.

"Group homes for abused women being shut down because the city wants to build an Arby's?" her mother asked in shock.

"Yeah. Then I'd be able to help them by protesting against the shut down while calling attention to the plight of abused women."

"Well, that's sweet, Kay, but what you should be worrying about is who you'll ask to the Sadie Hawkins dance next week."

"I told you," Katie had said, "I'm going with Dawn Rayburn."

"That girl from the next town? My, you two do spend a lot of time together…"

Midway through her junior year at Columbia Katie took an internship at the Warren Williams Foundation, a not-for-profit organization dedicated to the cause of homelessness. She learned how to run soup kitchens, the ins and outs of how the City's shelter system worked and the complexities of setting up food and clothing drives that encompassed all five boroughs. During the winter she and other Foundation workers would troll the streets in a van distributing blankets to anyone they found trying to stay warm outside and during the summer she helped pass out free bottles of water. She was a tireless asset to the Foundation, full of compassion for those less fortunate and full of ideas for helping the Foundation better fulfill its mission.

Homeward Bound was her idea, coming to her one afternoon not long after she'd earned her Bachelor's degree and was enrolled in the Masters program. While waiting for a cross-town bus she noticed a Help Wanted sign in a coffee shop window, and sitting outside on the sidewalk just beneath that very sign was a homeless person asking for loose change by shaking a tin cup. The connection made she stayed up until 2 a.m. drafting a proposal, presented it the next day to the Foundation's board, and despite her youth was selected as the obvious choice for setting up and running it.

That was six years ago and her commitment has never wavered. Helping the homeless may not pay very well—in fact it paid like shit, especially when the company signing the paychecks used a negative adverb in conjunction with the word "profit"—but the work made her happy and in her mind there was nothing quite like making a difference.

🍁   🍁   🍁

By six-thirty most evenings the Homeward Bound office was empty and it was Katie, as director, who usually locked the doors behind her and pulled down the metal shutters before leaving for home. At six-thirty on the Tuesday after Thanksgiving, however, she answered a knock on the front door and opened it to let Danielle in.

It was the first time these two had seen each other since their dinner at Yen Ching's back in June. Katie noticed that Danielle had had blonde highlights added to her hair and that she was accentuating her eyes more with liner and shadow. Other than those changes it was the same woman whom Katie had thought often of during the past several months usually in extremely erotic vignettes that sometimes involved whipped cream. What's more, the passing of time had done nothing to diminish that desire; seeing Danielle now in November gave Katie the exact same electric thrill as when she first met her way back in June.

Katie led Danielle into her office and tried to commence with the obligatory small talk.

"So, how are our clients working out at ARCL?" she asked.

"God, Katie, what the fuck do I care?" Danielle said. "That's Gail's problem now. I'm not here to talk about homeless people."

Katie laughed at Danielle's bluntness, was even turned on by it. When she got that enigmatic e-mail from her yesterday Katie knew right away it had nothing to do with business and spent last night imagining all sorts of delicious possibilities.

"Okay, fuck the chit chat then," Katie said. "What's really on your mind?"

"You."

"I like it so far."

"It gets better."

"No way."

"Way."

"Pray tell."

"What if I told you that I've suddenly become available?"

Katie's eyebrows raised.

"Is that so? Did you and the great Max Bland have a fight over the last piece of pumpkin pie and break up?"

"What if I told you that no, we haven't broken up, that we are not even close to breaking up but that I'm nonetheless available, and that any night of your choosing this week I'm free to come over and see what you taste like?"

Katie's mind may have been confused but her body responded to that "taste" comment by making her wet. She said, "Then I'd tell you that I wish I didn't have a sink full of dishes, three loads of laundry by my door and dust everywhere because I choose tonight."

"Would you?"

"Life's too short, Danielle. I'd rather wait to hear the explanation behind all this until after you've made me come."

This time it was Danielle whose body responded but in addition to getting wet she had to take a deep breath to calm herself and this made her breasts heave, something which Katie's eyes drank in hungrily. Danielle stood, putting on her coat and collecting her purse.

"Not tonight," she told the surprised blonde. "I want you to think about it first and then call me tomorrow. If we hook up tomorrow I'll give you all the details. But think hard, Katie. If you say yes I want to be sure it's what you want. Till then, good night."

"You're leaving?" Katie asked, getting up. "After only a few minutes?"

"A few minutes were all I needed," Danielle said. "It's been months since you've seen me…I wanted to be sure you remembered how tempting I am."

And with that the brief visit was over.

🍁 🍁 🍁

When Katie got home later that evening to the tiny flat she sublet on Eighth Avenue she solved the laundry problem she mentioned to Danielle in no time by just stuffing it all into the coat closet. The dirty dishes—stacks of them, most covered in dried spaghetti sauce or remnants of scrambled eggs—were similarly dispatched by being moved from the sink and hidden in the cupboard underneath. Her housecleaning done Katie went into her bedroom and dug out all her nightgowns from the bureau, laying them on the bed and scrutinizing them with a critic's eye: "The black lace is nice but maybe too cliché, she'll be expecting it," she said aloud to the empty room. "The red satin one was an unfortunate purchase because it makes me look fat and the pink one has that mysterious stain on it. That leaves the black satin one and the pink baby doll. The black satin is classy, the baby doll is definitely slutty. Safer to choose classy over slutty, at least until I get to know her better."

The black satin put aside for tomorrow night Katie filled the tub in the bathroom and soaked for twenty minutes before commencing to shave her legs and her pubic region leaving only her customary landing strip of tight blonde curls on her mons. She hated women with hairy bushes, not only did they give the impression that some kind of wild animal was nesting between the legs but they smelled bad to boot. So as she guided the Venus razor very carefully along the flesh on either side of her vaginal lips Katie hoped to Heaven that Danielle was shaved, although she felt certain she was. Looking at that woman, she considered, one can just tell she was very well groomed, even down to her private parts. Probably even went to a special salon where some gay guy snipped them for her while she read *Vogue*.

Staring at her toes Katie decided to paint the nails a little later while watching television and she also made a note to wash all her dildos. In the meantime she'd just soak and think.

Danielle had said that her and the great Max Bland were not even close to breaking up. Yet she also said that she was available. *I wonder how she swung that?* Katie thought. *But then again, maybe she didn't have to swing anything. Maybe I'll just be a little secret. Instead of her cheating on the great Max Bland with another guy she's planning on cheating on him with a woman.*

When she had first laid eyes on Danielle way back in June Katie had right away wanted her. That reaction, of course, was purely sexual—Danielle was, after all, stunning—but when that first flush of physical attraction subsided and her hormones relinquished control of her brain Katie had been surprised to find herself thinking of things she hadn't thought of in a long while; things like the word "couple", and matching tattoos, and Hers and Hers towels in the same bathroom, and a most-likely-to-be-nullified-by-the-State-Superior-Court gay wedding in California. In other words, stuff she hadn't dared think about since she and Nina had broken up.

But even though it was nice to daydream about being in a long-term and solid relationship with someone she clicked with, like Danielle, Katie was simply not at a point in her life where such an arrangement was in the cards. For now, work was everything to her and she was content devoting the lion's share of her energies to helping the homeless, and Homeward Bound was only the tip of the iceberg when it came to Katie. There were also fundraisers she organized; volunteer work she did on weekends; City Council meetings she attended; research she conducted on how other municipalities were addressing the problem, grant proposals to write, et cetera. Thus, the few attempts she'd made during the past few years to have meaningful relationships with women had ended disastrously: Emily, Aisha, Perdita, Nina—each of them eventually felt that she was Katie's second choice behind the city's panhandlers and vagrants, cried tears of frustration and resentment, and left.

As disappointing as this was (certainly when she was a kid she imagined being firmly attached romantically to someone by age twenty-eight) Katie nonetheless was comfortable with the choices she'd made. She knew someday her priorities would shift but until then she'd make do with gaining physical satisfaction from the toys in the box by her bed and from what she classified as "fuck buddies": various women she knew who, like herself, were only available for, or only interested in, brief sexual connections with no strings attached.

And I guess Danielle wants to be one of those women, Katie thought adding more hot water to the tub. *Fine by me. In fact, I'd be happy if she was my only fuck buddy.*

Katie had no idea what Danielle's motivations were or what had happened to suddenly make her available for a lesbian tryst, but she wasn't going to worry about that now. What she was most concerned about was whether or not she could still squeeze into the black satin nightgown after the huge Thanksgiving meal she'd eaten last week.

The bath water, hot as it was, was sensuously relaxing. All this thinking about Danielle made Katie want to masturbate and she even got as far as making a few strokes across the top of her clitoris with her middle finger but then, with an impressive show of will, she stopped. She wanted it to build up. For tomorrow.

CHAPTER 23

❃

The next day Max's cell phone rang while he was in his office writing. The caller ID informed him it was "Dani @ Work" calling.

"Hi Max," Danielle said in greeting, somewhat hesitatingly. "Am I disturbing you?"

Actually no, she wasn't disturbing him. He was at a particularly difficult part of his new novel, describing his main character's rationale for resigning as President of the United States to pursue a career as a circus clown and he wasn't having much luck doing it effectively. He was considering packing it up for the day and going to the movies with the hope that tomorrow Inspiration won't call in sick and show up for work. But he lied when he answered her. Long ago they had made an agreement that barring an emergency she would never call him between the hours of ten and three, typically when he was at his most productive. It wasn't that he disliked talking to her but just that he knew enough about women to know that when they get bored at work or start feeling mushy because they saw a butterfly the first thing they do is call their boyfriends. But on the days when the words were pouring out of him like water from a faucet he didn't need his rhythm disrupted by having to listen to Danielle wax poetic about daffodils or to tell her for the umpteenth time that yes, she was the light of his life. So when he answered he put an annoyed edge to his voice that he didn't really feel, just to cover up the fact that in truth he was glad for the disruption.

"What do you need, Danielle?"

"God, I'm sorry I called, I know I'm not supposed to but it's kind of a time-sensitive thing."

"What's up?"

"Are we doing anything tonight? I mean, do we have any plans I may have forgotten?"

Max rolled his eyes, wondering if Mayzie Witherspoon Incorporated had now diversified into dinners as well as brunches.

"No…" he said cautiously.

"Okay, good." She paused then and Max heard her take a deep breath. "Um…that's good because I have a date."

For a moment relief at not hearing Mayzie's name confused Max and that word "date" caused a pang of alarm to pierce his heart. But almost instantly he recovered and figured it had something to do with the Fountain Hills discussion.

"Oh…oh, right," he said. "You mean with a woman."

"Yeah, with a woman."

"Okay. Wow, that was fast, come to think of it."

Danielle gave a nervous chuckle. "Yeah, I guess it was. I probably should have told you earlier but I had someone in mind when we were talking about this in Arizona."

"No harm done. Well…look, we have no plans tonight, like I said, so there's nothing stopping you."

"Are you sure?"

"Absolutely. Have a good time."

"This still feels weird."

"It'll pass. So will you be coming home tonight?"

"I'm not sure yet but something tells me no. God, that makes me sound like a tramp."

"I always knew you had a bit of the tramp in you, the way you pounced on me that first night we had sex."

"I know—"

"I mean, one minute I'm sitting there having a perfectly reasonable discussion with you and the next I'm sucking on your tits."

"I know—"

"Caught me by surprise, quite frankly, I always assumed—"

"You're straying, honey," Danielle interrupted. "Max, are you *sure* you're okay with this? *Really, really* sure? I can cancel."

"And break the poor woman's heart? Don't be absurd. If you've built up her hopes only to turn her down now she may get suicidal."

"I'm serious, Max."

"Okay, okay. Yes, I'm fine with this. Go out and have a good time. Really. And if you wanna make me extra happy, take plenty of pictures."

"What are you going to do tonight?"

"Either enjoy having our place all to myself or call up my buddies in the Bronx and see if they wanna go bowling tonight instead of tomorrow."

"Do the bowling. I don't like the thought of you all alone in that great big apartment while I'm…you know…look, just go bowling, 'k?"

"You don't know me very well, Edwards. Being alone in great big apartments is what I like best."

Danielle sighed. "Okay, I have to go now, I have a meeting with Margot. I'll call you later, before my date. I love you."

"And I you."

"I guess I'll see you tomorrow then."

"Till then."

❦   ❦   ❦

"*OH, FUCK!*" Danielle shouted, arching her back as her vagina orgasmed around the hot pink dildo inside it. Katie instantly stopped sucking on her clitoris but kept her lips around it, feeling the tiny organ throb rapidly like a miniature heart.

"*FUCK!FUCK!FUCK!*" Danielle's shouts grew in volume with each passing wave of pleasure that washed over her body, up from genitals, and her eyes were squeezed so tightly shut a headache was forming behind them. Finally she couldn't take it anymore; her vagina was way too sensitive. She forcefully pushed Katie's head away from her crotch, yanked the dildo out and in the same motion flung it onto the floor. She enjoyed the rest of her orgasm whimpering into a pillow, her legs drawn up to her chest. Fatigue suddenly gripped her; she could sleep for days, she thought.

Katie lay down beside her, feeling the satisfaction that all accomplished lovers feel, and embraced her companion. She was drowsy herself.

It was still early, only nine o'clock. Their date had started innocently enough a couple of hours earlier: after leaving work Danielle had taken a cab to a Mexican restaurant on Eighth Avenue that Katie had recommended. Katie was waiting for her outside the place and when Danielle approached they both spent a few moments looking over the menu posted in a glass display case next to the front door.

"So how did you find this place?" Danielle asked.

"It wasn't hard. The apartment I sublet is two doors down."
"Is that so?"
"Yep. That way. Still feel like eating?"
"Definitely not burritos," Danielle said taking Katie's hand and leading her "that way."

🍁   🍁   🍁

As soon as the door had latched shut behind them they were all over each other. Danielle had purposely worn clothing that was simple to remove; nothing with lots of buttons or hooks: her sweater was a pullover, her slacks had an elastic waist and her shoes could be kicked off. Her foresight was rewarded when after their first frenzied moments of kissing Katie easily pulled Danielle's sweater off and gave a gasp.

"Like what you see?" Danielle purred, proud of her breasts in their black lace bra (which, by the way, had an easy open front snap closure). She sighed as Katie answered her by burying her face in her cleavage, biting the two mounds of flesh and then tugging the fabric of one cup to the side in order to free an erect nipple which she then sucked on deeply. Shortly thereafter Katie dropped to her knees, kissing Danielle's toned abdomen, tonguing her navel and then slowly sliding her slacks down being sure to scrape Danielle's flesh with her nails as she did so. When she had gotten the pants down to just past Danielle's pubic region (shaved, thank God!) Katie stopped and pushed her face into her groin, locating and then licking her clitoris with the very tip of her tongue.

"Good girl," Danielle murmured, grabbing Katie's hair and forcing her face tighter onto her body.

🍁   🍁   🍁

Katie had been afraid that Danielle would turn out to be a pillow princess. That was a term she used to describe a woman content to just lay back, let others please her and not concern herself much about pleasing them in return. It was a condition prevalent in women like Danielle: those who swung both ways. Even when they moved into the bedroom and she was stripping the rest of Danielle's clothes off a small voice in Katie's mind was warning her not to expect too great a time.

But then Danielle pounced and pinned Katie down on the bed. Taking the stockings Katie had been wearing and which had been tossed onto the floor within easy reach Danielle bound the other woman's wrists together and then tied them to the headboard. For the next hour Katie was blissfully helpless and all worries about pillow princesses were gone. Using her tongue, lips and fingers expertly Danielle spent that hour bringing Katie to the brink of orgasm repeatedly only to cruelly stop each time, stare up at her mischievously from between her legs and say, "Not yet," and then proceed to start all over again. When Danielle finally showed mercy and allowed her to come Katie's body was glistening with a sheen of perspiration and the orgasm wracked her so hard her ovaries ached.

🍁 🍁 🍁

Later, after Katie had gotten Danielle off with the hot pink dildo and her own mouth the two dozed contentedly in an embrace. It was Danielle who stirred first, around ten-thirty, and kissed Katie's forehead until the other woman's eyes fluttered open.
"It can't be time to get up for work already!" Katie moaned, stretching.
"No, baby, it's not even eleven yet. We just napped a bit."
"Mm, good," Katie said and then frowned suddenly. "Jesus, I'm starving!"
"So am I. Does your Mexican place deliver?" Danielle asked.
"Yeah, but I don't want to call just yet. I'm too comfortable right here," Katie answered and then kissed her new plaything deeply. When their lips parted Danielle sighed heavily and said, "Thank you, Max Bland."
This took Katie by surprise.
"You mean to tell me the great Max Bland knows you're here?" she queried.
"Mmmm-hmmm. He knows all about it." She then related to Katie the whole story: her telling Max about her bisexuality in the spring and the results of the recent Fountain Hills summit over Thanksgiving.
"So you have a pretty nice thing going for you, huh?" Katie said. "You already had a man available to you whenever you wanted and now you want the same arrangement with a woman."
"That's right."
"You greedy bitch!" Katie said in mock derision.
Danielle laughed. "Anyway, I called him this morning to say I had a date and that I probably wouldn't be coming home. Or was that presumptuous? Would you like me to leave?"
"Fuck you, are you kidding?" Katie said, kissing Danielle deeply again, this time cupping a breast also. "Do you realize how much I've thought about you

the past few months? There is no way I am not waking up with you tomorrow. Jesus, your boobs are so perfect, I hate you. What are they, a C cup?"

"34D."

"Fucking bitch. Look at me, I have the chest of a small boy compared to you. When I was a teenager I kept praying for tits like yours but I never got them, that's why I stopped going to church. I figured a God who thought 32B was sufficient wasn't worth worshipping."

"Come on…" Danielle said. "I hate you for how perky your boobs are."

"Well there's not much for gravity to get a hold of."

"Stop and be grateful. I'll be thirty in June and already I can feel my breasts heading towards my knees. Anyway, you have a perfect model's body, you know that? You're so graceful."

Katie spent a few thoughtful moments outlining Danielle's nipple with the tip of her finger and then changed the subject. "So…is this a one night thing?"

Danielle kissed the tip of the other woman's nose.

"I was hoping not," she answered.

"You haven't gotten me out of your system?"

"I think I've gotten you more *in* my system."

"So what are the rules then? How often can I call you? When do I get to see you? Do I first have to fill out a requisition form and send it to the great Max Bland for his signature? Blah, blah, blah."

Danielle shook her head. "I don't know. Max and I never really hashed those kinds of details out, maybe we will when I see him tomorrow. And, um…speaking of Max…you realize that my first priority has to be him, right? I mean, I love him very much; in fact, I can't imagine my life without him, and my being here with you doesn't change that."

"I know," Katie answered softly still twirling her fingertip around the nipple. She herself wanted to tell Danielle that right now her first priority was the homeless, that that was why she hadn't been seriously involved with someone for quite some time; that she viewed this thing with Danielle as a casual fling, just something (or rather, someone) to do to break the monotonous string of nights spent masturbating, and that one day she fully expected to meet a woman she'd fall in love with and possibly marry, even if they had to go all the way to Spain to do so, at which point Danielle would be kicked to the curb so to speak. But even though the words were right there in her throat ready to come out in perfectly formed sentences Katie didn't want to say them. For now she was content having someone to share her bed with tonight.

❦ ❦ ❦

For someone who had intended on spending the night at Katie's from the very beginning Danielle hadn't really planned it well. Upon awakening the next morning she realized she had no change of clothes, no makeup, nor even a toothbrush. In fact, she hadn't packed anything. The toothbrush issue was resolved easily by Katie offering her own for Danielle to use pointing out that considering the places on each other's bodies where they had their mouths last night they shouldn't feel squeamish about sharing dental implements.

The clothing dilemma was a bit more complicated, however. There was no way in hell Danielle was going to walk into a gossipy office wearing the same clothes as yesterday but because she was so much bustier than Katie none of Katie's tops fit, a discovery which left the Nebraskan feeling even more depressed about how flat-chested she was. Shirts or sweaters that had breathing room on Katie made Danielle look like a pin-up girl or simply didn't button over her breasts. Danielle thought it was funny; Katie thought it was a tragedy on par with finding a gray hair. In the end Danielle decided to hell with it, called in sick and after breakfast kissed Katie goodbye at the door. The two women promised to call each other in no more than 48 hours to plan their next assignation. As soon as Danielle was outside, vainly trying to hail a cab, she called Max's cell phone.

"Hi, where are you?" she inquired when he picked up. "Do you want to meet for coffee?"

"Can't. I'm at my office working," he told her.

Danielle was surprised and checked her watch. It was only 7:45.

"Why so early?" she asked.

"Well, it's like this: Me and the old gang went to Pino's up in the Bronx for dinner last night before we went bowling and I must've ate some bad oysters. I spent most of the night after I got home on the toilet and while I was sitting there thinking things over I got all sorts of ideas to get me through this writer's block I've been having. So I jotted down some notes, got up early when your alarm went off and I've been writing ever since."

"Well, listen, I'm coming over. I want to see you."

There was a pregnant pause then. Danielle knew that Max was trying to come up with a diplomatic way to tell her to kiss his ass, he was writing. So she said, "Look, Max, I just spent last night fucking someone else when I'm supposedly in a committed relationship with you and it's kind of messing with my mind now so get over it, I'm on my way."

❦   ❦   ❦

In all the time they've been together Danielle had never been to Max's office, and when she entered the studio apartment he had bought in a renovated brownstone to serve this purpose she was surprised at how empty and unadorned it was.

"God, Max, what the hell?" she said. "How can you stand it being so *boring*?"

"It's supposed to be boring. It's where I write not where I stage *La Boheme*. And don't you have a job? Aren't you supposed to be in the Financial District doing whatever the hell it is you do for a living?"

"I called in," Danielle said and then crinkled her nose. "Yep, this place definitely needs a woman's touch," she declared.

Max looked longingly at the spiral notebook and number 2 pencil on the desk and sighed. "Look, did you just come here to criticize me or is there something else?"

"There's something else."

"Okay, what?"

"I don't know."

Max sighed; then, figuring that the only way he was going to get her out of here so he could get back to writing was to pretend to care about what was bothering her, he led her to the couch, sat down beside her and encircled her in his arms.

"Okay, tell me about your date," he prodded.

"Wasn't exactly what I'd call a date," Danielle answered. "I mean, we did eventually get around to eating Mexican food but at the start we pretty much went straight to the sex."

"Really? Wow, women are so efficient; maybe I should become a lesbian. So lemme guess…this morning when you called you were feeling a little guilty and wanted to see me just so you can be sure I hadn't changed the locks on you."

"Bingo."

"Do we have to have this conversation again?" he asked. "I already told you it's okay."

"I know, but…I wanted proof. You have to remember, I'm a woman in love and for a woman in love there is no such thing as casual sex. If I hated your guts that would be one thing but as it is the entire cab ride over here I kept thinking you were harboring resentment towards me and I was all set to tell you that you could go fuck another woman if only you'd promise not to leave me."

"I'll remember that the next time you piss me off by saying Woody Allen is a narcissist whose films have no redeeming value. So, since you didn't have much of a date tell me about what did happen. Was it any good?"

Danielle took a deep breath, remembering the taste of Katie and how expertly she used that hot pink dildo. "God, good doesn't begin to describe it. Although now I'm wondering if it was good because it was good or because it's been so long since I've had a woman."

"Don't overanalyze it," Max said. "Just enjoy it."

"You're right, I will. Anyway, she asked me last night what the rules were, about her and I seeing each other. I told her that was something you and I had yet to discuss."

"Do you want to see her again? And, by the way, don't you think it's time you told me who 'her' is?"

"Katie. Her name is Katie Shaw." Danielle thought it bizarre that this was the first time Max had heard her name. Considering that twelve hours ago Katie's index finger was rubbing Danielle's anus while her tongue was tickling her G-spot made it seem as if a step or two had been skipped. "And yes," she continued, "I do want to see her again. We really hit it off right from the start. I really like her."

"And how'd you meet?"

"Through work actually. It was months ago."

"Oh? Is she also a…whatever the hell it is you are?"

"God, Max, don't you know anything about what I do?"

He shrugged. "All I know is you work for a bank of some sort. Are you a teller?"

"Fuck you."

"Is she a teller?"

"No, she happens to help homeless people find jobs."

"Wow. Well, I may not know exactly what you do for a living but I'm sure it's not as noble as that."

"Fuck you again."

"And you say you like her?"

"Yeah. A lot."

"Well, in case my opinion counts, if you're gonna keep doing this I'd prefer you choose to do it with someone steady whom you like. Face it, it'd be better for both of us. As far as when you can see her again, I don't care. Just don't let her monopolize you. Remember, I saw you first." He stood. "And now, my dear, I may have shown you that you are still welcome in my life but you are not welcome in my office. I was on a roll before you arrived and I'd like to get back on it. May I remind you that it was proceeds from my last book which paid for the Mercedes I bought you for your birthday?"

Danielle stood also and made for the door.

"Fine, Max, but I'll be back in a few hours."

"What? Why?"

She looked at him pityingly. "Silly man. I have the whole day off and a platinum credit card. I'm going shopping for things to liven this place up. Toodles!"

CHAPTER 24

✿

November turned into December, Christmas gifts were exchanged, and then January came. It was a particularly harsh one that year; two blizzards slammed the city and even Max daydreamed fondly of the mild winters in the Sonoran desert where a cold day was defined as one in which the mercury dipped to sixty-five. When February arrived it was not much better but instead of snowstorms it was rainstorms and each time they ended the soaked metropolis would freeze over with a treacherous sheen of ice.

During these months Danielle and Katie pretty much played things by ear, seeing each other every so often when schedules and previous commitments allowed them to sate their desires. At first, all three parties involved kept word of their little arrangement to themselves but eventually chance comments and offhand remarks forced them each to open up to their friends:

🍁　　　🍁　　　🍁

"Alright, I don't understand what exactly is going on," Max's best friend Mikey confessed one evening in January over drinks at a bar in the Bronx. Mikey was a thickset Puerto Rican who looked a lot like the comic Paul Rodriguez and who had been Max's friend since kindergarten.

"What's to understand?" Max answered, signaling the barkeep for another gin and tonic for himself and a second Heineken for Mikey. "Danielle lives with me, she's my girlfriend but I allow her to have a little fun on the side."

"No, I get that, boss, but what I don't get is you not benefiting from it. A bisexual girlfriend is like a gift from the gods, man. You're in prime position, boss, to—"

"I know, I know," Max cut in. "Prime position to fulfill the one fantasy every straight male has had since the dawn of time: a threesome."

"Don't you want one?" Mikey asked, but in a way that made it clear he was feeling his old friend out for latent homosexual feelings. Real men want to have sex with more than one woman at a time, his question seemed to be saying. Max recognized this but still he answered honestly.

"To tell you the truth I'm ambivalent about it. Sure, on the surface a threesome sounds like heaven but, really, who needs the aggravation? Suppose Danielle and I do invite another woman into bed with us, Mikey…and suppose we like it so much we invite her back for more. God forbid the second woman develops an emotional attachment to me as well; then I'd have two women to try to figure out, two women complaining I don't open up enough to them and two women wanting me to watch *Gilmore Girls* with them. I got enough problems. Besides, you're wrong: I do benefit from this whole thing."

Mikey couldn't see a benefit and he told Max so. He also told Max that if his own girlfriend Wanda was half as good-looking as Danielle, bisexual and didn't have girlfriends who were all fat loud-mouthed bitches he'd beg on his knees for a threesome. But Max explained.

"Look," he said, "I benefit because now I have more breathing room, you see? For example, I know you love Wanda but don't you sometimes just wanna not be around her?"

"What the fuck you think I'm in this bar for?"

"Exactly. Well, ever since Danielle got hooked up with this Katie woman I suddenly have all sorts of time to myself, you know? It's like my bread is buttered on both sides; I get to enjoy the benefits of being in a committed relationship but I also get some of the benefits of being single. When she's off with Katie I can do what I want, when I want and not have to worry about being home by a certain time or her feeling ignored…it's great. And I'll tell you something else: this arrangement helps cut down on the tension. Danielle and I don't fight often but when we do I know it's because we're both burned out from one another. The littlest thing will set us off. Our last fight was over which Darren was better on *Bewitched*. We slept in separate rooms. Anyway, I think that's why most couples fight; all that time spent together gets on people's nerves and makes them edgy, makes them moody." He took another drink, asked his companion to pass him the pretzels. "I dunno, Mikey, but I think I've discovered the secret to successful male/female relationships."

"And that is…"

"Bisexuality," Max said as if it were obvious. Then he explained. Not only is all the time spent together to blame but because men and women are so extremely different, with extremely different wants and needs but with no real capacity to understand one another it's a miracle couples stay together more than a few years. "And those rare couples who stay married for, say, forty years, only do so with a lot of screaming and name-calling and trial separations through the years."

But, he continued, if at least one member of an otherwise typical male/female couple were bisexual…

"Then you have a situation where the bisexual member gets to go off occasionally to spend time with someone who really gets where he or she is coming from while the other member not only gets some time alone but is also released from the burden of being the only one on Earth expected to understand his or her mate."

Mikey took a swig from his Heineken, mulling this over. Suddenly he shook his head.

"I don't get it, boss," he said. "Why does bisexuality have to be the secret ingredient? Why can't Danielle get this understanding and stuff from her normal buncha friends?"

"Because there are limitations to the emotional depth of the bonds Danielle can form with her straight friends," Max told him. "There are certain emotional bonds that can only be created in a sexual relationship, you follow? So, Danielle's sexual attraction to Katie *guarantees* me two things: One, that she'll want to spend a lot of time with her. Two, that a deep bond will develop between them which will make Danielle realize that I, a man, am far too stupid to understand what she, a woman, is all about."

"But then that leaves you out, boss," said Mikey. "Who gets to understand you? You get the short end of the stick in this deal."

"*I* get to understand me," Max informed his friend. "All the free time I now have allows me to better explore what makes me happy and to indulge in my own hobbies and interests. I think it all balances out."

Shrugging, Mikey downed the rest of his beer, signaled for another. "Sorta makes sense, Max. But tell me this: why is that you—"

🍁   🍁   🍁

"—are okay with sharing her with a man, even if that man is Max Bland?" Katie's best friend Moira asked one evening in February over coffee at Katie's apartment. Moira, like her friend, was a lesbian but there the similarity ended because Moira, unlike her friend, took pains to hide all traces of her femininity, did not own a single skirt or dress, kept her hair cropped military-style and was often mistaken for the opposite sex in public. Like most of America's lesbians she was a big *Pope Anne* fan; in fact, when she first read the book Moira was certain that the "Max" in "Max Bland" was short for Maxine and thus was disappointed upon reading a profile on the author in *Time* and learning that she was a he. But that disappointment was overcome when she noted that Max often used the publicity which the book gave him to speak out for gay rights.

"What's to understand?" Katie answered, dipping her biscotti into her mug and taking a bite. "They've been together for quite a while now, they're very much in love, she's bi and he's open-minded and liberal enough to allow her to get some female action on the side."

"Fine, I get that, Kay, but where's the benefit to you? You say you really like this chick but how can you expect to have a future with her? You do still imagine yourself ending up with a woman, right?" Moira asked, but in a way that made it clear she was feeling her friend out for latent heterosexual feelings. Real women only want to have sex with other women, her question seemed to be saying.

"You mean the same future I was planning to have with Nina? Or Aisha? Or how about Emily?" Katie asked sarcastically. "Those worked out great, didn't they? Did I tell you…Nina and I are going house hunting this weekend up in Connecticut *and* we're adopting a puppy from the shelter!"

"Very funny," Moira said. She held out her mug for a refill.

Katie went on after pouring the coffee. "Look, Mo, I was kidding myself before, alright? I'm sad that I lost Nina and even sadder that I lost Aisha but my work is extremely important to me and at this very moment in my existence I find it impossible to say to myself, 'Fuck the homeless, I need to hurry over to Brooklyn because my girlfriend wants to talk about her feelings.'"

"So are you telling me that if this Danielle chick and Max Bland broke up you wouldn't try to convince her to take you on full time?"

Katie had to pause before answering because during the moments when she was completely honest with herself she could indeed imagine a full time life with Danielle, whom she was growing fonder of with each night they spent together; but then she shook her head.

"Number One: Danielle and Max are not going to break up. You should hear how reverently she talks about him. It's sickening. He'd have to fuck her mother to make Danielle want to leave him and even then I doubt she would.

Number Two: even if it did happen Danielle is bi, remember? And trust me when I tell you that she is full-blown bi. She may get off on only being with a woman for a while but eventually she'd get to craving men and asking me if it's alright if she gets a boyfriend." Katie poured herself a refill, added two Sweet-N-Lows and selected another biscotti from the cookie tin. "I'll tell you, Mo…" she started again, thoughtfully, "The more I think about it the more I'm certain that I've stumbled upon the secret to my having a successful and meaningful relationship. Finally."

"And that is…"

"Bisexuality," Katie said as if it were obvious. Then she explained. Her devotion to her job, her devotion to helping eradicate homelessness was as important to her as breathing. "I've always been like this, even when I was a kid. Seeing societal injustices and seeing the appalling lack of empathy people have for their fellow man makes me work all the harder." However, she added, this commitment to helping others has been problematic when it comes to having a relationship.

But, in being involved with a woman like Danielle, who is bisexual and has a man available to her…

"Suddenly I have a situation where I not only get to be involved with someone and have my sexual needs met but I also never have to feel guilty about the nights I spend working late at Homeward Bound, or the hours I spend organizing fundraisers and what not. I can still remain just as devoted to fighting homelessness without worrying about Danielle feeling marginalized because if she wants attention one night when I'm, I don't know, handing out blankets on the street, she can go get it from the great Max Bland."

What's more, she went on, Danielle's bisexuality is a guarantee that she will always wish to divide her schedule between male and female companionship thus always giving Katie the time she needs to fulfill her professional duties.

Moira took a swig from her coffee, mulling this over. Suddenly she shook her head.

"But then you miss out, Kay. You get the short end of the stick in this deal. This Danielle chick gets all the attention she craves from you and Max Bland but you have to take whatever you can get."

"True, but so what? Even on the nights when I'm not too exhausted to feel lonely I can at least go to sleep knowing I tried to make a difference in the lives of some very unfortunate people *without*—and this is key!—*without* making my girlfriend feel as if she wasn't important. So it all balances out."

Shrugging, Moira downed the rest of her coffee. "It sort of makes sense, Kay. But tell me this: why are you—"

🍁   🍁   🍁

"—such a lucky bitch!" Syb exulted to Danielle one evening in March over the phone. "Max is so cool! How long has this been going on?"

"Since late November," Danielle answered, blowing on her freshly painted toenails.

"And you don't feel at all like you're taking advantage of them? Or that you're spoiled?"

Danielle thought about this for a moment.

"Spoiled yes. As for the other thing, no, actually I don't, Syb. Something tells me that they both kind of like this situation."

"Unbelievable."

"I know."

"So, tell me…how's it work, exactly? Do you just ring up Katie whenever you're feeling horny for a woman?"

Danielle had to think for a moment again.

"Well, it started out like that, just being sex, I mean. She'd call me or I'd call her, we'd meet at her place, fuck our brains out and then say goodbye in the morning. But lately, though, we've been having more of a real relationship, you know? Like, we go to movies now or to off-Broadway plays. Last week we went to see a new exhibit at the Modern, the week before that we saw Ellen DeGeneres in concert at Radio City. Sometimes now when we meet up we don't even have sex; we'll just spend the time doing whatever and then fall asleep together."

"Hmmm…" Sybil said.

"What?" Danielle demanded, knowing that her friend was turning something over in her brain.

"Nothing, it's just that I can see it now: Max and Katie will one day fight for ownership of your soul. It will be an apocalyptic battle, man against woman, yin against yang, ESPN against Lifetime. New York City will be destroyed and innocent lives lost. Oh, the horror!"

"Shut up," Danielle said, but in all honesty she too had wondered if just such an event, minus the theatrics Syb included, would ever happen because (in all honesty) her and Katie were becoming more than two women who met for casual sex. A romance was developing. It used to be that when it came to

Katie Danielle expended mental energy only on devising new sexual tricks to make the other woman orgasm; now (in all honesty) she also expended mental energy in coming up with ideas to make Katie feel…loved: sending her flowers at work, for example, or surprising her at dinner by having the waiter at the restaurant place those Ellen DeGeneres tickets on the plate with Katie's entrée. And Katie herself did similar things for Danielle. The two women were, in short, becoming a couple.

What did that mean long-term? And was Syb right? Would there someday be a battle of sorts between her two lovers for the right to claim Danielle as their own? *God, I hope not*, she thought.

But things really didn't seem to be heading in that direction and she told Syb so. "For instance," she said, "opening day at Yankee Stadium is still, like, a month away but Max has already given me the date and suggested I make plans with Katie if I want to do something that night. And just yesterday Katie told me that on Saturday she's volunteering at a soup kitchen in Queens in the morning and at another one in SoHo in the evening so I'd better make plans with Max. I'm telling you, Syb, I think those two are pretty happy with the way things are."

Sybil said, "And poor little you in the middle, right? Gee, I wonder if Vic would let me have a second boyfriend. There's a cute new guy at work who can't seem to take his eyes off my tits. He kind of looks like Taye Diggs so obviously I'm sorely tempted to let him see them *au naturel*."

"I doubt Vic would go for it."

"Yeah, you're right. Hey, I know…how 'bout you let Max be my boyfriend? He'll let me do anything."

"Very funny, tramp."

"Worth a shot, spoiled bitch."

CHAPTER 25

❈

Katie had actually forgotten about her stable of fuck buddies. Her involvement with, and enjoyment of, Danielle ensured that she just didn't need that kind of variety anymore. So over the months the various other women Katie used to keep available for sexual release fell out of her consciousness as she focused her attentions on the one from Arizona. And by some strange quirk of fate none of those now forgotten fuck buddies gave Katie a call during this time either. Maybe, Katie mused one night while soaking in the tub, they'd all moved on as well.

Then one evening in April the phone rang and it was Mary.

"So what's it like?" Mary asked in greeting.

"What's what like?" Katie asked back.

"Falling off the face of the Earth and coming back. Is it true what the shuttle astronauts say about the stars being so much brighter once you've left our atmosphere?"

Katie laughed and then reminded her caller that she, too, has neglected to keep in touch.

"I know, but Peter got laid off in December which meant I had to pick up an extra shift a few times a week at the hospital, and don't even get me started about the kids. It's been one crisis after another with them. Anyway, Peter took the little monsters to their grandparents' house in Jersey for the weekend and I suddenly find myself available."

"That so?" Katie asked, recalling an image of Mary from her mind's library. She was a nurse, very pretty and very Italian, a closet lesbian who only married her high school sweetheart and kept her true sexual orientation hidden because she didn't want to risk banishment from her devoutly Catholic family.

She was also a fitness fanatic so even though she delivered two kids her midriff was still as taut as a cheerleader's and her breasts as perky as a prom queen's. She only managed to sneak away for sex with women a couple times a month, if that, and so she was a very eager lover once she had a female in her arms.

"I was thinking I could come over?" Mary prompted.

Katie hesitated before deciding on responding with, "That may not be a good idea, honey. Bad time."

"Period?"

"No, not that. Something else."

"Well, are you sure? I'm wearing that sweater you like to see me in and I'm feeling very subservient today. I'll probably do anything your little heart desires if you let me."

Taking a deep breath Katie silently counted to ten because now this was getting hard. Mary, she remembered, was into role play and on the nights when she wanted to be dominated there was something about seeing that proud Italian woman meekly following every sexual command given her that tapped into the darker recesses of Katie's psyche and made her orgasms that much more intense.

She needed another set of ten before she was able to say, "Look, Mary, it's really not a good time, okay? In my life, I mean. I'm kind of seeing someone."

"Oh." The disappointment was evident over the phone. "Well, I guess that was bound to happen eventually. Good for you."

"Thanks, and sorry."

"No, not at all. I'm happy for you. Of course, now I have nothing to do the rest of the night. I'm in that coffee shop just two blocks over from my place, the one that serves the cheesecake we both like, remember?"

"I remember," Katie said. The shop was only three blocks east of her own apartment.

Mary paused a moment.

"Listen, forget about sex. Since I'm here already why don't you just meet me for dessert? The hairy Iranian guy behind the counter is giving me dirty looks because I haven't ordered anything yet. How 'bout it?"

Katie was hungry (and the cheesecake in that place really was fabulous); what's more, she still had mounds of paperwork to get through before bed. Coffee would help. So she decided.

"Sure," she told Mary. "Give me ten minutes."

After all, it was only coffee.

🍁 🍁 🍁

Figuring it had been a while since she and Katie had done anything spontaneous Danielle got up the next morning and instead of preparing for another day at ARCL she left a message on her secretary's voice mail that she was taking a vacation day and not coming in. She dressed in jeans, sneakers and a sweater, and with her hair pulled back into a ponytail caught a cab to Katie's apartment. She thought it would be fun if they pretended to be tourists today. They'd ride the Circle Line; visit the Bronx Zoo; ferry out to Liberty Island; share passionate kisses at the top of the Empire State Building; maybe even ride one of those Big Apple tour buses or hire out a hansom cab for a jaunt through Central Park. Then, to cap off the day, they'd get a room at the Plaza and spend the rest of the night having sex and ordering room service.

That, anyway, was the plan.

But when Danielle arrived at Katie's place to convince her to play hooky it was not Katie who answered the knock on the door.

🍁 🍁 🍁

Max was sleeping when suddenly he was jolted awake by the bedroom door slamming. Thinking that the evil Mayzie Witherspoon clones from his nightmare had come to life he was, naturally, quite alarmed and sat up in bed with a shout looking around for something heavy with which to bash their blue-blooded skulls in.

"Fucking bitch!" he heard through the haze of grogginess, a phrase he thought unusual for brunch-obsessed genetically-engineered beings to say. So he focused on the creature standing at the foot of the bed and felt his heart rate slowing upon discovering it was just Danielle.

"Thank God," he said, still breathing heavily. "You startled me, I thought you were an evil creature escaped from a genetics lab in the Hamptons." He wiped his brow. "Hey, wait a minute," he said, noticing the clock, "don't you have a job? Aren't you a teller or something?"

"That fucking bitch!" is all Danielle said and for the first time Max noticed how angry she was. And not just angry…livid. She looked as though she'd like to hit something. His very first reaction was fear and his hands moved protectively over his crotch, but then he remembered that when she was angry with him she called him prick, not bitch, so he figured he was safe and that a particular woman whose first initial was K was in for it.

"Trouble on the set of *The L Word*?" he asked.

"She's cheating on me."

"Oh, boy," Max said. "I'm sorry to hear that. Are you sure?"

Danielle looked as if that was the stupidest question ever put to her.

"Of course I'm sure! I went over to her place this morning and another woman answered the door."

"Well, that could've been anybody," Max reasoned. "Could've been her sister."

"She doesn't have a sister."

"Could've been an old friend from out of town."

"She was wearing a negligee."

"An old friend from out of town might wear a negligee."

"And a dog collar."

"That seems a bit unlikely."

"And when she saw me standing there she looked me up and down and said, 'You must be the day shift, I'll just go clock out.'"

"Well, you have to admire her wit," Max offered.

Danielle gave him the finger and then started pacing, muttering something unintelligible under her breath. Her cell phone rang and she stopped, looked at the caller ID and then answered it with a, "FUCK OFF!" that was screamed so loud Max winced. Danielle then threw the phone across the room where it clattered into a corner.

"You know, those cost money," Max chided, looking over at the wreckage.

Suddenly Danielle stopped pacing as it seemed an idea came to her. She approached Max's side of the bed and sat next to him.

"Whoa, whoa, whoa!" Max protested, turning his head away and covering his mouth. "I just woke up! I've got morning breath!"

"Forget about that. I need your permission for something," she said earnestly.

"I believe murder is still illegal even if someone gives you permission," her boyfriend said, keeping his head turned away. "At least I think it is."

"No, to retaliate. Since Katie cheated on me I want to cheat on her, it's only fair. I need your permission to sleep with another woman."

"What?"

"Come on, Max, tell me I can sleep another woman!"

"Is this what you'd do if I cheated on you? Fuck another man?"

"Absolutely. And somehow I'd make sure you saw us."

"Nice. Anyway, I don't think that you doing that to Katie is the best idea."

"Why not?"

"Because it's an idea born from anger. You need to calm down first before you decide how best to respond to this."

Danielle glared at him. "Prick. I can't believe you're taking her side. What the fuck?"

Putting up his hands in protest, but still directing his breath away from her, Max exclaimed, "I'm not taking her side, for chrissake."

"So I can retaliate?"

"Jesus, you sound like Patton! What, did you steal some of my testosterone while I was sleeping? Listen, I want you to calm down and, and wait right here." He scrambled out of bed and jogged into the bathroom. Danielle saw him take a generous swig from the Listerine bottle and swish the stuff around his mouth for a few seconds. When he came back to the bed he took hold of her hands and rubbed them in his own. "Calm down," he repeated, pulling her all the way into bed with him and embracing her protectively. "I'm not taking her side, sweetie. But I am going to point out that your relationship with her is not exactly orthodox to begin with and you need to take that into account."

"Yeah, but—"

"I mean, think about it, sweetie…this morning you find out that by all appearances Katie had sex with another woman last night and what do you do? Run home to your live-in boyfriend and tell him how upset you are."

"Your point is?"

"Are you blind? My point is that this whole thing between you, me and Katie is a little bizarre and certain allowances have to be made. What's more, you need to—"

"But I felt there was something good between me and Katie! It's not just sex anymore, Max; we're a couple and I thought we were exclusive."

Max was surprised. "Danielle, you're not exclusive to anybody."

"What?"

"You're not exclusive to anybody. You're not exclusive to her and you're not exclusive to me."

"Yeah, but—"

"I mean, one night you and I have sex and the next night you and her are doing it."

"Okay, but—"

"And then there was that one day in February when you left work early, fucked me in the afternoon, showered, and then went to fuck her that night."

"Okay, okay...I get your point. But you know what I meant...that her and I were exclusive the same way you and I are exclusive."

"Jesus, how greedy can you get?" Max asked. "Look, if I were you I wouldn't complain too much. You got a pretty good thing going here, after all, with your two lovers. So Katie wants to have some fun on the side, so what's wrong with that? I mean, you're expecting her to share you with a man, why shouldn't she expect you to share her with other women?"

"You're taking her side again," Danielle accused.

"Fine, I am taking her side, dammit, because unless you two specifically declared—under a full moon, with violins playing the love song from *Ice Castles* and all that romantic crap—that you would be exclusive to one another then I'm sorry, she did nothing wrong. Did such a thing happen?"

"No." Petulantly.

"But lemme guess, you'd like it to happen, right?"

"Yes." Defiantly.

Max laughed mirthlessly. "You people who grew up without brothers or sisters crack me up, you know?"

"In what way?"

"In the way that people like you enter adulthood with such a fucked up and skewed perspective on the world it's amazing those of us who *did* have brothers or sisters don't shoot you. I mean, let's look at the facts: when you were coming up you never had to share your toys; you never had to share a bedroom and every Christmas all the gifts under the tree were yours. Even when you people do grow up—if that phrase could be applied—you continue to think the world is your oyster and you harbor resentment every time you're not the center of attention or you have to share something. Well, I'm not sure you're gonna get what you want this time, sweetie. You may have to deal with things the way they are. If you like Katie as much as you claim you do you just need to shut up and be grateful she willingly stepped into 'Danielle's Perfect Little House of Self-Indulgence.'"

She gasped and looked up at him, mouth agape.

"Why are you being so mean?"

"Oh, I think you deserve to have a little meanness thrown your way on occasion. But that's neither here nor there. What's important now is for you to decide just how devastating Katie's infidelity (if you can call it that) is."

Danielle fell silent, a sure sign to Max that she was processing information, attempting to reach a conclusion. He let her do so, stroking her hair in the meantime. This is exactly what he had been afraid of, actually…that some kind of issue would develop between Danielle and Katie that would put him in the middle of two warring factions. Bound to happen, he considered. Two women and what not. Still though, he had to figure he was lucky. At least he only had to deal with calming one of them down at a time.

He chuckled silently. *Can you imagine if I lived with both of them?* he asked himself.

CHAPTER 26

❀

As her own cell phone was shattered in a corner of her bedroom Danielle had to borrow Max's an hour later when she left the apartment to take a walk in Central Park as a way of further blowing off some steam. After making a couple of circuits around the Reservoir she called Homeward Bound from Belvedere Castle, was told that Katie had taken the day off (ironic, Danielle considered) and then reached her at home. The women arranged to meet in the park by the Delacort Theatre.

"Max says I should talk to you," Danielle said when Katie arrived. "He actually said a lot of things but that was the gist of it."

Katie nodded. "Okay, let's walk and talk," she offered. So they struck north, leaving behind the castle and the theatre and moving past the Dragonfly Preserve and the softball fields.

"I'm sorry," Danielle said, breaking a long silence.

Katie was surprised. "You're sorry?"

"For telling you to fuck off earlier when you called. And for screaming it the way I did. That was childish. I'm sorry."

"Thank you," Katie said. "I tried calling you right back."

"My cell phone was destroyed in the moments immediately following me telling you to fuck off. I was upset. Naturally. I guess one of the things you have to learn about me is that when I'm upset it's best not to call me for a while and let me cool down a bit. Max knows this."

"Max has had more time with you."

"True. In any case, I'm sorry."

"Thank you again."

Another long silence developed and then it was Katie's turn to break it.

"I'm sorry, too, by the way."

"Thank you."

"Do you want to know who she was?"

"No," Danielle said quickly, and then, "Okay, I'm lying. Yes, I want to know who she was." She then listened to Katie give her a brief history of Mary as a fuck buddy and an even briefer recap of the previous night's events, starting with the phone call from the coffee shop.

"I met her for cheesecake," Katie said. "Cheesecake turned into flirting and then flirting turned into sex."

"It doesn't matter," Danielle said, waving her hand vaguely in the air, hoping to give an impression of unconcern.

"Yes, it does."

"No, no it doesn't, Katie," Danielle insisted. "Max made me realize that you and I never agreed to be exclusive."

"Kind of hard under the circumstances, don't you think? I mean, hello!, you have a boyfriend."

"I just assumed, is all. Things were going so well between us and—"

"So well that you were thinking about leaving the great Max Bland for me?" Katie asked.

"No!"

"So well that you were thinking about giving up men entirely?"

"No."

Katie smiled. "I didn't think so."

"It's just that—God, no wonder Max thinks I'm a spoiled brat. I even *sound* like a spoiled brat."

"I'm liking the great Max Bland more and more. Look, honey..." here Katie stopped walking, faced the other woman and took hold of her hands, "things *are* going good between us and I want them to continue to do so. The fact that you assumed we were exclusive kind of makes me thrilled because it means you have feelings for me. And guess what? I have feelings for you, too. We clicked, remember? I'm maybe even falling in love with you, despite my better judgment, not to mention all the warning sirens going off in my head. I don't know. But..." She started walking again.

"What?" Danielle prodded.

"But I can't promise that what happened last night won't happen again," Katie stated flatly, stopping in the middle of the path and facing her companion head on. "You and I haven't seen each other in *five* days, Danielle, and I know that's because you and the great Max Bland had engagements but last night I was horny, really, really horny. I had some work that I brought home and that distracted me for a while but the next thing I knew my phone rings and a beautiful woman is on the other end, just as horny as I am."

"Oh."

"And if it makes you feel any better I initially resisted by telling her I was seeing you but then when I met up with her later…well, you can imagine the rest."

The only thing Danielle could imagine was that dog collar around Mary's neck.

Katie continued.

"I'm not resentful of your relationship with the great Max Bland," she told Danielle. "And I'm not resentful that I have to share you with him or resentful of the constraints that this arrangement puts on our own relationship. To tell you the truth it's all I want right now because it allows me to get a lot of other stuff done that's important to me. But be warned: if I need someone in my bed—I mean, *really* need someone in my bed and you're not available then I won't feel guilty if I take advantage of an opportunity. Maybe I won't *look* for an opportunity, but if one looks for me like last night…"

"I get it."

"And you know what? Maybe there will be times when I do look for opportunities, now that I think about it. I mean, if I'm needy why should I stay home like an old lady just because you and the great Max Bland have theatre tickets?"

"Yeah, well…Max says I shouldn't have a problem with it because if I do then it means I'm too greedy."

"He's right."

"And what if I fall in love with you?" Danielle asked softly.

"What if you do? What if I fall in love with you?" Katie sighed as if that particular issue exhausted her. "Let's not even try to handle that problem until it happens. If it happens. And if it happens then we'll work something out."

"Like what?"

"God knows."

Danielle had no choice but to agree. Then she said, "I guess all the gifts under the tree aren't mine anymore. Time to share."

"Is that something Max Bland said today?"

"Yes." Danielle told her about Max's disdain for only-children. "He's quite clever sometimes."

"You don't have to tell me; I'm rereading *Pope Anne* for the third time."

After a while Danielle asked: "So what did we agree upon just now?"

"We agreed on: A) You'd better make damn sure you fit me in as often as you can because B) if you don't you won't have a problem with me finding someone else to take your place, if only for a night."

"God damn it."

"I know, life's unfair."

"Don't remind me," Danielle muttered before asking Katie brightly: "So tell me…have you ever been to the Bronx Zoo?"

CHAPTER 27

❦

Eventually everyone turns thirty and on June 10 of that year it was Danielle's turn. Not surprisingly, Danielle viewed the occasion with the typical emotional cocktail of one part anger, one part fear and one part bitterness, served very chilled with a splash of existential fatalism. In fact, way back on the morning of January 1 she awoke (a little hung-over) with the following thoughts in her achy little head:

> Resolution Number One: Always stop at four champagne cocktails.
> Resolution Number Two: Spend less money on shoes. Okay, spend less money on Blahniks. No, how about spend less money at Bergdorf's on shoes? Or maybe…oh, fuck it.
> Resolution Number Two (modified): Every time I buy shoes write a check for the same amount and donate it to charity.
> Resolution Number Three: Stop aging. This is the year I turn thirty.

Between the beginning of the year and June she very often succeeded in forgetting about the unspeakable event and would spend several happy days in blissful ignorance. Such a condition was aided of course by the distractions inherent in having two lovers, a rapidly rising career in the business of international finance, and attending classes for her doctorate in Economics at Fordham University; even the disaster of nearing thirty years old could be overlooked when one has two relationships to tend like gardens and two different sexual appetites to satisfy, not too mention when one is daily dealing with multi-million dollar (or yen, or euro, or pound) transactions. But every now and then something would remind her of the impending date: a meeting at work, for example, would be scheduled for two-*thirty*; Mayzie Witherspoon would arrange a brunch on the *thirtieth*; a new wall hanging she bought for her office cost, with tax, forty-seven dollars and *thirty* cents. Even *Cosmo* was the culprit once. Upon finding the March issue in the mailbox at home she was horrified to see on the cover, "Make-Up Tips For Women In Their Thirties." These little reminders, silly as they were, would inevitably give her enough of a reason to stew in a funk ranging from a few hours to a few days.

Max understood completely. He too had been dreading June 10 and spent a lot of mental energy during the first six months of the year wishing that date would hurry the hell up and arrive so Danielle would stop acting like a loon. But he kept his irritation to himself and whenever he noticed her feeling sad about exiting her twenties he'd embrace her and let her know how beautiful she was and then remind her, for instance, of the time recently when they ordered wine with dinner and the waitress asked for her ID. "Or how about the other day?" he said on another occasion. "That idiot Mayzie Witherspoon asked what skin cream you used because according to her you don't look a day over twenty-five."

Katie understood completely, too. But whereas Max worked hard to cure Danielle of this unreasonable fear of thirty Katie helped foster it by often inviting Danielle over when she was in one of her funks. The two of them would then eat ice cream and sob uncontrollably about their disappearing youth while working on schematics for a temporal impedance machine which they planned on selling through Sharper Image.

🍁 🍁 🍁

When June 1 arrived Danielle suddenly became upbeat about her birthday. Finally accepting that her turning thirty was going to happen whether she liked it or not (and also having made no progress on reversing the space/time continuum to her advantage) she conceded defeat and decided it would be best if she entered her fourth decade with smiles and aplomb, no matter how fake the smiles were or how phony the aplomb felt. Max should have been delighted at this change but he remembered reading once how Ted Bundy used to get overly cheerful just before he committed yet another murder and he instead grew fearful for his life, especially when Danielle started humming to herself. Didn't Dahmer also hum?

In any case, Danielle's idea was to have a bash that would, in effect, tell Thirty to kiss her ass while simultaneously showing everybody that she can age with as much dignity and class as Diane Keaton, who was practically ancient.

To that end she rented her favorite restaurant, an Italian joint on Madison Avenue, out for a private party, ordered a huge cake from a baker who was also a hostess on the *Food Network* and then set about inviting all her friends in New York, many of her co-workers, particularly Margot, and even Syb and Liz from Arizona. Max promised to fly her parents in as well.

"What about Katie?" he asked one evening while dressing for dinner.

Looking up from the magazine she was reading Danielle asked what about her.

"I just wanted to be sure that in all the excitement and planning of your party," he said, "that you didn't neglect to invite her. I'm sure she'd love to come."

❦   ❦   ❦

"Isn't the great Max Bland going to be there?" Katie queried Danielle when, the next day, she did indeed invite her to the party.

"Baby, it was his idea to invite you. Said he was sure you'd want to come."

"Really? He said that?"

"Swear to God. Of course, I wanted to invite you but…I don't know…I wasn't sure how he'd take it, wasn't sure how you'd feel about it. I never really considered the idea of you two meeting, have you?"

"Only at your funeral."

"Gee, thanks, and what would I have died from?"

"Overspending."

"Bitch. Anyway, he also said he'd been looking forward to meeting you for some time and that the birthday party seems like the perfect venue."

Katie narrowed her eyes. "You don't think he wants to poison me, do you? Slip some arsenic in my punch? Get rid of your lesbian lover?"

"Maybe. You know how these artistic types are. Very moody and unpredictable."

"Do you think we'll get along?"

Danielle shrugged.

"It's hard to tell with Max," she answered. "I don't think he tries to get along with anybody. He just tolerates them."

CHAPTER 28

Michelangelo's Trattoria on Madison and 67th Street was a very simple Italian restaurant: good food, good service, no gimmicks, no celebrity chefs in the kitchen and an advertising budget of zero dollars and zero cents. When they opened thirty-five years ago the proprietors simply unlocked the doors and let word of mouth do the rest. The bill of fare held no surprises: every variation of spaghetti or linguini; veal cutlets and sausages; meatballs the size of your fist; garlic bread, and for dessert spumoni or tiramisu. Naturally, wine was plentiful but they also had a fully stocked bar. The simplicity of the restaurant was evident everywhere: the brick walls were unadorned, the wood floors unpolished, the tablecloths white, the chairs unpretentious cushioned jobs like you'd find at a garage sale, and the laminated menus had been handled by countless hands over the last three and a half decades.

Danielle had stumbled across this place soon after she moved to New York, during one of her solo treks exploring the city. She had stopped in for lunch because it looked as good a place as any and then was charmed by how un-hip and old-school it was. Michelangelo's became her restaurant of choice. Even now she and Max ate there twice a week, sometimes more. The owners knew them, the wait staff knew them, the bartender started mixing their favorite cocktails as soon as he spotted them entering: amaretto spritzer for her, gin and tonic for him. Max and Danielle were treated so well, in fact, that Max actually wrote about the place in his third novel, a gesture which earned the couple a bottle of wine sent to their table with each meal compliments of Gianni and Sylvia, the sixty-ish owners.

So naturally, when it came time to pick a venue for her birthday bash Danielle thought of Michelangelo's. What made it even more perfect was that inside there was a balcony overlooking the main dining room. Usually it was put into use for corporate lunches or graduation parties, that kind of thing, but Danielle had Michelangelo's staff rope it off for another reason on the night of her party. She wanted Max to have a quiet sanctuary to escape to once he got fed up with socializing and making small talk. It would cut down on his complaining afterwards.

Despite June 10 falling on a Wednesday she had a pretty good turnout. Syb and Liz made it from Arizona, as did her parents, and just about everyone locally showed up. Told to arrive at seven that night by eight-thirty there were enough of them to make Max beat a retreat upstairs with his well-worn copy of *The Grapes of Wrath* and a snifter of brandy in order to take a breather from all the pleasantries.

Danielle, however, was in her element, effortlessly playing hostess, moving from one cluster of guests to another, easily joining different conversations, telling amusing anecdotes and seeing that the restaurant's staff tended to every possible need. Between the open bar and springing for the guests' meals this soiree was going to cost a fortune but by this point Danielle cared not a whit. The way she saw it, you only turn thirty once (thank God!) but upstairs in the balcony Max wondered dryly how much her turning forty was going to set him back.

❦   ❦   ❦

Katie arrived at nine and promptly ordered a drink to calm her nerves. Then she quickly snatched Danielle from out of the crowd and the two snuck off to a quiet corner.

"So…" Katie said, scanning the faces in the dining room, trying to inconspicuously spot her favorite-author-slash-lover's-boyfriend. "I don't see him anywhere. Did he come?"

"Of course he came," Danielle replied. "Granted, I had to bribe him with a blowjob this morning to be nice to people but he's here." She paused. "I just don't know where, exactly." Looking up at the balcony she saw that it was empty which meant he had deigned to immerse himself once more in the crowd. "I'll go look for him but before I do I need to go over some things with you for when you meet him."

"You mean there are guidelines to follow?"

"You have no idea. Meeting Max for the first time is an occasion fraught with pitfalls and if you handle it wrong you end up on his List."

"List?"

"Yes. He keeps it in his head. He can remember everybody who has ever pissed him off going back to kindergarten."

"Fuck," Katie said nervously, taking a stiff swig of her vodka gimlet.

"Okay, first off, don't call him 'the great Max Bland' like you're always doing with me. It'll just make him think you have your priorities screwed up and he'll go off on this spiel about how he's only a writer and that he hasn't cured cancer or invented a clean-burning car engine that runs on Kool-Aid or done anything else beneficial for mankind."

Katie nodded. "I know...I once read an article about him in *Newsweek* where he said that people grossly overestimate the contributions artists make to society."

"Which brings me to Rule Two," Danielle said. "Don't quote anything he said in an interview. It'll make him think you're a psychopath with *way* too much time on your hands."

"Oh."

"Rule Three: don't ask him what he's currently working on. He hates talking about a new book until he's finished it. If you are stupid enough to ask him he'll just bullshit you and tell you that it takes place a long time ago in a galaxy far, far away and then it'll be game over, end of discussion, automatic inclusion on the List. You look really hot tonight."

"That was the idea," Katie purred, momentarily forgetting her nervousness. "I wanted to put on something clingy and short, not too mention the kind of dress I couldn't possibly wear a bra with, and turn myself into a delectable piece of eye candy that you'd want to unwrap later at my place." She reached up and stroked Danielle's hair. "I suppose, though, there's no chance of that happening?"

"God, I wish; you smell soooo good. What is that?"

"I didn't notice. The first bottle I put my hands on."

"Whatever it is buy some more. You know, after this party I'm sure Max will like nothing more than to get rid of me for the night but that means leaving him home alone with my parents but if I did that he'd break up with me for sure." She leaned forward slightly and very discreetly brushed the back of her hand against Katie's right breast. "Fuck it, I'll sneak out after they all go to sleep," she whispered.

"Promise."

"Cross my heart. Anyway, Rule Four: no questions about *The Remarkable Reign of Pope Anne I.*"

Katie protested. "But why not?" What was the point, really, of sharing your girlfriend with the great Max Bland if you couldn't probe his mind about the one book that was being held up as a symbol of gay rights and empowerment?

"He's tired of talking about *The Remarkable Reign of Pope Anne I*, that's why," Danielle answered. "It's like when John Lennon stopped answering questions about The Beatles. Max never wanted to be a folk hero in the gay community and he thinks everybody has blown that book way out of proportion. Anyway, look, promise me you'll be good, okay? I want him to like you and he's such a misanthrope that he really only likes a handful of people: me, his buddy Mikey up in the Bronx, and all those dead authors he's always reading. His parents aren't even on that list and I think I'm more or less on the bubble. So…stay here and I'll go find him."

But no sooner had Danielle gone off in one direction then from the opposite direction the corner of Katie's eye alerted her of a figure in black approaching. Turning towards it Katie instinctively shook the outstretched hand it bore.

"Hi, you must be Katie," the figure greeted and then added, even though under the circumstances it was completely unnecessary: "I'm Max Bland."

CHAPTER 29

❊

Technically, Katie had met Max before. It was a few years ago, when *Pope Anne* was still brand new. Moira called her one night to say that "the writer of that really cool book about the lesbian pope" would be appearing at the Barnes and Noble on Fifth Avenue the next day to sign copies. Katie showed up two hours early only to find that already the line stretched around the block. But she had no problem waiting; *Pope Anne* was such a delightful read for a bookworm (not too mention gay woman) like herself that she knew an autographed copy would hold a treasured place in her library.

She very nearly didn't get it, though. The signing was scheduled from one to three and at two-thirty the store manager came out into the street and announced up and down the line that at three sharp anybody not already in the store would, unfortunately, be turned away. This led to much disappointed groaning on line, including some from Katie because, quite frankly, she was still nowhere near the store's entrance and the queue was not moving along very speedily. Then, not more than five minutes later, the store manager reappeared and said that Max Bland himself had said that to show his appreciation for the huge turnout he would continue signing books until everybody on line had come through, no matter how long it took. Suddenly, applause broke out, everyone was cheerful again and they eagerly awaited their chance to meet the writer.

When her turn finally came Katie approached the table inside and said, "Thank you so much for waiting for us. I was afraid I wouldn't get in. I love your book."

He had smiled, very politely, and said in a disarming manner, "I'm just glad you waited. Of course, it would've been more impressive if there were a blizzard outside and the city were under attack by Martians but I appreciate your persistence nonetheless." Then he had beckoned her to lean forward and whispered conspiratorially, "To be honest with you I'm not sure the book is worth all this fuss. But I owe a lot of money to the Mob so it'll be nice to pay them back before the cops find my head in Hoboken and the rest of my body in Brooklyn."

Katie had burst out laughing.

Asking her name he then signed her book with: "To Katie…thanks for braving a blizzard and a Martian attack just to spend a few moments with me. Max Bland." It was then that she realized that the reason the line had moved so slowly was because Max was taking the time to chat up each autograph seeker and to write something witty just for them in their books. At other signings she had been to the writers would stick out their hands, snatch your book from you, scrawl their name illegibly and dismiss you without so much as a "thank you." But here was Max Bland, hotshot author du jour, wearing out his poor right hand signing all these books and making certain each of his fans walked away with a memory.

🍁   🍁   🍁

"You make me sound like a normal human being," Max said, laughing, after Katie related that anecdote to him. After introducing himself to her he had led her upstairs to his private aerie in the balcony so they could talk without interruption while the party continued below. A waiter was allowed up to bring a new vodka gimlet for Katie and another splash of brandy for Max.

"Well," Katie responded to Max's statement, "you certainly didn't strike me then as someone who finds people annoying and would rather sit in a balcony than mingle at a party."

"People *are* annoying, Katie," he said, scowling down at the guests in the dining room below. "Nevertheless, when you said that I wanted each of the fans at the book signing to walk away with a memory you were right," Max said. "Despite my somewhat rough exterior I'm very appreciative of anybody who reads my work and when that dickhead manager told me of his plan to send people home empty-handed I told him that if he expected me to speak kindly of this experience to my publisher he'd go back out and say 'Never mind.' However, I'll let you in on a little secret—and keep in mind that I can say this to you because I know you're a lesbian and thus won't think I'm hitting on you: if indeed I was extremely nice to you in particular it's because I found you attractive."

"Really?" Katie said, amused.

"You see, on occasions such as book signings or birthday parties, when I'm forced to interact with people I employ a double standard to determine how well I treat them. Beautiful women such as yourself get my A game: I'm charming, I'm witty, I'm glad to be in their company. Everyone else? It's up for grabs." He pointed. "See that guy down there in the brown blazer? If he were to come up here and act like the nicest man on Earth I'd probably treat him like a leper. On the other hand, if that cute redhead in the black dress by the front door were to come up here and sneeze on me I'd probably ask her to join me for a drink."

Katie laughed. She loved his sense of humor and how easily he made her feel comfortable in his presence.

"Most men wouldn't admit to all this," she told him.

"Most men are liars. Surely even gay women know that. Besides, all I'm admitting to is enjoying the company of beautiful women, and I really do. Being in the presence of someone with your looks and grace is like having permission to be alone with a great work of art. But that's where it ends, mind you. Danielle need have no fear I will stray."

"Yes, she told me about how you can't stand the thought of handling two women. How it would drive you crazy."

"Indeed it would."

"Well, I happen to agree," Katie said, taking a sip of her cocktail. "Women may be the superior sex but on the whole we're a handful. So is that why I was allowed up here? My aesthetically pleasing qualities?"

"Pretty much, yeah. If you had looked like my high school gym teacher, Mrs. Schneider, or any variation thereof, I would have introduced myself to you, spent ten minutes in polite conversation about the weather and then come up here alone."

"It's always a relief for me to hear I don't look like a gym teacher," Katie said, omitting that she owes much of it to the South Beach Diet and Maybelline.

"Not any gym teacher who works in the Bronx, that's for sure," Max replied. He then raised his glass. "To beautiful women," he toasted. "May both our lives always be blessed with them." They clinked glasses and drank.

"Your frankness is refreshing," Katie said after they'd shared a few moments together in silence, "especially from a man. No offense, but you men often make me feel as if there's a hidden agenda to everything you say."

"Gee, there's a newsflash. No one's gonna give you an award for figuring that one out so don't expect the Nobel Committee to call soon. Yes, most men would sit here bullshitting you because they harbor a hope of getting in your pants. That's their hidden agenda. But because I know you're a lesbian and I know that what's in your pants in inaccessible I'm free from having an agenda, I'm free from trying to impress you. In other words, I'm free to be myself."

Katie acknowledged that it was a good point.

"It's refreshing for me as well, you know," Max continued. "In fact, it's fucking wonderful. You are the first attractive woman I've met in my entire life with whom I feel so free. I didn't expect that when I came here tonight."

"What did you expect?"

"To be vilified, mostly. No offense but you gay women often make us men feel like we're worms."

"Sorry about that. I think it's in our rulebook. And you feel so free because I'm gay?"

"Precisely."

"But what about Danielle?" Katie asked. "She's attractive and I'm sure you feel free with her."

Max shook his head, wisely, like a philosophy professor going over for the umpteenth time why God doesn't exist.

"You can't possibly believe that, can you?" he asked pointedly. "Yes, for the most part I am honest with Danielle but let's be real. I cannot ever be my true self when I'm with her and before you ask me why let me tell you why."

"Obviously it has to do with sex," Katie said. "If honesty might get in the way of you having sex then you may distort the truth."

"You're right, yes. I mean, if I'm horny and I wanna get my hands on her I'm gonna tell her whatever she wants to hear to be sure she's amenable. There are times when I feel I'd do a commercial for the Ku Klux Klan just for one of her blowjobs. But sex is not the big reason, Katie."

"Then what is?"

"Harmony. Harmony is the big reason. Many times I'll agree with something she says simply because I wanna keep things harmonious in my home. There are enough aggravations in this world already."

"But I don't—"

"Yes, you do," Max interrupted.

"No, I don—"

"Yes, you do," Max repeated. "Katie, if you thought long and hard about it you'd realize there were plenty of times when you, I dunno…avoided a conversation with Danielle, or pretended to be in a good mood, or suppressed an opinion about something because you wanted to have sex with her, or you were tired and just wanted to go to sleep and not get into an argument, yada, yada, yada. We all do it. Displaying our true selves to our lovers is an impossibility because we have too much to gain by acting. It's why husbands put up with nagging wives and nagging wives put up with Monday Night Football."

"You have an interesting way of looking at things," Katie said.

"You're free to disagree, of course."

"Actually, I like what I'm hearing. It makes a lot of sense. I see why Danielle says she loves talking to you. She thinks the world of you, you know."

"I love her to death," Max acknowledged. "And your presence in her life has really had a positive effect on her. I don't quite know how to explain it except to say that she's happier. I think the fact that she can satisfy both sides of her sexuality, physically and emotionally, is what's doing the trick."

"I'm glad to be of help."

"I am curious, though…"

"Why I don't vilify you?" Katie asked. "Why I'm okay with this whole arrangement?"

"Yes."

"Because it allows me to continue devoting a lot of time to my work," Katie said and then gave Max the rundown on her recent string of romantic failures starting nine years ago with Aisha and ending eighteen months ago with Nina, doing so with the kind of detail she never would have imagined using in a discussion with a veritable stranger. In fact, she was telling him stuff that she had yet to share with Danielle. But there was something about Max Bland that was disarming, something that made her feel as if she could trust him implicitly. "So you see," she said, finishing up, "Danielle is perfect. Because of you."

"Therefore it can be argued that in some small way I am helping to fight homelessness," Max said. "Excellent. Now I wonder if I can use pimping my girlfriend as a tax deduction."

🍁 🍁 🍁

Later, after another refill of her vodka gimlet, Katie said, "I want to thank you, by the way. For what you did during that mess a couple of months ago."

"You're referring to the dog collar incident?" Max asked and then laughed when Katie blushed. "Don't be embarrassed. To tell you the truth I think she was most upset because it wasn't her wearing the collar, given that she likes being dominated."

"That's interesting…with me she likes to play the dominator."

"Really? Wow, she sure knows how to balance her life out. Must be nice. Anyway, all I did that day was calm Danielle down, have her take a couple of deep breaths and then make her realize she was a selfish bitch."

"True, but I'm in love with that selfish bitch," Katie admitted suddenly and then wished she could take the words back as she felt Max's eyes on her. But when she dared to glance over at him she saw that his eyes had no malice in them.

"I take it falling in love with her was not part of the plan?" he asked.

"No, it wasn't," Katie answered, relieved that he didn't seem angry. "I'm so sorry, though. I shouldn't have said that to you."

"No harm done. You were just being honest."

"Still, I should have checked myself."

Max shrugged. "It's really no big deal and it's definitely not surprising. Danielle, like the rest of us, may not be perfect but she's certainly worthy of earning someone's love."

Raising her eyebrows, Katie said, "You're being pretty casual about it."

"That's because I feel I've got nothing to worry about. So you're in love with Danielle. Big deal. It means zip to me because there's no threat in that situation. After all, you're in love with a woman who can never be your own."

"But so are you," Katie pointed out.

"True, but the difference is I made my peace with it a long time ago. It was, after all, my decision to allow her to enjoy her bisexuality to the fullest. Have you made your peace with it?"

"Almost but not quite," she answered in a whisper.

"Well, let me warn you that there's no sense in hoping her and I break up, or in you trying to get us to break up. Even if she dumped me for Colin Firth—as she often threatens to do—you'll still have to share her with Colin Firth. Right now it's not a problem, is it? You're devoted to your work so you'll share her with anybody. But one day—and this day may never come—you might wake up and say to yourself, 'The homeless can make do with less of me' and then what? Try to win Danielle away from me (or Colin Firth)? Gay wedding in Vermont? Buy a house in some lesbian-friendly community on Long Island? Adopt a kid, maybe get featured in a human interest story in the *Times Magazine*? It's not gonna happen, Katie; not with Danielle. Any life you plan on building with her is gonna include a man, whether it's me or Colin Firth. Or maybe Blair Underwood…she likes Blair Underwood, too."

There was truth in what he said, Katie conceded to herself privately. "Falling in love with her was never part of the original plan," she once more told the writer. "But it happened so fucking fast that I couldn't prevent it."

"And I don't have a problem with it," Max said. "Be in love with her as I'm in love with her. In fact, I welcome it because it's good for Danielle and I always want her to be happy. But if you decide to continue down this path you *will* have to change your hopes for the future so that they conform to Danielle's bisexuality."

"You're right, I know. I guess I need to ask myself whether or not that's possible. I suppose I should have been asking myself that already but like I said, I fell in love with her so fucking fast."

"Tell me about it," Max agreed with a groan. "There's something about her, you know? An admixture of sweetness, cockiness and deviance that seduces you. One day you wake up thinking you've got your life planned out and the next thing you know she's part of your carry-on luggage on your flight to New York."

"Not to mention she's great in bed," Katie said, chewing on the straw from her gimlet.

"I've had a lot worse, I could assure you."

"So have I."

"And those breasts," Max said.

"Oh God, aren't they beautiful? Sometimes I sit in my office daydreaming about them."

"Me too."

"And the way she carries them…" Katie went on, "she thrusts them out there when she's walking, like she's bragging."

"Wouldn't you? I know if I had that package I'd spend most of my time at home naked."

"Yeah."

"Yeah."

And the two of them just sat there in silence for maybe a minute, each enjoying visions of Danielle's breasts. Finally, Katie snapped out of it and said:

"So, Max, assuming that I don't want the gay wedding in Vermont or the adopted baby or any of that stuff, except maybe the house on Long Island…assuming all I want is Danielle I guess what you're telling me is I'm stuck with you and we need to become friends. Is that even possible given our circumstances?"

"Who knows? I mean, considering that the sex thing is not an issue with you and me I don't see why not. Great friendships have been built on less." He rose and offered her his arm. They began descending the stairs. "We have the freedom to be honest with each other, even more honest than either of us can be with Danielle, so it's possible. Let's just hope for the best and try not to step on each other's toes."

🍁   🍁   🍁

Meeting them at the foot of the stairs Danielle gave an exasperated sigh and said, "I'm sorry but I couldn't get away. I went off to find you, Max, and as I was doing that I noticed Margot and my mother sitting together talking. Can you imagine anything more ghastly? Your mom and your boss chatting away like old friends? I had this horrid image in my head of mom telling Margot about the time I was six and got a marble stuck up my nose and then Margot firing me because she doesn't want anybody stupid enough to get marbles stuck up their noses handling offshore accounts worth millions of dollars. Naturally I had to intervene so I joined them and stayed there just to make sure the topic of marbles or pee-pee blankets didn't come up."

"Wait a minute," Katie said. "Pee-pee blankets?"

"It's a long story," Danielle said, blushing. Then she noticed Katie's hand in Max's arm. The two of them looked real chummy. "Actually, scratch what I just said…I just thought of something even more ghastly than my mom and my boss chatting and that's the two people I'm having sex with chatting." Color drained from her face. "What were you talking about up there?" she asked.

Max said: "Katie was telling me about some trick you do to her with an electric toothbrush."

Katie said: "Yeah, and Max was telling me about your cucumber fetish."

"Fine," Danielle said. "Fuck you both."

"You already are," Max said and Danielle was appalled to see Katie dissolve in his arms in laughter and then give him a quick kiss.

The whole thing was ghastly.

BOOK III

MIXED NUTS

CHAPTER 30

❀

On the Wednesday morning two weeks after Danielle's party Katie was in her office at Homeward Bound tacking up another snapshot of a formerly homeless person proudly displaying his apartment keys and beaming like the Cheshire cat. This one was particularly special because he was employed at ARCL, where Danielle worked, and he represented the tenth—tenth!—vagrant placed at that company who by working hard, keeping his nose clean and saving his money no longer lived in a shelter or halfway house but rather in an apartment, the lease to which bore his signature. Katie posted the ARCL pictures separately from the others, on the opposite wall. She preferred viewing that group independently of the rest because they had special meaning for her, they made her think of Danielle, the woman she loved, and of the very first time they met, in this office about a year ago, a meeting which led to Katie being able to, at last, enjoy an uninterrupted stretch of time of both professional and personal satisfaction. Philanthropy during the day; multiple orgasms during the night.

Intruding upon her reverie the phone rang.

"Katie Shaw," she answered.

"Ms. Shaw, it's Harrison Mayhew."

Suddenly, Katie was all ears and she put an extra brightness in her voice when she said, "Oh, hi, Mr. Mayhew. This is a surprise." Harrison Mayhew was the chairman of the board of the Warren Williams Foundation, the organization funding Homeward Bound, and indeed a call from him instead of from Nicole Fuqua, the vice-chairwoman and Katie's usual point of contact at headquarters, was rare.

"What can I do for you?" she queried. And was it her imagination or did she suddenly feel nervous?

"I apologize for the short notice, Ms. Shaw," Mr. Mayhew started directly, "I know you're very busy but I'm calling all of the division heads to say that it's imperative you come uptown for a meeting at one o'clock today."

"I see."

"Of course, due to the short notice you will be forgiven if you have an urgent personal matter to attend to this afternoon that will prevent your being there. If that's the case you'll be e-mailed a copy of the meeting's minutes tomorrow. Otherwise, we'd like you to attend. Can I count on seeing you?"

"Certainly," Katie said, knowing she'd need to cancel two afternoon appointments, one of which was with her hair stylist. "Do I have to bring anything? Reports or other data?"

There was but the slightest of pauses, most people would not have even noticed it, but Katie did and when Mr. Mayhew answered with, "That won't be necessary, Ms. Shaw. See you at one," she had no question about it: she did feel nervous.

❦   ❦   ❦

The Warren Williams Foundation occupied office space in a mid-rise across the street from Columbia University's campus. The foundation was created posthumously by one Lenore Broward, a wealthy socialite whose will stipulated that a portion of her estate be set aside for the creation of a non-profit organization dedicated to discovering the causes of and fighting homelessness in New York City. The will also demanded that the foundation be named after Warren Williams, a vagrant who used to panhandle on Mrs. Broward's block for many years during the 1980s and to whom she gave five dollars each day. One night Warren Williams came to Mrs. Broward's rescue when a purse snatcher attacked. He chased the thief down and using badly executed karate moves he copied from a Chuck Norris movie he'd once seen sent the culprit away with a couple of bruises thus earning the elderly Mrs. Broward's gratitude. She rewarded him with all of the money in the purse he had rescued, a little over two-hundred dollars. Unfortunately, the story did not end happily. Warren Williams spent the reward on crack purchased in Harlem and while on the ensuing high jumped in front of a cross-town bus intending to subdue it with his karate chops. Technically, he succeeded. The bus did have to stop in order to call the coroner's office to come scrape what was left of Warren off the front grille and tires. The tragedy prompted Mrs. Broward to use her influence and wealth to address the issue of homelessness, holding Warren Williams up as the perfect example of someone who fell through the cracks and wallowed long neglected in the hell of poverty, vagrancy and drug abuse.

Upon arriving at the Foundation Katie was told by the receptionist to proceed to the conference room and there she found the entire board waiting along with several other men and women who, like herself, were in charge of the various help and outreach projects the Foundation funded: soup kitchens, shelters, thrift stores, rehab facilities. As usually happens when such a gathering is called Katie felt the comfort of being in a room full of like-minded people just as dedicated as she was. She greeted everyone warmly and when the final two individuals showed up and Harrison Mayhew called the meeting to order Katie took a seat next to her good friend Paige, who ran the soup kitchens.

Katie had forgotten her nervousness from this morning until Mr. Mayhew, after somberly thanking everyone for coming, quickly introduced the distinguished middle-aged man with a goatee to his left as Walter Rubin, the Foundation's accountant. Suddenly, Katie was exchanging concerned glances with Paige and her other colleagues as her heart rate shot up. Like herself, they were all veterans of the not-for-profit game and thus were savvy enough to know that when the board of directors summoned you to an emergency meeting to listen to what the accountant had to say it was like being told by your doctor that she needs to fly in a specialist from Zurich to look at those strange spots on your X-ray.

🍁   🍁   🍁

"None of us had ever met the accountant before," Katie told Danielle that evening. "I mean, Paige has worked for the Williams Foundation since '91 and even she'd never met him. That's how we knew we were screwed. We all kind of looked at each other like 'Oh no, this is going to be bad.'"

They were at her place, sitting cross-legged on the floor in the living room, a Billie Holiday CD playing on the stereo and candles providing the illumination. That was the first clue to Danielle when she arrived that something was wrong. Candles and Luther Vandross meant Katie was horny; candles and Billie Holiday, however, meant Katie was upset because, as she put it, nothing matched a sour mood better than Lady Day bitching about life. The second clue was more obvious: Katie was smoking, a lot, something Danielle had never seen her do. No sooner had Katie sucked all the nicotine out of one cigarette than she tapped another out of the pack and lit it up.

"What do you mean screwed, baby?" Danielle asked.

Blowing out a cloud of carcinogens Katie said, "Homeward Bound is funded by the Williams Foundation, okay? But the Williams Foundation is—or rather was—funded mostly by the Lenore Broward bequest."

"Was?"

"It's gone. The Foundation is bust. The bequest has vanished. According Walter fucking Rubin the money from the will was invested in a bunch of different stocks and shit to keep it growing but the fucking account managers or stockbrokers or whatever the hell they are weren't very good at their jobs and when the market got stuck in the rut it's been in for the past couple of years they just tried to ride it out, which apparently was okay for a while but then came that crash last week."

Danielle nodded. She was very intimate with the crash. Last Thursday the Dow fell by over 400 points—even with two trading halts triggered by the so-called "circuit breakers." At ARCL Danielle and her co-workers watched CNN in amazement and horror as the numbers kept falling and the financial analysts tried to make sense of it all, one of them even using the word "armageddon." It made for a very long day at work and a very long night at home when she logged onto her broker's website, typed in her account number and realized she herself had lost $25,000.

"Anyway," Katie continued, a newly lit cigarette between her lips, "the crash wiped the Foundation out. The stocks that were barely keeping us afloat are worthless and we have nothing. In short, love, I'm out of a fucking job."

"But you guys get a lot of money from donations, right?"

"Sure, but not enough according to Walter fucking Rubin. Not enough to pay overhead and certainly not enough to pay salaries. He said maybe we could stay solvent for two or three months but ultimately it's a lost cause." She got up, went into the kitchen and almost immediately began spouting curses. "God-fucking-dammit!" she spat. "Of all the fucking nights not to have any booze." She came back to the living room and plunked herself down onto the floor with a pout.

"Do you know what the worst part of all this is?" she asked. "That tomorrow I have to tell my staff to clean out their desks because as of July 6th they are jobless and then I have to tell all our clients that we can no longer be of any service to them, so sorry, thank you so much for trying to improve your lives and for not being alcoholics and druggies, better luck next time. That's the worst part."

Danielle gave her a kiss.

"And who do I refer them to?" Katie went on. "Nobody, because, believe it or not, in a city with the kind of homeless problem we have, Homeward Bound was the only fucking organization doing what it did. And how fucked up is that, huh? I want booze, dammit."

Danielle told Katie that considering how upset she was drinking was the last thing she needed to do, which was funny coming from her seeing how Danielle sought comfort in liquor anytime the twists and turns of life made her heart rate eke above ninety. Upon discovering last week that her investment portfolio was lighter by twenty-five grand she became so thirsty for tequila that when Max came home after a night in the Bronx he found her in an argument with the toaster about fiscal responsibility. And apparently losing.

🍁 🍁 🍁

Of course, Danielle wanted to spend the night but Katie wanted it to herself. Wallowing in misery, she felt, was something best done alone. It not only allowed one to do it right but it also saved one from having to listen to the banal bromides people spouted at these times like, "There, there, everything will work out fine" or "If you need anything just call." So after assuring Danielle she'd be okay Katie escorted her to the door, waited a few minutes to allow time enough for Danielle to walk downstairs and find a cab and then promptly headed to the liquor store on the corner, returning with a bottle of Wild Turkey and a six pack of Michelob Ultra. Wallowing in misery, she also felt, was something best done drunk, and after two shots of whiskey chased by an entire can of beer, Katie (a bantamweight soaking wet) was well on her way there.

Her eyes lighted upon the stack of files she had brought home from work the other day, the newest set of clients looking for jobs. She took them off the kitchen table and spread them out before her on the living room floor, flipping through the pages. She had talked to many of these people herself, conducting the preliminary interviews, gauging their skills as well as their commitment to finding employment. She had studied their faces to pick up signs of lying as she asked about drug use or drinking problems; she had read their body English as they told their stories about how they became homeless. She'd made them feel comfortable, let them know there was no reason to be embarrassed, that she was not judging them because, quite frankly, most of them were very intimidated, unsure of what to make of all these kind people willing to help them find jobs when it seemed everyone else in the city wished they'd fuck off. But after a few minutes with Katie they not only trusted her completely but felt optimistic about their futures.

Pouring and then drinking two more shots Katie shut her eyes as the room began spinning. How the hell, she wondered, was she now supposed to tell her clients that their optimism was a delusion? That this one avenue of hope was being closed with the only detour available leading them right back where they started? What would this do to them? What kind of message would it send? So she used her imagination, put herself in the shoes of a typical client arriving at Homeward Bound tomorrow, a homeless woman who had spent the previous night in a dangerous shelter or sleeping sitting up on a bench in a subway station, a newspaper propped on her lap hoping the Transit cops would be fooled into thinking she was just reading and not chase her out into the street. She'd come to Homeward Bound because tomorrow was Thursday and when she first applied she was told to check back every Tuesday and Thursday to see if a position had been found for her. She'd arrive hopeful, maybe even certain that she had a job and could start dreaming of a new life.

But instead she'd find herself in an office with Katie and Katie would be telling her that Homeward Bound was shutting down and Katie would say how sorry she was and Katie would be saying that she herself is in the same boat because now she doesn't have a job also. But the homeless woman would think that's a bunch of bullshit because even though Katie may be out of a job too she's hardly in the same boat. Katie, after all, is a nice looking, well-dressed, educated white woman with practical work experience; Katie can get a job as easily as most people catch colds. She, the client, however, is most probably a minority, is wearing castoff clothes, is not very well bathed, dropped out of high school and has a ten-year old criminal record for possession. Homeward Bound was her only chance. Now that it's being shut she feels as if there are forces at work in the universe whose sole aim is to keep her down.

Katie moaned and kicked out angrily at the files in front of her on the floor, scattering them. She then stood and lurched into the bedroom, collapsing on her bed. To further hasten passing out she took a hefty swig straight from the whiskey bottle and sighed as her blood warmed. The last thing she felt before blackness overcame her was the same feeling of helplessness she had years ago when that stray cat ate the wounded bird.

🍁 🍁 🍁

It's hard to enjoy a good passing out when the phone keeps ringing. All Katie wanted to do was remain unconscious until tomorrow morning but that damn ringing wouldn't stop. And because the phone by her bed was one of those old-fashioned ones with an actual bell inside that gave off an earsplitting jangle when someone called the noise managed to bore through the wall of whiskey she had built around her cognitive center and wake her up.

"Fine!" she yelled to the phone, fumbling around on the nightstand for the receiver. "Shudda fuck up, already!"

Finally managing to take hold of the instrument Katie stole a glance at her alarm clock. It was only ten-thirty; she still had a good seven hours of passed-outedness to enjoy before having to wake up, go to Homeward Bound and tell her staff they may all have trouble paying their rent next month.

"H'lo! Whoziss?" she demanded. She had to pause a moment while the name of the caller registered in her brain, then she said, "Oh, hi, Madeline…thississa s'prise. I said thississa s'prise! S'prise! Uh-huh…uh-huh…uh-huh…fuck…y'sure? Okay…uh-huh…fine…not much I can do, right?…uh-huh. Okay, well I 'preciate you callin'. I said I 'preciate you calling! Yeah, a little, some whiskey. Okay…uh-huh. G'bye."

Katie just let the receiver drop onto the bed and sat up.

"God-fuckin'-dammit!" she said.

CHAPTER 31

❈

Max was laughing, which, he knew, was helping to lessen his chances of getting sex tonight, but he couldn't stop himself.

"Let me get this straight..." he said around his chuckles. "Yesterday afternoon Katie learns that she's lost her job and then a few hours later, on the same day, she learns that she's lost her apartment?" He broke into a new fit of guffaws.

"Max, it's not funny, you prick," Danielle chided.

"Oh, I beg to differ, sweetie. It's fuckin' hilarious. You see, us born and bred New Yorkers can appreciate such horrible twists of fate like that for the comic relief they are. As long as they happen to other people, mind you. For example, six years ago my brother was laid up in the hospital for a sprained back and second degree burns because he slipped on a banana peel while drinking a hot cup of coffee. When my mom told me that I laughed so hard I almost wet my pants. I mean, think about it, sweetie...who did Katie have to piss off in a previous life to lose both her livelihood *and* her home in the space of half a day? The possibilities boggle the mind." He got up from the kitchen table and extracted a can of ginger ale from the fridge. "Was it Christ? Was it Gandhi? Oh, I know...maybe she was the person who had the bright idea to get Abe Lincoln tickets to see *Our American Cousin*."

"Alright, enough," Danielle ordered.

"Not too mention the irony," Max went on, sitting back down and once more digging into the orange chicken he was having for dinner. "I'm a writer so I know all about irony, sweetie, and this is even better than my lesbian pope."

"What is?" his girlfriend asked, snapping her teeth down on a stalk of celery in such a manner as to suggest he'd better be careful where he asks her to put her mouth later on.

"Don't you see it?" Max asked. "Katie's career was helping homeless people find jobs, right? Now, she herself is homeless and needs to find a job. But according to you, hers was the only organization that provided that kind of service, but they're closing down. So you see, from a cosmic perspective it's the perfect storm of crappy luck."

In a huff, Danielle got up from the table and left the room. She returned a few moments later, however, with a DVD case that she tossed on top of Max's food.

"What's this?" he asked.

"Lesbian porn," she answered. "You're going to need it to help get yourself off tonight." And with that she turned on her heel and stalked out of the room again.

Max picked up the DVD, used a napkin to wipe off bits of fried rice and orange chicken and thoughtfully examined the pictures on the case.

"This is ironic," he said to himself. "But not funny."

🍁 🍁 🍁

It was earlier that evening when Danielle had arrived at Homeward Bound after work. She and Katie had had plans to go out for cocktails but instead Katie took Danielle into her office and proceeded to tell her the latest. The phone call that had awakened her from a drunken stupor the night before was from Madeline Crespo, the woman Katie sublet the apartment from.

"She's an artist, a sculptor," Katie said. "Not a very successful one but I guess they all can't be Rodin. Anyway, she was in Europe studying, trying to get better, I guess, living off of grant money she conned the federal government out of. Now she's coming back and needs me to be gone in three weeks."

"Fuck," Danielle had said.

"Yeah, fuck is right. So after telling my staff today that they would soon be jobless, after having to send Nadine to the dollar store to buy more Kleenex because everyone was crying, after having to put a sign on our front door announcing to our clients that if they're still unemployed by July 6th they're probably going to be unemployed for the foreseeable future I have to go home and face moving out."

Danielle had decided not to feed into any negativity. She was going to force Katie into thinking confidently.

"Baby," she began, "this is nothing, okay? All we're talking about is a new job and a new apartment."

"Oh, is that all?" Katie replied, recognizing Danielle's tactic and resisting. "It's really that simple, huh? Because I don't see it that way."

"Only because you're still upset," Danielle said encouragingly.

"No, only because I'm facing reality, Dani. Sure, the job thing is no biggie; I have experience and I have contacts, but the apartment? Dani, listen, I live paycheck to paycheck, okay? I worked for a non-profit company which means I have zero savings. It never bothered me before because, quite frankly, unlike you, I don't care about material things. Now, maybe not putting any money aside for a rainy day was irresponsible of me but to tell you the truth I was happy just earning enough to put a roof over my head and food in my kitchen. Now I wish I did save something. You know how expensive this city is…moving from one apartment to another is going to cost a fortune. A fortune I don't have."

"You're forgetting that I can loan you enough to cover any moving expenses, first and last month's rent, security deposits, that sort of stuff."

Katie laughed, reaching into her purse and pulling out a bottle of aspirin. She popped two in her mouth and washed them down with cold coffee.

"And be faced with paying you back? Thanks but no thanks."

"It'll be a gift, then. God, it's not like I'm here on behalf of the Mob; you're kneecaps won't be in danger."

Katie had leaned forward over her desk and looked at Danielle gravely. "Dani, listen…we've got a good thing going here between us, right? We love each other, the sex is great…let's not fuck it up by bringing money into it."

"Oh, come on…"

"No. Look, we're talking about a few thousand dollars at least that most likely will not be paid back. Ever. And, no offense, Danielle, but money is very important to you; there is no way in hell you'd be able to fork over three or four grand and forget about it because for the first time in your life you wouldn't be getting anything for your money, like a new pair of shoes or a Donna Karan suit."

"I hardly think that's fair, Katie," Danielle had protested, stung by the criticism.

"I don't care if it's fair or not, it's true. Face it, if you wrote me a check for anything more than a hundred bucks you may as well write 'Break-Up Money' on the memo line because that's where we'd be headed."

Danielle immediately felt defensive. She wasn't sure how this had turned into an attack on herself and quite frankly she heard enough cracks at home from Max about how materialistic she was. But instead of starting an argument here with Katie she wisely let the subject drop.

"Fine," she said, "then what about your parents? I know mine had to get me through some tight times when I first moved here, are yours able to help?"

Katie answered that she had already called them that morning, that they're sending a few hundred dollars. "It's all they can afford. My father's a mailman and my mother works in the high school cafeteria as a lunch lady, if you can believe that. Marcano, Nebraska ain't exactly Beverly Hills. Anyway, their money will help but it won't nearly be enough. Most likely I'm just going to sock it away and save it. When I get a new job I'll add to it each paycheck until I have enough for a deposit on a new place."

"And in the meantime…" Danielle prodded.

Shrugging, Katie said, "Don't know. Actually, I do know…I'm faced with hitting my friends up for accommodations until I'm back on my feet." She swore under her breath. "What a fucking nightmare that's going to be."

"In what way?" Danielle asked.

"In every way. Listen, I'm not like you, Danielle. I don't move among the upper crust, okay? All of my friends are just as poor as I am. My gay friends live in tiny flats much like mine and my straight friends live in equally tiny flats except they've managed to somehow cram husbands and kids in them as well. Sure, they'll open their doors to me but trust me, after a week of tripping over the extra body bunking on the couch it'll be made clear that I've overstayed my welcome."

"Well, how about—" Danielle began but was cut off when Katie stood up suddenly.

"Come on," Katie had said, coming around her desk and grabbing Danielle's hand. "I'm just not in the mood to talk about this anymore right now. I'm blowing off our cocktails date. I've still got way too much to do here and besides, I fucking hate blabbing about my problems non-stop; I'm not that self-centered. And when I get home I have a whole night ahead of me during which I have a lot of shit to figure out. I'll call you tomorrow."

❦   ❦   ❦

So, her date cancelled, Danielle had picked up take-out Chinese for dinner and then gone home hoping the great Max Bland could shed some light on how best to help Katie. Instead, she had to endure him making light of the whole situation which led her to spend most of the night behind closed doors in her office trying to read an Agatha Christie novel but finding it hard to concentrate because of her concern for Katie.

At ten o'clock, however, she sought Max out, locating him in the bedroom. He was reclining on the bed, remote in hand, watching something on the flat screen TV mounted on the wall opposite. Upon her entrance he looked over at her and said, "This is boring."

"Huh?" Danielle replied and then turned to look at the television. Her mouth dropped. On the screen a blonde was rapidly finger-fucking a brunette while kissing her. "You're watching the porn?" Danielle asked incredulously.

"Why not? I've never seen lesbian porn before, and since you gave me permission…"

"I was being sarcastic!"

"Be that as it may but I'm a man and when a man's woman gives him permission to indulge in a little pornography he takes advantage. But I have to say I'm quite disappointed. I mean, I'm all for seeing two sexy women go at it but it gets a little dull after a while. It's just eating pussy and biting nipples scene after scene, with the occasional dildo thrown in. Is this all you and Katie do?"

"It's a lot more fun in real life," Danielle answered, not bothering to add that Katie was quite good at eating pussy as well as biting nipples. Instead, she got into bed and immediately snuggled against Max. Naturally, this made him suspicious.

"I'm sorry I got upset earlier," Danielle cooed, kissing his neck. "Forgive me?"

"Okay, whaddya want?" he said.

"Nothing. God, you're always thinking I'm up to something." She began toying with his belt buckle.

"That's because when you go from being pissed off at me to unfastening my pants in less than twenty-four hours there's usually a reason behind it."

"Stop being silly."

"And the reason is usually Mayzie Witherspoon."

"I haven't heard from Mayzie in weeks, Max," she said, licking behind his ear. "I think she's in South America for the summer."

"Good, an entire continent for us to avoid, it's so much easier that way. What, pray tell, are you doing?" he asked as she expertly unbuckled his belt and opened his pants. She then reached her hand inside and cupped his penis and testicles.

"Making up to you," she whispered. She took the remote from him and used it to fast forward the DVD to a different chapter. "This is the best one on the disc," she assured him. "The Asian chick gets fucked in the ass with the vibrator while the redhead eats her out. I want you to watch it while I blow you."

Max laughed, gently pushing her away and using the remote to click the TV off.

"Okay," he said, still laughing, "what's up? This whole thing you do of using sex to get what you want was cute for the first couple of years we were together but now it's just annoying. Of course, since you teased me I'm still gonna make you give me a blowjob, but not until after you explain what it is you're after."

🍁 🍁 🍁

"Fine," Danielle said sitting up on the bed cross-legged. "Here's what's up: I want Katie to move in with us," she stated with determination.

"I'm sorry?"

"Only temporarily, Max. Just until she can find another job, save some money and get a new apartment. She has nowhere else to go. Her family lives in Nebraska and—"

"People live in Nebraska?"

"Apparently, and none of her friends here in the city have room. She has no money saved up and I tried to loan her some but she won't take it."

Max raised his eyebrows. "Whoa…you tried to loan her money? Aren't you afraid Chanel is gonna have a sale and you'll find yourself short?"

"Fuck you. I'm getting sick and tired of you and Katie making fun of me and how much I spend."

"That's because it's funny. What's even funnier about it is that if you weren't living here with me you'd probably only weigh ninety pounds and be close to being evicted yourself because of your whole 'Shoes Are More Important Than Food or Rent' philosophy."

"Can I continue or are you just going to be an asshole the rest of the night?"

"Probably an asshole. Look, you can continue to your heart's content but it's pointless. You want your girlfriend to move in with us and I think it's a fucking crazy idea."

"Why?" Danielle demanded.

"Why? Why? Are you insane?"

"She's in need, Max and I care for her deeply. It's the least we can do; it's the Christian thing to do."

"Okay, first all," Max began, "a woman who likes seeing Asian chicks fucked in the ass with dildos and who hasn't set foot in a church in twelve years shouldn't be giving lectures on the concepts of Christianity; I'm sure God disapproves. Secondly, Katie is not like any of the other women you hang out with, is she? She's not in the same category as, say, Vanessa, your Pilates partner or, I dunno, Debbie, that co-worker you meet for coffee every Sunday morning. Katie is a lover. She's someone with whom, in addition to me, you have sex. And you want to put her and I under the same roof?"

"Obviously I realize the complications, Max," Danielle said. "Give me some credit."

Max made a sound as if the idea of giving her some credit was on par with giving her his Visa card the same day Manolo Blahnik opened a new outlet store. He took a moment to collect his thoughts and then said:

"Sweetie, listen…I feel for Katie, I really do, and I'm sorry I was making fun of her earlier. I may never have lost my job and my apartment in one fell swoop but I do know what it's like to be in a bind and wonder what the hell I was gonna do. Remember, it wasn't so long ago that I was barely earning enough to get by and had creditors crawling up my ass because I was late paying this or that off. So I feel sorry for her but having her move in here is no solution."

"So name another."

"I dunno. Force her to take your money somehow, tell her you'll withhold sex unless she does so. Or maybe you can convince her to let you set her up in a hotel room, have you tried that?"

"No, I haven't."

"Or maybe one of *your* friends can accommodate her for a while," Max said. "Yeah, that's it. Didn't you tell me Debbie has a great big brownstone she got from her divorce?"

"But we have a lot of room, too!" Danielle insisted. "Even more than Debbie. Jesus, you'd hardly know she's here and it's only for a little while!"

"Why are you so bent on keeping her close, Danielle? The Debbie idea is a good one and you know it. Whatsamatta? You afraid the two of them will end up as playmates?"

"No," Danielle said. "I just see no reason to fob off the woman *I'm* intimately involved with on a total stranger. Under the circumstances I feel it's my responsibility to help her through this. I can promise you it won't be a bother; you'll hardly know she's here."

Max said he was sure Katie didn't take up a lot of space but that that wasn't the issue. The issue, he contended, was centered around the inherent awkwardness of having three people sharing the same address when two of the three are in separate sexual and emotional relationships with the third. It was a potential Pandora's Box of insanity and bullshit and he couldn't understand why Danielle was blind to it. But every point he made, every reason he stated, was stubbornly refuted by young Ms Edwards. She minimized all his concerns by looking only at the best case scenarios. She countered all his attacks by deftly making him feel guilty and whenever he got agitated she touched him gently, soothing him with caresses which carried the promise of sexual reward.

He had to hand it to her: she really stuck to her guns when she was passionate about something; he bet she was a real tiger at that bank she worked for, probably had all the other tellers under her thumb.

"This is my home, too, Max!" she insisted at one point.

"That argument is not gonna work and you know it," Max rebutted. "This being your home gives you the right to have a say in what color we paint the walls and the right to have the security code for the alarm system but it does not give you the right to open our doors to anyone you wish, especially if anyone you wish happens to be a sexual partner."

Eventually, after no less than an hour the argument ended in a stalemate but Max had no intention of trusting Danielle to drop it because afterwards she had indeed given him that blowjob, quite willingly, in fact. So, recognizing that women—especially this particular one—are not in the habit of sucking men off when they don't get what they want he knew she'd try to play another card soon. And he had a pretty good guess what that card was. All he had to do was remove it from the deck.

🍁 🍁 🍁

Homeward Bound was listed in the yellow pages under Social Services so Max didn't exactly have to bend over backwards to find Katie. Arriving by cab at the 47th Street address he had jotted down he saw this sign taped to the front door:

> **Dear Homeward Bound Clients,**
>
> **Due to circumstances beyond our control Homeward Bound will be closing for good on July 6th. We regret to inform you that Homeward Bound will not be able to continue providing you with job searching services after that date. If you are already registered with us we will make every attempt possible, to find you employment up until the very end. If you are NOT already registered with Homeward Bound we are no longer accepting applicants. Sorry for any inconvenience and God bless.**
>
> **Homeward Bound Staff**

Max thought it wasn't a very well written sign. It was too full of clichés like "circumstances beyond our control" and "we regret to inform you" and "sorry for any inconvenience." Additionally, the phrasing throughout was sloppy, the vocabulary was weak and there was a comma splice in the third sentence. And how many times, he wondered, could they possibly use the words "Homeward Bound" in the same paragraph?

He felt a presence near him and turned to see a rather shabbily dressed man also reading the sign.

"Shame them closing this place up," the man said. Max guessed he was in his fifties and that he had led a damned hard life. "They doing a good thing here, you know what I'm saying?."

"So I've heard," Max replied.

"I'se got an appointment, see. I'm waiting to talk to my case manager, see if she done found me a job yet, you know what I'm saying?" He had made an attempt at looking respectable but someone at the clothing donation center neglected to tell him that checked golf slacks worn together with a striped business shirt and white shoes had quite the opposite effect.

"My case manager, she trying to get me into a job filing papers or something like that," the man went on.

"I see. And what will you do if this case manager fails to find you work before the center closes?" Max asked.

The fellow waved the question off.

"Shit, man…I been making it like this for twenty years, you know what I'm saying? If these folks can't help then, fuck it, I'll make it for twenty more."

"Ah."

"But I don't want no job filing papers. I'se hoping to get a job with computers, you know what I'm saying?" he continued. "Futuristic stuff."

"Funny, that's what I used to do for a living," Max told him.

"No shit? Hey, how 'bout that? So is it a hard racket to get into, you know what I'm saying?"

"Well," Max began, "it does help if you've actually used a computer before."

"Shit, really?"

"And, I regret to say, they do tend to give preference to people who have finished college, although, interestingly enough, I never graduated from college and I ended up having a pretty good career."

"So you saying there's hope?"

"Yes, I suppose I am," Max said encouragingly, opening the door. "Now, if you'll excuse me."

"Cool, man. Cool."

Max went into Homeward Bound and asked the receptionist if he could see Katie Shaw.

"Name?" the receptionist inquired. Max didn't know it but she was giving his expensive duds the same distrustful look she had given Danielle's a little over a year ago.

"Max Bland," he answered.

Suddenly, the receptionist's expression changed and she said: "Max Bland? Are you Max Bland the writer?"

"No. Is she in?"

"You're not jiving me, are you?"

"Trust me, miss, I wish I was Max Bland the writer because I understand that in addition to being very talented he's incredibly good-looking."

"I don't know about 'very talented,'" the receptionist said. "I thought his last book was boring."

"What? His last book is still on the bestseller's list and—*and!*—was nominated for a Pulitzer," Max answered with a just a dollop of indignation. But the receptionist just shrugged.

"Katie liked it," she said. "You know, Max Bland is her favorite writer?" She leaned forward and whispered, "I bet she'd suck his dick if he walked in here."

"I'll take that bet. Is she in, please?"

🍁   🍁   🍁

"Wow, this is a surprise," Katie told Max once she had him in her office. She tried to sound cheery but Max could tell the strain of the past couple of days was taking its toll. Her face showed the fatigue of more than one sleepless night, particularly her eyes, which were red, and there was a noticeable slouch to her posture, as if she'd like nothing more than to collapse. Max thought all this was a result of the stresses she was under: losing both her job and apartment, and in a way he was correct because it was those stresses that made her very nearly finish off an entire bottle of Scotch last night. She was functioning today with a severe hangover which the four Excedrin she popped an hour ago were only now beginning to alleviate.

"So to what do I owe the honor?" she asked.

"Well, I'll get right to it," Max said. "Let me apologize, first, for arriving unannounced. I realize you must be very busy."

"Yes, well…you know how it is," Katie said off-handedly. "We're in the middle of our going out of business sale."

"Ah. Yeah, sorry about that, by the way. Damn stock market. Danielle lost a bundle but I came through it alright mostly because I keep my money under my mattress. Anyway, look…knowing how busy you are I'm still hoping that you have time to talk."

"Shoot."

Max hesitated. "Not here," he said, casting a glance over his shoulder at the hubbub beyond. "It would be best if your co-workers didn't overhear us. Are you up for taking a couple of laps around the block?"

Not really, Katie thought. She felt the only thing she was up for was a postmortem, but she was intrigued. Here was the great Max Bland in her office apparently needing to speak on some matter of import. So she agreed to the walk and told Charmaine, her deputy director, to take over for a bit. She and Max then left by the back door.

Outside, they headed east on 47th towards Madison Avenue.

"Has Danielle asked you to go out with her tonight yet?" Max began.

"Yes, she has, in fact. She called a while ago. Against my better judgment I said yes, primarily to get her off my back. We're having dinner and then going dancing. She somehow convinced me that the only way to get out of this funk I've been in the past two days is to paint the town and embrace the changes my life is undergoing, something like that. In any case, I was too tired to argue with her." She shrugged. "Who knows? It might do me some good."

Max said, "Her and I were supposed to go see the new Ben Affleck movie tonight. All week she's been begging me to take her and then suddenly this morning she breaks the date, says she wants to hang with you."

"I'm sorry," Katie said. "I didn't know you two had plans. I'll cancel."

"No, no!" Max replied hurriedly. "Don't bother. Quite frankly, you're doing me a favor. I can't stand Ben Affleck; I think the erasers on the Number 2 pencils I write with have more talent than he does. So please, go out, have dinner and save me the agony, but I just wanted to warn you that Danielle has an ulterior motive for wanting to see you tonight."

"And that is?"

"She's wants you to move in with us."

Katie stopped cold, her hangover forgotten. "What?"

"That's right," Max said.

"Impossible."

"I wish it was."

"What the hell is she thinking?"

"So I take it you're opposed to the idea?"

"Hmmm…let me think…am I opposed to the idea of staying in an apartment where there's a chance I may walk past the wrong door and overhear my girlfriend having sex with a man? Of course I'm opposed."

They started walking again.

"Can you imagine what a nightmare it would be?" Max asked.

"Or how awkward it would be?" Katie added. "What does she think we'd do, play rock-paper-scissor each night to determine who she sleeps with?"

Max shook his head.

"It's that selfishness of hers rearing its ugly head again," he determined. "I bet she's getting off on the idea of having her two lovers under one roof, you know? It's like you and I are sex toys to collect, like those fancy glass dildos from Japan she keeps in our closet."

"Tokushima dildos? She has Tokushima dildos?" Katie asked, stunned.

"If those are the ones that cost hundreds of dollars a pop and that you can warm up in a special heating unit then, yes. She's got, like, ten of them, dildos and anal toys. They look like art sculptures."

"They happen to be handmade by a Japanese artist in a little village outside Kyoto," Katie said expertly going on to tell him that each one is custom made, individually numbered and no two are alike. What's more, Master Tokushima tints the glass using pigments made from one of the rarest orchids in the world and inside each dildo he encases a preserved dwarf butterfly.

"I've wanted one for years," she admitted, "but the cheapest is five-hundred bucks, a little out of my league. That bitch has been holding out on me!"

"Well, maybe once you move in you can raid her stash of these things anytime you want," Max said sarcastically.

Katie looked as if suddenly she was indeed seriously considering moving in, just for the toys. But then she shook her head briskly. "No, no! It's fucking crazy!"

"Excellent, glad to see we're back on the same page. By the way, those are exactly the words I used during the argument we had about this last night. It *is* fucking crazy."

"And how did that argument end?" Katie asked.

"With an orgasm," Max answered truthfully, "but it was owed me. However, the matter of whether or not you can move in remained unresolved. I refused to budge in my opposition and she went to bed frustrated."

"Danielle doesn't like to be frustrated," Katie pointed out.

"Thus my appearance here. She failed to win me over so I know she'll try to have better success with you. Despite your obvious physical charms that's the real reason she wants to see you tonight."

Katie was angry and she started walking with more energized steps. Max needed to pick up his pace to stay beside her.

"Why the fuck can't she stay out this, huh? I've told her I'll be alright. I certainly don't need looking after."

"You know how she is. If she was a doctor instead of a bank teller she may have been able to put this stubbornness of hers to good use. She probably would have found a cure for death by now."

"Bank teller? I thought she was the vice-president for global strategy at ARCL."

"Really?" Max said, genuinely surprised. "Hey, that's impressive. I gotta congratulate her. Anyway, I tried to talk her out of it but she says she feels responsible for you. I dunno, at times it was actually kinda sweet."

"Sweet? What's sweet about making me feel like a goddamn child who still needs mommy to walk her to school? I'll admit I'm not in the best of circumstances, okay? I have no money and I'm faced with perhaps months of sleeping on couches and living out of a suitcase."

"Well then why don't you let her loan you some money?" Max asked gently. "It'll shut her up and make her feel like she's doing you some good. Most importantly, it may very well quash this idea."

Shaking her head Katie said, "No way. It makes me squeamish. I'll borrow money from my parents but not from my friends, especially girlfriends. Way too complicated. Been there, done that. Besides, with my luck, the day after she gives me the money she'll hear about a Bloomingdale's opening up on one of the moons of Saturn and resent me because I took all her spending money."

"Hey, that's pretty good," Max said, chuckling. He then shared with her the crack he made last night about Chanel having a sale and Katie started laughing. They ended up spending the entire 46th Street leg of their circuit around the block sharing yuks over Danielle's love of shopping.

Finally, Max changed the subject. "Any chance you'd accept money from me?" he said, taking Katie's arm and gallantly steering her around an open manhole cover as they turned the corner onto Fifth Avenue. "I mean, I barely know you so I don't qualify as a friend and because you're a lesbian I can't hope you'll be grateful enough to fuck my brains out. So you see, I'm the perfect person to accept a donation from."

Even though the danger of the manhole cover was past Katie was still holding onto his arm. She gave it a squeeze.

"That's sweet, Max, it really is," she replied. "But I'll be fine. I've struggled before, even worse than this. I'll get through it. I have a network of friends who'll help and before I know it I'll have a new job, a new place to live and this whole episode will just be something to look back on and laugh about."

"If that's how you feel..." Max said, acquiescing, but he gave her his card with his office phone number written on the back and insisted she call him should she change her mind.

"For now, though," Katie began, "you can give me pointers on how to win tonight's argument with Danielle."

"Be just as stubborn as she is," Max advised. "Wear her out with refusal, eventually she'll get frustrated and drop it. She may pout—"

"Oh, she'll definitely pout," Katie offered.

"Right, but fuck her. Let her pout. If she gets too overbearing send her back to me and I'll calm her down by letting her take my credit card on a pilgrimage to Saks."

A short while later they returned to Homeward Bound and shook hands to seal their commitment to thwart Danielle's plans.

Before he left Max pulled out his wallet and handed Katie a fifty-dollar bill.

"Do me a favor, would you? There's a guy in there, one of your customers. I didn't catch his name but you can't miss him: he dressed like his tailor was raised by circus folk. Give him this money for me, okay? And then tell him to come by here next week. I'm gonna have my old programming manuals and PC repair books delivered by messenger. Let him take whatever he wants."

CHAPTER 32

❀

"And up there," Danielle said, pointing up to the second of two loft areas that were opposite each other and connected by a bridge which spanned the living room, "is the library. Help yourself to whatever you want and if you really want to see something extraordinary have Max show you his collection of first editions. He's got first editions of Dickens and Tolstoy and a bunch of others—all his favorites, basically. And he owns at least one autographed book from each of them. I mean, he actually has Charles Dickens's autograph! Can you believe it?"

Sure, Katie thought, *I can believe he has Dickens's autograph. Perfectly normal for a successful writer to own memorabilia of his literary heroes.* What she couldn't believe, however, was this apartment. "Apartment", in fact, was entirely the wrong word for it, frankly. She had lived in an *apartment*; Moira lives in an *apartment*; the clients at Homeward Bound were looking for *apartments*. But this place...this place was a mansion in the sky. *It has a bridge, for Christ's sake!* Katie told herself, looking up at the rather artistic span of steel and wood bisecting the air above the living room diagonally from loft to loft. *A fucking bridge!*

It was the day after Max's visit to Katie, a Saturday, and Katie was moving in. That morning Danielle had called the Job Services office at NYU and hired a couple of college boys to come to Katie's place and help cart her stuff uptown to Max's home. There wasn't much. All the furniture belonged to Madeline, so did the cookware and the bath linens. Katie's possessions—amounting to clothes, books, stacks of papers and photos, a few knick knacks, CDs and old 45s, and her laptop with printer—all fit neatly into several boxes and suitcases.

Max wasn't home when they arrived just after two in the afternoon, a discovery which Katie greeted with a sigh of relief. She learned from Danielle that he was at a casting audition in the Village for the movie version of *The Remarkable Reign of Pope Anne I*, which Miramax was finally getting around to making. It bought her some time to come up with just how in the hell she was going to explain to him how this had happened. Truth be told, she wasn't sure she knew herself how this had happened. But suddenly here she was, on the sixtieth floor of an opulent high-rise, her jaw dropping open in amazement at how unbelievably *huge* the place was.

After paying the college boys and sending them on their way Danielle immediately began the tour. It wasn't long before Katie's head was swimming and she became disoriented. She felt like she ought to be leaving behind a trail of breadcrumbs. It seemed that there was always another hallway, another collection of rooms, another set of double doors leading to another hallway, another collection of rooms, another set of double doors, and so on. Danielle told her there was over 10,000 square feet of floor space and to Katie it seemed virtually all of it was either marble, Travertine or cherry wood. The windows throughout were all floor-to-ceiling jobs offering breathtaking and dizzying views of the city and Central Park while letting in huge amounts of natural light. There were two fireplaces in the living room alone, and another two in the master bedroom. One room just off the kitchen was identified as the maid's quarters. "He has a maid but Max doesn't like the idea of anybody else living here, so we use that room as our home gym," Danielle stated.

On and on it went with every inch being shown to Katie, her girlfriend's pride evident. Overall, the decor of the apartment was very urban and contemporary: a lot of dark colors, a lot of metal and stone accents contrasting nicely with very plush furnishings upholstered in distressed leather or corduroy. It was definitely, Katie thought, a man's pad, but even so it wasn't too overtly masculine. It was classy, sophisticated, modern. It spoke of Cary Grant, Humphrey Bogart and Ernest Hemingway, with just a touch of Sinatra and the Rat Pack. It possessed the aura of New York, the cutting edge metropolis, yet a woman could certainly feel at peace in it and indeed, Danielle didn't seem to have had much of an influence in the decoration even though Katie knew she'd been living here for quite some time. But then Katie reminded herself that her girlfriend wasn't really the type who went in for flowered curtains and fuzzy pink toilet seat covers anyway. The only room that was distinctly Danielle was her office which had a bunch of Winnie the Pooh stuff in it and bore a great big picture of the Grand Canyon on the west wall.

As for the other walls throughout the place, they were hung with tasteful black-and-white photos of the city and, in the most conspicuous places, masterpieces of art.

"Fuck, is that a Bruegel?" Katie had asked, standing before one particular piece.

"Wow, you have a good eye," Danielle complimented. "I didn't even know who Bruegel was before I moved in here."

"I minored in Art History in college," Katie told her before another painting caught her eyes. "Jesus, is that a Dali? And is that a Pissarro?" She moved from one painting to another, about seven in all, unable to believe she was in the same room as them. "Jesus Christ, are these the originals?" she asked, reverently touching the frame of a Manet and feeling lightheaded.

"All courtesy of that wonderful lady Pope Anne," Danielle replied.

Finally, Katie was shown the bedroom she'd be using. It was the largest of the four guest bedrooms and it alone had more space than the apartment she had been subletting.

"Bathroom's through there," Danielle pointed. "There's TiVo connected to the flat screen on the wall as well as a DVD player and VCR. The telephone is on a separate line from the rest of the house and it has long distance. There's a high-speed internet connection next to the desk—I know you do a lot of stuff on the web—and here's the remote to close the window shades."

"You're kidding me, right?" Katie said.

"No, I'm not. Look..." Danielle pressed a button on a tiny remote and with a barely audible hum window shades began unfurling from the ceiling to block out the sunlight and the stunning southerly view of midtown Manhattan.

"Ooh, I kind of like this," Danielle said when the room was enveloped in shadowy darkness. She pulled Katie to her and in a moment was probing her mouth with her tongue.

Katie pulled away reluctantly. "What about Max?" she breathed. "I mean, what if he comes home?" She moaned as Danielle began nibbling her neck. Suddenly Danielle stopped and looked at Katie with a wicked gleam.

"What? What are you thinking?" Katie asked.

"Are you really afraid he'll come home and catch us?"

"It's crossed my mind."

"In that case, come on," Danielle ordered, taking Katie's hand and guiding her all the way back into the living room (Katie swore she'd need a map to relocate her bedroom) where she shoved her up against a wall and started kissing her in earnest. Katie's first instinct was to protest but Danielle was a hell of a good kisser and soon it was like all self control had abandoned her. Besides, any struggling she did simply made Danielle push up against her harder to reassert control.

"To tell you the truth," Danielle whispered, hiking up Katie's skirt and grabbing her bottom, "I have no idea when he'll be back." She moved her right hand forward to Katie's pubic region and began rubbing a finger lightly just above her clitoris, almost but not quite in contact with the sensitive organ. Katie sucked in air through her teeth. "He may be gone for a few more hours," Danielle continued, ignoring Katie's pleas to stop, "or he may be in the elevator on his way up right now."

Katie looked across the apartment to the front door way off in the distance. Like a robot she obeyed when Danielle told her to lift her arms up. Her t-shirt was pulled off and in a flash one of her nipples was in Danielle's mouth hardening to marble. Keeping her eyes on the front door it gradually dawned on Katie that the very thought of it opening was making her exceedingly wet.

🍁   🍁   🍁

Max was rubbing the bridge of his nose between his thumb and forefinger, trying to stave off the headache he knew was standing on the platform waiting to board the train that would take it straight to his skull.

"Right," he said. "In the book, the book I wrote, mind you, I clearly describe Edna as being a frumpy housewife with a body that reminds you of two sacks of dirty laundry. I remember it exactly, Russell, because I was thinking of my Aunt Shantel when I wrote that."

Russell Meyers, the director Miramax hired to create the feature film based on *Pope Anne* nodded obsequiously, as if the sun rose and set depending on Max's opinions which, in this particular instance, wasn't far from the truth.

Before Max had agreed to sell the film rights a couple of years ago he and his lawyer had made certain that he would possess a measure of creative control over the film. *Pope Anne* was his baby and he had worked long and hard to create a successful book out of that story. He wasn't about to let Hollywood (as is their wont) give his novel a bad name by making a shitty movie out of it. He'd seen them do that to too many of Stephen King's books. So, not only was he to approve the screenplay adaptation but he also demanded approval rights for the cast. Cate Blanchett, who apparently was all set to sign on to play Anne, he had no problem with. But after the last two hours he was glad he wielded the power he did.

"I mean," Max continued, "if Edna is the type of woman normal men would have to be drunk to sleep with why have the past four actresses we've seen reading for that part looked like Dallas Cowboys cheerleaders? Somebody, please, explain that to me."

They'd been at it since eight in the morning, casting parts for the New York segment of the story. In a week, he was supposed to fly to California to repeat the process and help cast the remainder of the movie. He didn't even want to think about it now. Not that this was an entirely awful experience. In fact, most of it had gone well but the day hadn't been without controversy. To start, they had tried to convince him to let them cast a white guy for the part of Carlton Bailey, a black doctor, and then an argument ensued over the bra size of a teenager who read for the part of a twelve-year old girl.

"You want me to sign off on an actress," Max had said in disbelief, "who's, number one, *seventeen*-years old and, number two, has centerfold-sized breasts. In the book I describe someone like Tatum O'Neal in *Bad News Bears*, and you're trying to give me Jane Fonda in *Barbarella*."

So instinct had warned him that when the moment came for casting Edna (a character with significant screen time) these studio people would try to pander to the lowest common denominator in the movie-going public by hiring a bombshell actress to play the part.

Meyers tried to lob the blame over to the casting director; she became indignant and backhanded it to the screenwriter; he became pissy and put the onus on the various acting agents who sent clients down here, saying that obviously they didn't read the character descriptions in the screenplay very well.

Max opened his copy of the script to the point where Edna is introduced and then showed it to the screenwriter.

"'Edna is a housewife in her early thirties,'" Max read aloud. "Is that the highly detailed description the agents misunderstood? Jesus, they must be complete idiots, right? Shame on them."

The screenwriter said nothing.

Sighing, Max said, "Okay, fuck this. When are we set to meet again, Russell?"

"Bright and early Monday," Meyers answered.

"Fine." Max looked directly at Janice, the casting director. "I don't care how you do it, Jan, but you need to contact all these agents again and give them the description of Edna from out of my book, *not* from the script. When we pick up again Monday I wanna see thirty of Roseanne Arnold's ugly cousins waiting to read for this part. And you," he said to the screenwriter, "you need to revise the script so the descriptions you give in it match the descriptions in what now?

"Your book," the screenwriter mumbled.

"Excellent. Another couple of training sessions and you'll be ready for *Jeopardy*. I don't wanna have to go through this again out in California, people. I hate California. I wanna spend as little time as possible in California."

And with that, he left, looking forward to returning home and showering all this Hollywood-type business off of him.

🍁   🍁   🍁

Stepping into the apartment and setting down his briefcase Max thought he heard a bump that came from somewhere in the vicinity of the living room, and he could've sworn his peripheral vision had picked up something scurrying quickly out of sight. Then, even more oddly, wasn't that giggling his ears were picking up?

Knowing that burglars rarely giggle he called out, "Sweetie?"

"Um…yeah, I'm over here."

"Are you okay? I thought I heard something fall." He thumbed through the mail waiting on the table by the door. "Sweetie?"

"Yes…I'm fine, I'm fine," he heard her call back. "Sorry, I just stumbled a bit." Finally, Max saw her emerge from behind a wall. He frowned, bemused. She looked disheveled. Not only was her hair tousled but her blouse was done up all wrong, buttoned crookedly. She hurriedly tried pushing some stray bangs back into place. "See, here I am," she said, trying to sound normal and innocent.

Max crossed the foyer and living room intending to give her a kiss hello but he stopped suddenly when from behind the same wall from which Danielle had come Katie unexpectedly revealed herself.

"Oh, and Katie's here," Danielle said, once more trying to sound normal.

"Yes, I can see that," Max said.

Katie gave him a tentative wave. "Hi, Max."

"Yes, hi, Katie. Good of you to stop by." Motioning towards her he then said: "You might wanna…"

Katie looked down and swore. She was topless. In her haste of a few moments ago she had managed to get her white bra back on but had left off the t-shirt. It was still in her hands. "Sorry," she said bashfully, putting the shirt on.

"I guess there's no use pretending we were just watching Saturday cartoons, is there?"

Max held up his hands.

"Hey, look…none of my business. So," he said, directly to Katie, "are you here picking Danielle up for a date?"

"Uh, no," Danielle jumped in. "She's not. Max, listen, I know that we discussed this a couple of nights ago but I was sure you wouldn't mind. Katie's going to stay with us. Just until things are back to normal for her."

Max smiled but both women knew how false it was.

"Of course, she can stay, darling," he effused. "After all, we have plenty of space. Tell me, have you got her situated in a bedroom, showed her where we keep the towels, given her the remote for the window shades? Got that all taken care of?"

Danielle looked dubious as she responded.

"Yes, I took care of all that, Max." She came close to him and whispered, "Are you sure you're not upset?"

"You'll find out later," he hissed so only she could hear, keeping the smile on his face.

Danielle felt her stomach sink. The last thing she had wanted to do was give Max a reason to pick a fight with her. She had been optimistic that once Katie was here Max would forget his reservations and be okay with this arrangement. At most it would only be for a month or two. And since he's been so busy lately finishing his current novel *and* dealing with Miramax about the *Pope Anne* movie, the time, she felt, would go very quickly as far as he was concerned. It seemed, however, that he was of a differing opinion and she involuntarily gulped at the underlying threat his last statement carried.

But before she had a chance to placate him her purse, left on the same table as the mail, started to ring. Danielle extracted her cell phone from it.

"Christ," she said, reading the caller ID, "it's Margot. And on a Saturday. Will you two excuse me? I'm going to take this in my office…Hey, Margot, what's up?…Uh-huh…Uh-huh…Okay, if that's true that may be a problem come Monday…"

❧   ❧   ❧

Making sure Danielle shut her office door Max marched over to Katie and whispered, "What the hell?"

"I know."

"Wasn't it just *yesterday* when we had this big talk about what a rotten idea this was?"

"I know."

"So what...just because I don't have nice tits like Danielle everything I say goes in one ear and out the other?"

"Look, I don't know what to tell you," Katie whispered back defensively.

"Tell me you're packing your bags and getting the hell outta here. Fuck, couldn't you have done something to talk her out of this?" he insisted.

"Like what?"

"Jesus, anything. You could be in a nice hotel now if you'd only agreed to that in the first place."

"No thank you. Besides, you think I want to be here? I'm a twenty-nine year old woman who has to bum a room off her girlfriend—"

"*Our* girlfriend," Max said.

"Whatever. The point is, this is uncomfortable for me on a whole lot of levels."

Max snorted. "Yeah, you were the picture of discomfort a moment ago when your *shirt* was off."

Katie glared at him but Max didn't notice, he was pacing now, looking as if he was ready to pull out his hair.

"I just don't understand it," he said, "You strike me as the type who can stick to her guns, put up a good fight. I told you all you had to do was be stubborn and outlast her and eventually she'd give up. How the hell did she convince—" He stopped suddenly and looked at Katie, comprehension dawning on his features. "Did she go down on you?" he asked irately.

"What?"

"Last night, did she go down on you?"

Katie colored bright red and said, "I don't think that's any of your business, Max..."

"Aha! She did, didn't she?"

"I'm not answering that." But she said it somewhat sheepishly because she could see where he was going with this. Suddenly the events of last night came back to her and she could see what had made her fail to stick to her guns.

There, in her mind's eye, were her and Danielle in the bedroom.

There were her and Danielle making out on the bed and Katie thinking, what the hell, guess we'll argue after we have sex.

There was Katie, completely nude, arching her back in pleasure with Danielle's head between her legs and her finger rimming Katie's anus.

And finally, there was Katie, sweating now, the quivering in her loins ready to skyrocket her into orgasm and Danielle keeping her on the brink by licking her clitoris lighter and lighter until she was barely grazing it with her tongue before saying, ever so sweetly, "Baby, there's something I want to talk to you about."

Max knew from the expression on Katie's face that he had hit the nail on the head.

"Jesus!" he ejaculated. "Couldn't you recognize what she was up to? Or do you lesbians believe there's only honor among the sisterhood? That's her fucking trademark trick! Get you hard as stone, ready to burst and then stop so she can talk to you about something. That's how I ended up with this earring!"

"Fine, you're right," Katie admitted. "I was manipulated and I'm sorry I let it happen because I was just as interested in not moving in here as you were. I fucked it up, sue me." She took a breath. "But I'm here now and you know there's no way in hell Dani is going to let me leave, no matter what excuse I give, so we have to—"

"Make the best of it?" Max interrupted. "Is that what you were gonna say? We have to make the best of it? Jesus Christ. And how do you propose we do that, Katie?"

"I don't know."

"Great, fucking great! How, exactly, are two people in the same house supposed to share the emotional and physical attentions of a third? Hey, I know…let's make up a schedule that we can put in the kitchen! 'Monday: Danielle fucks Max, shares deep and tender conversation over coffee with Katie. Tuesday: Danielle fucks Katie, shares hopes and dreams over dinner with Max.'"

"That might work, you know," Katie said, "if I could find the kitchen."

"What's that supposed to mean?"

"It means this place is *huge!* You ought to be ashamed of yourself!"

"What for?"

Katie huffed. "What for? There are thousands of people right now sleeping on the street and you've got an apartment the size of a city block, that's what for."

"What the hell kind of place did you think I lived in?" Max asked. "Did you think I was another Thoreau, living in a fucking lean-to in the goddamn woods?"

"I was hoping you lived somewhere reasonable, yes. You know, Arthur Miller was a famous writer, too, but he lived in a modest one bedroom apartment."

"Arthur Miller was, what, three-hundred years old when he died?" Max shot back. "He was old enough to have once been married to Marilyn Monroe who dropped dead even before I was born. Anything larger than a one bedroom place and he risked not getting to the phone in time to call the paramedics during a stroke."

"Funny," Katie said sourly.

"Think whatever you want but I'm not going to have you make me feel guilty for people sleeping out on the streets. That's not my problem and it's not my fault. And as far as all this goes, I've worked hard for what I've got."

Barking a harsh laugh Katie said: "Please. You sit at a desk and make up stories. I work harder going to the store to buy your books." She pointed towards the entranceway. "You could sleep thirty people in your foyer alone, do you realize that?"

"Don't even think about it," Max ordered. "I don't need you bringing your work home with you. I'm not running a halfway house."

"Fear not, Max. I'm sure the gorilla of a doorman downstairs has orders to chuck poor people into the moving traffic on Fifth Avenue."

"As a matter of fact he does," Max teased. "It's what earns him that nice Christmas bonus at the end of each year."

"Stop being a jerk."

"Me being a jerk? You're the one laying into me about the size of my house, you psycho. Is that how you give thanks to a host that's forced to take you in because you couldn't keep your legs closed?"

"I don't have to listen to this," Katie sneered. She turned away and began walking in the direction she thought her bedroom was in. But Max called after her.

"Besides, tell me...since you're so perfectly charitable and so quick to look down your nose at those of us with fat bank accounts...how many homeless people did you used to bring home each night, huh?"

Katie stopped in her tracks.

"What did you say?" she asked.

"How many homeless people did you used to bring home each night?"

Katie felt the blood rushing to her face.

"I don't understand," she squeaked.

"It's very simple," Max said calmly. "You'd see, what, dozens of homeless every day, correct? In your office, I mean. Heard all their sob stories; felt sorry for them? Surely you'd bring at least one home each night, right? Especially during the winter, when the shelters are full and the weather outside is frightful? Surely you always gave someone needy a nice warm bed and a hot meal; made her feel safe; made her feel as if someone cared, because you strike me as the type of person who likes to lead by example. I mean, I can't imagine that you just go around the city preaching to everyone to open up their hearts and do more to help the homeless when, in fact, your own compassion never extended past working hours. Right?"

Max walked away, done with her.

Katie was taken aback, breathless and weak-kneed even. She watched him go up the nearest flight of stairs and cross the bridge to the library loft. She opened her mouth but nothing came out; as much as she wanted to she was at a loss to respond because Max had struck a nerve. Not only struck it, hammered on it. No, she had never invited a homeless person home with her. No, it had never crossed her mind. She knew, of course, that Max had said that tactically, used it as a bomb to wreck the foundations of her argument by throwing her self-righteousness back in her face. She also knew that realistically, she had nothing to feel guilty about; that she had never been expected to open her own home to Homeward Bound's clients, no matter how much pity she had for them; that it would have been considered going above and beyond, not to mention potentially dangerous. Yet the accusation of hypocrisy stung and she had to concede defeat to Max because for the first time in her entire life someone had made her feel as if she hadn't done enough.

Katie sighed, mentally cursing Danielle's proficiency at oral sex.

CHAPTER 33

❀

When Danielle reemerged from her office to find Katie on the balcony and Max upstairs in the library it raised alarms in her head, for there seemed to be a vibe of negativity charging the apartment's air. But Katie explained she merely wanted to relax a bit, get some fresh air and Max explained he merely wanted to begin reading *About A Boy* by Nicholas Hornby. Danielle was 99.9% sure she shouldn't believe either of them but was able to forget about it for a while when her mother called to ask if Max would make a guest appearance at her book club next week.

"Our club leader chose Max's third novel as the featured book this month. Of course, no one else in the club knows Max like I do so I feel I have a distinct advantage when we begin critiquing the book."

Danielle rolled her eyes.

"And you should have seen how envious they all were when I brought out my personally autographed copy of the book that you sent me. It was quite a hit."

"Yes, well, Mom, I'm not sure Max—"

"Anyway," Mrs. Edwards said, barreling over her daughter's turn to speak, "I figured Max showing up would give our little group a big boost and, just between you and me, would make our club leader forgive me for telling her that the apple streusel she made for our last meeting tasted store bought."

"I see, but—"

"I eventually took her word for it that she baked it herself but I'm still suspicious. I mean, you can taste preservatives, you know. And really, it's the easiest thing in the world to bring home an apple streusel from the store, pop it into a Tupperware container and pass it off as your own."

"Mmmm-hmmm—"

"Anyway, Muriel is one of my best friends and a big Max Bland fan so I think his coming would make her feel less hostile towards me for finding her out. I was even thinking maybe he could read a few passages from the book he's writing now? Sort of like a sneak peek?"

"That'll happen when hell freezes—"

"Then next year I'll be a shoo-in for club leader! And when I get elected I can finally open up the works of Barbara Cartland to thorough critical analysis."

After forty minutes of this, with her mother having a considerable edge in the final tally of words spoken, Danielle was at last able to interrupt long enough to disappoint her properly by informing her that Max was unlikely to schlep all the way to Arizona just to hear a bunch of middle-aged southwestern housewives offer up their mangled interpretations of his book even if it helped salve the wounds caused by the apple streusel controversy. Danielle ended the conversation by claiming the building was on fire and some very insistent rescue workers were urging her to evacuate.

🍁   🍁   🍁

They had Chinese delivered for dinner, Danielle thinking it would be nice to welcome Katie with a feast of sorts. When it arrived, Danielle asked Max to help her set the dining room table and dish out the food.

"Are you okay?" she asked him, handing him a plate to spoon Mongolian beef onto.

"Oh, I'm fine," he answered brightly.

"It's just that you've been quiet today."

"Has that become a crime?"

"No," Danielle said. "I just thought I'd make sure nothing was bothering you."

He didn't reply, just carried on emptying a carton of fried rice onto a serving platter.

"*Is* anything bothering you?" she prodded but again it was as if she were talking to herself. "Max, please, if there's—"

"Whew!" Katie said, arriving then, "I would've been here sooner but I took a wrong turn somewhere near the shopping mall and found myself in a whole wing of the apartment I've never seen before."

Without even deigning to favor her with a look Max replied, "It is a little disorienting for a newcomer, I apologize. My own mother, God bless her, could never remember where the bathrooms were. Please, have a seat and help yourself." He pulled out a chair for Katie. "Perhaps in the future we can arrange accommodations for you and my mom at Arthur Miller's old flat."

"Do you think so?" Katie said. She topped off two scoops of fried rice with some sesame chicken. "You know, I met him once at a fundraising event at the Javits Center a couple of years ago. He was a remarkable man, really dedicated to fighting homelessness."

"You sure he didn't think he was at an Alzheimer's symposium? Men his age are so easily confused." Max poured her a glass of wine.

"Doubtless," Katie acknowledged. "But, no, he was in the right place. He may have been elderly but he was still very mentally acute. We had a fascinating conversation about the responsibility of artists in helping to improve society."

"Well, when you're not busy bearing the weight of the world upon your shoulders you must tell me how that conversation went," Max said.

"It was simple enough. Would you like me to share it with you now?"

"Please do," Max said, as if his whole life up until now had been a mere dress rehearsal for this one spectacular moment.

"Well, Mr. Miller's thinking was that artists such as, let's say, novelists, whose livelihoods depend upon public opinion should feel an obligation to reward the public by doing things that in some measure benefit humanity. A kind of one-hand-washes-the-other sort of thing."

"Oh, Max is already very charitable," Danielle interceded. "He's a top donor to United Way, the American Cancer Society and the Boys and Girls Club. And just last year he paid for a new library for his high school up in the Bronx."

If Danielle was hoping Max would acknowledge her amicably for her compliment she was disappointed. Instead, he took a sip of wine and then bit into his egg roll before addressing Katie again. "I suspect you and people like Mr. Miller would deem that not enough, though, right?"

"I think it's wonderful that you donate so much money. I'm impressed."

"But?"

"But, let's face it…writing checks is easy and considering how wealthy you seem to be the money you donate is hardly a sacrifice. Besides, it's tax deductible so you end up getting it back in a sense."

"Go on."

"Well, what really turns people in my profession on are the volunteers; individuals who give up their time to help out. After all, time is something you can't get back; once it's gone, it's gone, so a donation of time is often more valuable than one of money."

"So the only way you and the Arthur Millers in this world would be happy is if I devote my weekends to ladling watered down beef stock at the nearest soup kitchen."

"For starters."

"That way, not only will the unfortunate souls be fed but apparently they'll feel so grateful they'll be willing to plunk down $25.95 in nickels and dimes at their local bookseller's to buy one of my novels."

Katie smiled.

"I'm afraid you missed the point a teensy weensy bit," she said. "The idea is not to get the homeless to buy your books but simply for you to make a positive contribution to our world. You shouldn't be looking to gain anything from it, like book sales."

"But," Max went on, "I fear you're overestimating people, Katie, darling. You're assuming that *everybody* wants to give up their nights and weekends to help out. You're placing more of a value on time than money—and perhaps you're correct doing so—but wouldn't you rather have volunteers who are enthusiastic about the work they're doing? Volunteers who think it's a pleasure to ladle soup or tuck the homeless in at night in a shelter?"

Nodding, Katie said, "Of course."

"But I'm not like that, Katie, my sweet. I don't wanna spend my free time in a soup kitchen. I don't wanna give up a Saturday afternoon working the register in a thrift store. Now, maybe that makes me inferior in some ways when compared to others but it's who I am and at least I do recognize that flaw in my character. And, okay, maybe I don't volunteer my time for any good causes but at least I do something: I write checks. And I'm sure that to the accountants of these organizations who help the homeless or feed the children my money is worth just as much as your time. And it could be worse. I could be one of these people who do nothing at all. Danielle, your phone is ringing."

Danielle, of course, knew her cell was ringing; it was attached to her belt, only a couple of feet from her ears. It's just that she was reluctant to answer it. The bad vibe she had detected earlier was certainly present once more but Margot had told her that she may be calling back and because the issue at hand involved fine tuning the particulars of a billion-euro account it just would not do to let it go to voice mail. Even on a Saturday. Even when her two lovers were at loggerheads. So she unhooked the phone and flipped it open. Sure enough...

"Yes, Margot...No, don't worry about it, have you talked to Devon?...Uh-huh...Uh-huh...He's wrong, the count should be higher; Jesus, why does he still work for us?...Yeah, I will fire him on Monday because I know circus animals that are brighter...Right, I'll check, just give me a moment to get to my office..."

🍁   🍁   🍁

With Danielle gone Max felt free to take his meal into the living room so he could watch television while eating. He discovered Woody Allen's *Everyone Says I Love You* playing on cable and finished his dinner a man temporarily content with the world.

Then Katie showed up.

"Just on my way to my room," she said. "I figured I'd start now so that I get there in time for bed."

Max smiled.

"Now, now, Katie," he said. "What makes you think you can just skulk off to your room? You know Danielle would like nothing better than to come out of her office and see the two of us sitting here together in perfect harmony, and since you got us into this mess the least you can do is have a seat and make her happy."

"Since *I* got us into this mess?"

"Well, certain parts of you, anyway." He looked at her crotch.

Katie colored and took a seat on the couch next to him.

"Wow, this is a remarkable TV," she said after a few minutes. "There's so much clarity in the picture you can almost count the pores on Woody's face."

Max said he was glad she liked it.

"May I ask what a set like this costs?"

"Certainly. This particular one ran me fourteen thousand dollars. That's, let's see...280,000 nickels in case any of your homeless friends ask."

"Wow," Katie cooed. "And how big is it?"

"Seventy-two inches."

"Wow," she cooed again. Then she frowned. "Must have been a bit of a letdown once you got it home, though."

"How's that, Katie?"

"It's just that I bet it looked much bigger in the store, right? I mean, a seventy-two inch set in the store looks *enormous*. A seventy-two inch set in any normal sized apartment looks enormous but in a living room like this, which is the size of a movie theatre, it looks so…average."

"You know, that's a good point," Max replied, in his most agreeable tone. "And now suddenly I do not feel as if I'm getting my money's worth with the TV being in this huge area. Hey, I know…since I'm rich, maybe I can help you out, Katie."

She made like she was all ears.

"Really? How?"

"Well, here's what I have in mind: I'll fill all this empty space in the living room here by stacking homeless people on top of one another. This will create the impression that the room is smaller than it actually is and as a result the TV will seem larger. Let's see…I'll pay the people on the bottom of the stacks ten bucks a day because, after all, the poor bastards are on the bottom, but I'll only pay the guys on the top a buck or so, just enough to get their daily bottle of cheap malt liquor."

Katie reached over and smacked her favorite writer on the arm.

"All homeless people do not get drunk on malt liquor every night, you know," she hissed. "That's an ugly stereotype which prevents many people from helping them."

"Relax, I know that," Max said, "But since it appears you're not gonna shut up about how good I got it I figure I'd better get my digs in at your sore spots. You're forgetting, sweetheart, you're talking to a native New Yorker. There's no way in hell I'm gonna let someone from Pig's Scrotum, Nebraska outtalk me."

"Fuck, can you blame me?" Katie queried, casting a look over to the door of Danielle's office to make sure it was still shut. "When you've spent as much time around the kind of poverty I have you'd hardly be able to keep your mouth shut, too." She then told Max about one of her clients who works sixty hours a week at Danielle's bank just to be able to afford to live in a crime-ridden building in one of the worst sections of the city.

"She's already been mugged twice in the elevator but she's just happy to have a home," Katie finished.

"I see your point," Max conceded. "Ours is a fucked up society that rewards people like me disproportionately more than others. I've long felt that teachers, in particular, should be paid the same kind of salaries major league ballplayers earn. However, I am hardly the person to bring this up to. I suggest writing our Congressman."

"And how dare you criticize Danielle's spending habits!" Katie went on. "Fourteen-*thousand* for a television? An original Gauguin in the dining room? First-edition autographed books by Charles Dickens?"

"Hey, you make fun of her also. In fact, have you ever jumped down her throat because of all the money she spends?"

Katie had to admit she never did.

"Aha! So as long as you're having sex with a person she can thumb her nose at the world's poor as much as she likes, is that what you're telling me? All I have to do now is convince you to go straight and then seduce you so I can get you off my back. But did you know that the only time Danielle makes a charitable contribution is when she buys a new pair of shoes?"

"No, I didn't—"

"And that when I asked her recently if she was gonna start volunteering with you at the soup kitchens she made some wisecrack about being afraid the bums will steal her Gucci purse?"

"Well, fine," Katie said. "I'll talk to her about that but in the meantime I want you to try to understand what is upsetting me. So many people in this world can't get what is needed to survive and here you are in a sky mansion filled with expensive baubles, none of which a normal person like myself can afford."

Max pointed to a spot just over her right shoulder.

"What?" Katie asked, twisting her head to look in the direction indicated.

"The lamp. On the table next to the easy chair over there. Picked it up for twenty bucks at K-Mart in the Bronx. Surely you can swing that."

Katie made a snide comment about being surprised that Max set foot in such a low end store.

"Look," Max replied, sighing, "I'll admit I've bought a lot of expensive things, okay? The paintings, the books, this apartment, the Ferrari in the garage downstairs (Jesus, you haven't seen that yet; something else for you to have a heart attack about.) And maybe I can ease up on the Danielle jokes but you, my dear, are in no position to judge me."

"Oh, I think I am," Katie insisted.

"No, you're not," Max shot back. "because, as you are so fond of pointing out—endlessly, I might add—you are poor."

"And that's relevant because…"

"Because you're in no position to show me that you would do things differently. If you were rich like me but lived frugally, in a modest home, with no fourteen-thousand dollar television sets, no Gauguin paintings and no maid service then you can cast aspersions. If you were rich like me but spent most of your fortune on helping the homeless or trying to cure the stigma of bedwetting, leaving only enough for yourself to live on then you can cast aspersions. However, you're not rich like me. You're a hard-working young lady who has trouble making ends meet. And because you think that elevates you to some higher plane of morality naturally you feel as though you can step into my home sounding like a disciple of Karl Marx, accusing me of everything from wasting money to the Kennedy assassination."

Katie opened her mouth to interrupt but Max forged on.

"But how do you know," he continued, "what kind of lifestyle you yourself would lead if you possessed my wealth? Would you really be as charitable as you are now? Would you really pass up owning your own Gauguin and would you really not spend as much money as Danielle does on clothes? And how many weekends would you spend in the soup kitchens if you had a house in the Hamptons?"

He rose from the couch, deciding that he no longer cared about letting Danielle see a picture of perfect harmony when she came out of her office. He looked down at Katie. "Look, I'll acknowledge that you're a good person, and that your heart is in the right place but your sanctimoniousness is beginning to bore me," he said, "so I will end by saying this and then bid you good night: I did not steal this luxury apartment, nor did I steal my Gauguin or the Ferrari or anything else. Though it may offend your sensibilities I have earned every ostentatious display of wealth that you see here because people like you fell in love with my lesbian pope and bought my first book by the millions. And unless you can prove to me that you would behave differently under similar circumstances you have no right trying to make me feel bad. Enjoy the remainder of your evening."

CHAPTER 34

❀

She has a lot of moxie, Max considered, thinking of Katie as he made himself comfortable in his bedroom. He was surprised to find that he had rather enjoyed their interaction. Katie may be on a high horse of colossal proportions but her attacks on him were harmless, hardly worth thinking about. In fact, he had delighted in their repartee. He could never have engaged in anything like that with Danielle without his girlfriend breaking down into tears and him ending up feeling rotten. Katie, on the other hand, had some balls despite being a Nebraskan, not to mention a quick wit, tough skin and a smart mouth. She may have been a little on the maddening side with her "I'm-better-than-you-because-I'm-poor" shtick but she had demonstrated enough chutzpah today to have earned the highest honor in Max's mind: in his estimation she was a New Yorker.

Danielle, on the other hand, was not a New Yorker. Not yet, Max mused. She was still a mere Arizonan only pretending to be a New Yorker; like a kid dressing up in her mommy's clothes (if mommy happened to be Carrie Bradshaw from *Sex and the City*.) And though Danielle had demonstrated some moxie of her own by going behind his back and convincing Katie to come stay with them it was the type of moxie that couldn't go unpunished.

When she discovered him in the bedroom after her phone call ended, reading the Hornby novel in the easy chair by the bay window overlooking Central Park, he was amused to see her approach him warily; so he put a scowl on his face to make like he was going to tear her a new asshole.

"You're pissed," Danielle began. "You're, like, really, really, pissed, aren't you?"

Max said nothing, just stared at her like Dirty Harry about to waste some punk.

"Fuck, I knew it," she said her voice full of worry. "God, Max, I'm sorry but what was I supposed to do? I knew it might piss you off but I thought maybe you'd see my point of view. Can you?"

He still said nothing.

"Sweetie, say something, please! I know I fucked up; I know we should have talked about it more. I'm sorry, okay? Please say it's okay."

Max saw that her eyes were beginning to water.

"I dunno, Danielle," he said, shaking his head.

"Come on, please!"

"This just isn't good, Danielle. You really disappointed me not, to mention gave me reason to doubt your dedication to our relationship."

She sniffled. Max went on.

"How do you propose I forgive you?" he asked, with mock derision.

Another sniffle.

"I don't know," Danielle said meekly. "Name it, I don't care, I'll do it. But if you could just be nice to her I'll think you're a god. She's going through a really scary time and I brought her here so she could feel safe. I want her to be able to sleep peacefully at night and I want her to feel as if this one apartment is not part of the fucked up world outside where people lose their jobs *and* their homes at the drop of a hat. I don't know how else to help her but I can't just stand back and not help her."

Max's eyes widened. For the first time he was aware of the depths of Danielle's feelings for Katie. Sure, Danielle had told him only a couple of days ago that she cared for Katie strongly but Max hadn't been sure how much stock to put into it (she also counted the personal shopper at Bloomingdale's among her closest friends, after all.) He had always imagined that when it came to the two women Katie was the one who believed she had a significant other and Danielle was the one who believed she had a pet. Apparently he was wrong.

"Okay, sweetie," he said. "I'll accept your apology but there will be consequences."

Danielle came to him and sat on his lap, relieved. She gave him a kiss. "What consequences?"

"Well you need to be punished. Can't have you getting off scot-free."

"Punished?" Danielle said, raising her eyebrows saucily. "Sounds like fun. I'll get the handcuffs." And she attempted to hop off Max's lap but he restrained her.

"No, no, no," he said, laughing. "When I say 'punished' I mean punished."

"Like how?"

"Like how 'bout you're not allowed to buy shoes for two months?"

She pouted. "Two months! But that's insane! I'll-I'll need to attend some kind of support group to make it that long."

"The sad part is you're probably right," Max retorted. "But the shoe embargo is only one part of your punishment. There will also be no Mayzie Witherspoon brunches until after the new year."

"But that means missing her pre-Thanksgiving 'Bruncheon' at the Mayflower Club!" Danielle whined. "And she told me that this year Karl Lagerfeld was going to be there."

"And yet I'm unmoved," Max said.

"But Max…"

"You have to learn a lesson, Danielle. And besides, who's more important, me or Mayzie Witherspoon?"

"It's more like who's more important, you or Karl Lagerfeld."

"I feel myself getting angry again," he said, pushing her rudely off his lap.

"Okay, okay…fine! No brunches till next year." Danielle regained her former position sitting on his legs. "Is that all?"

"Hardly. Victoria's Secret," he said.

"What about it?"

"Every week for the next two months I expect you to come home with something really naughty from Victoria's Secret and then be prepared to be ravaged that night."

Danielle smiled. "Gladly," she replied. "At least I get to do *some* shopping."

Max sighed and pinched the bridge of his nose with his fingertips. "Jesus, Danielle," he practically moaned. "Why'd you have to pull this stunt, huh? I mean, I know this isn't a crisis on par with Rwandan genocide or school shootings but you've put both me and Katie in awkward positions."

"I know."

"And not the good kind of awkward positions, either. Like the ones you find in the *Kama Sutra*."

"I know. I'm sorry." Danielle gave him a kiss. "Now can I get the handcuffs?"

"And some aspirin. Please."

❦   ❦   ❦

"Oh, my God!"

Katie was on the bed in her bedroom and that was her second rapturous use of God's name in vain in just under a minute. However, Danielle's tongue was not between her legs doing a dance on her clitoris, nor had Katie just bitten into a bite of Ben and Jerry's Cherry Garcia. She was simply lying on the bed but in this case it was enough to send her over cloud nine because it was without doubt the most comfortable mattress she'd ever laid on.

"Fuck! This is good!" she uttered, stretching her frame out as if she were just waking from a long slumber. Suddenly, she was feeling more kindly towards Max and his riches for if this was what money could buy then how on earth can she fault him for it?

After Max had left her in the living room a couple of hours earlier Katie had remained watching *Everyone Says I Love You* until Danielle's phone call with Margot ended.

"Are you sure this is a good idea?" Katie queried Danielle when the latter came out of her office.

"Why?" Danielle had asked. "Did Max say something?"

Katie decided to lie. "No! Not at all. He's been a perfect gentleman and we had an interesting conversation about economic diversity. It's just that I've read what a private person he is. I feel like I'm intruding. It would really be no bother for me to stay with Moira. She said she'd put me up."

Danielle had given an emphatic shake of her head and Katie laughed.

"What's wrong? Jealous?"

"Of Moira?" Danielle had asked, truly flabbergasted. She couldn't help laughing herself. "Please! She looks like Drew Carey, only more masculine." Then Danielle took hold of Katie's hand. "It's just that I want to be the one taking care of you, is all," she insisted. "As the woman who loves you it's my responsibility, not Moira's."

The idea entered Katie's head then that if Danielle had simply said those words last night there would have been no need for any trickery involving oral sex because Katie would have said yes to anything.

"But I think Max is upset about it," Danielle had added. "Don't get me wrong, he's not a bad person but I kind of went behind his back to get you here. We hadn't exactly agreed on it yet."

No kidding, Katie had thought. She felt like telling Danielle that when a man of Max Bland's stature makes a special trip to the less than magnificent digs of Homeward Bound to visit his girlfriend's lesbian lover it's pretty clear he doesn't agree on something. Instead Katie asked Danielle just how upset she thought Max was, to which Danielle shrugged and said, "Don't know...hopefully not too much. He's a pretty mellow guy. God, if I were a different type of woman I'd be able to get away with anything I wanted."

"But you love him too much to treat him like that," Katie had suggested.

"I do, I really do. He's amazing and he's really good to me." She looked over at Katie. "This kind of talk isn't bothering you, is it?"

"No. You already told *me* you loved me tonight so I'm happy."

"Good because unless he kicks me out I think I should spend the night with him. Is that okay?"

"Absolutely okay," Katie had answered. "You'd probably just be disappointed if you slummed with me anyway. It's been a really interesting day to say the least and I'm so bushed all I want to do is pass out."

So Danielle had gone off to face the music and Katie finished watching the movie alone. After figuring out which button on the so-complicated-it-must-have-been-designed-by-NASA remote control actually turned the TV off she herself retired to her room.

When her initial delight with the bed wore off Katie lay there feeling drowsy and musing at this odd turn her life had taken. Quite unbidden, a memory of two or three years ago popped into her head. It was back when she was dating Nina. The two of them were out at a restaurant and Nina, a clinical therapist, was asking one of those weird questions she liked to ask, the kind meant to provide clues to your personality, such as, "What kind of tree are you?" and "If you found out you only had an hour to live what would you do?" This time the question she put to Katie was "If you could have dinner with any famous person you want who would you choose and what would you talk about?"

Katie's first response, "Anne Heche, and I'd ask her if she's single," was intended as a joke but it didn't go over very well, so Katie thought for a moment and then said, "Max Bland, the writer. I'd ask him how the hell he, a man, created such a believable and complex female character and then I'd want to know what gave him the idea for a lesbian pope. Then I'd ask him what it was that made him so antagonistic towards Christianity in the first place and does he really feel indifferent about the furor he caused among the religious right like he says in his interviews. Oh, and I'd also like to know why he thinks most male writers can't create female characters in novels that are little more than one-dimensional paper dolls."

Recalling all this now Katie frowned, feeling a bit ashamed. Before Danielle's thirtieth birthday party the idea of sitting down and talking to the great Max Bland was something Katie used to daydream about. Then, when such a meeting actually happened at the party she was too awestruck to remember all the clever questions she had told Nina she wanted to ask him. Not only that but the fact that she was dating his girlfriend seemed to naturally focus the conversation in other directions. But what about today? Today she had spent a considerable amount of time in his company—in his home, no less—and instead of engaging the writer in a smart discussion about his book and about literature in general she had attacked him like a rabid pit bull.

"Fuck," Katie said with a sigh, suddenly remorseful. Of course, she still felt she was in the right. It was reprehensible how the wealthy chose to spend their money when there were so many people who needed to subsist on handouts and charity. Of course, Max had had a point too, she conceded, about her not knowing how she would live should she ever find herself in possession of a fortune. *Would I pass up owning a Gauguin?* she asked herself now. *Or a place like this?* In any case, Katie was feeling that irregardless of how much this grand apartment offended her it was not her place to proselytize the great Max Bland, whom she barely knew, and if she wasn't certain that he was now in his bedroom making up with Danielle she'd knock on his door and apologize.

That was the last thought she had before succumbing to the mattress and drifting off into a dreamless sleep still fully dressed.

CHAPTER 35

❀

On a Wednesday morning three weeks later Katie had this phone conversation with Charmaine, the woman who formerly was her second in command at Homeward Bound:

"Two interviews this morning," Katie was telling her, "and there were, like, twenty other candidates waiting their turn at each place."

"Where'd you go?" Charmaine asked.

"The Village Help Center and St. Vincent de Paul."

"Well, we just missed each other because I interviewed at the Help Center yesterday and there were also a lot of other people there."

"Fuck." Katie cursed.

"Girl, there is just nothing out there. I can't remember it ever being this bad. Do you know I started sending out résumés the day *after* you told us Homeward Bound was closing and I've only been offered three interviews? Three! And at each place they tell me the same thing: there's been a lot of interest in the job and they'll get back to me when they've made a decision."

Katie could empathize; her luck hadn't been much better. The stock market crash that brought about the demise of the Warren Williams Foundation also forced other non-profits to either shut their doors or tighten their belts by scaling back their workforces. The result was a glut of unemployed people with much the same skills and experience as herself vying for the few open positions available in the industry. Katie, because of her Masters degree from Columbia and her managerial background, had gotten a few more interviews than Charmaine but also had yet to see anything pan out.

"Are you getting along alright?" Katie inquired.

"I'd be better if I had a job, I won't lie to you. But at least Cliff is still working. We've had to cut back some and my kids may feel a little cheated in a few months when Christmas comes but so far we're still on our feet. And you?"

Let's see, Katie thought about saying, *you know that writer I used to always talk about? Well, I'm living with him because it turns out he and I share the same girlfriend. His apartment is so big that a phone call from my bedroom to his is considered long distance and if he sold all the masterpieces he owns he'd be able to feed Zimbabwe.* Instead, she told Charmaine she was living with that woman she's been dating.

"Danielle?" Charmaine asked. "The one from ARCL, our favorite client?"

"Yep."

"Well, I could tell she makes good money. I bet her place is nice."

"You have no idea," Katie answered. "Listen, honey, I'll be thinking of you and if I hear of any good openings I'll give you a call."

Charmaine made the same promise and the two women said goodbye.

Looking at her day planner Katie sighed. It was only Wednesday but already she was done with interviews for the week; she had nothing scheduled until next Tuesday, six days from now.

"Fuck and double fuck!" she swore softly. Charmaine was right, there was nothing out there and competition was fierce. It was so bad, in fact, that yesterday she had done the unthinkable: started answering ads for job openings in New Jersey.

After changing out of her business suit into a pair of jeans and a Columbia t-shirt Katie went to kitchen to fix herself some lunch and was startled to see Max rummaging in the fridge.

"You gave me a fright!" she said, laughing. "I didn't know anyone else was here."

"Sorry about that," Max said, withdrawing an apple from the appliance and shutting the door.

"You're home early."

"Yeah, I am," he replied listlessly. "It was one of those days, you know? Just wasn't feeling it. I got to my office, wrote about a hundred words and got stuck. So then I thought I'd take a walk to clear my head and come up with ideas because that usually works. I ended up walking all the way down to Union Square with zilch to show for it, so I gave up, caught a cab and came here. How's your day going?"

Katie shrugged.

"Two more interviews, two more we'll call yous."

"I know what that's like. There's crap in the fridge, by the way, in case you were here for lunch. I'll send Magda shopping tomorrow," he said, referring to the maid. "In the meantime, how 'bout we order a pizza?"

"So not on my diet," Katie said.

"Alright, how 'bout I order a pizza and you smell the box?"

"Or how about I make us some omelets? I noticed eggs in there last night."

It didn't sound as good as pizza but Max told her to have at it anyway.

Over the past three weeks Max and Katie had gotten over their rough start as housemates and settled into a much more amicable association, something akin to U.S.-Soviet relations near the end of the Cold War. By the terms of an unspoken détente Katie did not attack Max on his wealth or on how he spent his money, and Max did not make fun of homeless people or further threaten to hire them as human Legos. Sure, they slipped up every now and again but on the whole life on the sixtieth floor was peaceful. Moreover, there was Danielle to consider. Neither Max nor Katie wanted her in the middle of a skirmish between themselves so that was further inducement to keep things civil.

As far as them sharing her affections went while living under the same roof, it was remarkably easy. Max still enjoyed having time to himself so if Danielle came home from work with a taste for Katie he simply shrugged and happily occupied himself in other ways. Similarly, since Katie still volunteered at soup kitchens and shelters throughout the five boroughs of New York as well as being preoccupied with finding a new job it bothered her not one whit when Danielle had a hankering for Max. Every now and then the three of them would go out dining together or to see a movie but usually Danielle would do such things with one or the other and that would signal whom she was planning on having sex with later. On the nights they all stayed home, however, Max and Katie learned that the signal was a bit more subtle: Danielle would sleep with whomever she asked to suggest something to have delivered for dinner ("Katie, who should we order from, sweetie?"; or "Max, Chinese or Indian?")

🍁   🍁   🍁

"I guess I could start waitressing," Katie said, serving Max a cheese omelet and then sitting beside him at the small butcher block table in the kitchen. "It got me through college."

"No!" Max ejaculated, surprising Katie. "What are you, crazy?" he added.

"But, fuck, this is so maddening, Max. I've haven't earned a proper salary in weeks, my unemployment check is a joke, and yet I've been eating your food and using your electricity, contributing nothing to the household."

"Okay, that's all stupid stuff to worry about, alright?" he replied around a mouthful of omelet. "Whaddya think, you're creating a hardship for us because you eat a few eggs outta the fridge and plug your hairdryer into a socket? Gimme a break."

"But almost every night for dinner we order in take-out..." Katie reminded him. "And you guys pay for it all."

"Hardly worth talking about," Max assured her. "Twenty, thirty bucks a night, not even that sometimes? I'm sure my accountant's losing sleep."

Katie was shaking her head. "I was raised to earn my keep, Max; now I feel like such a fucking freeloader."

"Yeah, but at least you're freeloading off of people who can afford it. I mean, look...if Danielle and I were normal middle-class folks and we couldn't pay our rent due to our ConEd bill being ten bucks higher because of you then we'd have a problem. Not only would I tell you to start waitressing but I'd demand you bring home free food every night."

Katie gave him a quick smile. "I appreciate you treating this so casually," she said, "but I'm afraid it's not making me feel any better. Fuck, I can't even enjoy this omelet because I feel guilty about eating your eggs."

"Well, technically I don't own the eggs," Max told her.

"I don't understand," Katie said.

"What I mean is, I don't pay the food and utility bills here, Danielle does. When she moved in with me she volunteered to take on those expenses because otherwise she'd be living here free and clear. I guess she didn't wanna feel like a freeloader either. You see, this place is paid for in full. There's no mortgage payment I need her to fork over half of or anything like that. All I pay for this apartment are the luxury taxes, the insurance and the building association fees. When it comes to eggs, however, and anything else edible in the kitchen, Danielle takes care of that. But fuck her, she can afford a few more dollars for food and electricity. She makes over a hundred grand a year, Katie, and whatever doesn't go to Uncle Sam is hers to do with as she pleases and trust me, groceries and power don't eat up a lot of it. That's how come she can buy shoes that cost six-hundred bucks and expensive glass dildos from Japan."

"Which she still hasn't shared with me, by the way," Katie huffed.

Max laughed. "You can bring it up during our next tenants meeting. Anyway, the point I was trying to make is don't feel you have to take any crappy job you can find just because you think you're costing us money. I got nothing against waitresses but you're too good to be a waitress."

"Thank you," Katie said.

Max got a faraway look in his eyes, one of recollection.

"You know, I can remember being out of work myself—and it wasn't too long ago, either," he said. "It wasn't an easy time even back then but I guess now it's worse what with the job market the way it is."

"Trust me, you have no idea." Katie bit down hard on her forkful of omelet.

"No, you're wrong there. I know what it's like to be unemployed and frightened, hoping to find the perfect job. Excuse me." Max got up to answer the ringing phone. Just before picking up the receiver on the other side of the kitchen he said, "You may be a sanctimonious bitch but when you leave here I'd rather you left happy. Hello? Hey, babe...I give up, where?...What? Why?...Well...Uh-huh...Uh-huh...gimme the room number...Okay, sit tight and we'll be right there...Love you too. Bye."

Max hung up.

"I know that was Danielle," Katie said, getting up from the table. "What's wrong?"

"Maybe they'll have an answer to that question by the time we get there," Max replied. "Our girlfriend is in the hospital."

CHAPTER 36

Arriving at Lenox Hill hospital Max and Katie were told by the spinster manning the information desk that they'd find Danielle in a room on the seventh floor. Finally locating it they were about to hurry in when suddenly Katie stopped. She held Max's arm.

"Maybe I should go in first alone," she suggested.

Max looked at her as if she were crazy. "Why should you get to go in first? And alone? She's known me longer; if she sees anyone's face first it should be mine."

"No," Katie insisted.

"Why not?"

"Because she's a woman, Max. And chances are she's not looking her best right now. The last thing she'll want is the man she loves seeing her under less than desirable circumstances."

"Yeah, but what makes you think she won't be equally self-conscious with you? You're the woman she loves."

Katie shook her head.

"Max, women are used to seeing one another when we're not at our best. When you men aren't around we just let ourselves go. We don't put on makeup, we don't do our hair, we sit with our legs apart and we belch."

Max opened his mouth to protest but Katie cut him off.

"Surely the man who showed such an amazing understanding of the female nature to have created Pope Anne will get where I'm coming from, right?"

Max made a face, his teeth hurting from the saccharine sweetness Katie was trying to con him with.

"Fine," he relented with an irritated sigh. "Go in first and get Tyra Banks all dolled up. Heaven forbid I see her looking peaked."

"Thank you," Katie said opening the door to Danielle's room just wide enough to slip inside and then shutting it quickly in Max's face.

No sooner was Max abandoned when a nurse who had been standing nearby counting pills approached him.

"Excuse me," she began, "but I couldn't help overhearing what your lady friend said just a moment ago about Pope Anne. Are you Max Bland?"

God-fucking-dammit, Max swore inwardly. Over the years he had managed to train Danielle to never make references to him having had anything to do with *The Remarkable Reign of Pope Anne I* while in public and now it looked like he'd have to do the same with Katie. He thought about J.D. Salinger again and wondered if he'd like a neighbor. Giving the nurse a forced smile he said, "Yes, I am."

"Wow," the nurse gushed. "I'm a big fan of your book. I mean it, I really love your book. You're one of my favorite writers, you and Jackie Collins."

Oh good God! Max thought. Now his name was being used in the same sentence as Jackie Collins's? This was getting worse.

"Thank you so much for saying so," he said. "I'm glad you enjoy my work but if you don't mind I—"

"Hey, Estelle!" his new friend suddenly called out towards the nurse's station a few yards away, apparently forgetting that one is supposed to be quiet in a hospital. "C'mere!"

"There's really no need for Estelle to—" Max began, but before he knew it he was shaking hands with a plump fifty-ish woman also professing to be a devout member of his fan club.

"Oooh! You know who we should introduce him to?" Estelle asked the first nurse. "Mrs. Butterfass in 719."

"Oooh, yes! Mrs. Butterfass," agreed the first nurse.

Estelle turned to Max. "She's another big fan of yours, doll. She brought two of your novels to read during her stay here. Poor thing…she having gallbladder surgery."

"I'm terribly sorry to hear that," Max said, already trying to quickly think up a good enough excuse that would get him out of visiting Mrs. Butterfass and her malfunctioning gallbladder.

"Just yesterday," Estelle continued, "her and I spent a considerable amount of time discussing all your books."

"How delightful."

"I must say, however, that we were both somewhat disappointed with your last one."

Max blinked.

"Jesus, what is with you people and my last book?" he demanded, recalling the receptionist at Homeward Bound. "It was nominated for a Pulitzer!"

"Ah, but did it win?" Estelle asked sympathetically.

"Okay, that's enough for now," Max said, shaking both their hands. "If you ladies will excuse me I'm here to visit someone." And in a flash he disappeared into Danielle's room not really giving a damn how far from her best she looked.

❦ ❦ ❦

The diagnosis was appendicitis. Max and Katie each let out sighs of relief when the doctor informed them of this. It may have still been considered major surgery but both of them had horrible fears of more sinister things in their heads. Only Danielle had the audacity to complain. She had been hoping that the shooting pains and vomiting which forced Margot to drive her to the emergency room could be remedied without surgery. Now she'd have a scar and be forced to rethink every midriff-baring outfit she owned.

The operation took place first thing the next morning and when Danielle awoke both her boyfriend and girlfriend were there to welcome her back to consciousness.

"Your parents are on a 3 p.m. flight," Max said. "I mean, their only daughter was having surgery so I had to call them. I've sent a car to pick them up and bring them here."

"Are they staying with us?" Danielle managed to croak.

"Yeah," Max answered, and he couldn't help rolling his eyes at the thought, "but look...Katie and I talked about it last night. Now, I dunno if you ever plan on explaining to them what you two got going on but for now, when they get here, we're just gonna explain that Katie is a friend of yours who's staying with us while her apartment is being fumigated."

"I thought we agreed that my place was being painted," Katie pointed out.

"Whatever."

"Well, I think it's important we're in sync, don't you?"

"Okay, it's not like we're Iraqis trying to smuggle uranium through customs at JFK," Max told her.

"Anyway," Katie said to Danielle, "try not to throw yourself at me while they're here."

Danielle was released two days later and with her mother at the apartment there really wasn't much for Max or Katie to do. In fact, Max was even demoted to sleeping in one of the guest bedrooms because Arlene Edwards wanted to spend each night of her stay by her daughter's side. Of course, concern for her daughter didn't entirely prevent her from trying to get some inside information from Max that she can take back to Fountain Hills to improve her standing with the book club.

"Oh, come on, Max..." she prodded gently one afternoon when she had him cornered in the kitchen, "can't I have a little taste of what your next book is about? Just a *teensy* taste? It would mean so much to our club and give us something to look forward to."

"Okay, you really wanna know what it's about?" Max asked, and then he cast a quick glance over each shoulder, pretending to be on the lookout for eavesdroppers.

"Yes, indeed," Arlene said eagerly, also taking a look around to make sure they were alone. This was a coup she wanted to share with no one.

"Fine, I'll tell you. Now, understand that I'm only doing this because of my deep respect for you."

"Max, I am truly honored," Arlene assured him solemnly.

"Okay, here it is: my new book is a kinda fantasy story, you see. It's about a princess, okay?"

"A princess. Got it."

"And this princess lives in a castle with her stepmother, the evil queen."

"Evil queen. Got it."

"And one day the evil queen tries to have the princess killed..."

"Oooh!"

"But the princess escapes into the forest and ends up hiding out with these seven midgets."

"I think they like to be called 'little people' now, Max."

"Whatever. Anyway, things go happily along for awhile until the evil queen finds the princess and manages to poison her. The rest of the book after that is basically a suspense story concerning whether or not the seven pipsqueaks can find the one man whose kiss can reawaken the princess from her sleep of death."

Arlene, frowning, took a few moments to digest all this. Suddenly, she said: "Wow! That's amazing! Simply amazing!" She was looking up at Max with awe.

"So, basically, it's an allegory of the dynamics of modern parent/child relationships while at the same being an examination of our need for rescuing by the restorative powers of love."

"Precisely," Max said.

"How creative and yet, how simple, but in a comforting way, you know? Like soup. But what do the seven little men represent?"

"Well, as a group they symbolize the smallness of mankind but individually they represent different things, really. One represents happiness, for example, another represents stupidity, one signifies anger or grumpiness, and yet another one represents sneezing."

"Sneezing?"

"The violent expulsion of bad things from our bodies," Max explained. "More allegory."

"Of course! Sneezing! How very clever of you. I really admire your skills, Max. I just know our little book club will be so surprised when I tell them all this."

"I guarantee it," Max said.

🍁   🍁   🍁

One evening, when they were both more or less cut off from Danielle because her mother insisted her daughter get some more rest, Katie invited Max into her room to watch television. During a commercial break Max said: "I hope this whole thing about you just being a friend isn't bothering you. I actually feel bad about it."

"Don't," Katie replied. "Under the circumstances I understand."

"I never even thought about Danielle telling her folks about you and her. I wonder if they even know she's bi."

"They don't," Katie answered. "She says she's pretty sure her father would be okay with it but her mother? No way."

"That sucks."

"Yeah." Katie shrugged. "But that's how it is in my world, Max. There's a lot of secrets. *My* parents know I'm gay but there are a lot of women out there still stuck in the closet." She told him about Mary, the former fuck buddy who spent most of her life living a lie at home with a husband and two kids.

"It seems so strange, though," Max said pensively. "I mean, when I was a kid back in the seventies being gay was something you hid otherwise you'd get the shit kicked out of you, especially in the Bronx; being called a fag was one of the biggest insults you could hit a person with. But today it's so different. I mean, this is the era of *Will and Grace* and *Queer Eye*; nowadays it's hip to be gay; you almost can't be cool unless you're gay, am I right?"

"Only to a degree. What you don't understand is that a lot of the same people who love, let's say, Jack on *Will and Grace*, will throw a hissy fit the day they see someone in their own family act like him. For a lot of people, Max, it's okay to *know* a gay person, it's just not okay to be *related* to one. It implies a defect in the family's genetics."

Max tried to imagine how his father—ex-Marine, retired city detective—would respond if Max told him he was gay then decided to do it just for the fun of seeing the old guy turn purple and lose the faculty of speech. Maybe over Thanksgiving. Right now, though, he asked Katie how she came out to her parents.

"Very blatantly," she said with a bit of a laugh. "I brought my girlfriend home with me to Nebraska for spring break during my sophomore year and I said to my parents 'This is my girlfriend Aisha. We're a couple and we'd like to be welcomed into your home as a couple. If that's not going to happen then we will find somewhere else to spend spring break and in the future you can count on me returning home to visit you less and less.'"

"Brilliant!" Max lauded. "Either they had to accept you for who you are or risk losing you entirely."

"Bingo."

"But what if they had chosen option B?"

"It would have been devastating," Katie answered truthfully. "And I don't think that even now I would've gotten over it. But I had to take the chance."

"And did this Aisha do the same with her folks?"

Katie shook her head.

"Aisha was black and if you think white gays have trouble coming out to their families it's even harder for blacks. Of all the women I've dated, Max, I've only met two sets of parents."

"Son of a bitch…"

She shrugged again. "I know. It's not the ideal situation but I think it would be unfair of me to force my girlfriends to come out to their families when they're not ready. So sometimes I have to ask myself 'What's more important: gay pride, or having love in my life?' I've always chosen love."

"Bravo. Love should win out," Max said. "But I still wish everything here was on the up and up."

Katie nodded. "Well, I'm not holding my breath," she said.

Max and Katie then fell silent, watching the *Are You Being Served?* rerun playing on BBCAmerica. Finally, Katie looked over at her companion and, thinking about that dinner with Nina, began tentatively with: "Look, Max…is it alright if I ask you some questions about *Pope Anne?*"

"Sure," he answered, surprisingly nonchalant.

"Really? Because Danielle told me that was a taboo subject."

He shrugged.

"You caught me in a good mood. Shoot."

"Seriously?"

"Yeah."

"You're really going to let me ask you about the book?"

"I'm beginning to lose my good mood…"

"Okay, okay," said Katie apologetically. "Um…well, first of all I'd like to know how it is that you, a man, was able to create such a great female character."

"I'm a good listener," Max said. "One immutable fact about the female sex is that you all like to talk. Yet at the same time you pick who you tell certain things to. To some people you'll only talk about the weather, to other folks you'll get more intimate. But there's always been something about me in particular that makes women wanna tell me everything. Whether it's a gift or a curse I can't decide. I mean, I've had women at bus stops pour out their life stories to me without even introducing themselves. I've had women tell me personal stuff about their sex lives, their bad marriages, their bank accounts, their periods, you name it, all within a few minutes of shaking my hand at a party."

This struck a chord with Katie and she remembered the first night she met Max, at Danielle's party, and how she couldn't seem to stop herself from relating to him very intimate and private details about her past romances.

Max went on: "I remember once, a lady at some party or another told me that I just look like the kind of person anyone can trust and then proceeded to tell me she was having an affair. I guess she was right because all my life women have used me like I'm a priest in a confessional. Men too, for that matter, but men are stupid; all they wanna talk about are football and big tits. Gets boring after a while. Women are much more interesting so I pay attention more. Classmates, girlfriends, co-workers, wives of friends, strangers…they've all opened themselves up to me. Anyway, like I said, I listen real good and when a man has had women of all ages opening up to him his entire life he kinda gains an understanding of what makes your sex tick."

"So when you created Anne," Katie said, "you just drew upon the lessons you learned from listening to women."

"Precisely. Anne was an amalgamation."

"And what was it that set you off against the Church?" Katie then asked and for the next hour she finally got to experience the thrill of learning more about her favorite book, straight from the author who wrote it. And during it all she was not looking at him as a man whose wealth offended her but as an artist whose skill she admired.

CHAPTER 37

❊

After a week the Edwardses flew back to Arizona. Max drove them to the airport himself in order to be sure, in his words, "they get on the fucking plane." A week of playing host to them was enough what with Arlene's incessant kowtowing to Max and Danielle's father's incessant farting. By then some of Danielle's strength had returned and she was tired of being babied by her mother anyway and even more tired of being bedridden, but during a follow-up examination the day after her parents left her doctor recommended two weeks more of staying home after which she *may* give Danielle permission to return to work on a part-time basis, depending on the results of her next follow-up visit in ten days. As far as physical activity—including sex—went, the doctor insisted Danielle wait until six weeks after the date of the operation.

Normally, six weeks without sex would have made Danielle insane and would have represented the kind of drought she formerly had to endure only during those times in the past when she was between lovers. But recovering from major surgery thankfully eliminated any sexual desire from her system; even watching Max undress each night in their bedroom did nothing for her because usually she was so doped up on prescription meds she could barely see straight. And she certainly didn't feel sexy. She felt achy; she felt nauseous; she felt dizzy. And because she'd been confined to bed, she felt fat. In short, from the standpoint of doing without sex, the six weeks was a breeze for her; it may as well have been six days.

However, six weeks without sex was just the type of thing to make both Max and Katie insane and sure enough it did because for the forty-five or so days Danielle was convalescing they felt perfectly fine and the absence of hardcore carnal activity with their mutual girlfriend was maddening. It affected their sleep, their appetites, their moods. For example, upon watching the Yankees lose an important late season game against a division rival Max spat at the television and then stepped out onto the balcony and hurled the remote across Fifth Avenue into Central Park. And upon finding absolutely no jobs in the want ads one day that she could apply for Katie screamed in frustration, tore the entire newspaper to shreds, placed the remains in her bedroom's fireplace and gleefully watched them burn. No amount of masturbating could compensate for this forced hiatus, either; by the time the six weeks were done both Max and Katie were pleasuring themselves four times a week which did hardly anything to curb their cravings for Danielle.

Finally, it ended. In September, Danielle's doctor declared her fully healed and able to return to her normal activities—sexual or otherwise. On the morning when Danielle left for ARCL for her first full day of work in nearly two months Max looked out his bedroom window at Central Park and sighed. The last time he had had sex with his girlfriend the thousands of trees in the park bore boughs full of healthy green summer leaves. Now all he saw were the yellows, oranges, browns and reds of branches dressed for autumn.

🍁 🍁 🍁

In the living room a few minutes later Katie accosted him on her way back to her bedroom from the kitchen.

"Did you see Danielle this morning before she left?" she inquired.

Max nodded. "Yeah, I got up with her," he said, failing to mention that the reason he got up with her was because he was hoping she'd fancy a morning quickie. But Danielle was so excited about "being released from prison," as she put it, that she couldn't stay still long enough for him to get his hands on her. In record time she had gotten herself washed, dressed and coiffed, kissed him goodbye distractedly and vanished.

"How did she seem?" Katie asked. "Is she feeling okay? Does she feel like her old self? Did she look alright?"

"Lemme guess," Max said, dropping down heavily into an armchair, "you're just as horny as I am."

Katie laughed nervously. "What? No. Why do you say that? I'm just worried about Danielle, is all."

"Please," he chided. "You're so obviously desperate for sex that you're checking me out and wondering if it would really be so bad to make it with a guy."

"I am not!"

"Said the blonde, gazing at his crotch."

"Okay, fine...I'm horny as hell," Katie admitted, dropping into an armchair next to Max's. "I'm so horny I can barely function but can you blame me?" She turned to him. "This is the twenty-first century, right? Why the hell does it take six weeks to recover from appendix surgery?"

"Beats me."

"Don't they have laser beams and other shit they can use to zap out a fucking appendix in, like, two minutes?"

"You'd think."

"We really ought to complain," Katie continued. "There's got to be someone we can complain too, right? How dare they put my girlfriend out of commission this long."

"*Our* girlfriend," Max corrected. "You haven't convinced her to go total lezbo yet, remember? Anyway, now that Danielle is back on her feet don't get any bright ideas. I'm first in line to get on that ride."

"Says who?" Katie challenged.

"Says me, that's who. This is my house and I've known her longer. It's the only logical thing."

"That's such bullshit! Who was the one staying here every day taking care of her while you were off writing?"

"Yeah, writing books to help pay for what? This house."

"So? The point is I deserve some reward for my efforts and I'll take my payment in the form of one five foot five brunette in my bedroom tonight."

"Go get a hooker," Max advised, "because Danielle's gonna be occupied."

"And you're looking at the occupying force."

"In your dreams, Shaw. Why don't you work off your sexual frustrations by knitting booties for the homeless or something?"

"And why don't you work off yours by driving your Ferrari really, really fast down city streets?"

"Jesus, whatever happened to age before beauty?" Max said.

"Well, what ever happened to ladies first?"

At an impasse, this battle waged for ten more minutes, neither party gaining ground. Finally, Katie said, "Flip a coin?"

Max sneered. "Fuck you. I'm not leaving this up to chance. Fate's already shown me what a fucked up sense of humor it has by letting you move in here. Uh-uh, no way."

"Well, how about a game then?"

Eyeing her suspiciously, Max asked, "What kind of game?"

"Anything."

"Okay, how 'bout who can write the best novel? My entry is *The Remarkable Reign of Pope Anne I*. What's yours?"

"Very funny. But seriously…we'll challenge each other in a game and whoever wins the game wins Danielle tonight."

Max mulled this over, sure it was trap.

"Alright," he said hesitantly, "but let's not make it just one game. You could get lucky at one game. Let's make it a series. Best two outta three and each game is different."

Now Katie mulled, sure it was a trap.

"Fine," she said after a while. "Now all we have to do is decide on the games. How about checkers?"

"No."

"Gin?"

"No."

"Hearts? Ooh, I know…Old Maid?"

"Jesus Christ! Listen…unlike kids in Gopher's Armpit, Nebraska I had an interesting childhood, okay? I didn't spend my evenings with Granny Gumms and Uncle Cletus eating rhubarb pie and playing checkers or gin."

"Fine, you jerk, you suggest something."

"Pinball."

She rolled her eyes.

"Air hockey."

She stuck her finger down her throat and pretended to gag.

"Skelly."

"What?"

"Skelly. It's a game we used to play on the streets up in the Bronx. You play it with bottle caps." And he gave her a quick rundown on how the game was played, telling her that it had similarities to playing marbles. When that was done he said, "I always used Yoo-Hoo caps because it was my favorite drink as a kid. I'd fill them with the wax from melted crayons and my secret weapon: two dimes, to give 'em more punch. Boy, with one of those caps Mikey never knew what hit him; I could blast his caps all the way down the block. One time—"

Katie sighed in exasperation. "You're straying, honey," she said, employing the method she'd seen Danielle use countless times. "How the hell am I supposed to play a game I've never even heard of? And were you and your friends so poor growing up that your parents couldn't afford a proper game? Like Scrabble?"

Max's eyes lit up. He told Katie that he and Danielle used to play Scrabble all the time and that he had a set in his den. "A real nice set, too. Imported from Italy, made of ebony with pewter trim, and sterling silver letter tiles. I hesitate to tell you how many homeless people it could feed. Anyway, we used to play that game and Trivial Pursuit a lot. Then you came along."

"I love Trivial Pursuit!" Katie exclaimed. "This is great. We have two games, now all we need is a third."

"Pinball," Max tried again.

"Wait a minute," Katie said following a moment of deliberation. "Don't you go up to the Bronx a lot to bowl?"

"Once a week," Max replied.

"There's our answer," she told him. "It just so happens I'm a pretty good bowler myself. In fact, me and a few of the other women at Homeward Bound were in a league and I feel very confident in saying that I will kick your ass."

"Gee, surprise, surprise...the redneck from Nebraska bowls. Lemme guess, you couldn't graduate high school unless you were able to pick up a dime store split."

"What have you got against Nebraska, Max?"

"Nothing. It's just a waste of real estate is all. You see, what they oughta do with Nebraska is sell it to Disney, let them make something fun out of it. I feel the same way about Mississippi."

"God, I wish I could tune you out sometimes. So are we settled on the competition? Scrabble, Trivial Pursuit and bowling?"

Max nodded. Looking at his watch he said, "We got about ten hours before Danielle gets back, unless she pops a stitch. Plenty of time." And he left to go get the board games from his den.

❧ ❧ ❧

At the outset Katie recognized the folly of engaging in a Scrabble contest with a man who makes his living using words. He played confidently and demonstrated such an impressive vocabulary that he led the game from the start. Nevertheless, she managed to keep the score close and when she played *hatter* on a double word square for 26 points to pull within 10 points of Max late in the game she was certain she'd have a chance to overtake him, especially since the last two words he had played, *mete* and *ant*, could be taken as signs that he was flagging. Unfortunately, *hatter* was her undoing. It was like hanging a curveball to Babe Ruth, and Max swung for the fences. Using her H he played *qoph* for a triple word score of 64.

"Whoa, whoa, whoa, whoa!" she immediately cried. "What the fuck is that?"

"It's the word I'm playing, you twit. For 64 points no less."

"Fuck you, that's no word!"

"Jesus, the mouth on you. Yes, it is a word."

"What's it mean?"

"It's a letter in the Hebrew alphabet."

"Suddenly you're Jewish? You made that up."

"Why would I make that up?"

"To cheat, obviously."

Max told her to wait right there. He got up, headed towards his den and in a moment came back bearing a huge dictionary which he dropped into Katie's lap forcing an "Ooomph!" to escape her lungs.

"Look it up," he told her while already drawing three more tiles from the bag.

"Fuck!" Katie swore, finding the suspect word on page 1107 of the enormous dictionary. "Fuckety-fuck-fuck!"

Having lost the challenge she had to forfeit a turn. Max used the opportunity to play *qiviut* off his own Q.

"Whoa, whoa, whoa, whoa!" Katie cried again. "What the hell is that?"

"Qiviut," Max told her. "It's a type of wool used to make yarn. In this case, nineteen points worth of yarn."

"Fuck you, I'm challenging," Katie advised him because suddenly, in an eye blink, she was looking at an alarming deficit of 93 points and there was no way *qiviut* was a real word. So it was in a state of mild panic that she once more turned the pages of the dictionary.

"FUCK!" she practically screamed at page 1107 again.

Another challenge lost, another turn lost. Katie tried to put a hex on him, waggling hr fingers at him while squinting her eyes, asking the universe's dark spirits to make him lose his mastery of the English language. Apparently, though, the signals got crossed.

"Aha!" he exclaimed triumphantly after a few moments thought. To her complete dismay she watched him place all seven of his tiles on the board to form *ventricle*, once again using a letter from her *hatter* to construct the word. Not only did it net him 28 points for the word itself but it was a bingo yielding him another 50. Just like that his 10 point lead had stretched to 171 points; he had gone three straight turns and, more importantly, used 15 tiles from the dwindling supply in the bag, eliminating any chance Katie had at making a comeback.

In the best of three competition to determine who got to have sex with Danielle tonight Katie was down 0-1.

🍁 🍁 🍁

Conceding defeat after the *qoph-qiviut-ventricle* debacle Katie went to the nearest bathroom to splash some cold water on her face and regroup before taking Max on at Trivial Pursuit. When she returned to the dining room the game was all set up and Max was calmly sitting at the table. He didn't seem smug, didn't seem arrogant; he just seemed like a guy patiently awaiting his opponent. But there was something about his preternatural serenity that unnerved Katie because it warned her more forcefully than anything else could have that after the drubbing he had administered to her in Scrabble he had her right where he wanted her: needing a victory to stay alive.

Before she knew it, however, Max had a two wedges to none lead on her. It didn't surprise her that a wordsmith like him knew what the Inuit word for "hunter's boat" was (kayak), but it blew her mind when he correctly identified the author of *On Conoids and Spheroids* and *Quadrature of the Parabola* (Archimedes). She, on the other hand, when trying for the Science & Nature wedge, was tripped up on a trick question.

"What color is a polar bear's skin—black, blue or white?" Max read from the card.

"A polar bear, you said? White. Give me a wedge."

"Sorry, the answer is black. Black. No wedge."

"Fuck you! A polar bear is white, you prick! Stop trying to cheat me!"

"A polar bear's *fur* is white, you psycho. The question, however, asked for the color of its *skin*."

Despite her poor start, which she attributed to nerves, Katie finally took command of the game. The two wedges to none deficit was erased and with some propitious rolls of the dice she collected three more in quick succession:

"What reedy plant has a *madake* species that produces flowers only once every 120 years?"

"Bamboo." Green wedge and a "Damn!" from Max.

"What capital city sports a suburb called Montreuil?"

"Paris." Blue wedge and a "Shit!" from Max.

"What nation did the Netherlands win its independence from, in 1648?"

"Spain." Yellow wedge and a "God fucking dammit!" from Max.

After collecting all six wedges she led her opponent by two and began heading to the center of the game board to try for the win. But she had trouble landing in the center by exact count as demanded by the rules; every time she rolled she'd overshoot it and spit curses at the die. Meanwhile, Max got a Wild Card wedge on a question about Jane Goodall and needed only one more to make his own attempt at winning. Fortunately, though, he missed his next question, about an Elton John song and Katie then rolled a five. With a squeal of delight she dramatically hopped her piece into the board's center.

"Okay," Max said, "I get to choose the category."

"Fire away," Katie responded and then stuck her tongue out at him.

Max, recognizing the importance of the situation, spent some time considering.

"Lessee...you're good at History, I don't think you got one wrong there, so, fuck you, that's out; and you did well at People & Places, too, so, fuck you again, that's out. You're also a television junkie like me so I'm not risking giving you anything entertainment-related."

Then he smiled wickedly at her.

"But sports...you suck at sports knowledge. Rather a disappointing cliché if you ask me. It took you, what, five chances to finally get that wedge? You don't know a football from a baseball and you think Yogi Berra's an Italian swami. So Sports & Leisure it is."

"Just get on with it," she hissed.

"Fine." He selected a card from the box and smirked when he looked at the question. "Okay, here is your Sports & Leisure question that no lesbian on Earth could possibly answer because it has nothing to do with the WNBA or Brandi Chastain taking her shirt off: What's the only brand of baseball cards marketed continuously since 1957? And your wrong answer is..."

"Topps," Katie said with no hesitation.

Max's chin hit the floor. "How the fuck...?"

"Both my father and brother are avid baseball card collectors. It just so happens that this particular lesbian knows the approximate value of a rookie Bob Gibson."

Max's face fell. Katie gave him the finger. Contest tied 1-1.

❧   ❧   ❧

So bowling would decide it. Max asked Katie if she objected to traveling up to the Bronx for the game. After examining this request for any possible trickery on his part she agreed but asked him why.

"My buddy Mikey owns a one of those shops that sells computer games and it's right across the street from the joint we bowl at on Gun Hill Road," he said. "I'm thinking it'll be a good idea to have him score the game; just so neither one of us can accuse the other of cheating."

"You want one of your cronies in charge of scoring?" Katie asked incredulously, ready to rescind her agreement to bowling in the Bronx.

"Relax. Everything'll be on the up and up. If anyone should be worried it should be me. Mikey's got a soft spot for pretty women, he may give you a couple extra pins just to get on your good side."

"Okay, Max," Katie said. "But just so you know, I'm not some Bronx bimbo in a remedial math class. I know how to score a game myself so you better tell your little weasel of a friend that I'll be double-checking his work. I'll go get my ball out of my room."

Max then called Mikey to explain what he wanted and Mikey was only too glad to close down his store early. As he stated, how many chances does a guy get to score a game between his best friend and his best friend's girlfriend's lesbian lover?

Finding an open lane at the alley was easy considering it was 2 o'clock on a Wednesday afternoon and league play didn't start till eight. While Katie went off to the restroom and Max polished his personal 15 pounder Mikey leaned over and whispered, "That's a waste of a woman, boss. A cute thing like her being gay, I mean."

"You're not wrong there," Max had to admit. He looked up from his polishing and noted how gracefully Katie moved as she walked to the ladies room on the other side of the alley. More than a few of the other men in the place stopped what they were doing to admire her as well. "Danielle definitely has good taste," he said with a bit of an appreciative sigh. Then he told Mikey, "She wouldn't be interested in you anyway. You make too much money. Whatever you do don't tell her you just bought a Jaguar because she'll rip you a new asshole."

Before the game even started both Max and Mikey silently thought this match-up was lopsided, and Max felt he'd walk away the victor by a large margin. Katie was far too thin, they thought, to put any power behind her delivery so there was no way she'd be able to counteract Max's ability to shoot the ball down the lane like a cannon shot and blast the pins into submission. But neither of these men had ever bowled against a woman; their weekly matches were men-only affairs with a few other guys from the old neighborhood, so naturally it never occurred to them that whatever strength handicaps a woman might have could be overcome with precision.

This was proven when, three frames into the game, Katie led by twelve pins. Max may have had the power advantage, bowling like a Neanderthal, but Katie bowled like a surgeon, slicing her ball into the set of pins with such exactitude it gave the impression that she was using one of those smart bombs guided by laser beams and GPS systems. And sure enough, after every frame, Katie could be found looking over Mikey's shoulder making sure he tallied her score accurately. When her lead reached double digits she smiled smugly at Max and cocked an eyebrow. It rattled him. His next delivery went straight down the center of the lane with no English on the ball whatsoever. It continued straight through the triangle of pins and when the smoke cleared he was faced with a seven-ten split. In his attempt to pick up at least one of the pins he again failed to direct the ball properly and it went harmlessly between both of them.

"Field goal!" Mikey shouted, raising his arms like an NFL referee, Katie snickering happily beside him.

But the humiliation galvanized Max and before she knew it Katie was struggling to stay in the game because after that open frame Max fired off five booming strikes in a row annihilating the lead she once enjoyed. However, she kept her cool and in that same stretch had three straight strikes of her own. The lead changed hands four times and even Mikey was so tense that he broke the point of his pencil and called a time out to go sharpen it.

It came down to the final frame. At stake was the end of a six week sex drought. Both combatants knew that if they lost it may only mean going without sex for 24 more hours but considering how horny each of them was a wait of even one additional day was unacceptable. Katie bowled first and apparently the pressure was getting to her because her first delivery toppled only two pins. Faced with making an eight pin spare she stood a little longer at the approach, taking deep breaths, focusing on the task ahead. Then she fired and it was like she had the ball on remote control; the offending pins were obliterated with a loud crash, lengthening her lead. But her next delivery was even better: a surgically executed strike that momentarily took all of the air out of Max's lungs.

Scampering over to the scorer's table to watch Mikey tot up her score she then squealed in delight at the final number.

Mikey cast a rueful look at his best friend. Mathematically it wasn't impossible for Katie to lose but that would involve Max putting on a clinic.

"You wanna know the score?" he asked Max as the writer got up to retrieve his ball from the ball holder.

"Am I still in it?" Max inquired.

"Technically."

"Let's put it this way, Max," Katie said, her voice dripping malevolence, "you have about as much chance of winning as you do in making me straight."

"Trust me, Katie," he answered. "Men are better off with you being gay." He then zipped his ball down the lane for a strike. When the ball was returned to him he wasted no time. He lined up his approach and delivered again, all ten pins falling once more. Suddenly Katie was biting her nails.

During their weekly bowling games with the guys Max noticed that in close games Mikey had the habit of telling the last guy up how many pins he needed to knock down in order to win. On the surface it was a harmless habit but sometimes it had the effect of causing the guy whose turn it was to choke. He'd knock down three pins when he need four; eight pins when he needed nine. So when Max noticed Mikey opening his mouth to speak he growled, "Don't tell me how many fucking pins I need; just lemme bowl." But with his ball once more in his hands and him about to make his final delivery Katie quickly said, "Just seven pins, Max. That's all you need, seven pins." It had the desired effect for it made him abort his approach and nearly stumble. He glared back at her and she smiled innocently. "Oh, I'm sorry," she said, batting her eyelashes, "did you say you *didn't* want to know how close you were? Silly ole me, I misunderstood."

"You want something to misunderstand?" Max challenged. "Misunderstand this." A moment later his ball was rolling down the lane and in split second Katie's face fell. The speed, the trajectory, the sheer perfection of the delivery…Katie was able to compute the rather simple Newtonian physics in her head to see that more than seven pins would be upset.

"Noooo!" Katie screamed. "Fuck! Fuck! Fuck!"

"Yessss!" Max exulted, pumping his fist and dancing a jig. "Ha ha!"

"187 to 186," Mikey announced.

"One fucking pin! Ha ha!"

"I want a rematch," Katie demanded.

"Hey, fuck you. Rematches weren't part of the bargain. Now, come along, my dear," Max said after packing his ball, changing his shoes and accepting congratulations from Mikey. "If we leave now we can just beat the traffic back to Manhattan. I have a long night of pleasure to prepare for."

🍁 🍁 🍁

When Danielle reached home that evening shortly after six-thirty she found both Max and Katie watching television in the living room. Max seemed to have a rather smug expression on his face but there was nothing unusual about that; Danielle simply interpreted it as proof that he had had an exceptional day of writing and was confident of publishing yet another masterpiece. Katie, on the other hand, seemed a bit glum, but again, nothing unusual there; Danielle simply interpreted it as proof that once more she had had a frustrating and demeaning day of job hunting.

After kissing Max hello Danielle did the same to her girlfriend and then sat on her lap and said, "Katie, honey, what do you think we should order for dinner?"

Max started.

"What?" he asked. He couldn't help but notice that suddenly Katie was beaming from ear to ear.

"I just asked Katie what she thought we should order for dinner," Danielle answered.

"Yes, I know that but why are you asking her? What about me? I have a lot of damn good ideas about what we can have for dinner. Damn good ideas."

Danielle laughed and smiled sympathetically. "Oh, sweetie...you'll just have to wait your turn. I'll ask you what you want for dinner tomorrow, okay?"

CHAPTER 38

❦

A week later the worst storm to hit New York City in a dozen years arrived. Weather forecasters had been watching it develop in the Atlantic for six days, tracking its slow progress across the ocean. Thirty-six hours before it slammed into the city the National Weather Center warned residents to prepare as if for a siege: "Buy batteries! Buy water! Buy canned food! Board up your windows! Save your children!" In the Bland-Edwards-Shaw household there were no children to save but Max made sure there were enough flashlights and candles and he had the maid, Magda, make a special shopping run for bottled water, logs for the fireplaces and extra cognac because, "You can't enjoy a good storm without cognac," he said.

As a scornful response to the meteorologist's dire predictions, on the evening when the storm was due to hit Max took Danielle and Katie out for an "End of the World" feast at Michelangelo's. It seemed most of the city had been frightened by the frequent weather updates interrupting regularly scheduled programming into either staying indoors or visiting relatives in Ohio for the streets of Manhattan were eerily deserted underneath the lowering sky. The cabbie driving them uptown lamented that this was the worst night of his career and that they had saved him from going home empty-handed, so at the end of the ride Max tipped him fifty bucks. Why not? If the world is coming to an end what good is money? His flippant attitude made the women laugh and the cabbie drove away envious of this guy with a beautiful girl for each arm. At the restaurant, to further pay homage to the impending apocalypse, he ordered the waiter to bring them out one of every entrée on the menu and several bottles of wine they'd never tried before. And they all three did justice to that banquet. Even Katie, whose sensibilities would normally have been offended by the largesse partook willingly. There was something about the danger in the air, the threat of nature's full might about to be displayed that made her feel sexy and wanton, capable of, for one night, ignoring the thousands of homeless people who were even now scrambling to find shelter as she sampled a bite from this dish, a nibble from that one. She and Danielle kissed openly at the table; so did Danielle and Max. It was confusing for others to see. Who belonged to whom? In the end, every waiter in the joint wanted Max's life because apparently he was involved with two hot women, while all the waitresses in the joint simply wanted Max because of all the money he was spending, if it meant sharing him with two other women, then fine. Because the metropolis had been terrified by Mother Nature and dared not venture out there were only two other tables occupied in Michelangelo's, one by an elderly couple celebrating their sixtieth wedding anniversary; the other by a couple still in their teens on their first date. Max paid for both dinners, saluting them each with a raised glass of wine.

Sated, they decided to brave the inclement weather, which was becoming more and more inclement by the minute, and walk home. It felt daring and risky even though the full brunt of the storm would not hammer the city until shortly after ten and it was now only eight. But it was raining a little and the wind was beginning to gust somewhat strongly in their faces so it sufficed to make them feel intrepid and valiant.

During the elevator ride back up to the sixtieth floor Danielle and Katie, both tipsy from the wines, started making out heavily in one corner, something they'd never done in front of Max before, but what the hell...it's the end of the world, right? Under normal circumstances Max would have either told them to cut it out and get a room or simply averted his eyes to allow them privacy but instead he watched the deep kissing and the breast groping and the groin grinding. Even though he was the tiniest bit buzzed himself he never thought of joining in and trying to grasp the Holy Grail; that was their party, he wasn't invited.

Upon entering the apartment the two women disappeared instantly towards the vicinity of Katie's bedroom, stumbling and giggling as they went. Max didn't mind, though. For some reason or other Danielle had been smothering him a bit over the previous three days and here was his chance to breathe freely and enjoy some solitude. So, pouring himself a cognac at the bar Max went up to the library to choose something to read appropriate for a dark and stormy night. He settled on a collection of ghost stories by Charles Dickens, a slim volume he picked up recently at a used book fair, and then retired to the master bedroom with his cognac.

🍁 🍁 🍁

Around eleven that night Max was in that half awake/half asleep state common to people who enjoy reading in bed wherein he kept nodding off only to jerk back awake and struggle to finish one more page. Suddenly the door to the bedroom burst open and Danielle rushed in, completely nude. Drowsy though he was Max could tell she was in a heightened state of panic and when she scrambled into the bed and clung to him beneath the covers like she'd been the one reading Victorian era ghost stories he asked what was wrong.

"The building is moving!" she wailed. "Why is it moving?"

"Is it?" Max asked. He hadn't noticed it before but now that she mentioned it, yes, sure enough, the building was swaying ever so slightly.

"That's nothing," he told her. "The building we lived in up in the Bronx when I was growing up used to do that all the time. It's because of the wind; this storm is kicking ass out there."

"Make it stop!"

"Who am I, Spiderman? Just relax, sweetie. Look, these high-rises are designed to dance a little in strong winds, okay? That's what keeps 'em from toppling over. It's nothing to worry about."

"Oh God!" she yelped as the building gave a particularly stomach-churning lurch just then. Outside, a booming clap of thunder rattled the windows.

"Wow, did you feel that one, Danielle?" Max teased.

"Shut up!"

"We were almost perpendicular that time!"

"Shut UP!"

The skyscraper rocked again.

"Whoa!" Max said with mock seriousness. "That one almost knocked us out of bed; maybe we should move further away from the window."

"Max, I swear to God…" But Danielle was too frightened to let go of him and punch him in the ribs for making fun of her.

"Sweetie, listen…" her boyfriend said, chuckling, "I swear to you nothing bad is gonna happen. Just lay here and relax. Turn on the TV or something to distract you. I *was* about to go to sleep but now you've got me wide awake so I'm gonna finish reading my book and—"

Suddenly Katie appeared in the doorway, also in a state of alarm. She wasn't nude like Danielle but the NYU t-shirt she had chosen to put on in obvious haste was not only inside out but barely extended past her pubic region, exposing her lean long legs.

"Why did you leave me alone?" she asked Danielle.

"I'm sorry," Danielle said, "I panicked."

"Well fuck, do you expect me to stay in there by myself?"

"Jesus Christ! Not you too," complained Max.

"Can you feel how much this building is moving, Max?" Katie asked, as if he were the architect and it was all his fault. "This is not normal!"

"It is normal, you idiot! When you've got hurricane-force winds blowing outside this is what happens."

Another booming clap of thunder exploded and before Max knew it, before he had a chance to utter a single word of objection, Katie was clambering into the bed also, lifting up the covers and sliding in on his left side.

"Ooh, not a bad package you have there, Max," she said, catching sight of his penis.

Raising herself up on one elbow Danielle glared at Max sternly.

"Don't even think about it," she warned.

"I wasn't thinking about anything!" he protested. "She's the one making comments about my package!"

So Danielle threatened Katie: "Then don't *you* even think about it."

Katie made a face. "As if. He's a guy. I'd vomit."

"You'd vomit?" Max asked. "Really?"

"Only a little."

"Wonderful."

"Why are you naked anyway?" Danielle inquired accusingly.

"Since when have you known me to wear pajamas in bed? Besides, I wasn't expecting the lesbian to stop by."

"It's alright, Danielle," Katie said, "His penis may as well be a sausage for as much as it's turning me on."

"Good," her girlfriend retorted.

"But it is a good sized sausage…how big does it get?"

"None of your business!" Max declared but Danielle got up on one elbow again and said with obvious pride: "Nine and a quarter inches! I measured."

"Fuck, are you serious?"

"Swear to God. And the head is, like, huge!"

"Danielle!" Max pleaded.

"My gay friend, Roger, would love to meet you, Max," Katie said. "Apparently there's something of a shortage of well-endowed men out there."

"What a shame," Max replied dryly. "You can tell Roger, though, that should dealing with women ever drive me to homosexuality as I fully expect it will that I'll give him a call."

"It doesn't hurt?" Katie asked Danielle after a moment's consideration.

"You mean when we have sex? At first it did, yeah," Danielle answered. "For, like, the first month I was pretty damn sore but I got used to it a long time ago. Now you know why that hot pink dildo of yours didn't intimidate me."

"Fuck, that's only six inches."

"Right, which is a joke to me now. I mean, if Max died and I met a man who was only packing six inches he'd be getting a penis pump for Christmas."

"Can we change the subject?" Max asked.

But Katie said: "Well, I never thought about going larger."

"It's a completely different experience," Danielle stated matter-of-factly.

"It seems suicidal," Katie mused.

"Don't be silly. Trust me, sweetie, you'll never waste money on anything smaller again. In fact, we can go shopping tomor—"

"Okay, that's enough!" Max ordered, silencing the women. "Enough, enough, enough!" He let them believe he was upset at their indiscretion but what really motivated him to put an end to that conversation was the effect it was having on him. Two beautiful women discussing this type of subject matter, not to mention that their bare legs were rubbing against his own, was causing his penis to stir with desire and begin to inflate to that nine and a quarter inch size Danielle was so proud of. Quick as a flash he shut his eyes and accessed his brain's databank of emergency statistics kept handy for just such occasions:

Lou Gehrig had a lifetime batting average of .340 and hit 493 home runs including 23 grand slams. He led the league in RBIs five times…

Yankee Stadium Dimensions: 318 to left; 400 to center; 314 to right…

No-hitters thrown by Yankee pitchers: George Mogridge, 1917; Sam Jones, 1923; Monte Pearson, 1938—

He was almost back down to completely flaccid when suddenly a horrendous explosion of thunder rent the air outside. It was as if they were inside the storm cloud itself and if that wasn't bad enough, the lights flickered in the apartment and the building swayed so perceptibly that even Max felt his stomach lurch. The women screamed and clutched him, both digging their nails into his flesh.

"What the hell are you doing, Katie?" Max asked. "Let go of me!"

"Leave her alone," Danielle managed to squeak.

Katie said, "I'm sorry but whenever there was a bad storm when I was growing up I used to always go running to my dad to sleep with him." She kept her grip on him and Max felt her trembling.

"And didn't you stop at some point?" Max put to her. "Like around, I dunno…*puberty* because you were afraid Daddy would get *arrested*? Or do they ignore those kinds of things in Cow's Piss, Nebraska?" He tapped Danielle. "Ahem…doesn't this bother you?"

But his girlfriend was scared senseless and even refused to lift her head from where she had it buried in his armpit.

"Right now I couldn't care less," she mumbled. "She could give you a fucking blowjob just as long as we make it through the night."

"Do you realize," Katie began, "that if this building collapses there is no way we are going to survive?"

"The building is not gonna collapse!" Max insisted.

Danielle said, "No, she's right. Remember that high-rise apartment building in Vietnam that collapsed during a tropical storm last year?"

"Vietnam?" Max scoffed. "Jesus Christ, they build skyscrapers outta Play-Doh in Vietnam. This, however, is a three-million dollar home in one of the most modern buildings in New York City."

It was Katie's turn to scoff. Forgetting her terror for a moment she said, "You know, I almost wish the building would fall down now just to teach that smug attitude of yours a lesson. The rich aren't immune to mortality, Max."

"They are in three-million dollar homes in one of the most modern buildings in New York City."

"Fuck, you make me mad!"

❦   ❦   ❦

But Max didn't care how mad Katie was; he had a bigger problem; a nine and a quarter inch problem to be precise. Despite the distraction of having to deal with two nutty women and despite his excellent recall of every possible Yankees statistic available his penis was now as hard as a piece of rebar. No amount of recalling Mickey Mantle's home run totals year by year, or of mentally reciting how many base hits Elston Howard had in 1961 could convince his body to stop sending blood to that organ. Of course, Danielle had something to do with it. Three years of being her lover, of being familiar with every square inch of her body and of having sex with her quite regularly had done nothing to diminish his lust for her. However, if he was honest with himself, as much as Danielle's nudity and schoolgirl fright of the storm was turning him on it was only responsible for seven, perhaps seven and a half, inches of his erection. The rest, alarmingly, was thanks to Katie.

What the fuck is going on? he asked himself, nearing panic.

Calm down, it's perfectly understandable.

But she's a lesbian! It's not like I can expect any action from her.

True, but...

And she's got as much charm as a Mongol horde! What the hell was with her saying I got a smug attitude? All I was trying to do was ease her mind about the building collapsing.

True, but her being a lesbian and her being a holier-than-thou psychopath doesn't take away from the fact that she's one sexy lady.

No argument there.

She's cute as hell, has one of those sultry voices and right now she's embracing me for protection; her bare legs are up against mine and I can feel her breasts on my chest through her t-shirt.

And her nipples are hard.

So is it any wonder I am too?

Plus she smells good.

It's Moonlight Path from Bath & Body Works. Danielle tried it for a while herself but went back to Manifesto by Isabella Rosellini.

She's breathing directly on my neck. She shouldn't be allowed to breathe on my neck!

This is just great. It's every man's dream to find himself in bed with two women and what do I get? Two women about to wet themselves over a little storm, one of whom compares my dick to a piece of deli meat. Must be God's way of getting back at me for what I wrote in Pope Anne, *calling Him history's most successful fictional character after Mickey Mouse.*

Never mind that! I've gotta get rid of this thing!

Right! Okay, think now...what do I know about Joe DiMaggio?

"Why are you hard?!" Danielle barked, suddenly interrupting his recall of Joe DiMaggio data. While adjusting to a more comfortable position she had thrown her right leg over his body and felt his erection immediately. All at once, it seemed, the perils of the storm were forgotten as she sat up in the bed shooting him accusing glances.

Max was trapped and at a loss. He simply stammered, "I-I-I-" like he was a defective talking doll that had somehow made it past quality control.

Katie lifted up the covers.

"Fuck, that's impressive," she said appraisingly. She looked over at Danielle. "More power to you."

Max was red with embarrassment while Danielle was red with indignation.

"Stop looking at it!" she ordered her girlfriend in a high-pitched squeal.

"Yeah, stop looking at it!" Max agreed, even though he secretly felt pleased with Katie's compliment. It's always an ego boost for a man to hear that his equipment meets the standards of all women, even the lesbian ones, just as it's always an ego boost for a man (no matter how much he may protest to the contrary) to learn that he's attractive enough to be hit on by gay men. But Max grabbed the covers and pulled them down tight around his body. His erection, however, pushed up the fabric covering his crotch like a tent pole.

"So what the fuck, Max," Danielle began in her I'm-pissed-at-you-so-you-better-have-a-good-explanation voice. "What is so fucking stimulating in the bed?"

"I dunno!"

"Bullshit!"

"Honestly, I don't know."

"Is it her?" she said, indicating Katie.

"No! I mean...wait, yeah, that's the right answer...no, don't be silly."

"You son of a bitch..."

"No, now wait! Lemme explain!"

"I don't think you should say one fucking word," Danielle warned.

"I gotta say something if you want me to explain! It's not what you think!"

"What I think is that you're excited because Katie's in bed with you."

"Then it is what you think."

"How could you?" Danielle whimpered, her voice cracking.

"But it can all be explained," he insisted.

"Yeah, you want to fuck Katie. Fine. Go ahead you prick!"

But Max then decided he'd had enough. With a grunt he threw the cover off of them all and scrambled out of bed and then stood at the foot of it in front of the ladies, making no attempt to conceal his nudity.

"Max!" Danielle said in a panic. "What are you doing? Get back in bed now!" Katie, meanwhile, just sat up and looked like she was enjoying herself to the full.

"Max!" Danielle continued. "Put something on now!"

But he ignored her and stood there with his erection pointing upwards.

"I'm a man, Danielle," he said, "which means I inhabit a body that is rather unsophisticated in certain matters. It makes rude noises, for example; it grows hair in odd places and, yes, it will become aroused when it's least appropriate, like now as you can plainly see. But how was I supposed to help it? A few minutes ago I was ready to nod off to sleep and then you two show up and suddenly there's a new woman in my bed! Suddenly there's another pair of legs, and another set of breasts, and her nipples are hard, and she smells good, and her skin is soft! That's not something my penis can ignore! That's like asking one of Pavlov's dogs to ignore the dinner bell! Under these circumstances how could my penis not wake up and pay attention?"

"Max, you're pissing me off," Danielle warned. But her boyfriend ignored her and went on.

"You see, here's something you may not know, ladies: we men are not in control of our own dicks. The penis is pretty much a rebel and does whatever the hell it wants. There isn't a 'deactivate' button on the side that I can press to tell it to ignore the additional cute woman in my bed who's wrapping her legs around me begging me to save her from the storm. And even though my brain knows Katie is gay my penis doesn't give a damn. As far as it's concerned she's just a hottie who ended up in its playpen. This is what it's like to be a man, ladies; this is why we die before you, because throughout our lives our dicks use up a lot of blood that should have gone to our hearts."

"Bravo!" Katie exulted, clapping. "And may I just say that I am *so* flattered I have such an effect on you."

"*Shut up, Katie!*" Max and Danielle said together and then Danielle got out of bed and tried pulling her boyfriend back in with her so he could be covered up. But Max resisted, like a stubborn dog on a chain.

"No, fuck you, I'm not getting in that bed again."

"Max, please!" Danielle insisted, pulling him harder. "You've made your point. Katie and I will go back to her room and we'll leave you in peace. Just cover up!"

"And you're not gonna remain mad at me for getting hard?" he asked.

"No. Just cover up!"

"Swear on Prada."

"I swear."

"I don't want to go back to my room," Katie whined. "Things are far more interesting here."

"*Shut up, Katie!*" they both said again.

❦   ❦   ❦

Back in Katie's room Danielle was at first a bit surly. She was replaying in her mind the tableau of Max standing before the bed with an erection and of Katie's eyes taking it all in, never once looking at his face. As a result her moods were on a pendulum, swinging back and forth between distrust of Max for getting aroused and resentment of Katie for being attractive enough to make him aroused. There was, of course, a little voice in her head straining to be heard, telling her that she was being silly, that Max was right, you know...dicks have minds of their own, but her natural tendency towards jealousy was drowning it out and for nearly half an hour Danielle kept her back turned to Katie in bed while she tried to convince herself that her heterosexual boyfriend and her lesbian girlfriend would never cheat on her with each other.

Katie, sensing that Danielle was a little peeved and remembering what Danielle had told her that day in Central Park about letting her be for a while if she's upset did just that: let her be. But Katie saw no reason for her girlfriend to be so dramatic. The whole thing about Max getting an erection was hilarious, the kind of thing her and her friends could laugh about over cocktails. On top of that it was a bit flattering, although she'd of course never admit it to Danielle. But it is always an ego boost for a woman, even a gay one, to know that she can have that effect on a man.

It didn't take long for Danielle to come around, though. This was primarily because the storm showed no signs of abating and because one of the most modern buildings in the city insisted on continuing to sway. So eventually the two bed mates found themselves embracing again for protection and not long after that they were kissing for distraction.

Suddenly Danielle hopped out of bed, left the room and when she returned she was not empty handed. She carried with her a long rectangular box that had an electrical cord attached to it. She placed the box on the dresser plugging the cord into an outlet and then climbed on top of Katie who was still in bed, eyes full of anticipation. Danielle began by lifting up the t-shirt Katie was wearing and exposing the other woman's breasts. She sucked on one hard nipple while pinching the other tightly between thumb and forefinger, a mixture of pleasure and pain that made Katie pant to keep air in her lungs. Then Danielle kissed her way down her girlfriend's body, pausing a bit at the navel, pausing a bit at her hips, until finally she forced Katie's legs apart roughly and inserted her tongue as deep into her vagina as it would go.

Expertly, Danielle used her mouth to bring the other woman to the very brink of orgasm. By now Katie had hold of Danielle's hair, forcing her face harder onto her vagina, grinding her genitalia against Danielle's lips. Suddenly a bell dinged and cruelly Danielle pulled herself away, went over to the box on the dresser, opened it and came back to the bed bearing the most beautiful dildo Katie had ever seen. It was clear glass with swirls of indigo and pink, had a knob-like head and its gently curving shaft was pebbled with protuberances the size of pearls. And it was long. It made her hot pink dildo look like a thumb when compared to a forefinger.

Danielle didn't waste any time. Kneeling before Katie on the bed she began inserting the Tokushima dildo. Never had Katie had a warmed-up toy inside her before, usually her own collection of equipment was room temperature at best, so when she felt the sensual heat from this dildo radiating out from her vagina to spread over her entire pubic area she thought she might lose her mind. And never had her vagina been forced to stretch this much to accommodate a toy, and never had anything been in as deep. She knew from plenty of experience where the six inch point of her canal was but this thing kept boring in unrelentingly far past that point until she felt it bump against her cervix. When it did that she orgasmed so hard she rolled completely over, her hands between her thighs, holding the dildo inside of her.

When it was over and she could speak she said, "Definitely worth five-hundred bucks."

Then it was Danielle's turn and it was in this way that the ladies forgot about the building swaying in the storm.

※   ※   ※

In the glow of their satisfaction afterwards Katie was resting her head on Danielle's bosom.

"So..." she began, "I bet Max asks you all the time about the details of our sex life, huh?"

"Actually, no," Danielle replied sleepily.

"I thought all men had a thing for two women going at it."

"Mm, they do. It's an obsession with them." And she told Katie about Daryl. "But Max is no Daryl, thank God. He may ask me if I had a good time with you but he doesn't pry otherwise. What I don't understand," she then said after a moment, "is why it doesn't work both ways. I've never met a woman who told me she gets turned on by seeing two men have sex."

"Who would? Men are disgusting, hairy apes." Katie paused a moment. "So," she started up again, "have you ever had a threesome?"

"God, no."

"Ever wanted one?"

"As possessive as I am, are you kidding? When I first told Max I was bi I thought for two seconds that I might agree to one if he asked but just thinking about it gave me a panic attack." She frowned, suddenly suspicious. "Why? Are you trying to suggest you, me and Max…"

"Fuck no." And Katie pinched Danielle's nipple hard as punishment for even suggesting such an absurd notion. "I couldn't possibly get aroused at the thought of doing anything sexual with a guy. But…I don't know…"

Danielle sat up.

"Oh my God. Are you saying you want a threesome?"

"I don't know. Maybe. Yes. Look, I'm not expecting one, especially knowing how you are but I'll admit it's a nice fantasy: having two women at my disposal; having two women service me."

"God, you don't want one with Moira, do you?" Danielle asked, making a face. "If you have one with her you may as well have one with Max."

"I agree. I love Moira to death but…yuck." Katie paused a moment. "What about Jenny, though?"

"Who?"

"Jenny, remember? A friend of mine we ran into at Starbucks a couple of days ago? She writes for the *News?*"

"Oh, her…" said Danielle recalling the brunette with a caramel macchiato. "I got the feeling she had the hots for you, the bitch."

"She does, has for a long time but it was never convenient for us to get together. Anyway, when you went to the ladies room she gushed about how gorgeous you were and then let's just say she made an offer."

"Pretty forward of her."

"Subtlety has never been one of her strong suits. In fact, her exact words were that she'd fuck us both anytime we wanted."

"And you said…"

"'How about Tuesday?'"

"You did not!"

"And she said, 'My place?' and I said, 'Sure.'"

"Katie…"

"And she said, 'Bring your toys', and I said, 'Danielle's my toy', and she said, 'Yummy!' and I—ow!" Katie dissolved into laughter as Danielle started tickling her so she'd shut up. The matter ended there. Danielle never knew whether or not Katie had made the whole Jenny-wants-a-threesome thing up but decided it was best not to find out. Yes, there was something appealing about it (Jenny *was* cute) but she knew it would be inequitable. Being romantically involved with two people had taught Danielle something: the best way to keep the waters still and everyone happy was to adopt the same notions of justice and fairness employed by a parent with two children. Therefore, if Max couldn't have a threesome neither could Katie.

CHAPTER 39

❀

Max's nude speech on why men get erections had the unintended effect of breaking down a barrier between himself and Katie and over the next year a certain casualness became the norm inside Max's luxury home whereby both of Danielle's lovers began ignoring established conventions of propriety, particularly those conventions governing the use of clothing.

When she had lived alone in the sublet Katie preferred either wearing as little as possible or else being entirely nude, and post-storm she reverted back to this bohemian ideal. Many times Max caught sight of her naked form crossing a room or foraging for a snack in the fridge, and oftentimes after a shower Katie would join him on the living room couch to watch television clad only in a towel or a nightgown that made but a pretense of covering her breasts in delicate lace. Several times, when she had job interviews, she'd appear before Max in her bra and panties holding up a different business suit in each hand asking him to choose which she should wear. And Max himself was hardly more modest. If the urge for a late night snack came over him when he was already nude and comfortable in bed then nude and comfortable it was that he made for the kitchen, not even bothering to blush should he encounter Katie. One memorable night, in fact, they bumped into each other in the living room and had a forty minute discussion on the direction of contemporary literature, he totally in the buff and she wearing nothing but a pair of gym shorts.

Needless to say this initially upset Danielle who once more grew alarmed with visions of the two of them having an affair, a notion that did not seem beyond belief. Max did, she remembered (as if she could ever forget!), get a hard-on because Katie was lying next to him that night of the storm; and Katie, for a lesbian, had been more than a little admiring of his cock. But "Don't be silly," said Katie when Danielle chastised her for letting Max see her nude one night. "He's a guy. Sausage, remember?" And "Don't be silly," chided Max when Danielle got on his case about going into the living room naked to get a magazine. "She thinks my dick looks like sausage." Eventually, Danielle gave up worrying and joined in herself. The Bland-Edwards-Shaw household became a clothing optional exclusive club.

🍁 🍁 🍁

During that same year Katie found herself working again, having finally landed a job in December, five months to the day when Homeward Bound shut its doors. As relieved as she was to no longer be unemployed she was not entirely satisfied with her new position. Unlike at the Williams Foundation where her voice could be heard and her creativity exploited the charitable organization who hired her this time was huge, faceless and run like a Fortune 500 corporation, meaning that not only were the paper clips counted but there were several layers of bullshit to get through before anything got done. Despite being a bright woman with innovative ideas her brightness and innovativeness were diminished in a company with seemingly more vice-presidents and middle managers than there were members of Congress. She often felt as if she were spinning her wheels, if not wasting her time. Proposals she designed got lost in the bureaucracy, sometimes never to be heard from again, and her co-workers seemed less interested in helping the homeless than in stabbing each other in the back when an opportunity for advancement presented itself. But, it was a job and the company was prestigious. If she stuck it out long enough, she figured, it'd be something on her résumé that could launch her to better things.

However, although being without a job was what necessitated her moving into the great Max Bland's apartment, getting a job did not automatically necessitate moving back out. The months following her hire date came and went and still Katie occupied the largest guest room in the place. Twice she made mention of leaving: first Danielle talked her out of it three months after Katie was hired:

"Save up some more money, baby. If you go now all your savings will be eaten up by the deposits and crap; wait until you have enough to get properly settled." And because this made perfect sense the matter was dropped and so Katie continued taking half of her paycheck and depositing it in an account whose funds would one day be used to securing a new place of her own.

And then Max, of all people, talked her out of it *five months* after Katie was hired, when she mentioned that she had six-thousand dollars saved and would begin looking through the real estate ads that Sunday.

"Wait a minute," Max said, "you say you don't even like this job that much, right? So stay put until you find something better. You're not in anyone's way here." And because *that* made perfect sense the matter was dropped yet again.

Not long after that, the issue of when Katie would move out became non-existent. The truth was that, by this point, Katie wanted to stay because she liked living with Danielle; Danielle wanted her to stay because she loved her; and Max wanted her to stay because he had gotten used to her. Katie had become part of what made home *home* for him. He enjoyed their talks, loved their arguments and it was just plain nice having a woman in his house with whom he could truly be himself. He remembered that night at Michelangelo's, when Danielle turned thirty and he first met Katie. He remembered his spiel about being free with somebody when they are sexually inaccessible. That's what he and Katie had and it was therapeutic and he didn't desire losing it. Nor did she. To her, Max was a way of further understanding Danielle. Indeed, whenever she and Danielle got into a fight Katie would often seek Max out secretly and, like Luke Skywalker convening with Yoda, try to plumb the depths of his longer association and romance with her.

So by virtue of an unspoken agreement Katie became a permanent resident of the sixtieth floor apartment on Fifth Avenue, a circumstance which elevated Max's esteem in the eyes of the building's doormen who had no idea exactly what went on up on sixty; all they knew was that Mr. Bland had two cuties living with him.

Of course, the grandiosity of the apartment still offended Katie and she still busted Max's balls about it from time to time but it was home now. In fact, after getting her new job she began splitting the food and electric bills with Danielle so she'd no longer feel like a freeloader.

🍁   🍁   🍁

Also during that same year the bond between Danielle and Katie deepened to the point where their love was a twin to that shared by Danielle and Max. For Katie's part, no longer was there any question about remaining faithful. After the episode with Mary and the dog collar there had been others (including Mary twice more); brief one-nighters whenever Danielle got careless and neglected Katie's sexual needs for more than thirty-six hours. But by the time of Danielle's appendectomy Katie had completely weaned herself of the Marys, Carolines, Saras and the rest, preferring to focus her love and attention on the Arizonan. Besides, once Danielle introduced Katie to the insane pleasures that can only be gained from authentic Tokushima dildos and then suggested she keep them all in her bedroom...well, after that Katie's threshold for being deprived of Danielle (such as when Danielle and Max spent two weeks in Italy) increased.

For her part, Danielle viewed Katie as much more than a way to scratch her bisexual itch. As Max was her boyfriend, Katie was her girlfriend and Danielle made sure she devoted herself to understanding Katie's needs, her personality, her dreams, her uniqueness—just as she had devoted herself to understanding the same things for Max. Danielle strove to maintain the romance between her and Katie, leaving little love notes on her pillow, soaking in a tub with her in a candlelit bathroom, sending her flowers—the same kinds of things she did for Max. What's more, Danielle took pains to be creative with Katie, both in and out of bed, coming up with ways to keep their relationship fresh and exciting whether it was inventing a new sex game to play or suggesting a new activity outside of the home that they could both enjoy together—just like she did for Max. In Danielle's mind, the only difference between her two lovers was gender.

The love linking the women was further strengthened when Katie surprised Danielle by bringing home two airline tickets to Maine, a trip which occurred almost exactly a year after the big storm. Finally, Katie found herself at her favorite place in the whole wide world, the Inverness Lighthouse on the coast, with a woman whose heart she wanted to hold onto forever. Every morning they'd awaken in their room at the bed-and-breakfast on the shore, make love in the chill and then, taking a blanket with them, go to sit on the rocks in the lighthouse's shadow, feeling like the only two people on the planet. No matter how else they spent the rest of the day they always returned to the lighthouse. It became their Paris, their Venice, and for four days it was the one spot on Earth where they felt their love galvanizing.

CHAPTER 40

❀

"Why do you think you and I have never talked about marriage?" Danielle asked Max the night after she and Katie returned from Maine. They were in bed, had just had sex and Max was gently pulling on her pubic hairs.

"Well," Max began, "I can't tell you why *we've* never talked about marriage but I can tell you why *I've* never talked about marriage."

"And why is that?"

"Because it's an obsolete ritual with no practical purpose in today's society. That's my take on it anyway. I mean, people ask me all the time when you and I are getting married and it kinda offends me."

"Offends you? Why?"

"Because it makes me realize that other people can't validate our love unless they see us get married," he said. "That they're too stupid to believe that love can be real and permanent without an archaic ceremony to make it 'official.'"

"That's a good point," Danielle said.

"And what difference is it gonna make in our lives to have a piece of paper saying we belong to one another?"

"None, I suppose."

"Right. We already live together, we already know each other's habits and you already got me wrapped around your finger. As far as sex goes, fuck, our honeymoon would be anticlimactic."

"That's true."

"Look, all through history up until, I dunno, fifty years ago, marriage meant something different and it served a purpose for both parties. A man got someone to bear his children and keep his house clean, and a woman got someone to provide shelter, food and protection for her. Nowadays it's different, society's mores have changed and nowadays I think people get married just to satisfy their own vanity. Think about it...what is a wedding? A wedding is a chance for two people, but especially the bride, I mean, come on, who are we kidding?, to have the attention of all their friends and family members focused on them and them alone. It's ego masturbation with cake."

Danielle laughed.

"But it makes me wonder," she said, "if it's such a useless ritual now why do you think gay couples are always making a fuss about being able to marry?"

"The only reason gays are so bent on getting married is because they can't. They hate the idea that our laws prohibit them from making the same legal commitment to love another person for eternity as straight people can make. And they're right to be upset because it is wrong. But if the laws ever change and gays can marry I think that after a few decades many of those couples would say to themselves 'What's the point?'"

Max stopped playing with her pubic hairs to look up at her.

"Why are asking about this?" he asked with mock suspicion. "Trying to light a fire under my ass?"

"What? No. No, God no."

"You're not fishing for a rock from Harry Winston?"

"Sweetie, I'm always fishing for a rock from Harry Winston and anytime you feel so inclined please buy me one. But you can keep the proposal. When I first got involved with you I was hoping someday we'd get married but now I'm indifferent. I mean, you're right...it would serve no practical purpose and if our relationship ain't broke, why fix it? Although all of my friends are pushing me to marry you..."

Max scoffed. "That's only because I'm rich. If I made the same type of money you do they wouldn't give a fuck if we got married or not."

"You're cynical," Danielle said.

"So was Mark Twain but look at how well things turned out for him."

"Anyway," Danielle went on, "marriage is something I don't even think about now. I'm perfectly happy with the way things are."

"I find that hard to believe."

"Why?"

"Because women are more susceptible than men to brainwashing and society today still does everything in its power to brainwash women into believing one cannot be happy without a fairy tale wedding. That's why *Seinfeld* was such a great show: nobody got married in it."

"Well, you can believe it when I say it."

"But…" Max prodded. "I know there's a 'but' coming."

"It's nothing sinister like you're supposing."

"I'm not supposing anything, honey. So what is it? Why are we having a talk about marriage? Is it your pain-in-the-ass mother?"

Danielle hesitated and took a while to compose her thoughts and what she was going to say. Finally…

"Katie wants to do something and we were talking about it while in Maine. My pain-in-the-ass mother has nothing to do with it."

"Go on."

"It's not a wedding, like you're probably thinking," Danielle said quickly, to reassure him. "She told me that she wouldn't ask me to marry her out of respect for you and what you and I have. But she wants to do *something* and quite frankly I want to also."

"So what is it we're talking about here?"

"I don't know…the details haven't been worked out yet. But her and I want to do something, have a ceremony or something, that will commit ourselves to each other in front of people. Nothing official, nothing with papers to sign or licenses to get…just something romantic, something to show our loved ones that we're in love and that we want to stay together."

Max seemed dubious.

"And your mother has nothing to do with it?" he asked.

"No."

"What about Mayzie Witherspoon?"

"We won't even invite her."

"Fine," he then said in the same tone of voice he would have used if she had told him they were out of ginger ale, would he like a Vanilla Coke instead? "Knock yourselves out," he went on.

"It doesn't bother you?"

"Nah. I knew eventually you two would get around to wanting something like this. You're women. A woman who goes through life not declaring herself to someone else in front of people is…well, a man."

"We're not talking about anything large, Max," said Danielle, relieved, "or even fancy. A simple ceremony that will only have meaning for us."

Max was now kissing her pubic bone. Apparently he was in the mood again. Speaking between kisses he said, "Sounds…(kiss)…great…(kiss)…Just…(kiss)…send me…(kiss)…the bill." He was making his way south towards her clitoris but before he could reach it and distract her from the trickiest part of this whole conversation she said quickly, "We want you to be involved, too, Max."

※　　　※　　　※

It worked. He looked up, puzzled.
"What, you want me to give you away?"
"Not exactly."
"Well, I can't officiate, can I? I'm not a priest."
"I know."
"Although I hear you can become one over the internet."
"Yes, but…"
"Can you imagine that? Ten minutes online and boom!—you're ordained."
"Yes, but…"
"Even religion is fast food now. What a world we—"
"You're straying, honey," Danielle interrupted. "When I say we want you to be involved I mean that we want you to declare your love for me while I declare my love for you."
"Huh?"

Danielle told him to wait a sec and then got up and went to her closet. She came back carrying a little bag and from it extracted a small box.

"Katie and I bought these in Windemere, that's the town in Maine we stayed in." Opening the box she revealed four rings of silver. She went on, keeping a careful eye on his countenance in order to read his reaction.

"We thought these would be nice to give each other during whatever ceremony we have. They were made by a local artist. Aren't they beautiful?"

Picking one up Max asked, "What is this symbol carved all around it?"

"It's Native American," Danielle answered. "It's, uh…wait a minute…I have it written down." She removed a slip of paper, the receipt, from the bag and looked at a word written on the back. "It's Passamaquoddy, a tribe in Maine. That's the Passamaquoddy symbol for woman." She picked up another ring. "And this is the symbol for man."

"Ah. I see the man looks bankrupt. Figures."

"Very funny. You see, the idea we had was that you and Katie would both wear a ring with the symbol for woman. That means you're committed to a woman."

"I don't know about Katie but speaking for myself can the woman be Nicole Kidman?"

"Fuck you. Anyway, I would wear two rings, one with the woman symbol and this one, with the man symbol. That means I'm committed to both a woman and a man. I'd wear the man ring on my left hand, since that's tradition, and the other on my right."

"What a surprise…you get two rings. Lemme guess…you were in charge of this shopping expedition."

"Ha ha. Actually it was Katie's idea, smartass. So…the rings are beautiful, right?"

Max acknowledged in the affirmative.

"That one is actually mine," Danielle said, taking the ring he was holding and giving him the largest of the set. "Try it on."

He dutifully tried it on, holding his hand out at arms length to make a proper appraisal.

Taking a deep breath and even crossing her fingers Danielle asked the big question.

"So what do you think? Are you game?"

Max made a face, as if he'd just bitten into a bad piece of fruit.

"I dunno, sweetie…it's not my kind of thing, you know? I mean, hokey ceremonies and all that jazz. I don't even like showing up when some club or another is giving me an award for my writing."

Detecting danger to their plans Danielle took his hand.

"Max, please," she said. "You're right, you are probably going to hate every minute of it but, please, it's important to me and it's even important to Katie that you be part of this. She's willing to do whatever it takes to make it as painless as possible for you."

"I dunno…"

"Please, please, please, please, please! The way things are going it certainly seems like all three of us are going to build a life together so all three of us should be involved in declaring our intentions to do so."

Max wanted to continue arguing his side of the matter but made the mistake of looking into Danielle's eyes. When he saw the lack of selfishness and read the sincerity of her feelings about this he sighed.

"How many people are we talking about?" he queried.

"Maybe ten but maybe less. All we really need are witnesses and someone to officiate."

"Where's it gonna be?"

"Don't know. Someplace secluded, though, I promise."

"Well, if I'm being dragged into this I want it held somewhere in the Bronx, my native land. I'm sure you can find some nice spot at the Botanical Gardens or maybe Van Cortland Park."

"Fine."

"When's it gonna be?"

"As soon as possible."

"And how long will this screwball ceremony take?"

"Less than half an inning."

"I won't have to say anything corny, will I? Or act all mushy?"

"Katie and I will handle being mushy; you just handle looking conscious. Fair enough?"

"What about saying anything corny?"

"There may be some corniness involved, yes."

"Goddammit!"

"But we'll try to keep your end of it to a minimum. Deal?"

"Do I have a choice?"

"Not really."

"Then deal."

Danielle squealed in delight, hugging the writer tightly.

"I am so happy!" she exulted. "You have made me so happy!"

Max looked again at his ring.

"At least you ladies saved me a trip to Harry Winston's," he said. But Danielle gave a short laugh.

"I'll still have eight other fingers left," she reminded him.

CHAPTER 41

❀

In her cubicle at work the next day Katie was eating lunch and abusing her internet privileges. She was using Google to search for sites pertaining to the Wiccan ritual of handfasting, all the while keeping one eye open for anyone who may come in and see that she was wasting her company's high-speed connection for personal stuff, as if no one else here did—and worse. Just yesterday she had stepped into David Mason's cube to ask for details on a new homeless shelter being built on Long Island and though he was quick in closing the open internet window on his monitor he wasn't quick enough to prevent Katie from catching a glimpse of a cute blonde servicing two men with her hands.

It was Moira who was responsible for Katie's internet search. Moira was a Wiccan high priestess and as Katie had more or less denounced her Presbyterian upbringing because she recognized the same hypocrisy in Christianity that the great Max Bland so effectively brought to light in *The Remarkable Reign of Pope Anne I*, she had always kept an open mind whenever Moira spoke of Wicca and it's various beliefs and rituals. She had even attended a few of Moira's coven meetings.

"I know exactly what you should do," Moira claimed last night when Katie told her what her and Danielle desired. "Handfasting! It's perfect and it's even legal in some areas."

"We don't want anything legal, just symbolic."

"That's fine. I've presided over several ceremonies and I can help you plan it."

Katie looked askance at her friend.

"Is it romantic? I want romantic. What I don't want is a bunch of witches chanting around a cauldron in some Goth room with black candles." She suddenly frowned because she realized that she sounded so much like Max just then. He was beginning to rub off on her. Oh God.

Moira huffed. "You know Wiccans are not like that, Katie. And yes, handfasting is very romantic. I can plan a ceremony so romantic it'll probably make you cry." She then loaned Katie two books she owned on the subject which Katie brought home so that she and Danielle could research and plan.

Her desk phone rang.

"Katie Shaw, Charitable Funds Manager," she answered.

"Yes, Ms. Shaw, hello," began a woman with a British accent. "My name is Cassiana Lyndsay. We also have with us on the line my sister, Addison Rivers."

"Hello, Ms. Shaw, good day to you," greeted another woman.

Katie said hello to both and asked what she could do for them.

"Right," said Cassiana. "First off let me apologize for ringing you at work. I know you must be terribly busy but I, that is, we, wanted to catch you before you left to ask if you'd be kind enough to join us this evening for dinner, perhaps? Or maybe just coffee?"

"We apologize for the short notice." This time it was Addison. "But our business in New York is just about concluded and tomorrow afternoon we're off to London."

"Right. We'd only need about an hour of your time, maybe two. Is it possible you can fit us in?"

Katie wondered what it was about speaking to anyone British that made her feel as if she were central in a Le Carré novel and was about to be told where to drop off the secret documents. Must be James Bond's fault. Certainly these two Brits were merely students doing nothing more than working on their dissertation about how modern countries address the issue of homelessness and wanted to interview her for information before flying back to England to deliver their paper to the Lord High Chamberlain, or whatever they called the chap at Oxford who graded dissertations. Katie had done this sort of thing before for other students and was always eager to help so she told them she was free to join them for dinner but did ask what it was pertaining to in case she needed to brush up on some statistics.

Cassiana: "Right. Well, it's pertaining to a job offer we'd like to extend to you."

Katie was stunned. "Really?" she asked.

Addison: "Yes. Harrison Mayhew recommended you to us."

🍁 🍁 🍁

Katie suggested meeting at Michelangelo's; like Danielle and Max she had become addicted to its simple charm and good food. Besides, it wasn't a high-end restaurant and if for some reason she got stuck with the check she'd be able to afford it. When Katie arrived she was a bit baffled. She hadn't even been in the same room as Harrison Mayhew since Homeward Bound closed, though of course she'd heard his name discussed. He was one of the most outspoken advocates of doing more to help the homeless and was a big thorn in the sides of many of America's best known politicians as he lobbied them to break open the nation's coffers and start spreading the wealth. He earned himself guest spots on MSNBC and *Oprah*, he wrote Op-Ed pieces for the *Times*, and it was even rumored that every year, for two weeks, he lived on the streets, sleeping on benches and begging for food just so he'd always be able to properly empathize with those he tried to help. He was, in short, Katie's idol. So it was rather shocking for Katie to hear that a man like Harrison Mayhew had remembered her enough to recommend her for a job, let alone remembered her at all. She even said so to the two women joining her for dinner.

"Oh, Harrison spoke very highly of you," the one who had introduced herself as Cassiana said. She was an attractive brunette, late thirties, and when she spoke Harrison's name she blushed. Katie understood. For a lesbian she herself had been pretty damn attracted to Harrison Mayhew.

"Yes, very highly," Addison Rivers confirmed. This one was a redhead, a shade younger than the other, whose glasses did nothing to hide the sparkle of her green eyes. Katie noticed that their waiter was smitten and took particularly good care of Addison. "His words exactly were that we'd be unable to find anyone better."

"Wow," Katie whispered. To their credit, the two British women allowed a few moments to pass so that Katie could savor the honor of Harrison Mayhew's blessing. Then they went on to explain what it is they wanted with Katie.

"As I believe I mentioned, Addi and I are sisters," Cassiana said. "Our father was one of the most philanthropic men in England."

"Not to mention one of the richest," Addison contributed.

"Right. He was even knighted by the Queen."

"And when he died the nation mourned, don't forget that, Cassie."

"Right. In any case, he named Addi and I heiresses to his estate with the stipulation that we continue his charitable works. No problem there, I assure you…he raised us both to be very giving."

"That's where you come in, love," Addi said. "We've only now begun to turn our foundation's attention to homelessness in the U.K. and we want someone who can direct our efforts wisely."

Katie held up her hand.

"Um…in the U.K.?" she asked. "You mean the job is in England?"

"Well, based in Britain, yes; London to be precise, but our foundation services all territories of the United Kingdom. You'll become quite familiar with Scotland, Wales and the lot."

"Ah."

Cassiana nodded.

"Right. We feel that no one is doing enough in this field, that no one is even making a dent in the problem because to most everyone else it's just a job."

"It needs to be a passion," Addison tacked on.

"Right."

"We want you, love, to put the passion Harrison says you have to work for us."

"Right. For example, tell us about Homeward Bound, please."

So Katie detailed that program, from the moment she conceived it right up to the end, when she pulled down the iron gate and locked it for the last time; she went over how it worked, its organizational structure, who they helped and she even took from her purse the Polaroid snapshot of the very last person who gained an apartment thanks to Homeward Bound. The two Englishwomen smiled approvingly.

Addison said, "We want a Homeward Bound in every major city in the U.K. London alone could use three or four."

"Right," Cassiana said. "Your idea was brilliant. If properly funded and guided it could revolutionize the business of solving homelessness. Now tell us what you think about shelters here in the States."

"They're horrible," Katie answered with no hesitation. "They're very scary and unsafe, not to mention uncomfortable. A woman has less of a chance getting raped in a frat house than in just about any shelter in this country and a man has less of a chance getting shivved in prison."

"We want you to change that," Addison insisted. "We want you to oversee creation of a private shelter system in the U.K. that will not only put America's to shame and hopefully force them to change but that will also do what they're supposed to."

"Right. Provide a safe haven."

Next they asked Katie how she felt about the soup kitchens in the States.

Again, with no hesitation, Katie was quick to answer.

"They're demeaning, not to mention understaffed and under supplied. The homeless have to wait outside in long lines where everybody can see them lining up for free food and then once they get inside they're treated rudely."

"We want you to change that," Addison repeated.

"Right. But we also want you to go beyond shelters and soup kitchens. Those are old ideas that do have some merit but don't address everything. Harrison has told us you are one of the most creative and innovative people he's ever employed and with us you'll have total autonomy to use those traits and really attack the problem. We want to see stuff that's never been done before. And if anything new fails, no bother. At least we can say we tried and you can come up with something else."

Katie's head was spinning and she felt like she was going to float away. Certainly this was not happening. Certainly one does not awaken one day to find that yes, Virginia, there is a Santa Claus. Only he's not a fat white guy in a ridiculous red suit. He's actually two sisters from England who both sound like Mary Poppins. She had to shake her head to clear it and then said:

"I don't understand something. England's not a third-world country. You have smart, educated people there just like we do. Why aren't you searching for homegrown talent?"

Cassiana and Addison looked at each other and then replied in unison, "Harrison Mayhew."

Cassiana: "We trust him implicitly."

Addison: "There's no one we'd rather consult."

Cassiana: "If he says you're our girl, then you're our girl."

Addison (chuckling): "It's like a recommendation from God, love."

🍁 🍁 🍁

Katie's thoughts were racing, so was her heart. But she had the presence of mind enough to remember Danielle. As much as she wanted to throw herself at the feet of the two sisters and declare her undying fealty and then break into a rousing rendition of "O! Britannia" she had to consider Danielle.

"Can I think about it?" she asked, almost afraid that by doing so she'd insult them and they'd rescind their offer.

"Right. Absolutely."

"It's a lot to digest," Addison said. "Please do think it over."

"Right. However, not to attempt to sway you or anything but we are considering a starting salary of two-hundred and fifty thousand."

"Pounds, of course."

"Right. A little over one-hundred thirty-five thousand U.S. dollars."

"Current exchange rates, of course."

"Of course," Katie whispered.

"We'd even cover your moving expenses?" Addison said hopefully, trying to sweeten the pot.

"Right. And until you find a place to live we have a suite at the King Charles. You can stay there as long as you like."

"With a per diem."

"Right."

Katie said, "That's very generous."

Again the two sisters looked at each other and again they said in unison, "Harrison Mayhew."

"If he seems to think you're worth it," Addison added, "then you're worth it. And after meeting you we think you're worth it."

"I'm gay," Katie suddenly blurted out.

"I'm sorry?" Cassiana said.

"Beg your pardon?" Addison asked.

Even Katie hadn't known she was going to say that. But it was out there now so: "I'm gay," she repeated, somewhat breathlessly. "I just wanted to make that known right now. In case I accept the job and you expect me to show up at the office Christmas party with a model husband on my arm."

The sisters looked at each other and then burst out into trilling laughter.

Addison: "Oh, love, that's no problem."

Cassiana: "Makes no difference to us, really."

Addison: "You needn't worry about it."

Cassiana: "Half the people I know are gay."

Addison: "Including her ex-husband!"

Cassiana: "Right. Now that that's settled…we'd like an answer in one week's time, if that's at all possible. Is there a home number we can ring you back on?"

CHAPTER 42

❀

Yes, there was a home number they could ring her back on and Katie readily gave it. But just to be on the safe side she also provided her parents' number, Moira's number, Danielle's cell phone and office number as well as the number for Mrs. Edelstein, her old piano teacher in Nebraska; the old bat may be nearing ninety but she could hear a phone ring and go next door to fetch Katie's folks.

After leaving the restaurant Katie started walking. She remembered something Max had told her, that on the day he found out *The Remarkable Reign of Pope Anne I* was going to be published he was so excited that he couldn't stay still and so left his apartment and just started walking, even though it was August and 110 degrees outside. He told her he must have walked three miles in that unbearable heat one way and another three back just because he was so jazzed. Katie felt the same way now. It may not be 100 degree outside this evening but she was so jazzed that before she knew it she had somehow managed to travel all the way from the Upper East Side down to the Battery stopping only because continuing would have meant walking into Upper New York Bay.

She flagged down a cab to bring her home and entering Max's apartment took a deep breath and then sought out Danielle. Max told her she'd find her in the master bedroom trying to decide what to wear to Mayzie fucking Witherspoon's brunch on Saturday.

"Hey," he said as Katie was heading in the direction indicated. "Why don't you go this time? I mean, you and Danielle are a hot item and trust me, Mayzie would get a fucking kick out of having a lesbian couple in her set. She has two gay guys already but no lesbians. She'd think it was eclectic."

Katie smiled.

"I'll mention it to Danielle," she promised and then left him to his Yankees game.

The master bedroom looked like the third floor of Bloomingdales after a tornado. It was as if Danielle's closet had vomited. The bed, the settee, the armchair and much of the floor was covered in designer clothing and shoes. When she saw Katie enter Danielle emerged from this mess and rushed to give her a kiss.

"You're late tonight," she said in greeting.

"I had a meeting after work," Katie told her. "I tried calling to warn you but you never answered."

"I know. My cell phone has been lost in this disaster area for a while now and who knows when I'll find it. Anyway, I'm glad you're here. We have an important decision to make because Donna Karan will be at Mayzie's on Saturday and I can't look bad in front of Donna Karan. But I don't want to wear a Donna Karan outfit because that'll seem too obvious. So…do you think I should choose a Versace pantsuit, a Miyake dress or something more playful?"

"I have no idea but Max thinks I should go with you this time. As your lesbian lover, no less."

Danielle thought this over and nodded. "That's not bad. Mayzie will think it's eclectic and I bet even Donna will be impressed. Okay, so first let's decide what I'll wear and then we'll raid your closet to be sure you match."

"Sweetie, we need to talk."

Danielle stopped sifting through the clothes on her bed and looked up at Katie.

"You know," she said, "every time I say 'We need to talk' to Max he gets very paranoid, his stomach fills with bile and he's sure the news is bad. And then I say, 'No, it's nothing. Stop worrying.' So, is that what you're about to say?"

"Not exactly. There is something we need to worry about."

"You're not sick, are you?" Danielle inquired with genuine concern. "Because if you are I have two good kidneys and you're more than welcome to one. I'd offer you both but then I'd be fucked."

"I'm not sick," Katie said, laughing. "In fact, I've never felt better. So far, today has been one of the best days of my life." She spun a happy pirouette and landed on the pile of clothes on the bed. Danielle joined her.

"Why? Did you finally meet Anne Heche and she agreed to marry you?"

"No, but you do realize she's the only woman—"

"—you'd leave me for," Danielle finished for her. "Yeah, yeah, you've told me. Just so you know I'd drop you in a second for Halle Berry. So what made today so great?"

"I got a job offer."

"Fabulous!"

"It's a really good job, Danielle."

"Fabulous, fabulous!"

"It's everything I ever dreamed of. In fact, if I didn't take it I'd probably sink into a horrible depression, go on an ice cream diet and balloon up to four-hundred pounds."

"In that case I'm demanding you take it."

Katie nodded. "Believe me I want to. However, there is just one teensy-weensy catch…"

🍁   🍁   🍁

Max was upstairs in the library. The Yankees had won their game and he was celebrating with a gin and tonic and a good book, *The Remarkable Reign of Pope Anne I*. Sure, he had written it and sure, he had spent months poring over every one of its 112,379 words when revising it before sending the manuscript out for consideration to agents and publishers; and yes, he had spent the last few years speaking about it to fans at book signings, in college lecture halls, on television and radio, but since its publication he had never actually read the damn thing as a regular person would, just for pleasure and diversion. And thirty pages in he had to admit that so far it was quite good. What's more, it brought back all sorts of memories of that time when he was merely max bland, computer systems engineer, an anonymous guy spending his hours away from ProtoTech at the local park writing; or at the Tempe Library writing; or at his kitchen table writing—all in the hopes of finally changing his life.

Hearing footsteps on the stairs he looked up from what everybody considers his masterpiece to see his two housemates approach holding hands. He sighed, immediately wondering what was wrong now.

"Max, can we talk to you?" Danielle started. He noticed her eyes were red and damp.

"Jesus, why are you crying?" he groaned. "Can't I make it through one week without either of you crying about something?"

The two women took seats on the couch across from his easy chair and reluctantly Max put down his book. Katie confessed that it was her fault that

Danielle was crying and Max said, "Are you sick? Is that what this is all about? Whaddya need, a spleen? I got one and I'm pretty sure I'm not using it. Except, can they put a straight man's spleen in a gay woman? You see, these are the kinds of things they don't tell you about on the Discovery channel."

"I don't need a spleen but thank you," Katie replied. "And just so you know, you are using it. It has something to do with making the blood cells that fight off infection. Boy, you two are quick to offer up organs."

"It's kind of a running joke between us," Max told her. "Every time Danielle comes to me acting as if her world is falling apart I ask her if she needs a kidney or something."

"Katie got a job offer," Danielle said.

"And this is cause for tears?" inquired the writer.

"The job is in London."

"England's London?" Max asked and when Katie nodded he whistled. "Does the subway go that far?"

"I think it's the next stop on the D train after Coney Island."

"Boy, that's just like the Brits: they're still pissed about the whole Revolutionary War thing so they figure they'll take all our best gay women."

"Why not? America's not using us for anything."

"Would you two stop kidding around?" Danielle interrupted crossly. "This is serious."

Max apologized and then said, "So…are you considering accepting?"

"Yep."

"Must be a helluva job."

For the second time that evening Katie detailed her conversation with the sisters from England and the offer they made. She left nothing out, from Harrison Mayhew's recommendations all the way up to Mrs. Edelstein's phone number. She even took the trouble to enumerate several ideas she already had for obeying the sisters' mandate to be creative and really attack the problem of homelessness in the U.K. and then, hopefully, the world.

When Katie was done Danielle said, "She'll be making more money than me, if you can believe it. I guess they'll be two of us in Blahnik rehab."

Then, signaling each other with a look, Danielle and Katie knew it was time to get down to the hard part. Downstairs in the master bedroom, after Katie had given Danielle the rundown on the London job offer, Danielle had immediately said she'd move to England with her.

"Nothing could be simpler," Danielle had said. "ARCL has a London division, a huge division…Margot will definitely approve a transfer for me—she's even told me more than once that she wished I was over there because I'd run it better than stupid Jeremy Wilcox. I bet that by tomorrow evening I'll—"

She had stopped then suddenly and that's when her tears began welling up. Katie knew why.

"Max," she had said.

Nodding, Danielle answered, "I won't leave without him. I'm sorry, baby, but I can't. Before there was you there was Max, and before there was Max I was miserable."

"I know. You come with baggage."

"That's not fair. I come with a man I love and you knew that right from the very beginning. I never hid it from you."

"You're right and I'm sorry; that came out wrong."

"In fact, you're agreeing to formally accept him into your life with this handfasting ceremony we're planning."

"I know. Again I'm sorry. It's just that…I don't know…I think Max is great, I really do but I don't think I'd be willing to give up this job for him, sweetie. I just can't. If for some reason he's unwilling to move then—"

"You'd go anyway," Danielle had murmured.

"Fuck yes! This is too fucking good to pass up, Danielle! Far too good to pass up for some man. For you and you alone, yes; but for you because of him, no. Maybe that makes me a selfish bitch but too bad."

"Okay, I get it, I get it." Danielle couldn't fault Katie for her stubbornness on this matter. Though she knew Katie and Max had developed a nice little friendship over time they really hadn't forged a deep emotional bond yet. In fact, they still had to take each other in somewhat small doses or else their personalities clashed. No wonder, then, that in Katie's mind Max was a non-factor when determining whether to accept this job across the Atlantic.

"God, what if he won't agree to move?" Danielle queried. "What do we do then, Katie?"

"Maybe he will, sweetie. Let's not worry about it now."

"We have to worry about it now," Danielle had admonished. "You only have a week to tell them whether or not you're taking the job which means we only have a week to convince him to leave New York. And do you have any idea how much he loves this city? He's a member of the New York City Historical Society; he could tell you how to get anywhere in this city by subway; he's been to every museum and every art gallery; and he's already bought a burial plot for himself up in the Bronx: Woodlawn Cemetery, Plot 1577."

"Did he get one for you too?"

"No. He told me he doesn't give a fuck where I'm buried just as long as he's planted in the Bronx."

Danielle and her girlfriend then spent most of the rest of their time in the master bedroom strategizing like two conspirators. In the end, by virtue of her longer association with and deeper connection to Max it was decided that Danielle was their only chance of success in this endeavor and that Katie would be by her side for support. They also agreed not to consider yet the consequences of his saying no; one thing at a time.

But up in the library as Danielle took breath in her lungs to begin Max suddenly said:

"So, to make a long story short you want us all to move to London, right?"

"How did you know?" Danielle asked, genuinely surprised.

Max looked at his girlfriend as if she were a moron.

"Whaddya think, I'm stupid? You come up here with your eyes all teary because you think Katie's gonna go bye-bye; you tell me we need to talk about something serious; you let Katie explain in ass-numbingly boring detail what a dream job she's being offered...what other conclusion am I supposed to reach?"

The two women waited a few moments for him to continue but he just threw up his hands with impatience.

"Well?" he asked. "Aren't you gonna present your case? Don't I deserve to hear why I should pick up and leave my hometown to accommodate my girlfriend's lesbian lover who I don't even get to have sex with?"

"Because if I was the one with the job offer in London you wouldn't hesitate to make the move," Danielle said.

"Are you sure?"

"Max!"

"I mean, you are a bit of a pain in the ass, you know. I might be a happier man with a whole ocean between us."

"Fuck you. Plus, your career is portable. You can write anywhere."

"That's a popular misconception about authors. We cannot write anywhere. For example, it's damn near impossible to do it in the shower."

"Max, stop making jokes!" Danielle demanded and once more told him how serious a matter this was. "*And*," she continued, "you've always said you'd like to live in London, remember?"

"I meant London, Ontario, sweetie."

"Whatever. You hate Canada. You once said New York should annex the entire country and make it the sixth borough."

"Actually what I said was that New York should sell Staten Island to the Japanese and make Canada the fifth borough. I wonder why the mayor never answered my letter about that." He took a sip of his cocktail and then said ruefully, "I just don't know about this, Danielle. I mean, I waited twelve years in the cultural wasteland of Arizona to be able to return here and now you want me to leave almost right away?"

"Fuck, I didn't think about that," Danielle admitted softly.

"Why not?"

"I don't know; I just didn't."

"Figures. I bet if I was a famous fashion designer you'd be a little more considerate of my feelings."

"Max! Sweetie, that's not true! I just thought that under the circumstances you'd be willing to discuss the possibili—"

"I don't think you want to 'discuss' anything. I get the impression that you want me to make a decision right now. But you're outta luck. I'll need time to think about it."

"She only has a week, Max."

Shaking his head Max said, "I'll need at least a month, I'm sorry. Although…I may be willing to shorten that time in return for…"

"What?"

"Well, it's just that I know you were planning on spending the night with Katie, however, I'm feeling quite horny myself but my right hand and I got into an argument today so I'm not sure it's in the mood…"

Danielle looked over at Katie who nodded.

"Deal," Danielle answered.

"Fine, that brings the time I need down to three weeks."

"Max!"

"Well, I'm realizing now that you haven't dressed up for me lately. You know how I like to be enticed with lingerie, particularly that black lace nightie you own."

"Deal."

"Two weeks then."

"What?"

"I'll need more, sweetie. Throw in some thigh high stockings and high heels."

"Done. *And* I will give you the best blowjob of your life to finish you off. Now what does that get me?"

"Thirty-six hours," he said. "And you may wanna consider buying me something nice, too. Coincidentally, I happen to be in the market for a new digital camera."

♦ ♦ ♦

The negotiating done, Danielle went downstairs alone to answer a phone call and when she had gone Katie gave Max a grateful look and said, "Thank you."

"For what?"

"For doing this. Agreeing to the move, I mean. I can tell from the way you were giving Danielle a hard time that you were set to do it right from the start."

"Very perceptive," Max said, then he shrugged. "It's no big deal, really. I'd hate to bust up this happy family. Besides, America is really getting on my nerves. Any nation that would elect a Bush to a second term is one I'd rather not stay in. Next thing you know Blacks will be stuck picking cotton again and Jim Crow will be the law of the land. I think England will be a welcome change, if they'll have us. Anyway, she's right, you know. I always have fancied living there. Must have been all the Richard Curtis movies I've seen."

Katie crossed over to him, sat on his lap and wrapped her arms around his neck. She gave him a kiss on the cheek.

"I am surprised, though," she told him. "I may not have known you as long as Danielle but even I'm aware of how much you love New York. What gives?"

"I dunno," began Max. "I love New York, you're right. And if my arm hadn't been twisted by you getting this great job maybe I'd never leave but...what the hell, right? You only live once, why not spend part of it living in Europe?"

"This job is very important to me," she reiterated. "It's what people in my profession dream of."

"That depresses me because the only thing people in my profession dream of is the perfect adjective. Listen, I get to pick where we all live, understood? If I leave it up to you you'll have us in a sixth-floor walk up with no running water. If I leave it up to Danielle she'll have us living in the Women's department at Harrod's."

"Whatever you say."

"Now get off my lap. Remember what happened the last time we were this close."

CHAPTER 43

❀

When she called her parents in Arizona to tell them she would soon be moving across the Atlantic it occurred to Danielle that they had been kept in the dark about one very important thing. Upon her mother asking why she was making such a drastic move so far away Danielle's brain had composed the following answer: "Because Katie has a wonderful job offer in London and I love her enough to uproot myself for her sake." This response actually reached her mouth which got as far as speaking the word "Because" and was readying itself for "Katie" when suddenly it stopped abruptly upon receiving another message from the brain, this one marked "URGENT!" and demanding the mouth to cease and desist all operations immediately. Moving to London for Katie's sake may have made perfect sense to Danielle; it may have made perfect sense to Max but Danielle could just see the puzzled frown on her mother's face and the blank stare on her father's as they tried to fathom what it all meant.

"Because," her mouth started again after receiving new instructions from the brain, "I've been transferred. Yes, that's it. I've been transferred. The London branch is a mess and Margot believes I can turn it around. It's quite a step up, actually."

"Well, congratulations, princess," her father said. Danielle could always rely on him for the proper response to good news.

"But so far away," her mother whined. And Danielle could always rely on her for just the opposite. "I mean, really…it's a whole other country!"

"Don't worry, Mom. I'll try to make it back to visit once every ten years or so."

But when the phone call ended Danielle sat for a while in her office thinking things over and realizing that the time had come to reveal her bisexuality to her parents. She loved Katie deeply, after all, and they *were* in the midst of planning the nearest thing to a wedding they could have.

"You don't have to do that," Katie told her later when all three of them were in the dining room eating take-out Chinese. "It makes no difference to me one way or the other and I certainly don't want to be the cause of any animosity between you and your parents."

Max asked Danielle to pass the soy sauce and then said, "I think it's unavoidable at this point, though, Katie. There's no alternative, she has to tell her parents because we can't keep passing you off as a 'friend' whose apartment is being fumigated. I mean, what happens when her folks come to visit us in England? Are you supposed to hide in the basement or take a hotel room in town? Actually, that's not a bad idea…Danielle, can *I* hide in the basement or take a hotel room in town whenever they come visit?"

"Very funny. Anyway, it's not fair to you, Katie, for me to keep lying," Danielle added.

"I'm not worried about the fairness of it," her girlfriend replied. "I'm worried about the health of your good relationship with your parents. I know you think your mother's a Looney Tune and that your father's a pompous academic but you still love them."

"Which is why they need to know the truth about their daughter." Danielle said this with such firmness that it silenced Katie from making any more arguments. Max reached across and took hold of Danielle's hand. "I'm thirty-one," she continued, addressing Katie. "Someone my age should not be hiding who she is from her parents, like I'm afraid they'll ground me. Now, I've decided. This weekend I'll fly to Arizona and tell them face to face."

Katie nodded. "Can I come?"

"Absolutely. It'll give us a chance to show them how much we mean to each other."

Max sighed.

"Goddammit," he swore. "I guess that means I have to go too."

But Danielle put her hand on his shoulder in a gesture of restraint and said, "Honey, relax…I think Katie and I could handle this."

Max started laughing. "At the risk of discouraging you, sweetie, if you think your mother is gonna just sit back, listen to you tell her you're bisexual and then get up and bake cookies you got another think coming. New age concepts involving her daughter having both a man and a woman as lovers is gonna short circuit her brain. And after she's done torturing you with her lunacy I'll need to be there so I can buy you both something expensive to make you feel better."

🍁   🍁   🍁

"Oh, this is wonderful!" Arlene Edwards exclaimed when her visitors from New York entered her Fountain Hills home that weekend. "And I remember you," she said to Katie.

"Katie Shaw, Mrs. Edwards. So nice to see you again."

"Yes, same here. You're Danielle's friend who stayed with these two while your apartment was being painted."

"Fumigated," Katie and Max said in unison.

"Right, right, fumigated," Arlene said. "Well, come in and make yourselves comfortable. I have iced tea ready for the ladies and plenty of ginger ale for you, Max."

"Are your bags in the car, Max?" Danielle's father, Harold, asked.

"Uh, no, Dad," Danielle said. "We decided on staying in a hotel this time."

Arlene's face fell.

"Why on earth would you do that, dear? We have plenty of room."

The real answer to that question, that Danielle wasn't 100% sure she or Katie would be welcome to stay in the house after The Big Talk did not seem appropriate yet so she said, "I thought you told me Uncle Gary was coming down from Sedona."

"That's next week, darling, next week." She shrugged. "Oh, well. I suppose you've all checked in, huh? *C'est la vie.*"

Following a half hour of chitchat in the living room Max, at a prearranged signal from Danielle, got up and excused himself. He had some phone calls to make, he claimed, and would make them while taking a walk around the block.

"So…" Arlene began with a conspiratorial air, "why haven't you and Max been discussing marriage?"

"Arlene!"

"Hush, Harold. It's a perfectly valid question."

"You'll have to excuse Danielle's mother," Harold said to Katie. "She's never going to be satisfied until she knows our daughter has Max in her clutches."

"You make it sound so sinister, dear." Arlene swatted him lightly on the leg. "Is it sinister for a mother to want her daughter to marry well? Besides, I happen to believe they're a good couple who should make things permanent."

Before this got any further, Danielle decided to cut in.

"Mom, Dad...I need to talk to you about something."

"Ooh! Is it about a wedding?" her mother prodded.

"No. Well...yes, in a way, but not in the way you're probably hoping for."

"Now, look, I know I said I'd love to have a big wedding for you but there's nothing wrong with having a small private ceremony if that's what Max wants."

"No, Mom. I—"

"Last month we attended Cynthia Nisberg's wedding—you remember Cynthia, dear? Muriel's daughter? Anyway, it was so overblown that it was utterly tasteless. And it was little Cynthia's third! But Muriel likes to make a show of everything, of course. So if Max wants something simple then that's what we'll give him."

"Mom, it's nothing to do with a wedding, alright? Or Max, for that matter. It's about me. And Katie."

Arlene knitted her eyebrows in confusion while Harold simply steepled his fingertips in front of him in a scholarly manner. Next to Danielle on the couch Katie was trying her hardest to hide her nervousness with a calm, poised, perfectly pleasant visage so that whenever Danielle looked over at her she'd be able to draw strength from her.

"What about you?" Arlene asked softly. "And Katie?"

So Danielle blurted it out, employing the same ripping-off-the-bandage method she used when she confessed her bisexuality to Max lo those many moons ago.

"Mom, Dad...I'm bisexual."

Arlene tilted her head in confusion.

"Bisexual? What do you mean?"

"Oh, for God's sake, Mom...you know what bisexual means. It means I'm sexually attracted to both men and women and I have been for as long as I can remember."

"Nonsense," Arlene interjected. "You weren't bisexual when you were a little girl. Was she, Harold? Did you notice her being bisexual when she was a little girl?"

"Mom! Of course I wasn't bisexual back then, that's ridiculous. I meant that when I got older, in my teens, I realized it. I've just hid it from you, is all. Not that it's anything I'm ashamed of. I just wasn't sure how you two would view it. Ever since I was seventeen I've dated members of both sexes but I only told you about the guys. But in addition to all the guys there was a Lisa, a Melanie, a Sonia, a Crystal, a Jeanine, an Alexandra and a Susan. And now, a Katie. Oh, and maybe the reason little Cynthia Nisberg is already on her third marriage when she's only my age is because your friend Muriel keeps trying to convince her she's not gay; Cynthia happens to have been the first girl I had sex with."

"Oh!" Arlene exclaimed, growing pale.

"Anyway, like I said, now there's Katie." Danielle took hold of Katie's hand. "We've been together for nearly two years, are very much in love and she is the reason I am moving to London. And as much I would like your approval, as much as I want you to accept Katie as part of my life and then as part of yours I am willing to leave here without it. I cannot change what I am and I am not going to let you try to pull me and Katie apart. I love you but that love has limits, especially if it interferes with my happiness. Katie is a wonderful person who is bright, ambitious and extremely generous. She has brought a completeness to my life. If you'll only take the time to get to know her I believe that you will be proud that I have chosen so well."

Danielle took a deep breath and exhaled noisily. It was done. Finally. She felt as if only now were her parents aware of who this person they created was. And for the first time she herself became aware of what a burden it had been to carry this secret around. She literally felt lighter by several pounds; she felt exhilarated. Whatever other secrets she kept from her parents (her lesbian porn collection, for one, or her enjoyment of being tied up and spanked by Max, for another) could remain secret. This, however, was the big one and now she felt she could rest easy.

🍁   🍁   🍁

For several moments there was silence. Danielle and Katie were patiently awaiting a response from Arlene and Harold, but Arlene and Harold seemed to be awaiting more from Danielle and Katie. Arlene, in particular, looked as though what she specifically was waiting for was her daughter to tell her this was all a joke, a bit of harmless fun.

Finally, Harold, seeing that his wife was temporarily unresponsive and not wanting this already uncomfortable silence to become even more uncomfortable, shifted in his chair and said, "Are you also bisexual, Katie?"

"No, Professor, I'm not. I'm gay."

"Ah. So why don't you tell us how you two met?"

"Um…Danielle came to my office looking to hire some homeless people." And Katie gave Danielle's parents a brief recap of that first meeting. "But we didn't actually start dating until after Thanksgiving of that year, right, sweetie?"

"Right. When I got back from here, in fact."

"Oh!" Arlene uttered again, as if perhaps it was something she served at Thanksgiving that made her daughter this way.

"So," Harold went on, "This Homeward Bound was something you created, was it? And you got homeless people jobs? You know, that's a wonderful idea. I think it's admirable you've dedicated your life to those less fortunate. You're right, princess, she is a very generous person."

Danielle smiled gratefully at her father.

"And you're right to have said I'd be proud you've chosen someone like her."

"Harold..." Arlene began.

"Don't start, Arlene," Harold warned. "There's nothing wrong here, nothing for you to get upset about."

"But how did this happen? Danielle, how did this happen?"

"It didn't happen, Mom. Me being bisexual just is."

"Did you eat something wrong?"

"Mom!"

"Organic foods, maybe..."

"Mom, you're being ridiculous. Eating tofu doesn't change your sexual orientation!"

"I just don't understand, is all," Arlene continued. "You're attracted to women?"

"Yes."

"Well, are you attracted to me?"

"Oh God, Mom!" Danielle cried, cringing and shuddering. "Stop being disgusting!" She felt a horrible chill crawl down her spine.

"It's a valid question."

"No, it is not! God, why do you always have to make things so difficult?"

"I just don't know how to feel about this," Arlene wailed. "My only daughter flies all the way from New York to tell me she loves a woman! That's just the kind of thing to happen in New York, too! It's why I didn't like the idea of you moving there. You don't hear about women loving women in Arizona!"

Danielle was stunned; and she was starting to feel monumentally embarrassed because of the idiotic things her mother was saying. Organic foods, only in New York...really! She cast a helpless look in Katie's direction, begging the other woman with her eyes to not hold any of this against her. Katie squeezed

Danielle's hand for encouragement and then thought maybe it would help if she said something.

"Mrs. Edwards, from what I understand the Phoenix area has a thriving gay communi—"

"You be quiet!" Arlene ordered. "Our family has never been part of any gay community. All I know is I sent a perfectly good daughter to New York and you've ruined her!"

Katie was taken aback. "I-I had nothing to do with 'ruining' her, ma'am."

Leaning forward in his chair Harold said sternly, "Arlene, you need to calm down. Katie, I'm so sorry for—"

"I bet it happened when her apartment was being fumigated, Harold," Arlene sputtered. "Danielle was at home, in a weakened state after her operation…no wonder she was susceptible to subversive ideas."

"Subversive?" Danielle exclaimed. "Jesus, Mom, we're not trying to overthrow a government. We're in love!"

"In love subversively!"

"God, you're making no sense!"

"I am making sense! Good, Christian sense!"

"Please, Mom…you haven't set foot inside St. Joseph's since you lost the Spring Baking Contest to Muriel Nisberg ten years ago."

"The reverend's wife was biased! She and Muriel were bridge partners; my macadamia nut cookies beat those macaroons by a mile! But that's not the point! The point is I still hold to Christian ideals which make no mention of bisexuality."

"Arlene!"

"Oh, do shut up, Harold! This does not concern you."

Just then the front door opened and Max's head peeked in. He had stayed away for the agreed upon interval and was now returning to see if everything was hunky-dory. But as soon as Arlene caught sight of him she got up from her chair and ran to him, arms outstretched.

"Oh, Max, honey! I am so sorry about all this! You poor thing!" She embraced him as she would a man who'd just heard his cat died. "Now listen…I'm sure Danielle still loves you, Max. We just need to get this silly bisexual notion out of her head and then you two can go on as before, alright? And maybe someday there will be wedding bells ringing? I'm sure you have been such a patient man while Danielle sowed her oats with this Katie person and it was so good of you to be tolerant!"

Max, extricating himself from Arlene's embrace, said, "What are you talking about? Of course I know Danielle still loves me, who told you differently? And as far as her being with Katie I'm all for it."

Arlene raised her eyebrows.

"You are?"

"Yeah, didn't she tell you? That I'm the one who encouraged her to go out and get a girlfriend?"

"You did?"

"Yeah…I mean, she's bisexual. What else was I supposed to do? I really have no problem with her dating women."

"You don't?"

"No, why should I? I'm not threatened by it. All three of us have been very happy together. You should be glad she found someone as great as Katie. Could be worse, you know. I understand Sandra Bernhard is available."

"So, you're completely okay with this?"

"Perfectly."

Arlene considered this for a moment and then turned back to face the living room.

"Darling!" she squealed happily, coming towards Danielle. "This is wonderful news!"

"WHAT!" Danielle and Katie both said together.

"Katie, welcome to our family, dear!" And Arlene leaned down to embrace and then kiss the lesbian on the cheek.

"Mom, what the hell?" Danielle demanded. "Just because Max says he's fine with it all of a sudden you are?"

Arlene bestowed a sympathetic look on her daughter.

"Oh, honey…I've told you before: Max is special. He's an artist, after all, and his opinions carry more weight; I have to respect them. And if this little arrangement you have with Katie makes him happy then I see no reason to feel otherwise."

CHAPTER 44

❦

Max should have known better than to leave the planning of what came to be known as the "joining ritual" to Danielle and Katie. His mistake was in telling them that since A) he didn't want to do this in the first place that B) he didn't want to be bothered with all the details involved. Perhaps if his mind hadn't been preoccupied with finishing his current novel, planning their move across the Atlantic and continuing to deal with the Hollywood people about the Pope Anne movie he'd have reconsidered because as it turned out, it was like dropping off two teenage girls at the mall with a blank check.

Since Katie had to be in London two weeks after accepting the job she and Danielle decided why not kill two birds with one stone? And thus did they decide to blend the joining ritual with a going away party to make one big event. Of course, they didn't tell Max. Furthermore, using Moira as a consultant, they also turned the joining ritual into an elaborate Wiccan handfasting ceremony involving a "circle of love" and "callers of the four quarters", among other things. Of course, they didn't tell Max. And finally, because this was also a going away party Danielle and Katie invited every open-minded person they knew: friends, co-workers, even a couple of Katie's former lovers. Of course, they didn't tell Max. All Max knew was the date and time; he even had trouble remembering those between all the last minute revising he was doing on his book and all the information he was being e-mailed from London area realtors.

On the day of the blessed event Mikey, Max's lone invitee to what Max called "this stupid thing," bought his buddy a drink at a bar two blocks from the Botanical Gardens in the Bronx, not long before the ceremony began.

"I dunno how to toast this, boss," Mikey said, raising a glass of pilsner. "What should I say? 'Here's hoping the *three* of you live happily ever after?'"

Max raised his gin and tonic and said, "You wanna know what you're toasting? I'll tell you what you're toasting. You know how Wanda will come home from time to time and wanna talk about her feelings?"

Groaning, Mikey nodded.

"And," Max continued, "you know how Wanda will storm out of the bedroom from time to time saying you don't understand her?"

Another groan, another nod.

"And you know how Wanda will drag you from time to time to, I dunno…a tea party at her grandmother's, or the latest Goldie Hawn movie?"

"Fuck yeah."

"Well," Max said, clinking his glass with that of his buddy's, "we're toasting the end of that." He took a sip of the cocktail. "I tell you, Mikey, Katie is a godsend. She may be a sanctimonious bitch and maybe her idea of a good time is spending a Saturday with people who don't bathe regularly but ever since her and Danielle fell in love this arrangement has been working out better than I could have hoped. It's like I said before, the burden of being the only one expected to get where Danielle is coming from has been lifted from my shoulders. If I'm not in the mood to talk about her feelings I send her to Katie; if she says I don't understand her I tell her to go see Katie; and since I'm pretty sure England has its own Mayzie Witherspoon I can tell Danielle to bring Katie to those stupid brunches. That, my friend, is what we're toasting." And they clinked glasses again. "I only wish they could leave it at that and not make me go through this stupid ceremony."

"Well, you're a lucky bastard if things are really as convenient as you say they are," Mikey said, chasing the words with a swig of beer. "Still, it can't be pretty when they're both PMSing."

"Yeah, you're right. And they've been living together long enough for their cycles to be in sync, too. Five days out of every month I just try to keep my head down and blend in with the furniture, but they always find some reason to jump down my throat and then all three of us end up snapping at each other." Max shrugged. "Ah, well…it clears the air, you know?"

"Find a place to live in London yet?"

"I've narrowed it down to two places," Max answered. "Both of them are houses because the ladies thought it'd be nice to have yards and a garden which means I'll have to hire a groundskeeper and a gardener because Lord knows neither of them have green thumbs. When Danielle first moved here I bought her a cactus to remind her of home and she managed to kill it. Do you have any idea how hard it is to kill a cactus? Anyway, one of the houses I'm considering is apparently next door to George Michael's so guess which one the ladies want me to buy." Max rolled his eyes. "I can just see Danielle and Katie becoming fast friends with him, you know…going over to borrow a cup of sugar, that sort of thing…and then having lavish celebrity-filled parties at our place. I may have to keep an apartment elsewhere just in case."

The friends drank in silence for a while. The bar was a bit of a dive with a bartender straight from Central Casting and a waitress who'd seen better days. But it was dark and quiet and was the perfect place to stop in for a quick one. After ordering another beer Mikey said, "I dunno, boss…I can't see you living anywhere but New York. I think of this city and I think of you. Me, on the other hand, I'd like to buy a house up in Connecticut somewhere, have a dog, raise a coupla kids in the suburbs with all the white people."

Max laughed. "Where the hell are you gonna get good *arroz con pollo* in Connecticut, man? I once ate at what passed for a fine Italian restaurant up there and I may as well have stayed home and heated up a can of Chef Boyardee. Anyway, I'm thrilled to be going to Europe. I promised myself that I was gonna try to write a portion of my next book in every major city: Rome, Paris, Berlin, Zurich, Stockholm, Dublin, you name it. I wanna see how each environment affects my creativity. But as far as me missing New York goes, I got that all worked out too. Every other month I'm gonna fly back here and stay two weeks. I already talked it over with the boss."

Speaking of Danielle, Mikey glanced at his watch and told his buddy they'd better get going. They were due at the Gardens at one so after Mikey settled the tab they took off.

Outside again in the autumn sun Mikey put on some sunglasses and asked, "How come you didn't invite any of the other guys to this thing, boss? Omar's known you as long as I have, so has Esteban."

"I didn't even wanna invite you to this thing, pal," Max confessed. "But apparently this ceremony they got planned is more meaningful if we all bring a witness who's close to us, you know? Something about the spirit of kinship strengthening our bonds, who knows? I just wanna get it over with. Besides, it's a small thing. Danielle said there'd be no more than ten people involved, an intimate gathering, she said."

❦ ❦ ❦

The women had told Max the ceremony would take place in that region of the Botanical Gardens known as the Forest, which was what was left of the woodlands that long ago covered New York City back before the Dutch made the most famous real estate purchase in recorded history. They also told him it would take place on the banks of the Bronx River, in a clearing near the waterfall, a location which they scouted several days earlier and which was so beautiful they promised it would take his breath away. So after stumbling and meandering through thickets of trees and a forest floor slick with fallen leaves to reach the X on the hand drawn map Katie provided him with Max swore because he was certain he had made a mistake, gotten lost and come upon someone else's shindig in the woods.

"Ah, fuck…this can't be right," he said to Mikey. "Look at all these people. Must be a fucking family reunion." He began consulting the map.

"I told you we shoulda made a left at that knocked over tree," his friend admonished.

"We did make a left, you idiot. But I think we shoulda crossed the stream closer to those rocks we saw, remember? Damn!"

"Let's just—"

"Max! Max! Over here!"

It was Danielle's voice calling him and when he looked up he saw her waving to him through a crowd of people whose expectant faces were now all turned towards him. His mouth dropped open.

"Jesus fucking Christ," he muttered.

"Some intimate gathering," Mikey said in a commiserating tone.

"Who the fuck are all these people?" Max said, stunned.

By now Danielle had approached. She gave Mikey a quick peck on the cheek as a hello and then hugged Max. She was wearing a white gown with flowing sleeves that made her boyfriend think of the elf queen from the *Lord of the Rings* movies, and on her head was a wreath of wild flowers. Instead of Manolo Blahniks or Jimmy Choos her feet wore some strange leather footwear that could have been designed by one of Christ's apostles.

"Who the fuck are all these people?" Max put to her since Mikey couldn't provide an answer the first time.

"Friends," Danielle responded, leading him forward. "Some people from work, even a few of Katie's exes."

"What happened to ten? Ten. That's the number I was told, you twit! Ten."

"Max, honey, relax. Things just got a little out of hand with the planning is all. No harm done. This is a happy event, remember? Why shouldn't we share it with more people?"

Mikey was looking around as Danielle led them through the crowd.

"Sure are a lot of women," he noted.

"Down boy," Danielle said. "They're practically all gay. As far as they're concerned you've got sausage between your legs." And she laughed at the inside joke, expecting Max to join in also but he was too busy feeling ill at ease because of all the attention he was garnering. From the corners of his eyes he could detect women jostling to get a better view of him, and his ears could pick up their murmured exclamations to each other. It wasn't the first time he'd been in a crowd of lesbians, a demographic which treated him like a rock star thanks to *The Remarkable Reign of Pope Anne I*, but he'd never felt comfortable being an idol and wished to hell GLAAD was holding a rally somewhere now.

"Here we are," Danielle said, indicating a cleared area. "This, Max, is our circle of love. Isn't it clever?"

On the ground a circle had been described about fifteen feet in diameter. Max saw that it was composed of three equal sections which Danielle began explaining.

"See? This part is made up of copies of *Pope Anne* because you're a writer and that's the book that made you famous. This other part is made up of coins because I'm in finance and this last part is made up of clothes which all the guests had to donate, because Katie is in the business of helping others. You see? The circle represents the various things each of us have dedicated our lives to. Clever, huh?"

"Diabolically," Max muttered.

But the circle wasn't where the symbolism ended. Standing outside the circle were four women dressed in what looked to Max like the robes of cult priestesses. They each were carrying staffs with long scarves tied to the ends.

"These are our callers of the four quarters," Danielle explained. "They represent the four compass directions. You'll find out what they do later." In the meantime she called Katie and Moira over. Katie was attired in the exact same get up as Danielle. She also gave Max a hug and a kiss and even embraced Mikey. But Moira, on the other hand, was wearing what Max first took to be a clown's outfit. One half of her long magician's robe was red, the other green; one half of her tall conical hat was brown, the other blue. She also bore a staff, a gnarled length of pine with a crystal set on its top.

"Mr. Bland, it is such an honor to meet you," Moira said, pumping his hand up and down. "My name is Moira Templeton and I am a huge fan. It is such a pleasure to be part of this ceremony today."

"Moira?" Max said. "That's kind of a crap name for a guy to be stuck with. You must really hate your parents for that one."

"Actually, Mr. Bland, I'm a woman," Moira said, not appearing bothered by the mistake.

"Oh. Jesus. Sorry. Anyway, what are you supposed to represent?" Max asked. "Racial harmony?"

Laughing, Moira said, "No, not at all. Although I'm all for that, you understand. No, I represent the elements."

"Ah. So which one of these colors symbolizes iridium?"

Again Moira laughed.

"No, not those elements, Mr. Bland. The elements of fire, water, earth and air. I'm officiating today." She glanced up at the sky. "And you know what? We'd better begin. The sun is approaching Hera's Temple. Come on ladies," she said to Danielle and Katie, leading them into the circle of love.

Max looked up at the sky. As far as he could tell the sun was only approaching New Jersey.

"You see Hera's Temple up there, Mikey?" he asked his best friend as an aside.

"Nah. All I see are pigeons, boss."

"Maybe they're Hera's pigeons."

Max rolled his eyes, sighing, and then stepped into the circle.

❦ ❦ ❦

A gong was struck three times and the crowd gathered in close to the circle of love in which Danielle and Katie stood beaming and Max stood wishing he were dead. From somewhere among the folds of her robe Moira removed an index card and handed it to Max.

"These are your vows," she whispered. "I'll signal you when to read them."

"Uh-huh," Max muttered in way of acknowledgment. Then leaning over to Danielle he whispered sinisterly, "You are going to pay for this."

"We'll talk about that later," she replied, keeping the smile glued to her face.

At that point the gong was struck again and suddenly one of the callers of the quarters raised her staff and proclaimed with a loud yell, startling Max: "I am the east! I summon the powers of honesty and openness to this union!

Embrace these lovers and imbue them with the gift of always understanding each other, and when ill words are spoken between them let them be swept away!" East then ran twice around the circle of love, her staff held high so that the scarf tied to it fluttered in the breeze. Upon completing her second circuit another caller stepped forward. "I am the south!" she cried. I summon the powers of passion and love to this union! Embrace these lovers and imbue them with the gift of never-ending desire for each other, and when anger is present let it be burned away!" And then South also ran twice around the circle of love. Next came West who summoned the powers of feeling and compassion, and then came North summoning patience and endurance. When the callers had done their bit all four of them stepped into the circle to lay their staffs at the feet of Max and the ladies and then stepped back out again to stand like sentinels on the perimeter.

Again the gong was struck. This time it beckoned a pretty young woman bearing a pillow upholstered in purple velvet. On the pillow were two lengths of coiled cord, one red, the other silver. The young woman solemnly presented them to Moira who took one cord in each hand before dismissing the pillow bearer with a nod.

"It is by these cords," Moira told the three partners, "that you will be bound. The red symbolizes passion; the silver communication. With passion comes desire and commitment; with communication comes trust and honesty. These are the hallmarks of any successful union and by binding your hands together with these cords I am showing to all who are gathered here as well as all the unseen spirits who share our world that you three have accepted the responsibilities of passion and communication forever and always."

Moira approached the three and asked them to stand closer together and to hold out their arms. In a matter of moments she had expertly bound all six hands at the wrist with both cords, making sure the red and silver were entwined.

Again the gong. A woman dressed entirely in flowing black garments came to stand between Moira and the lovers. She was armed with a short-bladed sword and a stern countenance. Before Max knew what was happening she had the sword tip pointed at his breast.

"You, sir," she began, "if you do not intend to speak the vows truthfully I beg you to pierce your heart with my blade rather than deceive those you claim to love. Will there be truth in what you are about to speak?"

"Yeah, yeah, yeah. Jesus Christ," Max said, his eyes on the sword pressing against the fabric of his Hugo Boss suit.

The armed woman then did the same to Danielle and Katie who both answered her question with "There will be truth in my vows." Apparently satisfied, the woman left the circle of love without killing anyone and Moira continued the ritual.

"Danielle, as the central person in this relationship it is you who must recite your vows first. You will begin by declaring yourself to Max because you two have been committed to each other longer. When you are done you will turn to Katie to recite your vows to her. Please begin."

Danielle glanced down at the index card she was holding and said to Max, "You are my first love and I will never give you reason to doubt my commitment to you. I vow in front of everyone here that your love helps to complete me and I will always desire it. I ask your permission to bring another person into our family and I promise that she will not subtract from my dedication to you and the love we share."

Then to Katie: "You are my other love and I will never give you reason to doubt my commitment to you. I vow in front of everyone here that your love also helps to complete me and that I will also always desire it. I invite you to join my union with Max and I promise that he will not subtract from my dedication to you and the love we share. From this point forward I have two equal loves in my life."

🍁   🍁   🍁

Moira nodded to Max when Danielle was finished and he sighed, holding up his index card as best he could while being fastened to two other people.

"Okay, um…Danielle, you are my only love. No one will replace you in my heart. I vow to continue growing with you and to nurture our feelings for each other. Our love is steadfast in times of trouble; it is what I depend on when I am in need. I accept this other person you wish to bring into our family. I recognize her importance to you and I promise to always acknowledge the good her spirit brings to our union."

Moira indicated that next he had to speak vows to Katie.

"Really? Oh, yeah, I see it right here…okay…lessee…I promise, Katie, to be like a brother to you. I accept you without reservation into my family and promise also to give you friendship, love and support. We are now bound together with mutual love for Danielle and mutual respect for each other. Can I go now?" he asked Moira.

"Not quite, Mr. Bland. We're almost done. Katie?"

"Danielle, you are my only love," Katie said, looking her girlfriend deeply in the eyes. "No one will replace you in my heart. My love for you is my life and I will protect it from harm as I would my own life. Because my hands are now bound to yours on this day I am complete. May we both continue to grow in love and trust." Then turning to Max she went on. "Max, I promise to be your sister. I accept your invitation to join your family and I welcome you into mine. You have my friendship, love and support. We are now bound together with mutual love for Danielle and mutual respect for each other." She winked at him and Max rolled his eyes.

"There are many in the world," Moira said after the gong was once more struck, "who will view this handfasting with doubt and scorn. You three must promise each other to ignore ridicule or suspicion and stay true to the vows you have made here. Danielle?"

"I do," answered Danielle.

"Katie?"

"I do."

"Max?"

"Sure. You bet. Are we done?"

Apparently not for the gong was struck again and the same young woman who brought the red and silver cords returned with the pillow once more. This time it bore the four rings purchased in Maine. As solemnly as a priest offering the chalice of wine at Communion, Moira took each ring and slipped it onto the finger of its new owner. Then, raising her staff Moira also raised her voice.

"I present to you all the union of Danielle Edwards, Katie Shaw and Max Bland! Always honor and respect this new family! Wish them good tidings and protection from ill fortune." She touched each of the lovers on the shoulder with her staff. "You may now embrace and kiss."

🍁   🍁   🍁

When it was all over they were swarmed with well-wishers. Max particularly was besieged by many of the gay women in attendance who wanted simply to meet him and even ask him to autograph their copies of *The Remarkable Reign of Pope Anne I* which they all happened to have with them. Finally, he managed to work his way free and find Mikey.

"Congratulations, boss. But I gotta say…even if there hadn't been a bunch of gay women here that was the gayest thing I've ever seen."

"Thank God it's over," Max said and then: "Actually, it was…unique. I mean, it was a bit corny and all, and I'm pretty sure the Vatican would shit their pants over how pagan it was but…it was interesting."

"Well?" Danielle and Katie said in unison as they joined the men. "Are you mad at us?" Danielle asked, giving Max a kiss.

"Furious," he replied. "But in the spirit of the North who summons patience and endurance I will overlook what a pain in the ass you two are and forgive you. It was certainly different," he went on after a moment. "It's not every day a lady holds a sword to your heart and threatens to stab you if you lie about loving someone."

"Yeah, well if you had made some smartass comment then I would've taken the sword and stabbed you myself," Danielle informed him.

They all laughed and then Mikey said, "So, now that you three are married, sort of, which one of you is Danielle supposed to honeymoon with tonight?"

"Fuck," said Max.

"I hadn't thought of that," said Katie.

The two of them looked at each other, eyes squinted, like Old West gunfighters about to square off on Main Street. Finally Max said, "You know, we're in the Bronx and the Gun Post Lanes are only fifteen minutes away…"

"Best two out of three?" Katie suggested.

"You're on."

978-0-595-35448-1
0-595-35448-3

Printed in the United States
3094GLV00002B/97-102